A Game of Love and Betrayal
THE CHOOSING CHRONICLES
BOOK ONE

ELAYNA R. GALLEA

This is a work of fiction. Names, characters, places, and incidents either are the product of the author's imagination or are used fictitiously. Any resemblance to actual persons, living or dead, events, or locales is entirely coincidental.

Copyright © 2024 by Elayna R. Gallea

All rights reserved. No part of this book may be reproduced or used in any manner without written permission of the copyright owner except for the use of quotations in a book review. For more information, address: hello@elaynargallea.com

Cover and map designed by Elayna R. Gallea

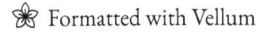

❦ Formatted with Vellum

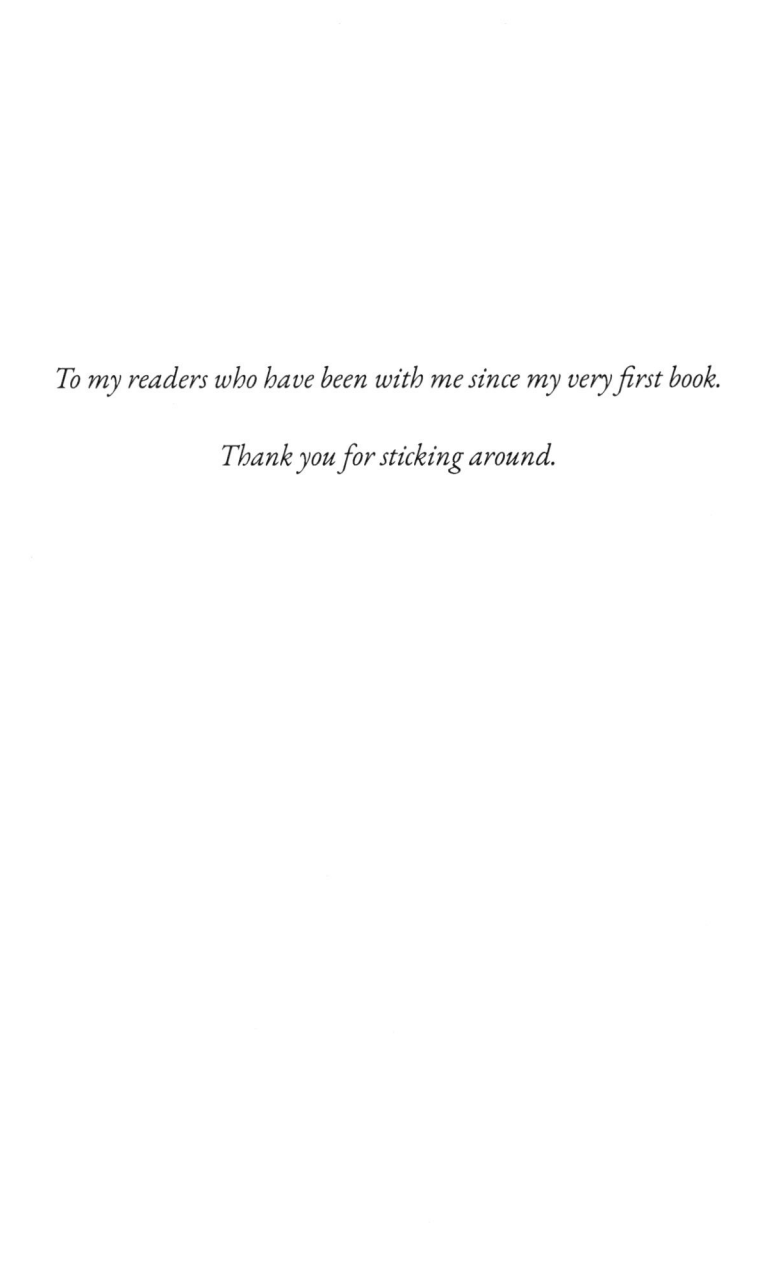

To my readers who have been with me since my very first book.

Thank you for sticking around.

Contents

Author's note	vii
Prologue	1
1. Fangs or Blade?	3
2. I Won't Let You Down	17
3. May the Gods Bless Your Choice	27
4. It Would Behoove You Not to Act Like Animals	40
5. A Curse and a Blessing	48
6. Today Would Change Everything	58
7. A Meeting to Remember	70
8. Butterflies and Silence	80
9. More Than She'd Bargained For	85
10. Game On	90
11. My Programming Does Not Allow Me to Discuss That	100
12. Unexpected Complications Arise	111
13. It Won't Happen Again	125
14. Breaking Rules and Guilty Consciences	134
15. Young Love	147
16. Pen Pals and Nicknames	157
17. Rule Number Eight	170
18. Universes Collide	179
19. Losing Was Not an Option	186
20. Retribution Would Be Hers	194
21. A Meeting for the Ages	211
22. Death is the Only Alternative	220
23. Protective Measures and Perfect Control	234
24. Nothing But a Physical Reaction	245
25. Welcome Home	259
26. Tendrils of Doubt	272
27. I Made My Choice	286

28. Complications Abound	299
29. Mistakes Were Made	306
30. A Visit to the Obsidian Palace	314
31. No More Rules	321
32. Wedding Bells and Blessings	327
33. Chocolate Cake, Happiness, and Suspicions	334
34. They Were a Pair	346
35. New Game, New Rules	358
36. The Cost of Silence	368
37. Questions and Answers	376
A Heart of Desire and Deceit	385
Acknowledgments	393
Also by Elayna R. Gallea	395
About the Author	397

Author's note

A Game of Love and Betrayal is a new adult fantasy romance set in a secondary world setting.

I never want my content to be harmful to any of my readers. This is a dystopian world and there are certain situations which may be triggering.

For a full list of content notes, please visit: https://www.elaynargallea.com/contentnotes.

THE REPUBLIC OF BALANCE

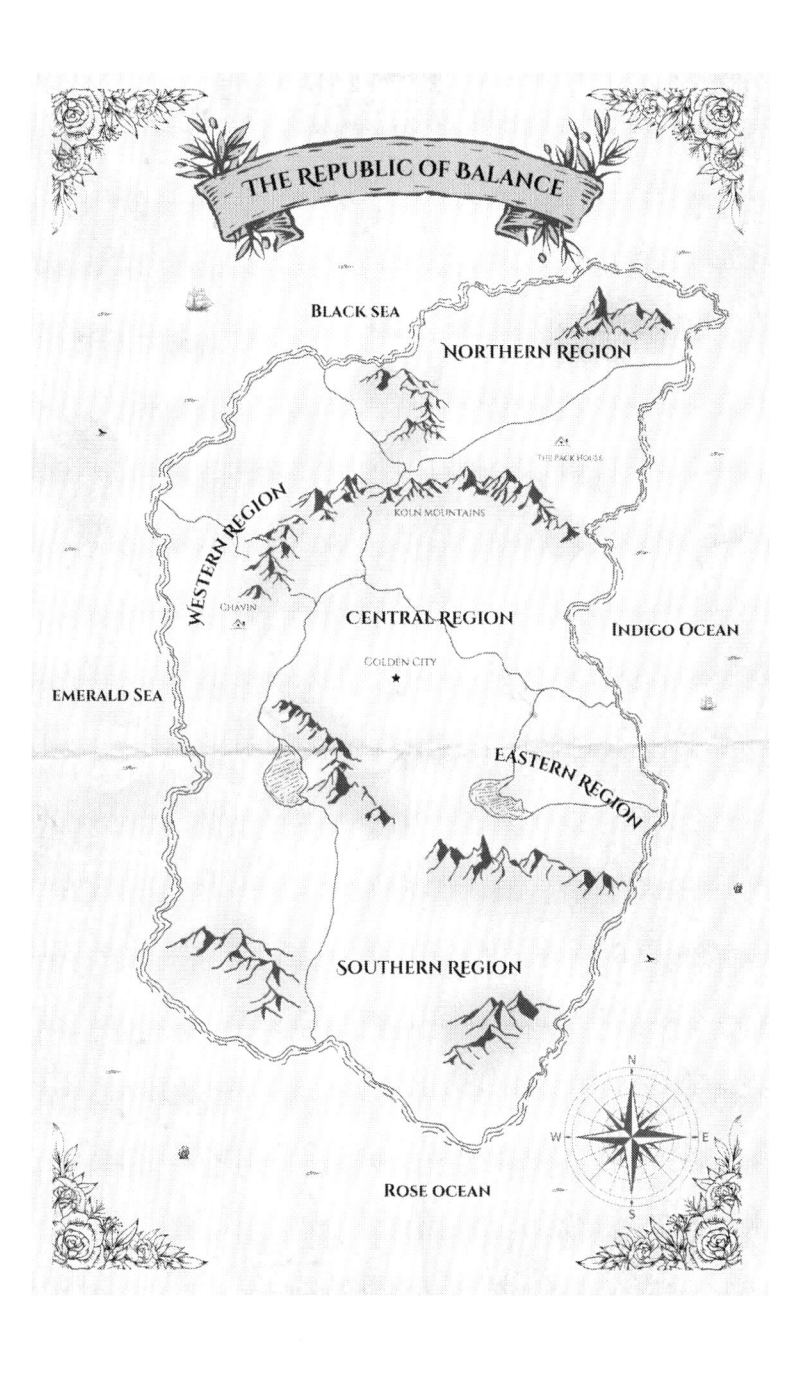

BLACK SEA

NORTHERN REGION

THE PACK HOUSE

KOLN MOUNTAINS

WESTERN REGION

CHAVIN

CENTRAL REGION

GOLDEN CITY

INDIGO OCEAN

EMERALD SEA

EASTERN REGION

SOUTHERN REGION

ROSE OCEAN

Prologue

Long ago, many centuries in the past, an Empress ruled over this continent. The Rose Empire was vast, prosperous, and generally a good place to live.

Until it wasn't.

Internal wars tore the Rose Empire apart. Elves battled dragons, merfolk staked their claim in the Indigo Ocean, werewolf packs settled across the continent, and vampires moved to the frigid, frozen north. The citizens of the former empire formed kingdoms.

Four of them, to be exact.

Prosperity reigned in the Four Kingdoms as well... for a time. All too soon, however, the pull of power and money became too strong for some to resist. Once again, tensions rose. Wars were fought. Power ebbed and flowed.

Time went on.

Elves Matured and Faded. Vampires were Made and died. Werewolves lived beneath the power of the moon, growing their packs over the centuries.

And humans?

They simply... existed.

Life continued. The balance was broken and then reformed. For a time, peace reigned over the continent.

Several millennia later, the Four Kingdoms evolved again and united beneath a shared banner. The fae crossed the Indigo Ocean in the Great Migration, bringing their impressive magic. Technology soared in this new time, and all the species coexisted in the Republic of Balance.

It was during this time that our story took place.

CHAPTER 1
Fangs or Blade?

"I'm feeling benevolent this evening, so I'll allow you to decide how you want to die." Brynleigh de la Point pinned the sniveling, half-dressed man with a glare that she hoped said, *This is the last choice you'll ever get to make.* Out loud, she added, "Fangs or blade?"

The man blinked from his position on the bed, his sluggish mud-brown eyes struggling to follow the vampire's movements across the dimly lit, shoddy studio apartment. The faint glow of streetlights several stories below filtered through the grimy glass of the single window above his head, adding a yellow tint to the space.

His inability to focus could have been caused by his half-mortal blood, the prohiberis Brynleigh had liberally sprinkled in his drink earlier to block his magic, or merely a side-effect from the pints of alcohol he'd consumed throughout the evening. Judging by the smell wafting off him, it was probably a combination of all three.

The shadows binding the man's arms and legs likely weren't helping matters either. They operated on Brynleigh's command, and there wasn't anything he could do to break the dark bonds.

If the man hadn't already concluded exactly how dire his situation was, he would shortly.

Brynleigh tapped her booted foot on the dirty floor, avoiding a questionable stain a few inches from where she stood. The sooner she got out of this apartment, the better. "What's your choice?"

He slurred, his voice pitifully weak, "I... uh... neither?"

Brynleigh barely suppressed a sigh. Did he have no self-respect? The least he could do in the face of impending death was be strong and fight with everything he had.

"That's not an option." Brynleigh withdrew the sharp, thin dagger sheathed on her thigh. It was one of the many weapons she'd hidden all over her person before venturing out tonight. "Choose, or I will for you."

Providing an answer would have been the intelligent option.

Instead, this man proved that not only did he lack self-respect, but he was anything but intelligent. His lecherous gaze raked over Brynleigh, starting at her head and dipping past her black tank top to her dark blue jeans. He smirked, probably determining that her choice of outfit meant that she was ready for a night on the town, not to kill a scumbag such as himself.

The bound man proved her suspicions correct a moment later. "You're not going to kill me."

If his response hadn't been so predictable, Brynleigh probably would have been disappointed. It was just like a man to take one look at her golden hair and curvy body, and decide that she couldn't be a killer because she didn't look like one. He wasn't the first to make that erroneous observation, and much to Brynleigh's dismay, she was fairly certain he wouldn't be the last either.

"That's where you're wrong." Brynleigh willed her shadows to tighten, their constrictive embrace proving her deadly point. "Only one of us will be walking out of that door alive, and it will be me."

He scoffed, rolling his eyes. "Come on, baby. I just wanted to have a bit of fun."

Yeah, she wasn't interested in his type of fun. Especially not in a place like this. She guessed he'd be a two-pumps-and-done kind of guy. Not what she was looking for. Besides, the atmosphere in this small space left everything to be desired. Yellowed wallpaper hung off the walls in clumps, chipped tiles demarcated the kitchen from the dirty living area, and the sheets on the bed looked like they had never seen the inside of a washing machine.

Not to mention the noise. The neighbors were far too loud. Tell-tale thumps came from the bedroom upstairs. The television next door blared, and a too-chipper voice filtered through the walls, announcing the arrival of a new, never-before-seen beauty serum. According to the saleswoman, it was designed to make even the most wrinkle-laden human young again.

Brynleigh barely stopped herself from rolling her eyes. That so-called miracle cure was probably made with vampire blood. Not that she had a problem with people doing whatever they needed to survive—obviously, considering her current predicament—but she wasn't a fan of hiding markers of age.

Getting old was a privilege many citizens of the Republic of Balance weren't afforded, including the halfling on the bed.

The man still hadn't decided, and Brynleigh's patience had run its course. Honestly, it was a miracle she'd made it this long. "Too late. Blade it is."

She spun the dagger in the air, catching the weapon by its engraved hilt before stepping towards the man. His eyes widened, and panic flashed through those brown orbs.

"No." His nostrils flared, and a hint of fear mingled with the apartment's musty aroma. "Please, don't do this."

The sigh that slipped from Brynleigh's mouth could probably be heard worldwide. Of course, this halfling bastard would beg. She should've known he was one of those.

Zanri, Brynleigh's handler, had probably laughed when he selected this mark for her. He knew how much she hated whiners. She would rather deal with someone who fought back any day. It felt... better when they fought back. Easier, somehow, to deal that

5

killing blow. She liked when they tried to stop her, especially when she knew what they'd done.

Still, Brynleigh had to be certain. She didn't believe in killing innocents.

She crossed her arms, and even though it was the last thing she wanted to do, she leaned against the filthy counter. Her dagger dangled from her fingers as she eyed the man on the bed. "Your name is Geralt Warsh, correct?"

He stared at her.

Fine. Two could play at this game. With a flick of her wrist, Brynleigh silently commanded the shadows to tighten. "Halfling Death Elf, originally from the Northern District of the Republic?"

The man swallowed, his eyes darting back and forth. That scent of fear grew stronger until the bitter, cloying aroma was all Brynleigh could smell. During moments like this, she wished vampires didn't have such strong senses.

"N-n-no, you're wrong." He shook his head.

For Isvana's sake. This was getting ridiculous.

"Don't fucking lie to me, it's unbecoming." Brynleigh uncrossed her arms and moved across the room in a blur. She slashed her dagger across the halfling's hair in a movement too fast for anyone but a vampire to see.

A long copper lock fell onto the mattress that was three shades of brown too dark to be sanitary, revealing a pointed, pierced ear. A red swirling tattoo crawled down the side of Geralt's neck. It was a mark of his Maturation and served to confirm his identity. The three earrings hanging from his ear were additional proof that this was the man she sought.

"I know who you are," Brynleigh said, done with his games. Between the lecherous gaze, the lying, and the whining, she wanted to leave. She'd have to take a dozen showers to rid her skin of the disgusting feel of this place. "*What* you are."

Geralt Warsh, half-Death Elf, half-human, was not a good man. He was a hardened criminal, the likes of which Brynleigh rarely encountered. When Zanri had shown her Geralt's file, her fangs had burned in anger. The halfling had been convicted of several crimes against minors, which had led to him spending over three decades in Black Prison in the Western District of the Republic. Earlier this spring, Geralt had been released. Apparently, his time in prison hadn't taught him any lessons. He'd gone right back to his old ways.

The photos Brynleigh had seen were enough to turn anyone's stomach, including hers. She might have been a vampire, but she still had feelings, for the moon goddess's sake.

And Geralt? He was so fucking cocky he wouldn't get caught that he wasn't even covering his tracks. Finding him this afternoon had barely taken any effort. After studying the paperwork, Brynleigh had located the halfling at the Falling Star, a local dive bar. He'd been indulging in copious amounts of bottom-shelf liquor, happily telling anyone and everyone that he'd recently been released from prison.

As if that was a bragging point.

Being imprisoned meant he'd been caught, which by definition, was not something to boast about. Brynleigh, on the other hand, had never been caught. She'd never even come close to it. That was one of the many reasons she was confident she'd be the one walking out of here tonight.

Once she had arrived at the Falling Star, all Brynleigh had to do to procure an invitation up to the grungy apartment was slide next to the halfling and flirt a little. Honestly, it was child's play.

The criminal had been in the middle of removing his jeans—which, no, thank you, Brynleigh didn't have sex with pedophiles—when the vampire released her shadows and bound him to the bed.

Which brought them back to the present.

Geralt studied Brynleigh. At first, his eyes were dull and brown, like the stains on his mattress. He wailed and struggled against the shadows binding him, even going so far as to fabricate a story about a wife and two children he claimed waited for him in the suburbs.

It was all a lie.

Brynleigh had memorized his file. Like her, the halfling had no one. He was a lowlife criminal who preyed on those less powerful than him.

Eventually, Geralt seemed to realize his weeping would not get him anywhere. It was like a switch flipped inside the halfling. One moment, he was a sobbing, snotty mess. The next, his tears dried up as if they'd never been there at all. His back straightened, his chin rose, and an evil glint entered his eye. The facade of the weak, confused halfling vanished like a thief in the night.

A smile tugged at the corner of Brynleigh's mouth. *There he is*, she thought, almost gleefully. *Finally.*

Now, she'd see this man for who he truly was.

Geralt's eyes narrowed, and his mouth twisted into a sneer. "You fucking vampiric whore. You think you can do this to me?" He tugged on his bindings as if he could break free. "Don't you know who I am?"

Brynleigh raised a brow and calmly said, "I know exactly who you are."

Her response seemed to enrage him further. He wiggled and thrashed against her shadows.

It wouldn't work. Brynleigh was a doubly blessed vampire. The night of Brynleigh's Making, Isvana, the moon goddess, had gifted the new vampire with both wings and shadows. Most vampires had one or the other. A few had none. Some, like Brynleigh, had both. Even now, darkness pulsed a reassuring melody through her veins.

"Who is your Maker?" Geralt snapped, his face turning beet red. "I'm going to drive a stake through your shriveled black heart, and then—"

The end of his threat never came.

Tiring of the halfling's antics, Brynleigh slashed her silver blade across his throat from ear to ear. Arterial spray painted her and the walls. It would've been enough to kill a regular human, but Geralt Warsh was a Mature Halfling.

Elves, fae, merfolk, werewolves, shifters, and witches all Matured around twenty-five years of age. Maturation extended their lifespans and gave them increased access to their powers. It also made them harder to kill.

Brynleigh sighed. She hated this part of her job even more than the whining.

Maybe she should've picked fangs. It would've been cleaner, although she was certain that ripping out Geralt's neck wouldn't have been a pleasant experience. He probably had disgusting, sewer-flavored blood.

It was too late now, though. She'd made her choice.

Twisting the dagger in her grip, Brynleigh slammed the bloody weapon into Geralt's chest. It took significant force to drive a blade cleanly into a heart, but thanks to Isvana's blessings, Brynleigh had strength in droves.

When she was confident the halfling was the kind of dead there was no coming back from, even for a Mature being, she went to the sink and turned on the tap with her elbow. She washed her hands thoroughly and dried them on her jeans before slipping her phone out of her back pocket. She unlocked it, navigating to the camera before snapping a picture.

With a few taps of her finger, she sent the bloody image to Zanri.

> B: He was a whiner. You owe me.

Two check marks showed up, and three dots swiftly followed. Her phone buzzed a moment later.

> Z: You got it. Meet me at the usual spot.

No other instructions were necessary. Brynleigh was done. For now.

"Was it a clean death?"

Brynleigh had barely stepped out of the Void—the dark, empty space that some vampires such as herself could use to travel from one point to another, as long as they'd been to the second location previously—when Zanri's deep tenor reached her ears.

The man in question stepped out of the shadows. His red hair fell to his waist, the lamp illuminating the streaks of brown running through it. Z was handsome in the way that most Mature beings were. His face was chiseled, his nose sharp, and his blue eyes dark as they swept over her.

Zanri was some kind of shifter, but Brynleigh had never seen his animal form. She assumed he probably shifted during the day when she couldn't go in the sun. If she had to guess, she'd think he was a cat shifter. His eyes had a predatory, feline glint. Tonight, he wore tight black leather pants that were probably a pain in the ass to take on and off. They were paired with a matching black T-shirt that looked painted on his muscled form.

Brynleigh blinked and rolled her shoulders as her vision cleared. The shadows had brought her to their safe house, the wards surrounding the building recognizing her blood and letting her enter without issue. She'd gone straight into the living room. Her plan for the remainder of the night was simple. She'd shower, grab a bottle of blood wine from the fridge, and relax in front of the TV for a few hours.

"What do you think?" was her response as she pulled her hair into a quick ponytail.

He pulled out his phone, tapping the screen and drawing the photo she'd sent him. She could see the crimson that coated Geralt's apartment from across the room. No one could ever clean that space now, not completely.

A dark chuckle slipped out of the shifter. "I think he got what he deserved."

"On that, we are agreed. He was disgusting." Brynleigh looked her handler over, noting the ruffled appearance of his red hair and his flushed cheeks for the first time since she arrived. She asked knowingly, "How's Owen?"

"He's good." Zanri's blush deepened, and the corner of his mouth tilted up, confirming everything she needed to know.

Owen Farnish lived in a desert city in the Southern Region but often worked with Brynleigh's Maker, Jelisette. He and Zanri had an on-again, off-again situation. When they were on, they would disappear for hours whenever Owen came to town.

"Tell him I said hello." Brynleigh liked Owen. He was one of the kinder people that Jelisette dealt with, and he always took the time to talk to Brynleigh, even back when she'd been newly Made.

"I will." Zanri smiled for a moment before his mouth flattened. "I left as soon as I got your message. Jelisette will want to debrief, and I need to wipe the security feeds."

There went Brynleigh's plans of lounging in front of trashy reality TV. Usually, Jelisette was out until dawn, but apparently not tonight. "How long until she arrives?"

"Less than an hour." In addition to being Brynleigh's handler, Zanri was in charge of technology and communication for their little operation. He had a gift for everything electronic in nature and ensured everything they did stayed under the radar. "She'll be proud, B."

Something sparked in the depths of Brynleigh's stomach. Even if she didn't exactly like her Maker—Jelisette was cold and icy, even for a vampire—Brynleigh was destined to want to please her. That was the nature of Maker bonds. Every vampire felt that way towards the sire who'd given them the gift of immortality.

Besides, Maker bonds were some of the strongest ones that existed. Even more than a mating bond, the link between Maker and progeny was incredibly powerful. There had only ever been one person who'd successfully broken their Maker bond, which happened thousands of years before.

Brynleigh owed Jelisette everything. The older vampire had found her after the worst night of her life and taken her under her wing. Before, Brynleigh had been nothing but a mediocre human, and now she was skilled in more ways than one.

She allowed a small smile to form. "Good."

Zanri pulled his hair into a bun and strode across the room. He gave her a gentle shove towards the bathroom. "Go shower. You have blood splattered across your skin. You should clean up. You know how she feels about looking good."

If anyone else dared touch Brynleigh like that, she would bite them—or worse. But she and Z had an understanding of sorts. They weren't really friends—she didn't do friends anymore—but they were colleagues who didn't mind each other.

"I know." Raising the pitch of her voice, she mimicked Jelisette's melodic, lyrical voice. "Rule number three: vampires are weapons. We must always look our best and be prepared to use every gods-given gift to our advantage."

Brynleigh's Maker had *a lot* of rules.

The shifter's mouth twitched, and he looked like he was holding in laughter. "That's the one. Now go."

She wouldn't argue with him. A shower did sound appealing. Especially after Brynleigh remembered the caked layers of dirt and grime in Geralt's apartment.

Brynleigh hurried into the bathroom, turning on the shower while she removed her weapons, stripped, and threw her clothes into the hamper. By the time she stepped under the water, steam billowed around her like a cloud. It was hot, and her skin quickly turned red, just as she liked it.

Twenty minutes later, Brynleigh felt like a new vampire. There was something about hot water and soap that was utterly life-changing. She toweled off, pulling on a fresh pair of black leggings and a white crop top as Jelisette's magic swept through the safe house. Seconds later, a lilac scent reached her.

Brynleigh tensed, and her heart beat faster. This always happened when her Maker came near. It was a remnant from that first night when Jelisette saved her. Flashes of lightning, booms of rolling thunder, and memories of waves taller than her head swept through Brynleigh's mind like an unwanted storm before she banished them. This wasn't the moment to remember the worst night of her life.

Curling her fists, she forced herself to take slow, deep breaths. Inhale. Exhale. Repeat.

Again and again, Brynleigh continued the practice until her heart rate returned to its normal, measured rhythm.

She was a deadly vampire. A bringer of death. She needed to get a grip. She wasn't a child unable to control their emotions. She was twenty-three.

Well. Sort of.

She'd turned twenty-three six years ago, and then she'd been Made. Inside, she still felt twenty-three. She wasn't exactly sure when that would change. After a few decades? A century? Two? Eight, like Jelisette had seen?

Right now, Brynleigh couldn't imagine living for so long. The pains of her mortal life continued to haunt her, and she still experienced human emotions. Perhaps those would dull over time and lose their potency. Perhaps that was the key to living for centuries: letting herself get cold like Jelisette. Brynleigh had never even seen her Maker shed a tear, let alone laugh.

This wasn't the time for those kinds of thoughts, though. Jelisette did not take kindly to lateness.

Shadowing back to the living area, Brynleigh's stance was wide as she clasped her hands behind her back. Zanri leaned against the wall casually, studying the chess board that was a permanent fixture in the safe house.

Seconds later, shadows gathered on the mahogany hardwood floor near the entrance. Brynleigh's skin tingled. Her own darkness fluttered in recognition of the powerful magic entering the space.

Moments later, Jelisette's lithe form stepped out of the shadows. A shimmering crimson floor-length ballgown was draped over her tall body. The dress was sleeveless, sporting a V cut so low that it exposed the sides of her breasts and her navel. Long gloves ran to her elbows. Her chestnut hair was in an elaborate swooping bun, and a heavy black diamond necklace was her only adornment.

"Oh, good." The powerful vampire's midnight gaze swept over Brynleigh. "You're here."

Brynleigh nodded, keeping her shoulders straight. "Yes, ma'am. I finished the job."

"Good girl." Jelisette lifted a manicured brow. "It'll be the last one for a while."

The last one? Zanri usually had lots of work for Brynleigh. The Republic of Balance was extensive, spanning the entire continent. It used to be four kingdoms that had merged into one government long ago. There was no shortage of evil people who required their particular kind of deadly attention.

Although talking back to her Maker was never a good idea, Brynleigh questioned, "What do you mean?"

Something akin to a smile crept along Jelisette's face. "I did it. I got you in."

Brynleigh's brows creased as she tried to follow her Maker's words. Then, she gasped. "You mean..."

Jelisette crossed the room and gripped Brynleigh's shoulder. Her sharp nails dug into the younger vampire's flesh, but Brynleigh didn't care. Not if this meant what she thought it meant.

"Yes," Jelisette hissed, and her black eyes glimmered. "The gods have spoken, and the stars are aligned. Tomorrow, the Two Hundredth Choosing begins."

Brynleigh's heart, slow beating as it was, galloped in her chest like a wild stallion. Her mouth dried. Her fangs ached. She sucked in a too-shallow breath, taking in a sip of air instead of a gulp. "And I'm in?"

This felt too good to be true. She needed to hear it confirmed.

"Yes, my dear." Jelisette removed her hand and trailed a sharp nail down Brynleigh's face. The gesture was almost maternal. Almost. "This is the moment you've been waiting for."

It felt like Brynleigh's heart would explode out of her chest.

She'd been training for this for six years, waiting for the moment she could finally exact her revenge.

Willing her heart to steady, Brynleigh stalked over to the chess board. Zanri silently watched as Brynleigh picked up the black king. She rolled the wooden carving around in her hand before trapping it in her fist.

This plan had so many moving parts, and this game had so many rules that Brynleigh hadn't been certain they would actually pull it off. She hadn't dared give too much thought to what this day would mean until now, for fear that if she did, the barriers she'd built around her heart would shatter.

If Brynleigh had spent too long thinking about her family's murderer and the free life he was living, she would have gone on a deadly, bloody rampage across the continent and fallen into bloodlust.

Then, who would avenge her family?

Instead, Brynleigh had become a master of compartmentalization. She shoved all her feelings into a box deep within her soul as she trained to become a killer.

That would end now.

Her fist tightened until a *crack* echoed through the room. Brynleigh unfurled her fingers, one by one, until the now-broken king lay in the middle of her pale palm. She placed the cracked piece on the board, looking first at Jelisette and then at Zanri.

"I'm going to enter the Hall of Choice, make Captain Ryker Waterborn, Head of the Fae Division in the Republic's Army, fall in love with me, and then I'll kill him on our wedding night," she declared.

Six years ago, the captain had vanished from the public eye. He hadn't been very visible before, but no one had seen him since. Living a quiet life wasn't abnormal for Representatives and their families. Some, like Chancellor Rose, were so secretive that even their children's magical affinities were unknown.

The captain's disappearance had been so complete that even in this technological day and age, finding him had been impossible. Jelisette had been able to confirm that the captain still lived, but even when he was at work, he was never alone.

Brynleigh had spent years hunting him, trying to get close enough to kill the captain, to no avail.

Until now.

The participants of the Choosing were supposed to be kept a secret, but Jelisette had a way of uncovering things that were meant to be hidden. *He* would be one of the twelve men taking part in the event.

"Revenge will be mine," Brynleigh said calmly.

Hearing the words out loud made them real in a way they hadn't been before. Her shadows twisted in her veins, and her dark magic pulsed at the thought.

Zanri's face was grave as he studied her, but Jelisette's black eyes twinkled. "Yes. No matter what, the captain will die before the year's end."

Jelisette's commitment to helping Brynleigh get her revenge was sweet. Brynleigh's Maker cared for her progeny. That was why Jelisette was willing to help Brynleigh avenge her family.

This had been Brynleigh's destiny since the night of her Making. Only one outcome was acceptable.

For the crimes he'd committed, Ryker Waterborn would die.

CHAPTER 2
I Won't Let You Down

The following day, before sundown, Brynleigh perched on the edge of her bed. She wore a black robe, her hair freshly dried from her afternoon shower.

Jelisette stood inside the walk-in closet wearing a sweater that seemed incongruous with the summer heat. Propping her hands on her hips, she tapped her foot on the floor. "Red or black?"

It may have been posed as a question, but Brynleigh knew Jelisette didn't want any answers.

Rule number seven: your Maker always knows best.

Instead, Brynleigh sipped her blood wine, relishing the dry taste as she swirled it around her mouth before swallowing. A non-committal hum slipped from her lips, and she twisted her pendant through the fingers of her free hand.

"Hmm. You're right." Jelisette walked around the space, shadows following her like dogs as she touched several dresses.

Brynleigh didn't particularly enjoy wearing formal attire, but she had several fancier pieces since she was often required to attend events with her Maker. Personally, Brynleigh would rather live in leggings. They were comfortable and convenient, and she always felt beautiful in them.

Jelisette pinched a scarlet sundress between her fingers. "You want something special. It needs to say, 'I could kill you with a single nip of my fangs, but I won't because I'm a good girl.'" She laughed cruelly, dropping the dress. "Though we both know that isn't true."

Another hum. Her Maker was right. Brynleigh wasn't a good girl. She'd never been one, even before her Making. As a child, scarcely a week went by that she didn't get in trouble for one thing or another. And now? Since her vampiric re-birth, Brynleigh no longer cared about trivial, mortal matters like "good" and "bad." Revenge was the driving force in her life, her reason for being, her first thought when she woke, and the fuel for her dreams.

It was those sweet thoughts of vengeance that propelled Brynleigh off the bed. Her bare feet padded on the plush cream carpet. She sipped her blood wine, entering the closet to stand beside her Maker. She pointed at a glimmering sequined garment tucked towards the back, half-buried by other clothes. "What about that one?"

Jelisette tilted her head, her brown hair falling over her shoulder as she pursed her lips. She pulled out the dress, studying it like a beast assessing its dinner.

"Hmm, good choice." She turned the garment around, taking it in from all angles. "Yes, this is the one. It will stand out from the others. No one will be able to resist you like this." Her brow rose. "The public's opinion is important, you know."

"I know," Brynleigh said.

The Choosing was televised and broadcast to the entire Republic. Couples who participated in the once-a-decade event were often considered semi-celebrities when it was over. Tonight was about more than just entering the Hall of Choice. This was Brynleigh's first chance to make an impression on the press.

Jelisette handed the dress to her progeny. Hundreds of black sequins sparkled like an entire galaxy was embedded in the fabric. "Get dressed; you're leaving in an hour."

There was no warmth in either Jelisette's voice or her countenance, and her assessing black gaze was equally cold as it ran over Brynleigh. That was fine.

Brynleigh didn't need warmth or comfort. Vampires didn't rely on emotions as humans did. It was one of her first lessons.

Jelisette glided out the door, her retreat silent thanks to her immortal grace, and as soon as she was alone, Brynleigh discarded her robe. The dress she'd selected was a tight onyx number that would hug her curves in all the right places. She'd never worn it before, and tonight seemed like the perfect opportunity.

Brynleigh slid the gown over her head, letting the fabric fall to the ground. Long sleeves tapered at her fingers. The hem trailed on the floor. Three strategically placed cut-outs highlighted her stomach and the curve of her breasts. The back scooped low, practically non-existent, and the material started right above the curve of her bottom.

If Brynleigh hadn't been a creature of the night, she probably would've been cold in a dress like this. Midsummer nights, even in the Central Region, got cold. The garment wasn't exactly built for warmth. Luckily for Brynleigh, being a child of the moon meant she could walk outside in the middle of a snowstorm and not be affected by the temperature.

Finishing her wine with one final gulp, Brynleigh placed the empty glass on her desk and grabbed her brush. She styled her hair into long flowing waves that tumbled over her left shoulder. For jewelry, she wore her pendant. Nothing else was required.

Rule number two: Doubly blessed vampires do not hide behind jewels or makeup. They let their gods-given gifts speak for themselves.

This was a rule Brynleigh was happy to follow. As a whole, vampires had an unnatural, too-beautiful-to-be-real quality about them, and Brynleigh was no different. She was the same as she'd been before her Making... but not. Her skin was smoother, lacking all blemishes; her eyes were sharper; her nose was slightly more delicate; and her hair was shinier.

Brynleigh drew in a deep breath and squared her shoulders.

She reached within herself, pulling on the shadows that danced in her veins. They responded eagerly to her call, flooding out of her outstretched hands. Her wings were next. Those dark, bat-like appendages emerged and hung on her exposed back.

She rolled her shoulders, enjoying the added weight of her wings, before slipping her feet into three-inch black stilettos. Grabbing the matching clutch, she strode over to her dresser. It didn't take long to find what she was looking for. After all, very few of her personal mementos had survived the events of the night she'd been Made.

Gently picking up the yellowed piece of paper she sought, she studied it for a long moment before folding it on the creased lines. She worked carefully, not wanting it to rip, then slipped it in the clutch beside her phone and charger. Her packed duffle bag was on the floor by the front door. It would be sent to the Hall of Choice and arrive a few hours after her.

Brynleigh did not shed a tear as she left her room for the last time, nor did she worry about what she was leaving behind. Sentimentality was for the weak, and this was but a stop on her road to revenge.

Jelisette and Zanri were sitting at the chess board when Brynleigh entered the living room. Jelisette had changed and wore a long black sweater and a flowing skirt. Her sleeve slipped as she cupped her chin, revealing a thick black marking on her wrist.

Zanri, wearing his usual jeans and t-shirt, looked up. His eyes darkened as they swept over Brynleigh, and he whistled.

"I'll be damned, B," he said appreciatively. "If I didn't bat for the other team, I'd be all over you. No one will be able to resist you like that."

Brynleigh laughed, and her shoulders loosened as Zanri's comment diffused some of the tension running through her. "That's precisely the point."

Just because the Choosing was a blind love competition didn't mean Brynleigh couldn't let her competitors know she was willing to do anything to win. She was young and beautiful, confident in her body, and she didn't care who knew it.

Jelisette moved the knight before looking up. "Do you have everything?"

"Yes." Brynleigh's voice was cold and emotionless, like her Maker's.

"And you remember the plan?"

Another nod. "Of course."

They'd gone over it a hundred times. Brynleigh knew what she was doing. She would seek out Captain Waterborn and make him fall in love with her.

Zanri moved his bishop and folded his hands. "Your turn."

Picking up her rook, Jelisette slowly moved it across the board with predatory ease. "Very good. And remember, you can't—"

"Trust anyone." Brynleigh snapped her wings tight against her back and lifted her chin. "Yes, ma'am. Rule number one. I know."

She'd memorized the rules and knew them backward and forwards. This was her game to lose.

Jelisette released the rook, removing Zanri's knight from the board. The shifter cursed quietly under his breath, frowning as he studied the game.

Zanri would lose.

There were three paths to Jelisette's victory, all attainable within five moves.

"Then you're ready." Brynleigh's Maker stood and produced a golden envelope from her pocket. Handing it to her progeny, she waited until Brynleigh met her gaze. "Your ticket in."

The thick paper was cool to the touch, the embossed metallic filigree pressing into Brynleigh's fingers. "I won't let you down."

Brynleigh's shadows pooled at her feet, and she prepared to leave.

The last thing she heard was Jelisette's melodic murmur, "See that you don't."

Brynleigh sat in the back of the limo her Maker had procured, her fingers lying flat on her thighs as she stared out the window. The chauffeur wasn't talkative, which was fine with her. She was wholly focused on her task and happy to watch Golden City's sparkling skyline pass by.

The namesake triple arches rising above the city gleamed against the starless sky. Their gilded glow shone brighter than any other lights burning through the darkness of the night.

Golden City was the largest urban area in the Republic of Balance. It was the capital and housed the governing body that looked over the welfare of the entire Republic. The Council of Representatives met here, and millions of citizens called the sprawling urban area their home. It was one of the most prosperous regions on the continent, and the golden arches symbolized its wealth.

Some people said this was the most beautiful city in the Central Region. Others claimed there was nothing like it anywhere in the Republic, that its beauty was unmatched. Once, she'd even heard someone say that Golden City rivaled the ancient Emerald Palace in its resplendence.

Brynleigh did not see the beauty. She did not see the appeal of the golden arches or the glimmer of money found around every corner.

All she saw was a city fueled by bloodshed and deception.

No amount of gold could hide the broken aspects of this world. No money could stop the cracks in the gilded veneer from showing. The beautiful illusion of Golden City hid the inequality that reigned in this place. Death often visited those who were less fortunate.

When Brynleigh was a child, she'd learned about the formation of the Republic of Balance. They'd spent a year learning about the Unification of the Four Kingdoms. Many centuries after the Battle of Balance, the Founders of the Republic had dreamed of a country where everyone was equal and lived beneath a single banner.

It was all a fucking joke.

The limo turned a corner and passed a white marble government building. Two statues of the same material stood outside the building, facing each other. The ancient elves were the High Ladies, once responsible for resetting the balance. One was covered in green whorls and swirls, while the other's tattoos were red. Everyone in the Republic knew of these two and the lengths they and their mates had gone to restore the balance long ago.

The Republic's flag flapped above their heads, illuminated by solar lights. The white banner, nearly as large as a car, had four roses encircling a scale.

Brynleigh scowled. The citizens of the Republic of Balance lived under one government, but the equality the Founders had desired was nowhere to be seen.

The Representatives and their families held a disproportionate amount of wealth and power. They were the government, the law, the army. They were in charge, and those who had the misfortune of being born outside their glorious ranks—which happened to be the majority of the Republic's citizens—suffered greatly.

Brynleigh's fingers curled around her gilded invitation, and anger coursed through her veins.

She wouldn't let the emotion rule her, though. Grabbing that anger, she bottled it up and shoved it deep inside.

The limo slowed as it turned another corner, and the driver lowered the barrier between them.

His hazel eyes met hers through the mirror. "We're fourth in line, Miss de la Point," he said, his gravelly voice breaking Brynleigh from her thoughts.

"Understood." Unfurling her fingers, she smoothed out the invitation.

"It shouldn't be long now. I'll let you prepare." He rolled the divider back up.

Brynleigh ran her tongue over the tip of her fangs, letting the slight prick of pain ground her.

She was about to enter the Choosing. A flurry of excitement spun in her stomach despite her best efforts to remain cool-headed about the entire affair. It was fair, she reasoned, to be a little excited because this was the biggest event of the decade. Each participant would arrive at the Hall of Choice in a limo. Once they exited their vehicles, they would walk through an arch of shadows designed to hide them from view from the other participants. This was a blind love competition, after all.

Efforts would be made to keep the men and women separate before the official Unmasking on the night of the proposals. The Masked Ball was one of the most important moments during the Choosing when the participants finally saw their Chosen partners face to face for the first time.

That didn't mean they'd be invisible until then, however. Press events were a very real part of the Choosing. After all, the Representatives wanted to ensure their offspring had time in the limelight.

Even though the Republic prided itself on the technological advancements that had occurred ever since the fae migrated across the Indigo Ocean, the Choosing itself was an antiquated process. It was a relic of times past, a remnant of efforts aimed at ensuring that everyone felt unified. Watching people fall in love was supposed to help the Republic connect and find common ground. That was no longer the case. Now, the upper class used the Choosing as another way to hold their superiority over the rest of the world.

As much as Brynleigh was disgusted by the show of wealth in Golden City, she had no choice but to play along with it. She needed to get close to Ryker. This was her only chance. She'd searched for the fae all over, but finding him had been impossible after he'd gone underground six years ago. She'd never even seen a picture of him. Someone had gone to great lengths to wipe all evidence of the captain from any publicly available sources of information.

The limo moved closer, and the thick, black fog fell over the windows. Even Brynleigh's vampiric eyes couldn't see through the opaque mist. If she were mortal, she would've been afraid. She'd never much enjoyed the dark when she was human. But she was no longer mortal, and that kind of thing no longer bothered her.

She'd been reborn into a creature of the night, and the darkness was her home. Her safe place. It called to her.

She straightened her dress and smoothed out wrinkles. She kept her wings on display, wanting to show the press precisely who she was.

It wasn't long before the engine turned off. Hundreds of heartbeats were the melodic backdrop to the city's symphony. Most were the rapid, steady heartbeats of humans and elves, but a few other slow, rhythmic thrums told her other vampires were nearby.

The driver walked around and opened Brynleigh's door. Darkness rose above them, an arch of swirling night. Inside the shadows were dozens of people with cameras waiting to catch a glimpse of her.

She inched towards the open door, careful not to snag her dress. The moment Brynleigh's heeled foot touched the pavement, cameras flashed. The press' lights lit up the night like bursts of lightning in a spring storm. In one hand, Brynleigh held her clutch. In the other, she gripped her invitation. Her shoulders were back, and a pristine smile graced her face.

An elaborate, long, scarlet carpet led up the massive steps of the Hall of Choice. The path they wanted her to take was obvious, but Brynleigh wasn't an obvious vampire.

She took a few steps down the red carpet, smiled, and waved.

If they wanted a show, she'd give them one. Fanning out her wings, Brynleigh allowed them to stretch to their full length. They were heavy, capable of supporting her weight, and her favorite part of being a vampire.

A few murmurs rippled through the crowd, assuring her she had everyone's attention.

Only then, once she was certain they were watching, did she

release her shadows. The dark wisps pooled at her feet, eager to do her bidding.

"A doubly blessed vampire," one of the reporters murmured.

Several more cameras flashed.

"A creature of the night," was another remark.

"Beautiful."

The comments swirled around Brynleigh as she flapped her wings. She rose in the air, remaining within the black arch, enjoying how the wind caressed her like a lover.

Someone else noted, "This one will be a favorite."

Brynleigh didn't hide her expanding grin as she flew towards the guarded entrance of the Hall of Choice, bypassing the steps entirely. She wasn't here for fame, fortune, or any other perks.

She was here for revenge, and finally, it would be hers.

CHAPTER 3
May the Gods Bless Your Choice

Brynleigh landed on the top steps, waved at the press, and grinned as she retracted her wings. She kept a strand of shadows wrapped around her wrist like a bracelet as a reminder of her power.

"Good evening, Miss de la Point." A guard dipped his head. "Right this way, please. The women are gathering in the Crimson Lounge."

Brynleigh handed her invitation and clutch to the man. Looking over her shoulder, she waved at the cameras one last time. Thanking the guard, she smiled demurely. She would be kind, but not too kind. Happy to be here, but not exuberant. Present, but not overly talkative. There were many things Brynleigh had to remember. Her plan hinged on walking a fine line of truth and lies, falseness mixed with the barest amount of reality.

The guard entered the Hall of Choice, and Brynleigh followed behind. Keeping her head down, she discreetly took in her surroundings. Several flashing red lights blinked at her from within vases and above doors, hiding cameras that were probably displaying her procession through the hall to the members of the Republic.

In preparation for this moment, Brynleigh had spent hours

studying the blueprints for the Hall of Choice. The building was practically palatial, and not only did it house the participants of the Choosing, but it boasted an expansive ballroom, several staterooms, two prodigious libraries, and an industrial kitchen equipped to feed everyone needed to keep the building running. The residential area of the Hall of Choice was mirrored, with one section for men and another for women.

Hushed whispers filtered beneath closed doors as the guard led Brynleigh towards the Crimson Lounge. Most people wouldn't be able to make out their words, but the moon goddess had blessed vampires with the best hearing of everyone in the Republic. Even dragon shifters, with their extensive senses, couldn't hear as well as children of the night.

Tuning out the clicking of her heels on the marble tile, Brynleigh picked up snippets of conversations.

"My mother loves the Choosing…"

"… Another riot last night in the Eastern Region…"

"There are several elves…"

"… did you see…"

"He's so handsome…"

"… unrest in the Southern…"

Brynleigh's ears perked up at the final comment. News of riots and general unrest wasn't exactly new to her. One would have to be blind not to notice the inequality between the upper and lower classes in the Republic of Balance. Sure, the government said they were all for "equality," but it was all talk. Their actions showed how much they didn't value the lower classes.

In the real world—the one veiled behind a golden sheen—the Representatives and their families were the elite, and the rest of the population was considered less than. The upper class hid behind their rank and used the power of their names as shields from the laws that governed the rest of the continent.

Captain Ryker Waterborn was the perfect fucking example. If he hadn't hidden behind his mother's title, he would've been arrested and tried for the numerous deaths he'd caused.

But that never happened.

Brynleigh's family and their entire human village died, and no one paid the price for their lives.

One day, they were living happily. The next, they were gone. Dead, as if they'd never existed.

Brynleigh was finally taking matters into her own hands. For once, the archaic laws of the Republic were working in her favor. Captain Waterborn was duty-bound to participate in the Choosing, and sometime tonight, he'd be walking into the same building. He could hide from many things and become a recluse; he could wipe any trace of himself away, but even he had to obey the laws requiring the offspring of Representatives to join the Choosing.

"Here we are." The guard stopped in front of a golden door. He bowed. "Good luck, and may the gods bless your Choice."

"MY NAME IS YVETTE VIDENTIS," the redheaded Death Elf standing before Brynleigh exclaimed. Her voice was rather loud, and the vampire winced.

Yvette's hair was a loose, strawberry waterfall down her back, and she drank from a ruby goblet. While Brynleigh's dress was long and fit her like a glove, Yvette's dress was short and strapless. It did little to support Yvette's cleavage, and the material stopped mid-thigh. It was white, the traditional color most people wore to the Choosing.

The custom hearkened back to the Rose Empire when the Empresses would wear white on the day they met their potential husband during the opening ceremony of the Marriage Games.

Remembering her manners, Brynleigh forced herself to smile. "Nice to meet you."

When Brynleigh had initially entered the Crimson Lounge a few minutes ago, she'd been taken aback by all the red. The entire room was awash in it. The couches, the rugs, and even the paintings were all shades of the same color. Scarlet, crimson, maroon, and cerise were splashed throughout the space.

Their theme was probably love, but Brynleigh would rather interpret it as blood. Each Choosing had its own theme. Once, it had been a jungle. Another time, it had been fire and ice.

This one was good. Perfect, actually. The color reminded Brynleigh of her deadly purpose.

Yvette smiled kindly. "What's your name?"

Brynleigh didn't exactly want to share her life story with the Death Elf, but they were the only two here. After a moment, she said, "Brynleigh de la Point."

Her fingers went to her neck, twisting her necklace as a pang of agony ran through her. She shoved *that* emotion deep inside.

Once, she'd had another name. It was stolen by a rush of water in the middle of the night. Drowned, that name was forever gone. She'd given it up the same night her family had been taken from her. Now, following vampiric tradition, she used the name of her Maker.

The warmth in Yvette's voice was genuine as she said, "Nice to meet you. I like your necklace."

Brynleigh's hand fell, and she grimaced. "Thank you. It's an heirloom."

She really didn't want to get into it further.

"You're a vampire, right?" Yvette asked sweetly, her gaze sweeping over Brynleigh's. "I noticed your black eyes when you first walked in."

Obsidian eyes, sharp fangs, and a predisposed hatred of silver and wooden stakes were things all vampires in the Republic of Balance shared.

"Yes." Brynleigh nodded, hoping the questions would end soon.

Thank all the gods, a resounding gong sounded at the door, saving her from further interrogation. The exuberant Yvette went to greet the newcomer, and after exhaling and shaking out her shoulders, Brynleigh followed.

A beautiful elf with russet skin and silky midnight hair twisted in an intricate braid walked into the lounge. Gold earrings dangled from her pointed ears. Layers of gossamer white fabric hung over her shoulders, artfully covering the important bits of her body before pooling on the floor. She looked like a goddess brought to life.

The elf's gaze swept over the crimson room before landing on the pair. She smiled. "Hello, my name's Esmeralda Larousse, but most people call me Esme. It's nice to meet you."

Yvette handed Esme a ruby glass filled with wine of the same color. She seemed a natural hostess as she ushered Esme over to the couches. Brynleigh trailed behind, hoping that her lack of speed would save her from being the target of any more questions.

Luckily, it seemed Yvette was happy to learn about Esme. "What kind of elf are you?"

Esme sipped the wine. "A Light Elf, though my grandfather on my mother's side is a dragon shifter."

Yvette gasped and leaned closer, intrigue scrawled across her face. "Are you a descendant of the Carinoc dragons?"

"Mhmm." Esme nodded, taking another sip.

Yvette looked impressed, and honestly, Brynleigh felt the same way. As a child, she'd often heard the story behind the Carinoc dragons. Their miraculous survival and subsequent contribution to the Battle of Balance were the stuff of legend.

"Can you shift?" Brynleigh asked, unable to help herself. She'd never met a dragon before.

Esme looked over the back of the couch and shook her head. "Unfortunately not. My elven side is much stronger, but my brother can."

"Really?" Yvette's eyes gleamed.

"Yep." Esme took an enthusiastic swallow of her wine. "His dragon is emerald. It's stunning."

"Fascinating!" the Death Elf exclaimed. She asked Esme a slew of questions, making Brynleigh eternally thankful that she was no longer the target of Yvette's interrogation.

Esme didn't seem to mind the questions one bit. She told them where she grew up (the plains of the Western Region), her favorite food (chocolate cake, and honestly? That was also Brynleigh's favorite before she was Made), what she did for a living (unsurprisingly, her father was an Elven Representative, so she was training to take his place when he retired).

Thank all the gods, neither of the women seemed to notice Brynleigh's silence. The vampire procured a glass of blood wine from the bartender, a quiet human with black hair and kind eyes.

By the time Yvette had run out of questions, more women had joined them.

Armed with her beverage and a desire not to answer any more questions, Brynleigh stationed herself against the back wall. She studied the participants as they filtered in, taking slow sips of her drink. Blood wine, like all alcohol except for Faerie Wine, didn't really affect vampires, but Brynleigh didn't want to risk being anything but alert.

Soon, the room was packed. Some women were as tall as her, while others were shorter. A werewolf with glowing orange eyes entered, followed by four more elves, two fae, and a shifter of some kind. So far, Brynleigh was the only vampire. Eleven women were present, and they were just missing one.

Excitement filled the air as the women milled around and introduced themselves. No one seemed to notice that Brynleigh was standing off by herself, which was exactly how she liked it.

An elf with long silver hair twisted in an elaborate knot sauntered up to Yvette.

"So, who do you think the last one is?" She twisted a lock of her hair through her fingers. "A child of a Representative or a commoner?"

Standing a few feet away, Brynleigh scowled. How dare the elf draw such a blatant line between the upper and lower classes?

Yvette didn't miss a beat before she shrugged. "I don't know, but regardless, they'll probably be a wonderful person. You shouldn't be so quick to judge others."

Just like that, Yvette rose much higher in Brynleigh's books.

The elf sneered. "It's not judging if it's true. My mother always says—"

The gong sounded one final time, cutting off the classist elf. The door didn't open immediately, though, and something felt different. Narrowing her eyes, Brynleigh pushed off the back wall and stood beside Yvette. The vampire's shadows swirled in her veins, urging her to pay attention. Some people followed their gut, but Brynleigh followed the call of her darkness. It hadn't steered her wrong yet.

The next contestant to walk through the door would be dangerous. As someone who claimed that title herself, Brynleigh felt confident assigning it to another.

Rule number five: always trust your instincts.

When the door finally opened, a tall beauty strode into the room as though she owned it. Danger emanated from her every pore. Blue-black hair was piled on her head, highlighting her pointed, pierced ears. Sharp cheekbones and a long nose looked down on the room. Bright, ruby-red lips were pressed together. Violet eyes glimmered with the promise of violence. Unlike most of the other women, this one wore a scarlet gown. When the light hit it, it sparkled like a thousand rubies were sewn into it.

Next to Brynleigh, Yvette gasped. "The Chancellor's daughter."

Shock rippled through the room.

One of the fae murmured, "I had no idea she was participating in the Choosing."

Brynleigh's heart, which usually mimicked a turtle, sped up. Now, *this* was interesting.

Dangerous but interesting.

There wasn't a single person in the Republic of Balance who didn't know about Valentina Rose. After all, her mother was Chancellor Ignatia Rose, the head of the entire government. The fae had kept her daughter sequestered and guarded for decades, only parading her out for select functions with the Representatives. She was so well hidden that no one knew which element her magic favored.

But now, Valentina was out in public. Here. At the Choosing.

Brynleigh studied the fae. Something about the other woman made her feel on edge.

Valentina's sharp gaze swung around the room. She silently assessed each participant until her violet eyes locked onto Brynleigh's black ones.

Those red lips twisted into an ugly sneer. "I thought this was a classy competition. Who let the bloodsucker in?"

Inhaling sharply, Brynleigh tightened her grip around her glass of wine. This wasn't the first time she'd heard that particular insult, or even the hundredth, but she hated it all the same.

Most people in the Republic of Balance didn't harbor much love for vampire kind. Growing up as a human, Brynleigh had seen some of the side glances directed towards children of the night. She'd heard the stories of vampires who ripped through the throats of others for fun. She'd learned about the Firsts who'd terrorized the previous Kingdom of Eleyta before being entombed in Hoarfrost Hollow, the evil Queen Marguerite and her Favorites, and the Last King and Queen who ruled Eleyta.

None of that knowledge could have prepared Brynleigh for the hatred she'd encountered since her Making.

No one seemed to like vampires, probably because they were Made, not born. Unlike the other species who would Fade after centuries of life, Isvana's children were truly immortal.

Those violet eyes drilled into Brynleigh as if daring her to respond. With every passing second, the vampire's anger grew. Was Valentina purposefully baiting her? Wanting her to lash out?

Brynleigh's spine straightened, and she drew a few dark wisps from her veins. They gathered around her palms, and she slowly placed her wineglass on the nearest surface.

The other ten women glanced between Brynleigh and Valentina before taking a collective step back. The tension in the room ratcheted up as the seconds passed.

Valentina raised a manicured brow and snorted. "Do you have nothing to say, leech? No way to defend yourself? How very *typical*."

Brynleigh snarled, and she clamped her mouth shut. A sharp burst came from her mouth, and she tasted blood as her tongue came too close to her fangs.

Get a fucking grip, she chided. *You're not a Fledgling anymore.*

Although technically, that wasn't exactly true. Jelisette had worked closely with Brynleigh to help her overcome the initial urges of being a new vampire, but she was still less than a decade old. The danger with Fledglings was that since they were newly Made, they were less in control than other, older vampires.

Historically, hundreds of Fledgling vampires had succumbed to bloodlust, embarking on murderous rampages that ended with stakes shoved through their hearts.

Definitely not the outcome Brynleigh desired.

With help from Zanri and Jelisette, along with a significant amount of meditation, Brynleigh had successfully kept her murderous impulses under control. That was one of Z's main jobs as her handler: ensuring she *only* killed the right people at the right time.

Too bad he wasn't here right now. At this moment, there was nothing Brynleigh would love more than to dig her fangs into Valentina's pale neck and teach the fae a lesson about respect. Unfortunately, that would have to wait. Brynleigh had a bigger kill in mind than some fae with definite mean-girl vibes.

Still, Brynleigh would keep an eye on Valentina. One day, when they weren't in the middle of a competition for love, she would destroy her.

"I have nothing to say to you." Brynleigh finally broke her silence.

Her mother, the gods be with her soul, had always taught Brynleigh and her sister that remaining silent was the best course of action if they didn't have anything kind to say. It had never been more difficult than it was at this very moment.

Valentina scowled. "Whatever. I'm going to keep an eye on you, bitch."

Brynleigh's nails dug into her palms, cutting open the flesh as she forced herself to remain still.

Thank Isvana, the gong above the door rang once more. This time, an older woman entered. She had silvery hair, her face was worn with age, and her cerise pantsuit matched the red theme of the room. The look would've been garish on anyone else, but somehow, this woman made it seem normal.

She strolled into the middle of the room, either oblivious to or ignorant of the crackling tension that had been building.

"Welcome to the Two Hundredth Choosing." The woman—a human—smiled at each participant in turn. "I'm Lilith, your Matron."

Brynleigh murmured a greeting along with the others.

"I see the gods have selected well for this year's Choosing," Lilith said. "The men will be blessed, no matter who they pick."

Yvette giggled into her wineglass, the drink clearly having gone to her head.

The Matron smiled kindly at the Death Elf before continuing, "Now that you're all here, tonight's itinerary is simple. Eat, drink, and get to know each other." A white brow rose to her forehead. "You're all adults, so I won't be enforcing a curfew. I trust you can behave?"

It was Valentina who smoothly replied, "We certainly can."

There was no trace of the earlier cruelty in the fae's voice, but Brynleigh wouldn't be fooled that easily. She would keep an eye on Valentina. In Brynleigh's experience, the worst types of people were the ones who waited in the shadows for the perfect moment to strike.

"Wonderful." Matron Lilith strode to the bar, picking up the last unclaimed glass of sparkling wine. "You'll be expected to hand over your cellular devices tonight, and your clothes will be delivered by breakfast tomorrow."

"We won't be able to contact anyone at all?" the werewolf asked from her position on the couch. Her orange eyes glowed.

"No." Lilith shook her head. "Outside interference in the Choosing is strictly prohibited. Is that clear, ladies?"

"Yes, ma'am," Brynleigh said, along with the rest of the group.

"Good. Tomorrow, the twelve of you will be split into three groups of four. You'll participate in a series of interviews with select press members." She smiled. "It'll help you ease into things before the Opening Ceremony the day after."

Excited whispers flowed through the room as the women speculated about what they might encounter during the Opening Ceremony. It changed every time, but one thing remained the same—the men and women would not meet.

Brynleigh didn't engage in the chatter. She sipped her wine, her mind already jumping to when she would finally meet the captain.

If the Matron noticed Brynleigh's silence, she didn't say anything. "It would be wise to rest while you still can."

The whispers ceased.

"The gods only know you'll need it in the days ahead." Lilith raised her glass and waited for the women to follow suit. "Congratulations on being selected, and may the gods bless your Choice."

Soon after that, the Matron departed. Brynleigh maintained her position against the wall. Like a hunter eyeing her prize, she assessed each of the women.

After all, they were her competition for Ryker's hand in marriage. She would never forget her reason for being here.

THE NEXT DAY, the interviews went without a hitch. At least, they did for Brynleigh. Others didn't fare so well.

After breakfast, the women were given directions and split into groups. They would each meet with six reporters in interview rooms that were miniature versions of the Crimson Lounge, right down to the red goblets and ruby couches. The first member of the press had been waiting for them upon arrival.

Once the questions began, they went on for hours.

Brynleigh was well-prepared for every single question that came her way. Her answers rolled off her tongue smoothly, sounding practiced but not overly rehearsed. Most of the inquiries directed at her were related to her Maker. Jelisette de la Point was a well-known vampire in the Republic of Balance, and the press was naturally curious about her newest progeny.

Some of the other members of Brynleigh's quad didn't fare so well. Hallie, one of the elves, stumbled over many of her responses. Like Brynleigh, she was not related to any of the Representatives and was instead Selected from the general population to participate in the Choosing. This was a way to keep the main populace happy while ensuring bloodlines within the Representatives remained fresh.

Hallie was a pale, white-haired Fortune Elf with emerald eyes that sparkled as she spoke. She was kind and had greeted Brynleigh as soon as they'd sat down. She was notably nicer than the other women, and there was a softness about her that Brynleigh hadn't seen in a long time.

The reporters were vultures. They picked on Hallie relentlessly when they realized she wasn't as prepared as the others. When the last reporter, a witch from the Eastern Region, closed the door behind her, Hallie was wiping away tears from her green eyes. Her nearly translucent white wings fluttered behind her, betraying her nerves. They'd been doing that since the first reporter started asking them questions hours ago.

"I don't understand why they kept pushing me," Hallie whispered, twisting a tissue through her fingers. "Why wouldn't they leave me alone?"

Brynleigh handed the Fortune Elf a fresh tissue. "Because they're predators." Just like her. "They saw your nerves and fed on them."

Watching the reporters tear into Hallie had been terrible. This only affirmed Brynleigh's belief that the Choosing, like everything else in the Republic, was unfairly skewed towards the Representatives.

Esme sighed from where she sat on Hallie's other side. "You should ignore them." She brushed a lock of white hair from the Fortune Elf's cheek. "They're curious about us. The Choosing only happens once every ten years, and people want to know about the participants."

"It's easier for you." Hallie blew her nose. "How long have you known you'd be participating?"

"Since I was old enough to understand what the Choosing was," Esme admitted. "It's my birthright."

Like Brynleigh, Esme's answers had been practiced and perfect.

The fourth member of their quad was Trinity, the werewolf. She was soft-spoken. Her great-uncle was the new Alpha of the Northern Werewolves. An extremely rude reporter had dared ask about Trinity's older sister Malika, who'd died last year. Malika had initially been the one destined for the Choosing.

Trinity had barely made it through her answers before bursting into tears. She, too, clung to a tissue.

"Maybe tomorrow will be better," Trinity said hopefully.

Hallie sniffled. "Maybe."

Probably not. Beneath the facade of caring about equality, the Representatives were cold, hard people who only looked out for themselves. That's what made them so dangerous and why infiltrating their ranks was so difficult. They were powerful, wealthy, and commanded the entire world.

If Hallie and Trinity were lucky, they would find strength within themselves before the others tore them to shreds.

If not, Brynleigh would add their names to the growing list of people she was avenging.

CHAPTER 4
It Would Behoove You Not to Act Like Animals

Captain Ryker Elias Waterborn, Head of the Army's Fae Division, wrapped a black silk tie around his neck with the smooth precision of someone who had attended dozens of lavish parties where younglings were to be seen and not heard.

His light brown hair, streaked with red, was still damp from the shower. The ends tickled his pointed ears. He raked a hand through his locks, letting them settle where they wanted before he pulled on the black suit jacket slung over the back of the only chair in his room. The space was much smaller than his apartment, but he hadn't come into the Choosing expecting the accommodations to be luxurious.

Striding over to the desk, he picked up the red rose that had been delivered this morning and pinned it to his lapel. Even though they wouldn't see the women today at the Opening Ceremony, they had to look their best. After all, the cameras were always watching.

That would be... odd. Difficult to get used to.

Many Representatives, including Ryker's parents, kept their families shielded from the public eye. He had been raised in private, and after the Incident six years ago, he'd allowed that same privacy to wrap around him like a shroud, hiding him from the world. Now, he was stepping out of isolation and letting the world watch him find a bride.

All because of a promise.

Once he was happy with the placement of the rose, he slid his feet into the black shoes matching his silk shirt. He meticulously tied the laces, taking care to work with precision.

When other children played tag and chased each other through parks, Ryker was learning how to tie a tie, ride a horse, and never speak to an adult if they weren't directly addressing him. By his tenth birthday, he already had a decent amount of control over his birthright water magic. By his eleventh, he accompanied his mother to the monthly meetings of the Representatives in Golden City. Always under guard and hidden from the press, of course. By his fifteenth, he was already training to join the army.

When he Matured and came into his full fae strength, Ryker was the youngest captain the army had ever seen. One did not rise in the ranks as quickly as he had without having an innate understanding that laws were the reason order existed in the world. Rules and regulations were the backbone of his life.

Through all that, Ryker had always known that one day, he would participate in this event.

Two thousand years ago, when the Founders of the Republic of Balance first established the Choosing, they decreed that each Representative's oldest eligible offspring would participate in the Choosing when they came of age. It was a way to keep the peace among the many people who made up the Republic.

It wasn't a completely choice-less process, though. Children of Representatives decided when they would participate in the once-a-decade event. Ryker had planned to wait another two or three decades before seeking a wife, content to live in his bachelorhood for a little while longer, but when his father fell ill...

Cyrus Waterborn had begged Ryker to enter the Choosing now and find a wife. He wanted to see his son married before it was too late. Ryker's father was many things, including a provider, and he loved his children deeply. He refused to Fade without knowing that his son was settled. It was an old-fashioned idea, but Ryker didn't have it in him to fight with his father. Not after everything else that had happened.

Reluctantly, Ryker had agreed. He hated that this meant he'd have to come out of hiding, but he would do anything for his family, including this.

With that thought in mind, Ryker rose and gave himself a once-over in the mirror. He adjusted his suit jacket one last time before slipping out the door to join the other eleven men in the Ruby Lounge.

Their group was a good mix, or so he thought. It was symbolic of the current mosaic of citizens that called the Republic of Balance their home. The merfolk were the only ones who didn't participate in the Choosing. They preferred to remain in the sea and govern themselves as they always had.

Ryker was the last to enter the Ruby Lounge. The men stood in clusters of two and three, murmuring amongst themselves as they glanced at the door. Nervous energy thickened the air as they waited for the Matron to arrive with instructions on how today would go.

Ryker went to the bar, where a Light Elf with spiked hair was serving drinks. "Coffee, sir?"

"Yes, thank you." Caffeine was part of Ryker's everyday routine. He needed it to function. His younger sister River teased him about his addiction to the drink, but she was only twenty-one and didn't yet understand how much he needed it. One day, she would.

The Light Elf passed Ryker a red mug filled with steaming brown liquid. Ryker's nose twitched at the decadent smell of freshly ground beans, and a smile spread across his face.

"Thank you." Ryker ceded his place at the bar as a blond shifter approached him and asked for the same drink.

When Ryker had first arrived at the Hall of Choice, the shifter had introduced himself as Therian Firebreath. If his name hadn't been enough of a tell, his size was proof of the dragon living beneath his skin. Even in this form, Therian made Ryker look lean.

Coffee in hand, the shifter turned. "Morning, Captain."

"Morning." Ryker shook Therian's hand.

Both men were in the military, although they were in different divisions. Ryker had heard of Therian before, but he'd never met him. The shifter was a skilled fighter, known for the size of his black dragon. Therian had a reputation for never starting fights but always finishing them. He could either be a good friend or a formidable foe.

Ryker had a rule that it was always better to befriend those who could possibly cause him problems in the future. That was how he acquired his two best friends, Atlas and Nikhail.

"Those interviews yesterday were something else, weren't they?" Therian asked as Philippe, an Earth Elf, came over to join them.

"They were long," Ryker confirmed.

Philippe asked, "How did your quad do?"

"Good. The questions were run of the mill," Ryker said.

He'd known all the answers. Ryker always knew the answers. It was his job. He'd long since memorized the right things to say, knowing that something as simple as a slip of the tongue could endanger him and his family. No matter what, Ryker would never let anything happen to them.

Especially River.

It was rare for fae to have children so close in age—Ryker was only seventeen years older than his sister. As such, he and River had an affectionate sibling relationship that many fae lacked. The day his little sister was born, Ryker had sworn he would do anything and everything to protect her.

He'd never broken that promise.

Sipping his coffee, Ryker took quick stock of the room. Besides Therian and Philippe, there was another fae, two werewolves, three elves, a witch, and a duo of vampires. All the men wore black suits and red roses on their lapels, like Ryker.

The clock struck the hour, and the door opened. Matron Cassandra entered, her scarlet ballgown swishing around her. Her white hair was elaborately braided away from her face, and she held herself with authority. Each Choosing, the Matrons were selected from the population to help the participants navigate the Choosing. It was an honor to serve the Republic in such a manner.

Cassandra smiled warmly, reminding Ryker of his grandmother, Fannie. She'd Faded when Ryker was six, but before then, she'd always showered him with love.

"Good morning, gentlemen. It's time for the Opening Ceremony." She raised a brow, meeting each of their gazes in turn. "Remember, your future wife will be attending as well. Even though you won't be able to see the women, it would behoove you not to act like animals."

STARING ACROSS THE GRAND BALLROOM, Ryker gripped the railing of the elevated box where he and the other men waited for the ceremony to begin. Two elevated opera-style boxes spanned the length of the ballroom, one on each side. The men were in one, and the women were in the other. An unnatural wall of shadows that must have been created by a vampire stretched across the ballroom. Even with his elevated senses, Ryker couldn't see through it.

He tried. No one could blame him for that. After all, one of the women veiled in darkness would be his bride. Ryker *would* find a match in the Choosing. He'd accept no other outcome.

Shuffling came from the floor below as a crowd filled the seats. There were at least a hundred people, judging by their shadowy forms. Hushed murmurs and quiet conversations rose from the crowd beneath them. Several bright lights illuminated the stage, and camera crews stood by, waiting for the Chancellor to take her place.

Minutes ticked by, and anticipation thickened the air. The hairs on Ryker's neck prickled, and his magic thrummed in his veins. This was unusual, and unusual things were never good.

"Do you think something is wrong?" Therian strode next to Ryker, his large hands gripping the railing. "It should've begun by now."

"I don't know," Ryker said honestly.

He reached for his back pocket, where he usually kept his phone, before recalling that it had been confiscated upon arrival two days ago. Damn.

"It's strange." The dragon shifter crossed his arms and frowned.

Ryker agreed. All his military training had taught him to be suspicious of anything that didn't go exactly as planned. He had a bad feeling about this, and his stomach was in tight knots. The last time he felt like this, he had to deal with a family crisis six years ago.

Peeling his gaze away from the empty platform, Ryker methodically searched for trouble. Even though he couldn't see anything wrong, that sense of unease remained within him.

Another ten minutes passed.

Ryker's fists were furled at his sides. He gnawed on the inside of his lip. This was a public event, and the tardiness was most unbecoming. Like most aspects of the Choosing, it was broadcast to the citizens of the Republic. People all over the continent would be waiting for the live stream to begin.

Eventually, he could wait no longer. He released the railing. "I'm going to find someone in charge and demand some answers."

"Alright," Therian grunted from his position at the railing.

Ryker was halfway to the door when the *click-click-click* of heels on wood came from below. His shoulders incrementally relaxed as he returned to his position at the railing.

Chancellor Ignatia Rose strode into view. Her blue-black hair was pulled back from her face, silver earrings dangled from her pointed fae ears, and she wore a tailored white pantsuit that looked like it cost thousands of dollars. A small microphone was clipped to her lapel, and she looked directly at the cameras, exuding confidence.

It wasn't the Chancellor herself that caught Ryker's attention, but the four soldiers, dressed head-to-toe in black, fanned out behind her. The Republic's sigil—a scale surrounded by four red roses—was on their chests, and each guard held a massive black gun. Their stern expressions gave nothing away as they coolly looked over the attendees.

Tension thickened, and the air practically crackled. The chatter from earlier was gone, and no one dared speak.

The door behind them clicked, and two guards entered the men's box.

Ryker walked over, his brows furrowed. "What's going on?"

The guards exchanged a look that set warning bells off in Ryker's mind.

The taller one said, "Nothing, sir. This is standard protocol."

Standard protocol, his ass. Ryker knew something was wrong. He could feel it.

Probing for answers would have to wait because the Chancellor cleared her throat. The microphone screeched. Ryker winced.

"Ladies and gentlemen of the Republic, I apologize for the delay." The Chancellor's smooth, melodic voice rang through the space. Like Ryker, Ignatia Rose was a fae, but her element was fire. "There was a slight incident."

That would explain the guards.

"Fortunately, the situation has been dealt with, and we can now begin." The Chancellor smiled, but nothing but ice came from the fire fae.

Ryker didn't believe the Chancellor. If everything was

resolved, why were there so many guards present? The problem, whatever it was, still existed. He'd bet on it.

He remained alert as Ignatia continued speaking. As was tradition, she regaled the attendees about the history of the Choosing, and of the Founders' desire that the Choosing would bring strength to all and unite the continent. The Chancellor reminded them that the Choosing wasn't just for the Representatives and their families. Six participants were Selected from the general population to join the competition. It was an honor that would elevate their status and lift them into the echelons of high society in the Republic of Balance.

The Chancellor was in the middle of explaining the timeline of the next three months when suddenly, a scream ripped through the air from the back of the ballroom. It was so sudden, so unexpected, that for a moment, no one moved.

Then, that sense of dread exploded in Ryker. He released the railing and spun around as all hell broke loose.

CHAPTER 5
A Curse and a Blessing

Brynleigh was in the middle of an internal debate about how bad it would look if she slipped into the Void to escape this wearisome ceremony when a high-pitched scream cut through the Chancellor's monotonous speech. Was it bad that, for a moment, she'd been happy because it meant she could focus on something other than the history of the Choosing?

As soon as the ceremony had started, Brynleigh was looking forward to its end. Not only was the speech ridiculously tedious, but all the women wore floor-length black strapless gowns and four-inch stilettos. The shoes seemed designed to inflict agony upon the wearer's feet, and Brynleigh wanted to take them off as soon as possible.

Another scream came seconds after the first.

Brynleigh's head snapped back, her eyes narrowing as she searched for the source of the cry. Her shadows pulsed within her, and she let a few slip as her fingers curled into fists. The damned shadows cloaking the middle of the ballroom, designed to keep them from seeing the men, made seeing anything at all nearly impossible.

There.

At the back of the ballroom, by the exit, a guest was on the ground. Even through the shadows, Brynleigh made out their prone form.

Her nostrils flared, and her heart raced.

Blood.

She'd recognize the scent anywhere. It was her life, after all. The source of her immortality. Her *everything*.

A snarl rumbled through the elevated box, and it took a moment for Brynleigh to realize the sound came from her chest. She stared at the floor, warring with herself.

Half of her—the monstrous, deadly, violent creature built for death itself—wanted to vault over the railing. She'd summon her wings and make it onto the floor in one piece. The other half—the rational, logical one—remembered that she wasn't there to feed. It urged her to leave before she did something stupid and endangered her entire mission.

The other women were yelling, and Brynleigh could've sworn someone was crying, but their voices were muffled.

Brynleigh battled the dueling desires within her. Like all vampires, blood was her weakness and her strength. A curse and a blessing. The giver of her life and the pulsing, never-ending need in her veins.

Her fangs sliced into her tongue as she stared at the growing pool of red on the ground below. It wasn't that far. Two, maybe three stories. She could be down there in a flash. Her shadows would protect her while she fed. She could—

"Ladies!" a guard shouted, his commanding voice snapping Brynleigh from her thoughts.

She jerked her attention away from the body, turning to face the soldier.

"Follow me," he ordered. "I have orders to return you to the Crimson Lounge immediately."

A sigh of relief slipped past Brynleigh's lips as she moved towards the guard. Each step took her further away from the crimson pool of temptation.

Three more guards waited in the hallway. Two took the front, and the other pair flanked them from behind.

The predator within Brynleigh had awoken at the scent of blood; now, it was on high alert. It prowled within her, writhing like the shadows in her veins.

She jumped when something brushed against her arm.

"What's going on?" Hallie's voice shook as she hugged her arms around herself. Her pale wings twitched behind her.

Brynleigh's stomach twisted at the sound of the Fortune Elf's voice. Hallie sounded so much like...

No.

Brynleigh refused to think about that. She couldn't risk letting those memories take hold. Not right now. She needed to stay alert and present.

Still, she could take pity on Hallie and try to protect her. The Fortune Elf seemed too frail for this world, as if all the inequality and violence surrounding them would break her.

Brynleigh leaned in. "I'm not sure," she whispered. "I think someone was shot."

That was the most plausible explanation for the amount of blood. Even though they'd moved far enough away that the scent was gone, Brynleigh's fangs still burned. She needed to feed, and soon.

In the old days, when the Kingdom of Eleyta was ruled by vampires, Isvana's children used to have Sources. They were able to drink from the vein whenever they wanted. Now, that kind of behavior was frowned upon. Blood banks were the intermediary between vampires and the vital liquid they needed to survive.

For a fee, of course.

Paying for blood was considered more "humane" than biting. In fact, Brynleigh had never actually bitten and fed from anyone before. She was fairly certain that the blood banks were another way for the Representatives to keep vampires in check.

When creatures of the moon drank blood that didn't come directly from the vein, their powers were significantly reduced.

Oh, their blessings of wings and shadows remained intact, but as Jelisette so often told her progeny, vampires had other gifts in the past. One of their blood ancestors had even been able to read minds. Brynleigh had never met Estrella de la Point, but she'd heard of her impressive skills.

Estrella, along with many of the vampires who'd lived in the Four Kingdoms, had voluntarily entered a deep sleep when the Republic was founded. Tales were told of the older vampires, who'd grown weary of life and required a rest. Their location was a well-kept secret, known only by a select few.

Hallie gasped, and several of the other women glanced her in direction. "Shot?" Panic flared in the Fortune Elf's eyes, and she stumbled.

Brynleigh caught Hallie's arm and righted the elf before she fell. "Don't draw attention," she cautioned.

Brynleigh knew better than most that flying under the radar was the best way to get through life. She didn't need anyone looking too closely at her.

"Oh gods," the Fortune Elf moaned. "This was supposed to be a safe place." Hallie wrung her hands in front of her, and worry leaked into her voice. "I never thought someone would get shot!"

So much for keeping her voice down. By the time Hallie spoke the last words, she was yelling.

Valentina appeared out of nowhere. "Aren't you a Fortune Elf?" she sneered. "You should've Seen this coming."

Hallie seemed to shrink in on herself. "That's not... it doesn't work..." Her wings flapped, and she was as white as a sheet of paper. "I can't... the paths of the future don't reveal themselves like that."

"Leave her alone," Brynleigh snapped. "She's in shock."

Not everyone was used to death like Brynleigh. Hallie obviously didn't know how horrible life could be, which was a blessing, in a way.

Brynleigh's innocence had drowned along with her family.

The mean fae wrinkled her nose. "Oh, I see how it is. The

Fortune Elf has acquired a fancy bodyguard. Two misfits finding solace in each other. The bloodsucker and the commoner."

"Fuck off," Brynleigh snarled as she reached out and drew Hallie towards her. The elf trembled as she drew in massive gulps of air. "Go find someone else to harass."

Valentina's violet eyes widened, and she bared her elongated canines. "You vile blood-drinking bitch. Do you know who I am?"

Brynleigh raised a brow and haughtily replied, "You look like dinner to me."

A very nasty dinner whose blood probably tasted like putrid garbage. But Brynleigh didn't care. She didn't know what kind of fae Valentina was, whether she took after her mother's elemental abilities or her father's, whoever he was, but right now, she didn't care. Her control was already hanging on by a thread.

Valentina should know better than to pick a fight with a vampire already inflamed by the scent of blood.

Brynleigh released Hallie. The Fortune Elf stumbled back as a growl rumbled through the vampire. Somewhere outside of herself, Brynleigh was aware of the other women stepping back.

The guards were nowhere to be seen.

The Chancellor's daughter didn't move. She smirked as if she knew a secret no one else did. "You really have no idea who I am, do you?"

Valentina's eyes glimmered with violence, and Brynleigh knew she should drop this, but she couldn't seem to stop herself from saying, "Other than a bitch?" Brynleigh snarled and drew shadows around her. "No."

Valentina opened her palm. A flame flickered above her hand.

Instinctively, Brynleigh stumbled back.

Of course, Valentina was a fucking fire fae. Why not? That was the worst possible scenario. Just once, Brynleigh would like for things to go her way. Being in the Choosing with someone who could kill her with a flick of her wrist was a sick, twisted joke.

Vampires were essentially immortal, but three things could

cause them significant harm and even death: silver, wooden stakes, and flames. Long ago, before electricity, vampires lit their homes with Light Elf magic to avoid fire entirely.

Despite her desire to remain strong, Brynleigh trembled at the sight of the small yellow flame. She hated that her stomach curled in on itself at the sight, and she despised the icy fear running through her veins.

She was a vampire, a true immortal that would never Fade, but *this* instilled fear deep within her.

And Valentina? Her horrible, red mouth twisted as an awful, mocking laugh left her lips. The sound was like nails running down a chalkboard.

Right then and there, the fire fae secured a spot at the top of Brynleigh's "to-kill" list.

"Not so brave now, are you?" Valentina sneered and took a step towards Brynleigh.

The deadly flame was now a foot tall.

Brynleigh staggered back and slammed into a wall. She didn't look away from the fire. Her fingers flexed, and she released even more shadows.

She prepared to fight.

If it came down to it, Brynleigh would do whatever it took to survive, including killing the Chancellor's daughter. She was aware that wouldn't go over well—honestly, she'd be lucky if she spent the rest of her immortal life in a prohiberis-lined prison—but she was being threatened. Rational thought had no place here.

"Ladies!" Matron Lilith screeched, appearing in the corner of Brynleigh's vision. "Enough!"

A long moment passed before Valentina smirked. She extinguished the flame and rolled her shoulders. "Don't worry, Matron," she said in a sickly-sweet voice. "I was just showing my new friend what I can do."

Boiling lava replaced the ice running through Brynleigh's veins. "We're not friends," she snarled. "I'll never be your friend."

The fire fae simply shrugged and sauntered into the lounge as if she hadn't been threatening to kill Brynleigh moments before.

Matron Lilith looked at Brynleigh and shook her head. She frowned. "You shouldn't let her get beneath your skin, dear. It will only make things worse."

Brynleigh knew she should answer—she'd been raised to understand the importance of manners, especially when dealing with one's elders—but her control was rapidly deteriorating. She dipped her head, following Valentina into the Crimson Lounge.

The other women were discussing the shooting, but Brynleigh ignored them and headed straight for the bar.

The Death Elf who was wiping down the counter looked up as Brynleigh approached. "Miss?"

"Blood, please," Brynleigh rasped, gripping the ruby countertop.

Thank Isvana, the elf took one look at her face and gulped. He ducked beneath the bar, pulling out two red bags. "Warm or cold?"

At that moment, Brynleigh didn't have any time to wait for the blood to heat up. "Cold," she replied. "Please hurry."

The bartender nodded and ran a knife along the top of the bags. He poured the crimson liquid into a goblet and slid it over. "Here you go, miss."

Brynleigh snatched the cup and took a long swallow. The blood settled in her stomach, taking the most brittle edge off her hunger. "Thank you," she breathed.

The bartender nodded as Brynleigh drained the contents of her cup. The anger subsided as she downed the blood. The burning in her fangs cooled, and although she still desired to teach Valentina a lesson, rationality ruled her thoughts again.

"Can I have some more?" she asked.

The elf nodded, grabbing another bag as the door opened. Brynleigh watched over her shoulder as Matron Lilith entered, flanked by two guards. Both tall guards were broad of shoulder, muscular, and had scary-looking guns holstered at their hips.

Their matching brown eyes swept through the room, and Brynleigh would've bet good money that they were brothers.

"Here you go." The bartender handed the goblet to Brynleigh.

Matron Lilith sat on one of the crimson couches, folding her hands in her lap. "As I'm sure you're all aware, the Opening Ceremony didn't exactly go as planned."

"No shit," someone snarkily replied.

Brynleigh didn't see who it was.

"What happened?" This question came from Esme, who had her arm wrapped around Hallie.

The Matron sighed and signaled for one of the guards to step forward. "Harper will explain."

The soldier cleared his throat. "This morning, we received a tip that there may be a threat on the Chancellor's life."

A flurry of horrified gasps ran through the room.

"What?" someone exclaimed.

"Who would do such a thing?"

Valentina paled, and for a moment, Brynleigh felt bad for her. She imagined hearing that someone wanted your mother dead wasn't pleasant. Then she remembered the way the fire fae had threatened to kill her, and the pity was dissipated like a morning mist.

If Chancellor Rose was half as much of a bitch as her daughter, it was surprising that it had taken someone this long to threaten her life. Brynleigh knew better than most that there was no safe place in the Republic of Balance. Not really.

"There's no reason to fear." Harper's voice was matter-of-fact.

"No reason to fear?" Hallie questioned. "Someone was shot!"

Brynleigh was surprised by the force in the Fortune Elf's voice, considering that Hallie had seemed close to fainting a few minutes ago. She was happy to see her new friend fighting back, though. Maybe Hallie did have enough mettle to survive in this cold, harsh world.

"I assure you; we are equipped to deal with any threats,"

Harper replied. "The woman who was shot was a rebel. She will no longer be a problem."

The undercurrents of his words were evident: the rebel was dead, and dead women couldn't cause problems.

Cold-hearted. To the point. Jelisette would approve.

"Due to the unusual circumstances, the Opening Ceremony is over." Matron Lilith gestured to the guards. "From now on, there will be added security around the Hall of Choice."

"There's no need to be worried," Harper added. "This is a precautionary measure, nothing more."

A hand raised in the corner.

"Yes, Calliope?" Matron Lilith nodded.

"What about the Choosing?" Calliope perched on the edge of a red sofa, twisting green threads of magic through her fingers. The Earth Elf's black hair had slipped from its bun on the hurried walk back to the lounge, and several strands dangled around her face.

Brynleigh stiffened. She hadn't even considered that such an act of violence could make the Chancellor halt the Choosing. She hadn't even met Ryker yet. She couldn't wait another decade to avenge her family.

For some vampires, ten years wasn't a long time, but Brynleigh was young enough that time still had meaning for her. Ten years might as well have been a lifetime. If the Choosing ended now, the captain would return to hiding, and then what would Brynleigh do?

Twisting her necklace through her fingers, Brynleigh forced herself to breathe. Not for the oxygen, since vampires didn't precisely require air to live, but for normalcy.

The Choosing couldn't end prematurely. It just couldn't.

A memory flickered across Brynleigh's mind. Her heart raced. Her stomach knotted. Flashes of too-sudden lightning and a deluge of rain forced their way out of the compartment where she kept them. She shoved them back down.

After what felt like hours but was probably a few seconds,

Lilith smiled. "The Choosing will continue as planned. Chancellor Rose believes stopping it would give the rebels what they want."

Brynleigh's legs trembled in relief.

"And we're safe?" Hallie asked.

"Extremely," replied the Matron. "There has never been a single participant injury or death in the history of the Choosing. This one won't be any different."

Calliope asked a follow-up question, but Brynleigh didn't hear her. Relief liquefied the vampire's limbs, and she barely reached the empty seat on the couch next to Esme.

The Light Elf glanced at her, lifting a manicured brow in question, but Brynleigh shook her head. "I'm fine," she murmured.

And she would be. Rebels be damned, Brynleigh de la Point wouldn't be leaving the Hall of Choice without a ring on her finger.

CHAPTER 6
Today Would Change Everything

Ryker's alarm blared, the obnoxious tone pulling him out of sleep. He rolled over, blinking as his eyes adjusted to the darkness. His heart thundered, and he stared at the ceiling.

This was the day he'd been waiting for.

Today, he would meet twelve women. One of them would be his bride.

His stomach, which was usually rock-solid, was a churning mess. It took him a moment to realize what it was—nerves. That was strange. Ryker couldn't remember the last time he'd been nervous. He was a decorated soldier, for the gods' sake. He'd faced down entire armies without a trace of fear.

And yet, he was anxious. Even his magic roiled in his veins. Deep within him, he knew today would change everything.

That thought had Ryker rolling out of bed, quickly showering, and getting dressed in jeans and a black t-shirt. He raked a hand through his hair and headed to the Ruby Lounge.

He wasn't the only nervous one, it seemed. Breakfast was a rapid, loud affair as the men speculated about the women they'd meet. When the Matron entered a few minutes later, Ryker was polishing off a bagel with cream cheese.

Matron Cassandra's eyes sparkled. "Good morning, gentlemen. Are you ready for today?"

A chorus of "yes" rang through the room. Ryker joined them. Breakfast had eased his nerves, and now excitement flourished within him. He was eager for this day to get underway.

Smiling, the Matron instructed them to head to the ballroom when ready. There, they would check in with a woman named Lacey to receive their headphones, a necessary component for the Choosing. After confirming that no one had any questions, she departed.

Less than a minute after the Matron left, the first man followed suit. Ryker stood as well and was in the middle of the group as they made their way through the Hall of Choice.

The walk to the ballroom took a lifetime and a few seconds. Maybe Ryker was still nervous, after all. An armed guard stood at the ballroom entrance, his expression grim. Ryker counted at least three weapons on the man.

His fingers itched for his own gun, or even a knife, but he wasn't a captain here. He was a participant in the Choosing. Unarmed. Defenseless, but for the water magic that was his birthright.

He nodded at the soldier. "Good morning."

"Morning, sir." The guard opened the door. "Good luck, and may the gods bless your Choice."

"Thank you." Ryker had heard the blessing many times, but for the first time, it meant something more. He entered with a spring in his step, automatically scanning the dimly lit room for threats. He marked the exits, tucking the knowledge away in his mind.

The faint lilt of classical string music streamed out of hidden speakers, a backdrop to the quiet hum of conversation already filling the space.

A woman Ryker presumed was Lacey stood at a table nearby. Half a dozen white headphones were spread on the surface before her, and she held a clipboard as she spoke with Therian.

Two guards stood behind Lacey, and a dozen others were scattered through the room. They had their backs against the walls and were attempting to be inconspicuous. It was a nearly impossible task. The soldiers were dressed in black and had large guns holstered on their belts. They were a stark contrast against the ruby theme that surrounded them.

The rebel threat must have been more significant than Chancellor Rose was letting on. Ryker was aware of an undercurrent of unrest in the Republic. In the past, he'd even been part of quelling riots. However, this was his first time being on the other end of things. He didn't like it.

Therian and Lacey were still speaking, so Ryker took in the space.

The ballroom had undergone a complete transformation. The stage and microphones were gone, and in their place was a giant wall that stretched from floor to ceiling. It stretched down the middle of the ballroom, splitting it in two.

Instead of a typical partition that might be found in an office, this one featured a slow-moving walk-through of a garden at night. Vines dangled from trees. Night-blooming roses blossomed amid dark bushes. Fruit trees dotted the garden. The moon glowed above it all.

The visual wall wasn't the only change. Several people had gone to great lengths to make the ballroom as comfortable as possible. Ruby couches and crimson armchairs were spread across the expansive room. A long black bar stretched across the back wall. There was even a temporary kitchen set up, where a pair of chefs were busy plating some delicious-smelling snacks. Dim lights dotted the ballroom, the dark ambiance reminding Ryker of the high-end restaurants in the Western Region that his sister loved to visit. She would've called this lighting romantic.

A pang of longing went through Ryker at the thought of his sister. For as long as he could remember, even in hiding, he'd seen River multiple times a week. They met for training, and for the weekly family dinner their mother insisted on holding.

This separation would be the longest Ryker had ever gone without seeing his family. He'd known participating in the Choosing would mean he couldn't speak to them, but it was different now that he was in the middle of it. Ryker had instructed Atlas and Nikhail to watch over his sister while he was gone, but he'd rather be there in person. Between his father's illness and the Incident six years ago, Ryker's family responsibilities were heavier than ever.

Clenching his fists, he forced thoughts of deadly storms out of his mind. He couldn't focus on that right now.

Thank all the gods, it was his turn to approach the table.

"Name?" Lacey picked up a clipboard.

He cleared his throat. "Captain Ryker Waterborn."

She dipped her head, checking something off on the paper in front of her before grabbing a labeled pair of headphones.

"Here you go, sir." She handed him the headset along with a red notebook and pen. "These are noise-canceling, and they're matched with that of your first partner. The system will automatically connect you with your date in five minutes. We suggest grabbing a drink and getting comfortable before that happens."

"Thank you, I'll do that." Making his way to the bar, Ryker fit the headphones over his pointed ears, appreciating how the custom set molded around them perfectly.

As soon as the headphones were on, a chime sounded within them.

"Greetings and salutations, Captain Waterborn," a disembodied, robotic feminine voice said. "It is my pleasure to welcome you to the Two Hundredth Choosing."

Ryker jolted, stopping in his tracks. "Uh... thank you?"

"You are welcome, sir."

He blinked. "Who am I speaking with?"

"I am a Computer Engineered Logarithmic Support Technology Expert. You may call me Celeste. I am here to assist you through the Choosing."

An AI. Like the moving visual partition, this was technology that the army had access to, but Ryker had never seen it used by civilians. This must have cost a small fortune to set up, especially since he'd noted a multitude of blinking lights embedded in various surfaces. The hidden cameras were small but certainly powerful as they recorded and broadcast the Choosing to the world.

Not for the first time since Ryker's arrival at the Hall of Choice, he wondered how much money was being poured into this event. As the son of a Representative, he was somewhat aware of the Republic's financial situation. Even though he wasn't privy to the finer details, he knew the government had fallen on harder times of late.

Where were the funds coming from?

"Captain Waterborn, you have three minutes before your first date," Celeste said.

"Thank you." Arriving at the bar, he ordered a coffee and grabbed a plate. Several different pastries were laid out before him, and he perused them.

As he did, Celeste spoke quietly in his ear. "This is your moment, Captain. Remember, the purpose of the Choosing is to find a wife without worrying about societal pressures. While you are in the Hall of Choice, nothing else matters. Over the next twelve weeks, you will narrow your choices until you are left with your perfect match."

Adding a lemon pastry, two apple turnovers, and a hand-held berry pie on his plate, Ryker moved towards a couch stationed halfway between the entrance and the door marked with a glowing "EXIT" sign. "What if people don't find love?"

He was fairly certain he knew the answer but wanted to hear the AI's opinion.

Celeste paused, then sighed. The reaction was strangely mortal for what was essentially a robot. "The Choosing is focused on unity and love, sir. All participants are encouraged to Choose a partner."

"I see. Thank you for explaining that to me."

That evasive answer was essentially what he had expected. A Choice couldn't be forced, but it was strongly recommended. Marriage was the only option for Ryker, though. He couldn't let his father down. He sat on the crimson couch, placing his notebook, coffee, and snacks on the table before him. A blanket hung over the back of the couch, and he pulled it onto his lap, getting comfortable.

"Of course, sir. That is my sole—" A high-pitched bell chimed in his headphones. "Your first date is incoming, Captain." Celeste's voice returned to the same sickly-sweet robotic tone from before. "Please stand by. If you require my assistance, say my name. If not, I will give you privacy."

The AI's voice switched off, leaving Ryker staring at the garden wall. Waiting-room music began playing in his ears, the slow pop song one he'd heard hundreds of times before.

It was him and his thoughts. He was actually here, in the ballroom, about to meet his first date. He'd known he would participate in the Choosing his entire life, but knowing something and experiencing it were two very different things.

He tightened his hold on his pen. "Get a grip, Waterborn," he muttered under his breath. He counted back from five in his head. "You're a gods-damned soldier. This won't be difficult. You'll ask some questions, meet the women, and find your wife."

Failure was not an option, especially when it came to those he loved.

The music came to an abrupt halt. The silence was so loud that Ryker's heartbeat was a drum in his ears. He straightened his back and stared at the virtual garden as he waited.

Three long seconds went by before a sharp inhale echoed through the headphones.

"Hello?" a soft, feminine voice whispered.

That one word was all it took to make Ryker feel like a youngling again. He palmed the back of his neck. "Hi."

By the Obsidian Sands, that was an awkward response. Internally, Ryker chided himself for not being more suave. One would think he wasn't a Mature fae nearing his fourth decade of life with monosyllabic responses like that.

The woman on the other side of the wall chuckled, apparently unconcerned by Ryker's lack of linguistic prowess. "This is... weird, right?"

"I'm staring at a wall and talking to a woman I've never seen." He leaned forward and grabbed his coffee. "Yeah, it's fucking weird."

She huffed a quiet laugh, and instantly, Ryker felt more at ease.

He'd been on his fair share of dates, but knowing he would end up participating in the Choosing, he'd never sought anything serious.

Sensing his partner was shy, he asked, "What's your name?"

After a moment, she said, "Hallie. You?"

He jotted her name down in his notebook, underlining it twice. "Ryker. It's a pleasure to meet you."

She exhaled, and he could almost feel her nerves as she spoke. "Same. This is... a lot, you know?"

Hallie sounded sweet, and Ryker smiled. She must not have been expecting to be here. Filing that tidbit of information away, Ryker stretched his legs before him and settled in comfortably. A glance to his left and right confirmed the other men were doing the same.

Therian was on the next couch over, the dragon shifter's large form taking up the entire piece of furniture. Beside him, Philippe drew green threads of magic absentmindedly through his fingers as he spoke to his date.

"Yes, it is," Ryker agreed. The attack yesterday hadn't helped matters, either. "Tell me about yourself, Hallie. Where do you live?"

A rustling sound came through the headphones, and Ryker imagined that whoever this faceless woman was, she was rearranging herself. Was she on a couch like him? Or perhaps she was pacing back and forth in front of the wall like Luca? The werewolf didn't seem agitated, but clearly, he couldn't sit still. He sipped from his red goblet, his mouth moving as he spoke to his date.

"I grew up on the tip of the Southern Region, near the Sandy Flats," Hallie replied after a minute.

"It must be hot," was Ryker's reply.

He mentally slapped himself for such an awkward response. He needed to shake that, and soon.

She giggled. "Very."

"How are you finding the more moderate climate of Golden City?" Summer was nearly half over, and the nights were rapidly getting colder. While it didn't get as cold in the Central Region as it did in the north past the Koln Mountains, the four seasons were pronounced. "It must be a shock after the desert heat."

Nikhail was from the Southern Region. The fae often complained about the changing weather in Golden City and lamented the lack of his homeland's prolonged, dry heat. Personally, Ryker found the idea of living in a desert unappealing on several fronts, but he could understand why some people enjoyed the warmth it provided.

Hallie paused. "It's... alright, I suppose. I don't think I could live here all year round. How about you?"

"I was born and raised here, in Central Region."

"Oh."

Ryker blinked at the wall. Were all the conversations going to be this stilted? He hoped it was just first-date jitters. Otherwise, this would be a very long day.

"My mother is a Representative of the Fae," he told her. "She took over the position from her mother before she Faded."

"Did your parents meet during the Choosing?" Hallie asked.

"They did." Ryker sipped his coffee. "They took part in the One Hundred and Eighty-Ninth Choosing."

Fae were long-lived, thanks to their Maturation, and of all the different species that made up the Republic, they had fewer children than most.

Hallie laughed. "Wow. That must be strange, although maybe comforting in a way. My parents met through old-fashioned dating. All this is new to me. I mean, I watched the last Choosing, but I never imagined I would take part in this one. My sister applied for me. Imagine my surprise when I was Selected."

"That must have come as a shock."

"It was. I fainted, which my sister found supremely funny." She giggled. "Do you have any siblings?"

"One." Ryker smiled. "River is the light of my life."

"That's wonderful." Hallie seemed more relaxed now that the initial jitters were wearing off. "I have two sisters and a brother at home. All younger than me."

"Tell me about them?"

"I'd love to. First, there's Harlowe. She's three years younger than me, and she's the one who thought it would be funny to apply for the Choosing. She's..."

The more Hallie spoke about her family, the more she relaxed. The pair eased into a conversation, and time started slipping by.

Eventually, another chime sounded in his headphones. "This is your one-minute warning, Captain Waterborn," Celeste said pleasantly. "Please say your goodbyes. You will have a five-minute break before your next date begins."

Another chime.

"Well, Hallie, it was a pleasure to meet you." Ryker meant it. The Fortune Elf was shy, but she was kind, and he'd enjoyed getting to know her.

"Likewise," was her soft response. "I hope the rest of your day goes well."

The rest of their date passed quickly.

When the gods-awful waiting room music returned, Ryker stood and stretched. He made his way to the bar, intent on refilling his coffee.

Philippe, the brown-haired Earth Elf, met him there. He tugged his headphones off one ear and raised a brow. "How did it go?"

Ryker leaned against the counter as the server filled his mug. "Good. She was a little shy but very nice. I'd talk to her again."

The Earth Elf grinned. "Yours was shy? Mine was anything but that. She was loud and spoke her mind." Philippe leaned in close. "She was a fae, like you. I want to speak with her again."

He kept talking as Ryker added some cream to his coffee.

"Thirty seconds, Captain Waterborn," Celeste warned.

Ryker wished the Earth Elf good luck before he grabbed his coffee and returned to his couch.

He'd just settled into his seat when the music cut off again. This time, he was the first to speak. "Hello, my name's Ryker. It's a pleasure to meet you."

Full, proper syllables. This date was already starting better than the last.

A smooth inhalation of breath was followed by, "Hi, Ryker, I'm Esme. I'm glad we're getting a chance to chat."

He smiled. "Likewise. Your name is beautiful, by the way."

She huffed a laugh, and he leaned forward, intrigued. Their date flew by far faster than his date with Hallie. Soon, Celeste was back in his ear, warning him their time was almost over.

After Esme, he met several more women in quick succession. His notebook soon filled up. By the time Celeste informed him they would have an extended break for lunch, he'd already met more than half of the twelve women.

There were a few he already knew wouldn't be a match for him.

The energetic Yvette was kind, but they wouldn't be properly balanced. Their date had been less of a romantic first meeting and more of an interrogation. She'd had a lot of questions for him. He'd been exhausted by the time the music returned.

The soft-voiced shifter named Isabella seemed to lack all confidence. That wouldn't do for his wife. He needed someone strong and capable of standing up for herself. He was certain she would make someone a good partner—she was kind and smart—but it wouldn't be him.

A third, Demetra, was another fae. He hadn't met her before but had heard of her through the grapevine. She was powerful, which his mother would certainly approve of, but early on in their date, Demetra made an off-hand comment about one of the other women's weight.

Right then and there, Ryker had stopped taking notes. They wouldn't be working out. He didn't need a partner who made snide comments about other women. He'd been polite until their date ended, but that was it.

Of all the women he'd met so far, one stood out above the rest. Valentina Rose. Ryker knew who she was, of course. It wasn't as if hundreds of eligible fae were running through the Republic with that unique name. Her position of power wasn't what drew him to her, but her sharpness as they spoke. From his first impression, she seemed like a worthy companion. He'd enjoy spending evenings verbally sparring with her. Their date had been the most enjoyable so far.

Lunch was in the Ruby Lounge, and it was a light, airy affair as the men gathered and shared tidbits about their dates. Most seemed to have made at least preliminary connections, and a few men were already talking about setting up second dates.

Tonight, they would submit lists to the Matrons about which women they'd like to speak with again.

Ryker didn't contribute much to the conversation. He was focused on the two guards stationed at the entrance of the Ruby Lounge. They spoke quietly, shifting from one foot to the other. Their jaws were hard, their eyes like steel as they searched the room for threats.

Discretely angling his body towards the soldiers so he could hear better, Ryker listened intently.

"... another threat," said the guard with a sharp nose.

"Did they catch them?"

"Yes, but... there are more..." Sharp Nose scrubbed his face. "There was a protest in the Western Region yesterday, and today, there was another riot in the North."

"Fuck. Do you think they'll cancel—"

The doors opened, and Matron Cassandra entered. Instantly, the chatty soldiers split apart, their backs straightening as they returned to their stations.

Turning back to the table, Ryker shoveled mediocre pasta into his mouth. He barely tasted it, his mind working overtime to process the information he'd heard. There was always unrest in the Republic. After all, it was an enormous continent that housed millions of people.

But between the shooting yesterday and now this...

Ryker would remain on his guard.

Thank the holy Obsidian Sands, he still had his magic. Even weaponless, he was still a force to be reckoned with. Finishing his lunch, Ryker pushed back his plate and summoned a sphere of water to his palm. It gathered in a translucent orb, waiting for his next command.

He didn't have time to play with his magic. Matron Cassandra announced the end of lunch, and they returned to the ballroom for an afternoon of dates.

Ryker replaced his headphones and headed for a red hammock closer to the entrance. When the music turned off, he was studying the night-blooming roses on the virtual wall.

Having undergone this process several times already, he knew what to expect. He crossed his arms behind his head and closed his eyes. "Hello, my name's Ryker. What's yours?"

A sharp inhale was the only response.

CHAPTER 7
A Meeting to Remember

This was it. The moment Brynleigh had been waiting for ever since she learned who was responsible for her family's murder. The man she'd been searching for was on the other side of the wall.

It had been a long day. Every time the AI connected her with a man who wasn't Ryker, Brynleigh felt a little more deflated. She had taken cursory notes in case anyone was watching, but she hadn't paid too much attention to the other men. She wasn't here for them, after all.

At lunch, Brynleigh had enjoyed a double serving of blood—warm this time, which was how she preferred it—and listened as the other women shared about their dates. Brynleigh hadn't joined in on the conversations. She'd spent the time in contemplative silence, wondering how she would react when she finally met the captain.

Brynleigh had run dozens of scenarios through her head, but she had never anticipated this. The moment she heard his voice, she froze. Her heart thundered at the mere sound. Her shadows writhed. She gripped her pen so tightly that it snapped in her hand. Eyes wide, she let the broken writing implement fall before the ink could stain her fingers.

For all her preparations, all her plans, all her meticulous calculations, Brynleigh hadn't anticipated this.

Ryker's voice sounded *good*. His gravelly, almost smoky tone sent a bolt of desire running through her.

She would be going to hell for this. What kind of person was attracted to the man who killed their family? Her fangs pulsed and burned in her gums. A completely irrational desire to break the wall between them and look upon the fae nearly overwhelmed her.

He was so close, and yet, so far.

"Hello?" Ryker said again. "Is anyone there?"

Brynleigh jolted, realizing she had to act quickly if she was going to save this relationship. How ridiculous would it be if this entire endeavor ended before it started because she couldn't get her head on straight? She rubbed her temples and forced herself to get a grip.

"Hi. Sorry about that; I heard your voice, and I... forgot how to form words for a moment." There was nothing like a sprinkle of truth in a relationship built on deception, right?

She was here for one reason, and one reason only: to make her enemy fall in love with her so she could get close to him. To do that, to make him Choose her, she had to be perfect. Not too hard, but not too soft. Desirable and easy to love, but not such an easy catch that he felt she was too simple.

Whatever Ryker Waterborn needed in a wife, she would be that person.

There was a pause, and Brynleigh imagined this man—this powerful fae—considering her words.

Please, believe me, she silently begged him.

Her nails dug into the flesh of her palms as she waited. She prayed to Isvana and Ithiar that she hadn't ruined everything.

Jelisette would never forgive Brynleigh if she destroyed years of planning because of something as pedantic as *attraction*.

Rule number eight: emotions are for mortals, not vampires.

A frisson of icy fear ran through Brynleigh at the thought of her Maker's displeasure.

The last time Brynleigh had forgotten one of Jelisette's rules, she'd barely been a year past her Making. The incident was so minor that Brynleigh couldn't even remember what happened.

It didn't matter if she'd forgotten her transgression because she would never forget the punishment she'd endured.

Jelisette had locked Brynleigh in the cellar for a week and strictly forbidden Zanri from helping the Fledgling. Brynleigh had nearly gone mad from lack of blood so soon after her Making. She'd begged until her voice went hoarse. Screamed until her cries were nothing but air. Sobbed until she had no more tears. No one had come, no matter what she did or said.

Seven long days. Alone. Cold. Starving.

When Jelisette had freed her progeny, she'd simply said, "Remember, Brynleigh, rules are rules. We must always follow them."

Brynleigh hadn't replied. There was no point. Her Maker had proven her point. Follow the rules, and nothing bad would happen. Break them, and... well, the next time, she wouldn't be so kind.

A baritone chuckle rumbled through the headphones, snapping Brynleigh out of her thoughts.

"I like you," Ryker said. "You're funny."

Brynleigh sighed in relief, her eyes momentarily fluttering closed. Thank all the gods, she hadn't completely ruined everything. Now, all she had to do was make sure he remained interested.

"Honestly, that's the first time anyone has called me funny," Brynleigh admitted, the words slipping from her mouth before she could stop them. "I'm not usually one to make others laugh."

Scream? Yes. Run away? Also, yes. Laugh? Nope.

"Fascinating. I think you're quite humorous."

She wasn't sure whether to be delighted or insulted by that

comment. Was he laughing with her or at her? She supposed it didn't matter. He sounded intrigued, which was good.

"I shall endeavor to make you laugh again." If Brynleigh had to become a fucking comedian to make the captain fall in love with her, then she'd do it. She would be whatever he needed.

He chuckled. "Tell me, Oh Humorous One, what's your name?"

Had she forgotten to give it to him? Brynleigh blinked. Isvana help her, she must have been more affected by his voice than she'd originally thought.

She ran her hands over her braid, which hung over her shoulder. "Brynleigh de la Point."

He repeated her name slowly, like each syllable was a delicacy, and he was savoring each taste.

The vampire ground her teeth at the sound. Her name had no right sounding so good in his mouth.

He added, "It's a pleasure to meet you."

Why did it sound like he was being earnest? And why did she like the sound of his voice so much? A low, pulsing headache formed as Brynleigh puzzled through these new, troublesome developments.

"Agreed." Hoping to get back on track and regain control, Brynleigh took a large swallow of the blood wine she'd grabbed after lunch. Crossing her leggings-clad legs, she leaned back on the couch. "So, Ryker, how's the process agreeing with you so far?"

If any of his dates had been like hers, he'd already endured a hundred "get-to-know-you" questions. Brynleigh wanted to stand out and be remembered. What better way was there than to take a different approach than everyone else?

Several seconds went by in silence. Brynleigh imagined this faceless man with the intriguing, attractive voice mulling over his words. Was he on a couch like her or on a chair with his legs slung over the side like Yvette? Or maybe he was strolling up and down the length of the ballroom. The options were endless.

"It's been... more than I ever expected. This morning, I was nervous. I'm never nervous. It's not something I usually do. In my job, I need to be in control. But this is different." A choked sound came from him, and he groaned, "Gods. Why am I telling you this? We just met. It's strange, but I feel—"

"Comfortable," she provided before she could stop herself. The word slipped out of her mouth, and she cursed herself for speaking.

Stupid, stupid, stupid. Even though something innately easy came from speaking with this fae, she never should have admitted to it.

She was definitely going to hell.

"Exactly," he said on an exhale.

The problem was that Brynleigh felt it, too. It was like they'd known each other for years, not minutes. The vampire had felt varying degrees of awkwardness with all the other men. Aside from the first moment, where the sound of Ryker's voice made her forget how to speak, she didn't feel anything like that with the fae.

But maybe it was because she knew him. Not personally, but she'd been aware of Captain Ryker Waterborn's existence for years. She'd met him, not in person, but in the form of the magic he wielded.

That horrible night, with its sky-high waves, burning lungs, and floating bodies, was forever imprinted on her mind. Jelisette found her that same night, half-drowned and soaking wet.

After her Making, Brynleigh learned all there was to know about the captain. She had studied him like he was a difficult equation, and she was the mathematician determined to solve it. Even after he'd become a virtual ghost, she'd searched for him across the continent. She spent every waking hour trying to find morsels of information about him. Jelisette, Isvana bless her soul, helped Brynleigh as best she could.

Every detail they unearthed, no matter how big or small, was like a nugget of gold as Brynleigh sought to familiarize herself with the captain she planned to kill.

Brynleigh knew Ryker was under constant guard, both because of his position as the son of a Representative and as a captain in the army, and he was extremely private. He had a sister—River—who was almost two decades younger than him. She wasn't even Mature yet. His mother was a Fae Representative and worked closely with Chancellor Ignatia Rose. Brynleigh even knew that Ryker's father was ill. He'd come down with the Stillness over a decade ago and hadn't been the same ever since.

Maybe that was why when he spoke, she felt drawn to him.

Yes. That had to be it. There was no other reason he made her feel this way. None at all. Certainly, it had nothing to do with the way her fangs burned with the need to bite, nor did it have anything to do with the curling ball of want in her core.

It was just because Brynleigh knew who the captain was.

He's a killer.

Jelisette's voice echoed through Brynleigh's mind. Yes. That was a good, solid reminder of who she was speaking with. Brynleigh could never, ever forget why she was here.

It was time to get the conversation back on track.

Twisting her pendant through her fingers, Brynleigh asked, "What do you do when you're not seeking a wife in the Choosing, Ryker?"

"I'm a captain in the army."

"Oh?" She feigned surprise. "Have you done that for a long time?"

She imagined him nodding. "Since before I Matured. It's my calling."

And there it was. He was a bringer of death. It was his fault her family had died, his fault she'd been Made, and his fault she was alone.

"Do you enjoy your work?" Brynleigh asked.

He didn't even pause before saying, "I do. I'm good at my job and like what I do."

Fae couldn't lie. Everyone knew that. Whatever warmth had been flourishing in Brynleigh was doused as if someone had dumped a bucket of ice water on her.

"I bet you're very good at your job," she said flatly, unable to even infuse a bit of warmth into her voice.

"Most of the time," was Ryker's response.

"Oh? When was the last time you made a mistake?"

Part of her felt like she was making one right now, but she needed to know what he would say. If he answered her instead of staying silent, if he *told* her something, it would be the reminder she needed that he wasn't a good man. That he made mistakes. That he was a murderer.

"A few years ago," he said.

Fuck. Was that remorse in his voice?

"What happened?" She didn't want to know, but the question slipped out of her mouth. It was like her body had a mind of its own.

He sighed. "People... died." He spoke slowly, and there was a hint of something that sounded awfully similar to regret in his tone. "I still think about it to this day."

A collection of curses that would make even the most hardened Death Elves blush ran through her mind. The question wasn't supposed to make her feel bad for him. That emotion had no business here. Brynleigh grabbed it and threw it away.

"Oh," was all she could manage to say.

Ryker shifted gears. "Enough about me. I'd love to know more about you, Brynleigh. You said your last name is de la Point, right?"

"Yes."

"Are you, by any chance, related to Jelisette?"

She nodded before remembering that he couldn't see her. She had anticipated this question—it inevitably always came after she revealed her last name, but right now, her tongue stuck to the roof of her mouth.

Most people were biased against vampires. Was he one of them? Part of her hoped he was because it would be easier to hate him. But the other part, the remnant of her humanity, wanted someone to see her for who she was, not what she was.

There was only one way to find out.

"Yes. She's my Maker. Following vampiric tradition, I took her last name after my Making."

A long moment stretched between them. Brynleigh dropped her necklace, twisting her hands together.

From the next couch over, Hallie glanced over at the vampire. The Fortune Elf's brows creased, and concern radiated from her. *Are you alright?* her eyes seemed to say.

I'm fine, Brynleigh mouthed.

There was no point in worrying her new friend, especially since it seemed like Hallie was fully engrossed in her date.

Luckily, Ryker didn't keep Brynleigh waiting for long.

"I bet you have a very sharp bite," the water fae said, a hint of humor in his voice.

Brynleigh *laughed*. The mirth burst out of her so loudly that she drew stares from several women around her. Sheepishly, she mouthed, *Sorry*.

She hadn't been expecting that at all. She couldn't even remember the last time she'd chuckled, let alone laughed. Not really.

She didn't have much to laugh about these days.

"You don't mind that I'm a vampire?" she confirmed. "It doesn't bother you?"

"Not at all," was his immediate response. "I'm a fae. Does that bother you?"

It fucking *should* bother her. Other things about him bothered her. But somehow, that wasn't one of them.

Brynleigh didn't care what someone was. Human or vampire, fae or mer, shifter or elf, witch or werewolf, it didn't matter. True, world-ending, soul-crushing evil could exist beneath anyone's skin. Darkness could find a home anywhere if the right circumstances presented themselves.

"No." She twisted her braid through her fingers. "What kind of fae are you?"

Obviously, she already knew the answer. However, since it was imperative Ryker never found out exactly who Brynleigh was, she had to keep up appearances.

"A water fae," he said.

"What does that mean exactly? Can you summon a few drops of water? A sprinkle?"

This time, it was his turn to laugh. The sound was as deep as his voice, and it washed over Brynleigh like the first drops of rain after a long summer's day. It woke parts of her that had no business being awake right now.

She yearned to hear that sound again and again…

And she wanted him to never, ever do that again in her presence.

"Not at all, sweetheart. More like storms."

The nickname registered in Brynleigh's mind, and she stared at the wall. Part of her rebelled against it, but the other couldn't help but preen. She liked it—a lot. That could possibly be problematic, but just like the issue of her burning fangs and twisting core, she gathered up that emotion and shoved it down, down, down until she couldn't feel it anymore.

Thank Isvana, a chime sounded in her headphones, and the AI interrupted them. The date would soon be over. They said farewell, and Ryker was kind as he wished Brynleigh a good rest of her day.

It was horrible.

Brynleigh chugged the remainder of her blood wine as soon as the connection broke. She closed her eyes and rested her head on the back of the couch. That did *not* go as planned.

The remainder of the afternoon went by in a blur. No matter how many other men she spoke to, she couldn't get a certain water fae and his deep voice out of her head.

In all her planning, Brynleigh had never anticipated that she might actually be interested in Ryker Waterborn. That she might actually... like him. He was nothing like what she expected. He wasn't hard or ruthless or cold.

That was frustrating, to say the least.

There wasn't a rule for this.

CHAPTER 8
Butterflies and Silence

"What's your favorite childhood memory?" Ryker reclined in the hammock as he waited for Valentina to answer.

A few days had passed since their initial introduction, and he liked the fae. Not only was Valentina sharp-witted, but she had a fire in her. Ryker had a gut feeling his mother would love Valentina if he brought her home. They'd already been chatting for a half-hour, and Ryker smiled frequently during their conversation. He liked that.

Valentina chuckled. "I don't know if you'll believe me."

Curious, he raised a brow. "Try me."

She paused, and for a moment, he wasn't sure she'd answer. He ran this thumb down the side of his mug and waited.

"Are you familiar with the goldback butterfly?" she asked. Her voice was different than it had been earlier. Softer, like a harsh edge had been scrubbed away.

Ryker's brows furrowed. "No, I can't say that I am."

A sigh. "They're rare." Valentina paused. "When I was younger, I was rather... isolated."

Ryker understood that. For the past six years, he'd gone to

great lengths to stay away from others. It was the best way to protect his family. "That must have been difficult."

Even as an adult, loneliness had often courted Ryker. He'd only kept it away during his prolonged isolation because of his dog Marlowe, his friends, and trips to his cabin.

"It was." Valentina drew in a breath through her teeth. "Anyway, I was alone a lot. Mother was often at work, and I spent time in the library when I wasn't at school. One day, I was reading an encyclopedia and found a picture of a goldback butterfly. It was beautiful. The wings shimmered in the afternoon sun like they were made of gold. The butterfly called to me."

"It sounds lovely."

"It was. The goldbacks were all I could talk about for months. I became obsessed with them, talking about them for hours. One day, Mother came home early. I'll never forget it because she'd abandoned her formal business wear for jeans and a yellow sweater. 'I have a surprise for you,' she told me." Valentina's voice took on a wistful tone, and he could've sworn her breath caught. "It was my first and only surprise ever."

A pang of sadness went through Ryker's heart, and he dropped his pen. He'd never had a great relationship with his mother—Tertia Waterborn was a fierce, sometimes cold woman—but she'd taken great care to spend time with her children. Enough that he never felt ignored by her.

Evidently, that wasn't the case for Valentina.

"I'm sorry," he breathed.

"Don't be. It was a beautiful surprise. She arranged an entire trip for me. I had her to myself for twenty-four whole hours. We went to a botanical garden in the Southern Region, where goldback butterflies were abundant. They flew around us in a flurry of shimmering gilded wings, landing on our heads and shoulders. It was amazing."

Ryker could picture the swarm of yellow wings caught in the afternoon sun. "It sounds incredible."

"It was," said Valentina. "I—"

"This date will end in sixty seconds," Celeste interrupted, her robotic voice jarring Ryker from the calm he'd settled into. "Please prepare to say goodbye."

The headphones clicked, and Ryker sighed. "I'm sorry, Valentina," he said. "But—"

"I heard." That harsh, polished edge was back. "It's fine. It was nice to speak with you, Ryker."

And as they wished each other well, he agreed. There was far more to this fae than he'd ever guessed.

After his date with Valentina, Ryker's next few were... not as wonderful. That wasn't to say he didn't enjoy talking to the other women, but there was no connection between them. His mind wandered. When Calliope, an Earth Elf, was telling him about her job, his eyes grew heavy, and he almost drifted off to sleep.

By the gods, he had to pay attention. He needed to find a wife. His father didn't have long. The Stillness...

"Good afternoon, Ryker," said Brynleigh.

He hadn't even realized the music had stopped. Nevertheless, Ryker smiled, eager to spend time with the vampire today. He'd already come to recognize her voice. A spark came to life within him every time they spoke. Whatever tiredness vanished as he settled in. "How are you today, Brynleigh?"

"I'm... alright." Her tone made it sound like she was anything but.

An alarm blared in Ryker's mind. Finding out what was wrong was the only thing on his mind. "What's the matter?"

A long, heavy silence stretched between them. Ryker rose from the hammock, needing to stand. To do something. He wasn't one to let the people he cared about be hurt, and even though the Choosing was barely underway, he already felt something for the vampire.

"You can tell me," he murmured after a few minutes of silence.

"This... today... it's a difficult day," she whispered, her voice cracking.

Were those... tears he heard? Ryker's chest seized at the thought. He balled his fists at his sides. His water magic, which was usually calm, thrummed within his veins. It wanted him to climb over this wall and find the woman hurting on the other side.

But he couldn't. One glance at the guards, the blinking lights, and the other participants conversing quietly with their dates reminded him of that.

"Do you want to talk about it?" he asked instead.

Another pause. Each one was longer than the last. Heavier. Was she sitting? Walking like him? Was she crying quietly in a corner?

By the Sands, he wished he knew.

"I lost someone," she whispered. "And this is... it's the..."

Her voice trailed off, but he had heard enough. Ryker recognized the grief in her voice, the depth of hurt, the old wounds. He was deeply familiar with the kind of pain that rooted itself so deeply within oneself that there was nothing one could do except live with it.

"The anniversary?" he guessed, wishing he was wrong. Hoping he was wrong.

More silence.

He returned to his hammock, letting his head fall into his hands.

Eventually, she sighed, "Yes."

He rubbed his temples. "Fuck. I'm sorry."

She drew in a shuddering breath. "Me too. I'm so fucking sorry. I wish... they should still be here."

"I'm here if you want to talk about it," he offered.

Sometimes, when the Stillness got worse, talking about his dad helped. Reliving old memories or sharing something simple.

On other days, words were impossible. Grief stole them from him, and he could barely get out of bed, let alone talk.

He would do whatever Brynleigh needed.

Another long moment passed before she said, "Can we be quiet?"

Her request was soft, and it went straight to his heart. He wished he could see her. Hold her. Embrace her until her grief passed. But he couldn't.

This, though, he could do. "Of course."

The rest of the date went by in contemplative, heavy silence.

That night, when Ryker went to bed, he realized there had been a comfort he'd never experienced before, even in that quiet. He hated that Brynleigh was hurting, hated that she'd gone through an entire day of dates with grief in her heart, but she'd opened up to him. Shared it with him.

And that made him feel... good.

CHAPTER 9
More Than She'd Bargained For

Red, puffy eyes stared back at Brynleigh in the mirror. She hadn't slept last night. She hadn't done anything after her dates except go to her room and cry. Once they had started, the tears had flowed and flowed and flowed.

She'd never cried on this day before. Never shed a single fucking tear.

It was him. The captain. His presence here. He was doing things to her. Twisting her up. She could feel it—even her shadows were responding to him.

When she woke up yesterday, she knew it would be a bad day. Her heart had been heavy, and she'd wanted to do nothing more than stay in bed all day and grieve.

Six years had passed since that fateful midsummer storm. Six years of being utterly and completely alone. Seventy-two months. Two thousand, one hundred and ninety days since she'd said goodbye to her family.

He'd stolen them from her.

After their date, where she'd revealed something she *never* wanted to reveal—not to him or anyone—she ran back to her room and wept. She hadn't known it was possible to have so many tears, hadn't known grief could slam into her like an unmovable wall and crush her.

She'd skipped dinner, forgoing nutrition in favor of sitting on the floor of her shower fully clothed.

Hours had passed, and even with her vampire blood, Brynleigh had been a freezing, frigid mess by the time her door creaked open. Hallie had cautiously poked her head into the bathroom and frowned.

"I Saw that you might want this," the Fortune Elf had murmured, holding out a bag of blood in Brynleigh's direction. "Let me know if you need anything."

Brynleigh had thanked the Fortune Elf through a veil of tears. She'd turned off the shower and shed her sopping-wet clothes as soon as Hallie had left. Naked and bone-tired with a grief that wouldn't leave, Brynleigh had climbed into bed. She'd inhaled the bag of blood, the food doing little to ease the emptiness within her.

She hadn't slept a wink.

Today, Brynleigh would do better. She needed to get a grip. Yesterday, grief had been a deep ocean of despair, but this was a new day. Things could only go up from here.

It was with that thought that Brynleigh showered again—this time with scalding, hot water, just the way she liked it. After, she dressed in black leggings and a comfy sweater. She brushed out her hair, letting the waves fall around her, before applying makeup. Arguably, vampires didn't need makeup because they were unnaturally beautiful, but sometimes Brynleigh liked how it made her feel. Strong. Powerful.

Today, she needed that.

Each brush of eye shadow and each swipe of lipstick was armor against the world.

Finally, she was ready.

Breakfast went by without a hitch. Brynleigh sat with Hallie and Esme, listening as they shared about the men they were seeing.

Everything was going alright until she put on her headphones, and Celeste connected her with her first date.

"Hello?" Brynleigh fiddled with her pen.

"Morning, Brynleigh." Ryker's concerned voice came through the headphones. "How are you feeling today?"

She barely bit back the bitter laugh threatening to burst out of her. Of course, the captain was her first date. It was just like the fates to play with her like that.

His concern would've been humorous if she were in a better mood. He was the reason she was upset. If it weren't for him, her family would still be here, she'd be human, and she would never have participated in the Choosing.

But there was no point in thinking about what might have been. She needed today to go better than yesterday, even if it killed her.

Casting aside gloomy thoughts of a life that could have been, Brynleigh forced a smile on her face as she settled into her seat. "Better, thank you."

It wasn't a lie, per se. She *was* better than yesterday.

His baritone voice rumbled, "Good. I was worried about you."

"Thank you." Brynleigh didn't want to dwell on yesterday. She wanted to set that overwhelming grief and aching heart aside. She rubbed a fist over her chest, trying to ease the ache. It helped... a bit.

Shutting her eyes and letting her head fall back against the couch, she asked the first question that popped into her head. Anything to keep the conversation moving and off her. "What's your dream travel destination?"

She didn't know why it mattered since they would never go anywhere after the Choosing—he'd be a rotting corpse before they could shadow anywhere or get on a plane—but it seemed like a safe question to ask. On a day like today, good and safe were all she could ask for.

"Are we talking about anywhere in the Republic of Balance?" he asked.

"Sure, why not." Whatever he wanted. Hopefully, he'd talk for a long time so she could compose herself. She didn't trust herself not to open up again and share something else she didn't mean to. "Where would you want to go?"

He hummed, and she focused on rebuilding the box where she kept her emotions. It had cracked yesterday, and she couldn't let that happen again.

"I'd love to visit the Black Sea," he said after a minute. "See the inky waters, skate on the ice, maybe even spend a few nights hiking the frozen mountains."

"Do you like to hike?" As a human, she'd enjoyed the activity, but she hadn't done anything like that since her Making.

"I love it." She could hear the grin in Ryker's voice. "I have a cabin in the mountains that I visit as much as possible. It's beautiful all year round, but especially at night. The bedroom overlooks the lake."

She smiled despite herself. "It sounds nice."

"It is. If we were in the north, we could go exploring. There are beautiful ruins in the Northern Region. Castle Sanguis, for one. Some of the old abbeys as well."

Warmth coursed through Brynleigh. Damn it all. She wasn't supposed to care about what he said, wasn't supposed to want to go on the trip he described. She'd never been to the Black Sea, even though the Northern Region was the ancestral home of the vampires. His trip sounded like fun, and Brynleigh hated that she wanted to join him on it.

So much for her simple question.

"That sounds nice," she said after a moment, realizing she needed to speak. "Does that mean you enjoy the snow? Is that a water fae trait?"

He snorted. "I mean, I like snow as much as the next person. I can turn my water to ice, but I feel the cold like any other fae."

"Hmm. Vampires don't feel cold," she told him, a touch of

smugness in her tone. "We're made for the snow. I could dance in it, I suppose."

She'd never tried. Jelisette wouldn't approve.

"I'd love to see that," he said. "Tell me, Brynleigh, would you keep me warm if we were trapped in an icy cave?"

A grin stretched across her face despite herself. She relaxed in her seat. "Maybe. If you're nice to me."

He laughed, the bass sound resonating through the headphones. It was beautiful, like a crisp winter's night after a stormy day. Once again, her fangs reacted to his voice, and a fire burned in her gums. This reaction was quickly getting tiring.

"Oh, Brynleigh. I could be *very* nice."

Damn it all, but she laughed, too. She didn't want to, but she couldn't stop the sound from bubbling inside her.

They chatted about the Black Sea, discussing various things they'd do on their trip until Celeste informed them their date was over. When the music started playing, Brynleigh leaned back and rubbed her temples.

"Fuck me," she groaned.

This would be far more difficult than she'd ever bargained for.

CHAPTER 10
Game On

A few days later, Ryker was back in the crimson hammock. He was settling into a routine. After breakfast, he would spend most of the day in the ballroom, getting to know the women. Eventually, when the Choosing was past the halfway point, they'd move onto actual dates, but for now, they focused on creating that connection.

Surprisingly, at least to Ryker, he was enjoying this process far more than he thought he would. Who knew talking could be so agreeable?

He crossed his arms behind his head and closed his eyes. "What do you do when you're not hunting for a husband, Brynleigh?"

The vampire was his first date today, and he'd be lying if he said an enormous grin hadn't stretched across his face when her voice came through the headphones.

He still didn't know what she looked like, but it didn't matter. They were building a connection that wasn't based on how the other looked. He wanted to know more about this humorous vampire that made him laugh. Of all the women here, Brynleigh and Valentina intrigued him the most.

Brynleigh chuckled, and the sound was tinged with a touch of darkness and the night. "I work for my Maker."

That wasn't inherently surprising. Most vampires in the Republic of Balance preferred to remain with others like them. In fact, outside of the Choosing, Ryker hadn't met many vampires. They had a division in the army, but the Night Corps tended to keep to themselves. It probably had something to do with their aversion to sunlight... or maybe their general dispositions made them better suited to working alone.

"What do you do for her?" he asked.

"Odd jobs, mostly. A little bit of this, a little bit of that. Whatever she asks of me."

That, he understood. Life in the army was regimented, and whatever his superiors said, he did. It was the way of military life.

The hammock swayed beneath Ryker as he glanced at the garden wall. "Do you like it? Your work?"

She paused. "Mostly."

"I understand," he murmured. "There are moments when I wish I were anywhere else."

Like that stormy night six years ago.

He frowned. That was... not something he liked to think about. He shoved the thought from his mind and focused on the vampire speaking with him.

Brynleigh sucked in a breath. "That makes sense. Sometimes the things I do for Jelisette... I wish things were different. That's all."

A comfortable silence stretched between them, an understanding that each saw the other and knew where they were coming from. Ryker had never considered that he might meet someone who would understand him so profoundly in such a short period of time.

"How about you?" Brynleigh asked after a few minutes passed. "What does Captain Ryker do when he's not searching for a wife?"

Ryker's lips twitched at the obvious change in the topic of

conversation. "Would you believe me if I told you I enjoyed playing games?"

A light, harmonious laugh rang through the headphones. It was like wind chimes tinkling in a night breeze. The sound of the vampire's pleasure seeped into his bones and stirred something deep within him. He would cherish her laugh and replay the memory repeatedly when he was alone.

"I have to admit, I wasn't expecting that," she said when her laughter died.

He chuckled and palmed the back of his neck. "No? What did you think I would say?"

"Honestly, anything else." There was a smile in Brynleigh's voice. "I, too, enjoy games. Especially chess."

Ryker's eyes widened, and he grinned. "That's my favorite."

There was no hiding the enthusiasm in his voice.

He'd been playing the game since he was a child. When he hadn't been at school, he studied strategies, memorized moves, and played against any willing opponent. Even now, he gravitated towards a chess board after a long workday.

Most people only played chess against Ryker once. Not because he was bad at it, but because Ryker played to win.

Every. Single. Time.

He firmly believed there was no point in playing a game if he wasn't trying to win. He was competitive, not just with others but with himself as well. He constantly strove to be the best at everything. He enjoyed games, liked the structure of rules, and he always aimed to defeat his opponent.

"You're joking," was Brynleigh's response.

"Not at all." Ryker sat up and placed his feet flat on the floor. Resting his elbows on his legs, he stared at the visual wall. Today, blue and pink flowers stretched as far as the eye could see. "I have a chess board from one of the ancient Eleytan abbeys. It dates to the time of the Vampire Queen who fought during the Battle of Balance."

Many artifacts from that age had been lost to time, having

disappeared when the ancient vampires chose to sleep. Ryker's father gifted him the chess board on his eighteenth birthday. Ryker cherished it, and it remained in his apartment to this day. He rarely played with the ancient set but often admired the hand-carved black and white marble pieces.

"Truly?" A hint of suspicion entered her voice. "Are you pulling my leg?"

"Not at all," Ryker smirked. "Fae can't lie, after all."

"Hmm. I suppose that's true."

He chuckled. "It is. I swear to you that I can't, even if my life depends on it."

But he was skilled at twisting his words. All fae were. It was a skill passed down from generation to generation, a way to remain powerful while still telling a version of the truth.

"I'll give you that," Brynleigh conceded.

Ryker sipped his coffee. "I'll have to show you the board. Maybe challenge you to a match?"

Was it presumptuous of him to make plans outside the Choosing already? Maybe. But he didn't want to ignore the connection between them. And this, her playing chess, felt like a sign from the gods.

"At your home?"

"Yes."

She sucked in a breath, then murmured, "I'd like that more than you know."

Ryker's smile widened. So would he.

Their conversation shifted to different chess strategies, which occupied them until the chime rang.

"Apologies for the interruption, Captain Waterborn, but your next date will begin in five minutes." Celeste's voice was crisp and to the point. "This date will be over in sixty seconds."

"Damn," Ryker growled. He didn't want to say goodbye. Not now.

"Our time's up already?" Brynleigh sounded as surprised as he felt. "It feels like we just started talking."

"Doesn't it?" He capped his pen. "I really enjoyed this, Brynleigh. I hope we'll get to talk again soon."

A pause, and then she breathed, "Me too. You know, Ryker, you're nothing like what I expected. This was... nice."

"It was." He raked a hand through his brown hair. "Have a good day."

"You too."

Later that night, as Ryker replayed their conversation, he tried to picture the vampire. Was her hair dark like his or light like his mother's? She must have had the same black eyes that all vampires did, but what did her face look like? Was it round or heart-shaped? Was she tall or short? Curvy or slim or somewhere in between?

Even as he considered the possibilities, he rolled over and buried his face in the pillow. It didn't matter what she looked like. Not really.

All that mattered was that the vampire was occupying more and more of his thoughts.

THE NEXT DAY, after lunch, Celeste connected Ryker with Valentina. "Good afternoon, Ryker. I'm so glad we get to chat again."

"Likewise." He opened his notebook and turned to the page where he'd been keeping notes about the fae. "I find it interesting that we've never crossed paths before."

There weren't millions of fae in the Republic of Balance, and even fewer ran in the upper echelons of society. Unlike the other species that called this continent their home, the fae hadn't always existed here. Their ancestors had made the Great Migration from the Obsidian Coast after a series of natural disasters had destroyed much of their land. They'd brought technology with them and shared it willingly. Their technological advancements had shaped the Republic into the country it was and earned the fae seats on the Council of Representatives.

The Republic of Balance was divided into five regions. Each had a Representative from each species. These formed a council, which was ruled over by the Chancellor. The position used to be elected, but that hadn't been the case for several hundred years.

"It is strange, isn't it?" Valentina hummed pensively. "I must admit, Mother was a little... strict with my upbringing."

"I can relate to that." Ryker's mother wouldn't be considered warm by any stretch of the definition.

"It's ironic, considering Mother's position, but she doesn't like the press," Valentina said. "She wouldn't let anyone take pictures of me, and I spent most of my youth in private schools."

Ryker palmed his neck as memories of running from the press flashed through his mind. After dealing with the fallout of the storm, he learned the value of privacy. He probably would've started living at work if it weren't for his dog.

The last thing he had wanted was to run into one of the so-called journalists from the Daily Dragon or any other news outlet in the Republic of Balance. They fed off salacious information like starving sharks. He was certain that if given the chance, they would drag his family through the mud.

He sighed. "That, I understand. The press is—"

"Awful," Valentina interjected, at the same time that Ryker said, "Terrible."

Ryker didn't trust the press. They always asked questions about his family, always wanting information, and they never took "no" for an answer. He'd always been worried they would pierce through his shroud of privacy and destroy everything he'd carefully built.

Valentina snorted. "Yes. The press is a... necessary evil."

He wasn't sure they were necessary, but they were a part of life. Every Representative and their family dealt with them.

Settling back in his seat, Ryker twisted the top of his pen.

"I'm glad we finally had the opportunity to meet." He liked Valentina's frankness. "Where did you go to school?"

"Mother wouldn't settle for anything less than the best. When I was six, she enrolled me in prep school," Valentina continued, telling Ryker all about how she attended Highmountain's School for Young Fae, a renowned preparatory school for girls in Golden City.

The Chancellor's daughter was everything a Representative's wife should be—well-educated, polite, and of a good pedigree. Ryker knew his mother would be overjoyed if he brought someone like her home.

But even though he tried to focus on Valentina and learn more about her, every so often, Ryker's mind slipped back to Brynleigh. He wanted to know more about the vampire, too.

Two weeks had passed since the Choosing started. Ryker stepped out of the shower, rubbing a towel over his hair as he mentally prepared for the day ahead.

Who knew dating was so exhausting? They weren't even leaving the Hall of Choice yet, for the gods' sake. But apparently, being emotionally and mentally available for days on end took a toll on one's body that was similar to the most stringent military training.

Whenever his parents talked about their Choosing, they never mentioned being this tired. Ryker felt as though he'd scaled the Koln Mountains with his bare hands, not spent the past fourteen days talking to women.

To call the experience abnormal would have been an understatement. Ryker did not ask the women about their appearances —he wanted to maintain the integrity of the Choosing and was enjoying getting to know them without thinking about how they looked—but that didn't stop them from invading his dreams.

Especially one particular vampire.

Brynleigh de la Point was a frequent guest in Ryker's mind during all hours of the day and night. He couldn't stop thinking about her.

He learned more about her each time they interacted, but it was never enough.

The vampire captivated him and made him comfortable. He always desired more time with her. Their conversations were easy, and their dates always passed quickly. When they weren't together, Ryker thought about her.

A lot.

He thought about the way she'd feel beneath his hands. About her body beneath his, pressed against a mattress. About the way she'd taste. About the sounds she'd make as he made her his in every way.

Ryker was becoming a master of listening. He'd learned that Brynleigh often sucked in a breath when she was surprised by something, that she laughed rarely, but when she did, it was a beautiful sound, and that in the morning, her voice was rougher than when they met in the afternoons.

He yearned to hear that voice after a night in his bed, hoarse from calling out his name as he spent himself inside her.

Ryker tugged on jeans and a navy sweater, turning to face himself in the mirror.

"You have it bad," he told his reflection.

Ryker hadn't officially made a Choice, but his decision was becoming clearer every day. It wouldn't be long before he knew which woman he wanted.

Pleased with his appearance, Ryker headed to the ballroom.

Matron Cassandra was waiting for him, standing next to the guards who had become commonplace around the Hall of Choice. The rebels hadn't attacked again, but Ryker had repeatedly overheard the soldiers discuss unrest throughout the Republic.

The Matron bounced on the balls of her feet, and the corners of her eyes crinkled as she smiled up at him. "It's ready,"

Cassandra whispered, her head barely coming up halfway on Ryker's chest. "She's going to love it."

Last night, he'd asked the Matron if he could send a gift to one of his dates. Evidently, Cassandra was a romantic because she'd eagerly agreed.

"Do you think so?" Ryker was surprisingly nervous about this, which was strange. He'd given hundreds of gifts throughout his lifetime, but none had meant as much as this.

"Absolutely." The Matron nodded enthusiastically. She clasped Ryker's larger hand between her wrinkled ones and squeezed. "Young man, if that beautiful vampire doesn't already feel something for you, this will certainly push her in the right direction."

He hoped she was right. "Thank you, Matron."

Grinning up at him, Matron Cassandra released Ryker's hand and tapped him affectionately on the arm. "Go get your girl."

He couldn't help but smile as he entered the ballroom and grabbed his headphones. As had become his routine, Ryker ordered a coffee while Celeste informed him his date was incoming. He picked up a breakfast sandwich and went to what had become *his* hammock.

The item he'd asked Matron Cassandra to procure was waiting for him on the table. His grin widened. It was perfect.

He slid into the hammock, getting comfortable while balancing his coffee.

Today, the visual wall was taking them on a tour of a desert garden in the Southern Region. It was filled with vibrant flowers that ranged from the darkest of blues to the lightest of yellows. He was certain each shade had a name, but he didn't know what they were. Still, the garden was relaxing, and tension left Ryker's body as he waited for his date to begin.

He'd finished chewing by the time the classical music clicked off. He sat forward, almost falling out of the hammock in his haste to talk to Brynleigh. He felt like a schoolboy who had sent his crush a note, except... not. This was far bigger than that.

Reminding himself that he was a fully grown, Mature fae who was more than capable of conversing with the woman he had feelings for, Ryker cleared his throat. "Good morning, Brynleigh."

"Morning, Ryker." The smile in her voice was evident. "How did you sleep?"

"Well, thank you." Wondering where all his confidence had gone, he quickly added, "I sent you a gift. It should be on the table next to you."

"Really?" She hummed, and he pictured her searching for it. It didn't matter that he didn't know the shape of her body or the color of her hair because he was getting to know *her*.

He knew the moment she saw it because she inhaled sharply. "Oh, Ryker. A chess board."

His lips twitched as he reached over and picked up the matching one. "Not just any board. It's part of a set. The pieces are holographic, and I thought we might…"

"Play together?" She finished the sentence for him.

Gods, how was it possible that they were already in sync? It felt like they'd spent a lifetime together. "Exactly."

"I don't know, Captain," she teased. "What will you do when you lose?"

A chuckle started deep in Ryker's chest and rumbled through him. "Sweetheart, you don't know this about me yet, but I don't lose." He slid his finger down the side of the board and pressed the hidden button. It lit up, and he added, "Ever."

She snorted as black and white pieces appeared, flickering before stabilizing. "Maybe that used to be true, but now you've met me. You should get used to losing, Ryker. You'll be doing it a lot in the future."

"Cocky much?" Smirking, he settled the board on his lap.

"Only when I know I can win."

Ryker grinned, watching the board carefully as Brynleigh made the first move. "Game on."

CHAPTER 11
My Programming Does Not Allow Me to Discuss That

Two weeks later, the Choosing was at the one-third mark. Ryker stretched out his legs before him as he got comfortable on the couch.

It was late morning, and he'd been chatting with Valentina for over an hour. This was their fourth encounter that week. She'd spent most of that time talking about her favorite stores in the Red Plaza, an upper-class district in Golden City.

"Enough about me," Valentina eventually said. "What do you do when you're not hard at work, Captain?"

Thank the gods, they were done with fashion. It wasn't that Ryker didn't appreciate good clothes—he admired the female body as much as the next man and recognized how certain garments highlighted curves and beauty—but he didn't care about fashion.

Leaning back, he closed his eyes. "Depends," he said after a minute.

"Oh?" Valentina purred. "On what?"

"On whom I'm with."

The fae laughed, but there was something strange about the sound. It was nothing like Brynleigh's and didn't make him feel anything inside.

Valentina was nothing like Brynleigh.

Over the past month, Ryker had slowly whittled his way through the other women, landing on these two as his best potential matches.

If he were smart, he would Choose Valentina. He knew that. On paper, she was the right wife for him. She was everything a proper partner should be. Well-educated, mannered, and already familiar with the way Representatives lived. He could hear his mother's voice in the back of his head, urging him to pick the Chancellor's daughter.

Valentina would produce heirs, which Brynleigh couldn't do since vampires didn't procreate. If he chose her, the Waterborn line would continue, mingling with the prestigious Rose line. Their children would be powerful, prominent members of society.

Theoretically, Valentina Rose was perfect.

Except every time Ryker spoke with the fire fae, he couldn't help but compare her to Brynleigh. They had nothing in common. Brynleigh was real in a way that Valentina wasn't. The vampire pulled on a part of his heart that no one else had ever touched.

Some of the other men had already chosen favorites. Therian and the shy Hallie spent every waking minute talking. Phillipe had taken an interest in Trinity, the werewolf. A few others were still dating several women, while it seemed some men weren't making the connections they desired.

"On a perfect day without work, one where the sun was shining, what would you do with me?" Valentina asked.

He knew what an ideal day would look like if he were alone. His days were regimented down to the minute when he was at work. Everything, from when he stepped onto the army base to when the gates closed behind him, was accounted for. When he was off, he preferred not to do anything strenuous. He liked to play games, relax with his dog, and watch sports with his friends.

Ryker knew Valentina well enough at this point to know she'd never be okay with that. If he Chose her, his life would be filled with endless parties, enormous credit-card bills, shopping, stuffy dinners, and high-society events. He'd never have a night off or a chance to play chess or relax.

He was exhausted thinking about it.

Taking a long drag of his liquor-laced coffee, Ryker rubbed his temples. "If I were with you, I'd probably wake up early and make you breakfast with all your favorite foods."

"Mhmm, I like the sound of that," Valentina hummed.

He figured she would. "After that, I'd take you shopping and let you buy whatever you wanted."

Ryker's mother, Tertia, and his sister, River, had expensive tastes and often went shopping together. It was one of the only times they weren't fighting. Although he hadn't joined them since the storm, Ryker often heard about their expensive escapades during family dinners.

He was certain Valentina would get along with them. She seemed like the type of woman with expensive taste who spoke eloquently and would enjoy the finer things in life. If Ryker picked Valentina, she would fit into the life his mother wanted him to live.

But was it the life he wanted?

A sigh of delight filled his ears. "Ryker, baby, you know the way to my heart."

It wasn't that difficult. The more Ryker talked to the fae, the more he realized the only two things she cared about were herself and money. Not that there was anything inherently wrong with either of those, but evidently, incompatibilities were rising between them.

Before Ryker could delve into his plans for dinner—he would take Valentina to an upscale restaurant with a chef's table, where they could watch their food being made in person—his headset dinged.

"Your date will be over in sixty seconds, Captain Waterborn," Celeste said.

A rush of something that could only be described as relief ran through Ryker. It caught him off-guard. He'd never felt this way after a date with Valentina before.

Raking a hand through his hair, Ryker groaned. This process was far more arduous than he'd ever expected. He never thought that the Choosing would leave him with such complicated feelings.

"Ryker?" Valentina's voice held an edge of sharpness, and he jolted. She must have been calling him. Irritated, she asked, "Did you hear me?"

By the Black Sands, he hadn't been paying attention at all. However, thanks to his mother and sister, he knew enough about the feminine condition to know that admitting to *that* particular flaw wouldn't go over well.

Instead, he said, "This conversation was enlightening, Valentina."

She paused, then sighed, "I hope we can talk again soon."

Ryker didn't answer. He couldn't lie to her and say the conversation had been nice. It had begun that way, but now, his stomach was in knots. Would Valentina be a good partner for him? He was having some serious doubts. If he Chose her, he'd always be doing something. Always be on display. With Valentina as his wife, Ryker would have no hope of privacy and quiet.

He wasn't certain he could live with that.

He could practically hear her frowning through the headphones. "Ryker—"

Strands of violin music swallowed the remainder of her words, freeing him from having to deal with the rest of that conversation.

Thanking all the gods for their perfect timing, Ryker rose from the couch and strode to the bar. On his way there, he counted the number of guards. They'd doubled during his date. Not only that but their faces were pinched with worry.

Ryker ordered another coffee, frowning as he scanned the room. Something was off. He could feel it in his gut.

Taking his drink, he made his way over to the red hammock.

"Celeste?" He summoned the AI.

"Yes, Captain?"

"There are more guards here than normal." He placed the coffee on a red coaster.

The AI said, "If you say so, sir."

"I can count, so yes, I know there are double. Why are there more guards here?"

A strange clicking sound came through the headphones, but there was no response. Ryker's lips slanted down. Had she misheard him?

He repeated the question.

After a moment, Celeste replied, "I am not at liberty to discuss the outside world with participants of the Choosing."

"I'm aware." His fingers twitched, and he wished for his phone. Damn the technological blackout forced on Choosing participants. "Still, can you give me an update on the riots?"

This morning, he'd overheard several guards discussing the ongoing unrest.

"My programming doesn't allow me to discuss that," Celeste said curtly.

He scrubbed his face. "What about the unrest in the region?"

"My programming doesn't allow me to discuss that."

Ryker groaned. He fought the urge to rip off the headphones and fling them against the wall. "What's happening with the lower classes?"

"My programming doesn't allow me to discuss that."

Again and again, no matter how he worded his questions, she gave him the same response. It was infuriating. He got nothing out of the AI. That knot within him twisted tighter and tighter, sending sharp shooting pains through him.

What was happening outside these walls? He knew his family was safe—they were well-guarded, as were all Representatives and their loved ones—but what about the rest of the Republic?

When it became apparent Celeste wouldn't answer his questions, Ryker abandoned this course of action. This line of questioning wasn't getting him anywhere, and his tolerance for hearing the same answer had rapidly become non-existent.

By the time Celeste's too-chipper voice informed Ryker that his date was incoming, he'd devised a plan. After this, he'd speak with one of the guards and see if he could use his position in the army to gain information. The plan was solid, and he felt confident in it.

The music faded, and a sense of peace instantly washed over Ryker. He closed his eyes and settled into the hammock. Unlike the early days, when his date was a mystery, he knew Brynleigh was waiting for him on the other end of his headphones.

He greeted her, his voice filled with happiness that hadn't been present during his conversation with Valentina.

"Hey," she breathed. "I missed you."

Any remaining tension Ryker had felt from Celeste's non-responses melted away. It was always like this with Brynleigh. Everything flowed between them. They'd played several chess games and were tied with three wins each. Ryker learned more about the vampire every time they faced each other. Not only was she funny, but she was thoughtful, strategic, and surprisingly fierce.

"I did as well," he murmured. "How was your day so far?"

She sighed but didn't answer. That wasn't like her. She was quick-witted and often made him laugh. Today, though, something was different.

"Brynleigh?" He opened his eyes and stared at the winter garden separating them.

"I... didn't sleep well last night," she admitted after a moment.

A growl rumbled through his chest, and he clenched his fists. "What happened? Did someone say something to you?"

If they hurt her, he'd find them and make them pay.

Once again, she paused.

Ryker hated that he couldn't see Brynleigh right now. Was

there indecision or fear in her eyes? Or worse, hurt? Was she curled in a ball on the couch, or was she pacing?

His brain had constructed an image of her, faceless and shapeless, and he wanted to fill in the blanks. He wanted to know more about her...

He wanted to know everything.

Big things and little ones, he valued everything Brynleigh shared. Each tidbit of information was a jewel he would cherish forever. No matter how much time they spent together, it was never enough for him. He always wanted more.

At that moment, Ryker realized he couldn't see Valentina again. His feelings for Brynleigh were far more potent than anything he had with the fae.

"No one hurt me," Brynleigh assured him. "I had a nightmare. It's... I get them a lot."

His chest tightened as visions of this vampire waking up screaming in the middle of the night ran through his head.

He'd had his fair share of nightmares, both due to his job and his father's illness. Waking up alone, tangled in sheets, was horrible.

"I'm sorry." His voice was rough, and his arms ached with the desire to hold her. "Do you want to tell me about them?"

A bitter laugh came through the headphones. "Why would you want to hear about my bad dreams?"

His brows tented, and he leaned forward. "Because they bothered you, sweetheart, and I care a great deal about you."

If he was honest, he could see himself more than liking Brynleigh. She made it easy for him to care about her.

This was the first time he had admitted to having feelings for the vampire out loud. He thought it would scare him to say something like that, especially after spending so many years without participating in the outside world, but it didn't.

His heart sped up as he waited for her response.

Their match was unorthodox. Ryker was the first to admit that fae and vampires didn't traditionally get along. But something about Brynleigh made him feel as if he could relax about the rules he so often followed, and the world wouldn't fall apart around him.

She hitched a breath, and when she spoke, her voice was quieter than before. "Ryker—"

"You know if I said it, it's true." He inhaled. "I—"

The ground beneath him trembled. A massive *boom* echoed. The walls rattled. Someone screamed, the sound audible despite the supposedly noise-cancelling headphones.

Jumping off the hammock, Ryker smoothly fell into a fighting stance. He called out, "Brynleigh?"

Harsh, abrupt static was the only thing he heard.

Time seemed to slow as the air in the ballroom shifted. Gone was the lightheartedness from earlier, and in its place was tense anticipation and worry.

Another tremor shook the ground. This one was worse than the last. A crack appeared on the floor in front of him.

"Earthquake!" someone yelled.

Again, Ryker shouted for Brynleigh, but there was no response. He tried Celeste next, but nothing happened.

"Fuck." He clenched his fists.

This was bad.

Philippe, the Earth Elf, dropped to the ground a few feet away. He ripped off his headphones. Tendrils of emerald magic slipped from his hands, and he placed his palms flat on the marble. The ribbons sank into the ground and disappeared.

Less than a minute later, Philippe raised glowing green eyes and shook his head. "No, this isn't an earthquake. The land has nothing to do with this."

A third tremor ripped through the building. This one was different from the first two. Closer. It stretched on and on.

Ryker's heart thundered as he fell back on his military training. He hurried towards the guards. The soldiers were already shouting orders at each other. Therian was picking up shards of glass where they'd shattered near the bar.

An ear-piercingly loud siren blared.

The image on the dividing wall shuttered, pixelating before transforming into a flashing red screen.

"Code Orange, Code Orange." Celeste's amplified voice came through a dozen hidden speakers. "Everyone within ten miles from the Hall of Choice must take cover immediately."

Ryker's blood was ice in his veins. He'd memorized these codes early on and knew them backward and forwards. Golden City was under attack.

His fingers twitched, and his magic pulsed in his veins. He needed to be out there fighting, not standing in some grand ballroom.

Ryker ran to the nearest guard. "I'm Captain Waterborn of the Fae Division." He rattled off his identification number. "What's happening?"

The guard's name tag read Orion. "I know who you are, Captain." Orion's voice was as harsh and unforgiving as his eyes. He was a military man through and through. "We're under strict orders to move all participants to the bunkers until the attack has passed."

Frustration was a churning storm within Ryker. They wanted him to sit this out like a civilian. That went against everything he believed in. "No. I can fight."

"Me, too," Therian growled, coming up behind Ryker. Black scales rippled on the shifter's skin, and his eyes flashed. His dragon was close to the surface. "Let me out; I can shift."

Orion said, "No. Today, you are nothing but men going through the Choosing."

Therian swore. "You can't do that."

"We can," said Orion smoothly. "You agreed to it when you entered.

"These are obviously extenuating circumstances," Ryker said through clenched teeth.

The guard's face was as firm as stone. "I have my orders."

Clearly, Orion wouldn't budge. On one hand, Ryker

respected that. On the other, worry coursed through him. Static still crackled through the headphones.

Another guard walked up, holding black strips of cloth. "I have them, sir," he said to Orion.

"What the hell?" Therian growled, exchanging a look with Ryker. "What's going on?"

The new guard, whose tag read Johnson, said, "We must take you to safety."

"We—" Ryker started, but Orion cut him off. "You cannot help," the guard said, his voice leaving no room for discussion. "The details of the attack are not for you to know. Outside these walls, you may be members of the military, but here, you are one of the twenty-four we are meant to protect."

Ryker snarled. His water magic bubbled up, demanding he fight.

A woman screamed somewhere on the other side of the wall.

Another yelled, "I'm not putting that on."

"Yes, you are," was a soldier's harsh, curt response.

The remainder of his words were muffled by distance, but another shriek echoed through the ballroom.

Ryker didn't think Brynleigh was the one yelling. She wouldn't do that. She'd probably bite someone who touched her without permission. And fuck if he didn't like that thought.

Not the time.

The siren continued to blare.

"We need to go." Orion turned to the participants, who were gathering around him. "You can't see the women. The integrity of the Choosing must be maintained."

Suddenly, the black strips of cloth and the woman's screams made sense.

"You're blindfolding us," Ryker said.

It was a statement, not a question.

"We are," Orion confirmed.

Another tremor shook the ground.

"No more talking. We need to go." Johnson clenched his jaw.

"If anyone fights us, we'll tranquilize you. There's no time for chitchat."

Allowing someone to blindfold him and lead him into a bunker went against every single grain of Ryker's being. Control was part of the very fabric of who he was. It was the reason he was so good at his job, and giving it up was not easy.

But when another woman screamed, he stepped forward.

"Do me first." He took off his headphones and placed them on the table. "I won't fight you."

Relief flashed through Orion's eyes as he lifted the black cloth and secured it around Ryker's face. The thick material was manufactured specifically so that even beings with strong senses, like fae, vampires, and shifters, couldn't see out of it.

Once Ryker was blindfolded, the others quickly followed suit. Blaring sirens and faint screams accompanied the group as they entered the basement.

Another tremor hit as they descended below the Hall of Choice.

Death was in the air today.

CHAPTER 12
Unexpected Complications Arise

The bunker was freezing. Even though Brynleigh's blood ran cold, and the dropping temperature wouldn't kill her, she was uncomfortable. She could only imagine how bad it was for the others. She wore a thin violet t-shirt and workout leggings, not having dressed to spend the day underground.

A musty scent tickled her nostrils every time she inhaled, and a suspicious dripping sound came from nearby. At least there wasn't any tell-tale scurrying from mice or other rodents.

After the guards had blindfolded them—many of the women had cried and screamed during the process—they had led them down several flights of stairs. From what Brynleigh could tell from her limited information, they were deep underground in a cement room. If there were any lights, she couldn't make them out through the material they'd forced over her eyes.

Hours had passed since they descended into the bellies of the Hall of Choice. At first, a few women had cried. Some, like Esme, were stoic. In a display that confirmed how horrible Valentina was, the fire fae had verbally berated the guards, assuring them they would hear from her mother if the threat was fake.

Hallie had nearly passed out from shock. Now, the Fortune

Elf rested her head against Brynleigh's shoulder. A shuddering sob occasionally ran through the smaller woman, but she seemed to have run out of tears.

The men were somewhere down here, too. Brynleigh could sense their presence, along with even more guards.

Another vampire must have been working with the soldiers. Their shadow magic crawled over Brynleigh's skin, and she sensed the presence of their darkness. They must have filled the bunker with shadows, adding another layer of security to keep the participants from seeing each other.

The guards had handed out protein bars and bottles of water, but they hadn't had anything for Brynleigh. She needed blood, and soon. Her stomach twinged, warning that hunger wasn't far off.

Instead of focusing on her need to feed because she couldn't do anything about it, she turned to Hallie. Keeping her voice low so no one else could overhear, Brynleigh asked, "How are you feeling?"

"I didn't See this," the Fortune Elf whispered hoarsely. "Mama told me I shouldn't Look ahead much while I was here in case I accidentally Saw my future husband. I shouldn't have listened to her. I should've walked the silver planes more often. If I'd known—"

Brynleigh reached out blindly and put her hand on what she thought was Hallie's knee. "You couldn't have changed anything. You heard the guards. The rebels attacked Golden City."

Brynleigh was surprised that it had taken them this long to attack a Choosing. It didn't take a genius to correlate the rebel attacks and the class disparity in the Republic of Balance. Issues were bound to arise, seeing as how the majority of the Republic suffered under the rule of the Council.

Even now, Brynleigh knew she and the other "commoners" were only Selected to take part in the Choosing to appease the citizens of the Republic. Valentina and the others whispered behind their backs, taking little care to hide how they felt about the women they deemed beneath them.

Still, it was frustrating that the rebels were causing problems during Brynleigh's Choosing. She'd spent years meticulously crafting her plan, and now everything was falling apart. This was an unexpected complication she'd rather not deal with... and wasn't the only one that had arisen.

Brynleigh and Ryker were forging a connection, which was her plan. What she hadn't seen coming was the way she couldn't stop thinking about him. He haunted her every minute of every day. Even while she slept, she thought about him.

The deep rasp of the fae's voice and the smoky quality that edged his words intrigued her. Her heart sped up while they talked, no matter how much she tried to stop it. Even though she imbibed blood daily, she couldn't get her fangs to stop aching.

Her body's reaction to Ryker was a problem, and she needed to fix it. He was supposed to want her, not the other way around.

Rule number six: let nothing distract you from your goal.

Today, Brynleigh had almost slipped up and told him about her nightmares. The words had been on the tip of her tongue. She'd been seconds away from admitting that when she slept, she dreamed of deadly waves and burning lungs.

The rebel attack stopped her just in time.

She needed to remember who Ryker was. What he'd done. Over the past month, he'd put on a good front of being a kind, caring man, but she knew the fae hiding beneath the surface was a cold-blooded killer. Her entire town was dead because of him.

Brynleigh was so caught up in remembering exactly why she hated Ryker that she didn't hear the guards moving at first.

"Can I have your attention?" a commanding voice came from the front of the room.

Silence fell. The bunker was so quiet that a pin dropping would have been as loud as a clap of thunder.

Brynleigh turned her head towards the voice. Hallie's fingers nudged hers, and she let the Fortune Elf lace their fingers together. Usually, Brynleigh refused to let anyone touch her like this, but between her friend's soft demeanor and earlier tears, she couldn't find it in her cold heart to refuse the elf.

The voice continued, "The situation has been contained, and it is safe to re-enter the Hall of Choice. The women will go first. Once you reach the residential sectors, head directly for your Lounges. The Matrons will be by shortly to deliver further instructions."

Hallie sagged against Brynleigh, her relief palpable. "Thank Kydona."

Brynleigh wasn't sure the mother goddess cared about the rebels or the Choosing, but she didn't say that. If Kydona brought Hallie peace, then that was all that mattered.

The soldiers gave a few more instructions before helping the women to their feet. They were herded out of the bunker.

A door clicked behind them, and the same guard said, "You may remove your blindfolds."

Brynleigh ripped hers off, her vision adjusting quickly to the faint fluorescent glow from the lights ribbing the ceiling. There were no windows, but several doors lined the concrete, gray hallway.

The soldiers split in two, half traveling at the front of the group and the other half at the back as they led the women upstairs. No one spoke as they climbed five stories. Pinched lips, furrowed brows, and tired eyes were all around Brynleigh.

"Remember, straight to the Crimson Lounge," the guard at the front reminded them, his hand on the door to the main level of the Hall of Choice.

Once everyone had agreed, the guard turned the knob.

Then it happened.

One moment, Brynleigh was fine.

The next, her world shifted.

A coppery scent slammed into her.

She stumbled and crashed into the cement wall.

The delicious aroma of blood called to her. It took over her, pushing aside rational thought as if it had never existed.

Blood permeated the air. This wasn't a paper cut or some minor injury.

No.

Multiple people had bled out and died nearby. Not miles away, in some unknown location, but right outside the building. Death would forever mark this place.

Brynleigh's fangs burned. They were fire.

An animalistic, predatory growl rumbled through her, echoing in the stairwell.

It felt like sharp knives were stabbing into her stomach as she clawed at the cement wall.

Brynleigh wasn't hungry. She was *starving*. Had she ever known, truly known, the sensation of requiring sustenance before this point? She thought not.

This new need, this deep-set desire to feed, was so potent that Brynleigh was certain she would die if she did not drink blood. Right. Fucking. Now.

Somehow, her feet started moving. Shadows flooded out of her. Her heart sped. She snarled. Red tinged her vision.

She shoved her way past the guards in a blur and made it halfway down the main corridor before realizing where she was going.

An iron grip grabbed her arm and twisted.

"Someone get this vamp some blood!" the guard holding her yelled.

Brynleigh snarled, trying to shake him off. The sound of her anger was foreign and vicious, like a dog unwilling to give up its prized possession.

Somewhere deep inside her, the remnants of Brynleigh's humanity were being dragged away by the bloodthirsty monster living inside her. The need for blood was so intrinsically tied to her, such an essential part of her being, that she didn't know where the bloodlust stopped, and she began.

She was becoming a creature of the night, through and through.

Brynleigh struggled to hang onto the thin strands of her control. At war with herself, she barely paid attention to her surroundings.

Someone shoved a bag of blood in her direction. The guard loosened his grip just enough so she could drink. It wasn't enough.

Her hunger was a steep cliff, and she teetered on the edge. Dancing between sanity and forever losing herself to the monster within her, she panted and growled.

That smell remained.

Another red bag was thrust in her direction.

She drank that, too.

It still wasn't enough.

Closer and closer, she danced to the ledge.

"Get a fucking grip!" someone screamed in her face.

Maybe she could bite them? They seemed angry. She wouldn't kill them. She just needed a little blood.

Brynleigh moved towards them, but that iron grip returned, this time around her waist.

"She's too young," the guard holding her said. "Little more than a Fledgling."

Shaking her head, Brynleigh tried to clear the fire in her fangs. If only she could shove this need aside, she could tell them it was fine. She was here for a reason. She couldn't lose control. Not yet.

But she was slipping, slipping, slipping away.

"I knew this bloodsucker would be a problem from the first day I met her," Valentina snarled.

Even through the bloodlust, Brynleigh recognized the horrible fae's voice.

Brynleigh's nostrils flared. She spun, growling and gnashing her teeth at the fire fae. "I'll kill you, bitch."

She'd have no remorse about it, either.

A flame appeared in Valentina's hand. "I'd like to see you try."

A snarl.

Someone kicked the back of Brynleigh's legs. She fell to the ground. A knee pressed into her back, forcing her to the ground.

Heartbeats.

So many gods-damned heartbeats. They got louder and louder until they were drums pounding painfully in Brynleigh's ears.

All these people had blood in them. Forget the dying ones outside. She could get what she needed here. She'd kill them all, starting with the one glaring at her with malice.

Deep inside, Brynleigh recognized this was a monumentally bad idea, but she couldn't remember why.

Feed.

The word echoed through her mind. Her body. Her spirit.

Feed, feed, feed.

People kept talking, but their voices were hard to hear beneath the pounding of the life-giving organs surrounding her.

"I can... it'll knock..."

"Do it." The order came from the guard, forcing Brynleigh to remain down.

Valentina shouted, "Let her..."

Something sharp pierced Brynleigh's skin.

An agony-filled scream burst from the vampire's lips.

Flames ran through her from the point of injury, burning her from the inside out.

Someone shouted. A softer, friendly voice cried out. Brynleigh's mind swam as she fought for control.

Then she tumbled headfirst into blessed darkness.

SOMETHING soft and pillowy was beneath Brynleigh. Yawning, she stretched her arms and arched her back. The softness surrounded her, and she decided she was on a mattress. A very cloud-like mattress, one covered in silken sheets and pillows. That was strange. She wondered where she was, but the moment she tried to think, a low throb started at the back of her mind.

That was not a good sign.

Even though she was in an unknown location, Brynleigh didn't feel tense. If anything, she felt... at peace. That was strange. She hadn't known a moment of peace since her family's passing.

Leaving aside the problem of where she was for another moment, Brynleigh cracked open her eyes and looked around. As suspected, she was on a bed. It was large and could hold several people comfortably. Massive windows stretched across two of the four walls, a black tint blocking the sun's dangerous rays.

Fuck, she missed the sun and its warming embrace. The way its yellowed fingers touched her face. The light it cast on the world around her. She'd only been a vampire for six years, yet she already longingly remembered the natural light she would never see again.

Because creatures of the moon had no business being in the sun.

Turning from the windows, she took in the rest of the space. High ceilings, elaborate crown molding, and golden picture frames spoke to a level of grandeur to which she was unaccustomed.

Maybe she *should* worry about where she was because this was not her home or anywhere she'd ever been.

Something urgent pressed at the back of Brynleigh's mind, begging her to remember. She tried to unearth the memory, but it remained out of her reach.

Then the doorknob twisted.

Instantly, Brynleigh was on high alert. Her heart thundered in her chest. Shadows were a sheet of darkness as they poured out of her. She kneeled on the mattress, and her wings formed effortlessly on her back. Peeling back her lips, she exposed her fangs.

Who dared sneak up on her?

Something slid across her thigh, and she glanced down, her eyes widening. Why was she wearing a thin black slip? This was far from her usual nightwear of choice: a tank top and shorts.

The door creaked open.

Her attention snapped back up.

"Brynleigh, are you awake?" a deep smokey voice asked.

That voice. It spoke to the deepest parts of Brynleigh and echoed in her soul. Her core twisted, and she stared at the shadowy figure entering the room. He was cast in darkness, and though she tried, she couldn't make out his features.

For some reason, that didn't bother her.

When she didn't respond, he said, "Sweetheart?"

Safe.

That was the first thing she felt when he spoke. This man, whoever he was, was a haven. He wouldn't hurt her. She wasn't sure how she came to this conclusion, but she knew it in the marrow of her bones.

"I'm right here," she breathed. She retracted her wings and called her shadows back. They were always present, always ready, but she didn't need them here.

Peace radiated all around her.

But she was forgetting something. It was important, this piece of her mind that had slipped away. There was something about this man with the deep, smoky voice, and the two of them...

She searched and searched, trying to shove past the strange mist clouding her mind, but she couldn't remember why she shouldn't trust him. She fought against her mind and sought the missing memories, but they remained out of her reach.

His hand trailed down her back. "What's wrong?"

The bed dipped as he kneeled behind her. She could see their reflection in the blacked-out windows but couldn't make out his face. He was bigger than her, taller by almost a head and bulkier. His ears were pointed, but she couldn't seem to focus on his individual features.

"I... I don't know," she admitted quietly. "I'm missing something, and my brain hurts."

What had begun as a low throb was now a rhythmic ache. Her

fangs bothered her, and there was a need present within her that she had trouble identifying.

"Let me help you," the mysterious man murmured.

But was he mysterious? Not really.

His voice... she knew his voice. It had haunted her dreams. The inflections, the way he hummed, the hitch in his breath when he spoke of something personal.

She knew *him*. Of that, she was certain.

They'd been... together? That mist formed a firm wall, slamming down on her memories before she could remember much of their relationship.

Before she could think through the ramifications, Brynleigh nodded. "Alright. You can help me."

The moment the words left her lips, the world around her swirled. She blinked, and everything had changed. The grand room was gone, and in its place, floor-to-ceiling windows looked out over a moonlit bay. Pine trees hugged the bay, their green branches swaying in the night breeze. Stars shone brightly, day having suddenly given way to night, and the full moon cast its silver glow on the water.

The gilded room was gone, and a cozy log cabin was in its place. The bed was sturdy, a lush carpet covered the floor, and she peeked a claw-foot tub in the bathroom through an open door.

"What?" Her brows creased. "How is this happening?"

This wasn't real... right? It couldn't be real. And yet... It felt real. She'd never felt anything more real than this.

That same hand trailed up her spine, each touch blazing a fiery path as he ran his fingers over the thin silk of her slip.

"You needed me, so I came," he said as if it was that simple. As if she knew exactly who he was, and they had something deep between them. "I'll always come for you, sweetheart."

Did Brynleigh need him?

She rarely needed anyone, but if he said she did, maybe he was right. Maybe he knew her and could tell her what she was missing. It certainly sounded like they had something between them.

And the way his fingers caressed her back...

His touch, though foreign, was comfortable. Protective. It was like he cared about her.

She leaned into him, needing more.

"Do you like that?" His breath warmed her ear and sent tingles running down her spine.

She hummed her approval, and his lips ghosted over her bare shoulder.

"Fuck, you taste divine," he murmured, a baritone rasp edging his voice. "Like the night and shadows and everything I've been missing in my life."

He kissed her other shoulder.

She shivered beneath his touch.

"I've been dreaming about this," he whispered. "The way you feel, your smell, your taste. All of it."

She exhaled a shaky breath, and her heart raced. Her fingers gripped the sheets. "And what do you think now?"

His lips skimmed her back, settling in that spot where her shoulder blades came together. "I think my dreams didn't do you justice."

His hand landed on her hip, grounding her and holding her still as his mouth trailed down her back. Everywhere he touched felt like it was on fire.

Brynleigh had had her fair share of sexual partners before, but none of them had ever made her feel like this. Flames licked her insides, warming her always-cold veins. Her fangs throbbed. Unbidden, a deep-set need rose within her. To bite. To feed. Not to inflict pain but to share pleasure.

Fuck, she wanted more.

She needed it.

Moaning, Brynleigh's head landed on his shoulder, and her eyes fell shut.

"That's it, sweetheart," he said encouragingly, nibbling on her ear. "Let me take care of you."

Brynleigh probably should've fought him more. She

should've tried to push past the fog and remember his name. Maybe if she'd wondered why she knew his voice but didn't know what he looked like, she would've realized this was a bad idea.

Except, she didn't care. If this man, whoever he was, made her feel safe, she would revel in that feeling for as long as it lasted.

Brynleigh nodded. Keeping her eyes closed, she inhaled deeply. He smelled of thunderstorms and bergamot, and the scent only made her fangs hurt even more.

She wanted to bite and taste him like he'd tasted her, but something told her doing that would bring this all to a sudden end.

She really didn't want to do that.

His hand tightened on her hip, his grip firm but not bruising. He kissed her ear gently as his other hand slid down her side. His touch was gentle but firm as he reached the hem of her slip and slowly dragged the material up. He exposed the swell of her ass, brushing his knuckles over her bottom.

She shivered, the action having nothing to do with the cold.

He froze, his voice a rasping caress as he breathed, "Is this alright?"

"Yes," she half-pleaded, half moaned. "Please touch me."

They'd already started. Why stop now?

A familiar low chuckle rumbled through him as his hand slipped beneath her, reaching for her core. His fingers grazed her inner thighs, brushing the lace of her undergarments.

His touch was all too brief as he teased her.

His fingers danced close—so gods-damned close—to her intimate flesh, but not quite there. Tracing the edges of her underwear, he explored her slowly as though mapping out every part of her.

She rubbed against him, trying to get him where she needed him the most. If she knew his name, it would be on her lips.

"More," she whispered, not caring that she was close to begging this unknown man for everything.

His lips found her throat, and he nipped her. Heat coursed through her, and she moaned.

"More, what? I need to hear you say it, sweetheart."

Isvana have mercy on her, but her heart raced at his demand. She loved the way he was taking control.

Swallowing, she forced her mind to focus. "Touch me," she requested. "I need to feel your hands on me. In me."

"Thank fuck," he groaned.

He didn't make her wait. Pushing aside the lace, he exhaled gruffly as he touched her. "Gods, you're so wet. Is this for me?"

"Yes." She didn't know how she came to this conclusion. His name was a mystery, as was his face, but the ache in her core was for him as much as his presence was her haven.

Finally—*finally*—his thumb found her sensitive flesh.

At the first touch against her clit, Brynleigh panted.

He pressed harder.

She moaned.

The sound spurred him on, and he slipped a finger into her wet heat. She moved against him, his hand firm on her hip as he held her in place.

He was hard behind her, his impressive length pressing against her lower back, and he slowly pumped his finger in and out of her.

"You're so fucking perfect," he growled.

She needed more. As if he sensed it, he added another finger. They drove into her, giving her more and more. She writhed against him.

Pleasure built. The fog in her mind remained, but she no longer cared.

There was just this moment, her and the man whose voice made her feel safe, and nothing else.

She was so close. So coiled. So ready.

It had been far too long since she'd been with anyone, and she needed this man in a way she'd never needed anyone.

"Fuck yes, that's it," he said encouragingly. He kissed the corner of her lips, her jaw, her neck. "Let go, sweetheart."

He added a third finger, stretching her as his movements sped up.

Moaning, her fingers curled in the sheets as she chased her release. It was so close.

He kept speaking as he touched her. Telling her how much he dreamed of this. How much he wanted this. How good she felt pressed against him. He told her how he'd take her next, lay her beneath him, and let her feel his full weight. He would take care of her, giving her everything she needed.

There was a forcefulness in his voice, a dominance that Brynleigh usually didn't enjoy from partners.

But here? Now?

She would let him do whatever he wanted to her.

His thumb found her clit once more, and she screamed.

"I'm so close," she whimpered.

He released her hip. She didn't have time to mourn the lack of his touch because he tugged down the straps of her slip, exposing her breasts to the night air.

"Fucking beautiful," he breathed.

His fingers grazed her hardened nipples. Every touch, every twist of his skilled fingers against her pebbled flesh, brought her closer and closer to that cliff. She kept her head on his shoulder, her eyes closed, with her mouth opened in a soundless scream.

His lips grazed hers. It was feather-light, a winter breeze against her mouth, not a kiss. It was airy, and she wanted more.

"Let go, Brynleigh," he murmured. "I've got you."

And she did.

He held her, never stopping his sensual touch, as she finally careened off that precipice. Waves of pleasure coursed through her until she was limp in his arms.

He kissed her and laid her down on the bed. "Sleep, sweetheart. I've got you."

He wrapped his arms around her and held her tight.

She drifted off to sleep instantly, the land of dreams welcoming her with open arms.

CHAPTER 13
It Won't Happen Again

Brynleigh's brain pounded against the confines of her skull, making a valiant effort to escape. She groaned, and her eyes opened. That only made things worse. The pounding increased as she took in her surroundings. Her brows knit together.

Wooden rafters stretched high above her head, and the bed was decidedly less cloud-like than before. The scratchy mud-brown blanket covering her wasn't delightful either. She wiggled her toes, the material itchy on her bare feet. White cabinets stretched along one wall, and the air was frigid. Several shiny medical instruments were displayed, and a doctor's coat was on a rack nearby.

She was in an... infirmary. How did she get here? And perhaps more importantly, why was she here?

"Hello?" Her mouth struggled to form the words, her tongue heavy like she'd eaten sandpaper.

A woman in pale pink scrubs with raven hair appeared in Brynleigh's field of vision. Kind blue eyes, much like Brynleigh's had been before she was Made, peered at the vampire through a set of wide-rimmed glasses.

"Oh, good. You're awake." The woman unceremoniously

grabbed Brynleigh's chin and shone a thin, bright light into each of her eyes before nodding to herself. "Your vitals are strong."

"I'm sorry, but who are you?" Brynleigh would usually be more polite, but between the headache and the strange surroundings, gathering information seemed more important than manners.

The woman didn't seem to mind as she smiled. "You can call me Carin, dear. I'm the doctor who's been looking after you."

Doctor Carin crossed the room to a desk Brynleigh hadn't noticed before. She picked up a black phone that looked like it belonged several decades in the past and quickly dialed.

Whoever was on the other line must have answered right away.

"She's awake," the doctor murmured. "What do you want me to do?"

Narrowing her eyes, Brynleigh tried to focus her hearing on the voice coming through the phone line. It was faint, but she picked up a few words.

"... keep... until it's passed... the Chancellor says..."

Carin dipped her head. "Understood. Do you want me to knock her out again?"

Brynleigh's heart seized. She would *not* allow that to happen, even if it meant going against the doctor. She needed to remain alert and figure out what was happening.

The doctor glanced at Brynleigh. "No, she looks normal. Pale, but they all are."

Brynleigh's fingers grappled at the sheet as she struggled to find her last coherent memory. The doctor's words insinuated they'd already knocked her out once.

She didn't remember any of that. She didn't even remember putting on the black sweater that currently covered her arms.

Her mind swirled as she sought her missing memories. Evidently, she wasn't in the Hall of Choice. This room was too small and quaint to be part of the massive building in the middle of Golden City.

Brynleigh had been on a date with her mark when—

"Fuck," she groaned.

Everything came flooding back all at once. The rebels. The bunker. And then... the blood.

Squeezing her eyes shut, Brynleigh fought the urge to scream. She'd been so close to falling into bloodlust and ruining everything. And then after...

The dream.

Heat rushed through her core.

Bad.

This was monumentally bad. Terrible, even. Brynleigh couldn't wrap her mind around how awful this was.

She'd sought the man she planned to murder for comfort in her distress. And she'd let him touch her and bring her to immense pleasure.

No, terrible was too simple a word for this. Catastrophic. That was more fitting. Had she thought the way she reacted to his voice was problematic? That was nothing compared to this.

Brynleigh recalled what she'd called him: her safe haven.

Gods damn it all.

She wanted to bang her head against the wall but decided the doctor probably wouldn't receive the action well. Instead, she rubbed her temples and attempted to talk some sense into herself.

The captain was not her safe place. He was the pinnacle of everything dark and dangerous in her life.

Brynleigh needed to get her head checked because mentally sane people did not find the man who killed their family attractive, let alone dream about him bringing them to orgasm.

The doctor hung up the phone and met Brynleigh's gaze. "You've had quite an eventful few days." Carin's voice was soft, and there was a trace of kindness in her eyes. "They tranquilized you in Golden City and transported you here."

Brynleigh's heart tightened, and a cold sweat broke out on her forehead. "Am I..." She licked her lips. "Am I still in the Choosing?"

"You are." A gentle, practiced smile likely meant to help her patients feel at ease danced on the doctor's lips. It didn't quite work, but Brynleigh appreciated the effort.

"Where are we?"

"We're in a safe place, dear. Your Matron will explain more when you're better. We're on a warded compound, and no one will get to us here."

Brynleigh blinked, her mind whirling as it attempted to keep up with this new information.

"You should rest," continued the doctor. "Now that you're awake and I've checked your vitals, there are a few things I need to take care of."

Carin went to leave, but Brynleigh reached out and grabbed her hand.

"My things." Desperation coated the vampire's words as she remembered her folded picture. She'd left it in the Hall of Choice. "Are they gone?"

She almost didn't want to hear the answer. If she lost the picture...

Grief cut off her airways and stole her breath.

No.

Tears stung the back of her eyes.

Panic rose and rose within her. This couldn't be happening.

She grabbed her necklace, but it didn't help. The picture... she needed it. It was too important.

Oh gods.

Her heart raced.

A warm hand covered Brynleigh's, grounding the vampire. "Not to worry." A squeeze. "Everything was packed and brought with you."

It was here. Not lost.

Slowly, so slowly, Brynleigh's heart slowed. Her eyes shuttered, and she exhaled. "Thank you."

"Of course." Carin strode to the fridge and withdrew a few bags of blood. "You know, I've been watching the Choosing. For what it's worth, I'm rooting for you and Captain Waterborn. The two of you make a handsome couple."

With a wink, the doctor handed Brynleigh the blood and pulled on a coat. "I'll be back soon. You should sleep. The tranquilizer they gave you is still in your system. Rest will help."

Brynleigh didn't move as the door slammed shut behind Carin. It closed too quickly for Brynleigh to see anything except for the dark outline of a man's body. A guard, she assumed.

Brynleigh frowned. Her gaze darted between the blood and the phone on the doctor's desk. Judging by the ache in her fangs and the hollowness in her stomach, she needed to feed, but she had no idea how long the doctor would be gone. This was the first phone she'd seen in weeks, and after the dream she'd had...

She had a call to make. Her lips pursed, and she quickly ran a dozen scenarios through her mind. In the end, her decision wasn't difficult. She didn't have long and needed to act now.

Her mind made up, she slipped her legs out from beneath the scratchy blanket. Her bare toes curled as they pressed against the frigid wooden floor, and she wondered where her shoes had gone. She banished the thought. There were bigger problems at hand.

Participants of the Choosing technically weren't allowed contact with the outside world, but this was one rule she was willing to break. If someone came in, she'd think of an excuse.

Brynleigh perched on the edge of the desk, keeping an eye on the front door as she lifted the phone from its cradle. It was nothing like the sleek, rectangular cellphone she usually used. This one was larger than her hand and had a long, coiled black cord that hung off the side of the desk. It reminded her of the one on the kitchen wall growing up.

At the memory of her familial home, a surge of acerbic anger went through Brynleigh. That kitchen, with its bright sunshine yellow wallpaper with daisies and light blue cupboards, was gone.

Destroyed.

By *him*.

The same man whom she'd invited to touch her in her dreams.

Bitterness burned at the back of Brynleigh's throat, and her grip tightened around the phone. She'd been an idiot but wouldn't make that same mistake again.

This time, she'd follow the rules to a T.

The only good thing about the dream was that it hadn't been real. She was the only witness to her extreme lapse in judgment. No one else had seen her break the rules.

Never again, Brynleigh vowed.

That was the first and last time Ryker would ever touch her, in dreams or reality. She would never let her guard down around him.

He was her enemy.

Dialing the number she'd memorized years ago, Brynleigh brought the phone to her ear and waited for it to connect.

It rang twice before someone picked up.

"Hello?" Jelisette sounded angry.

Shit. Little was more dangerous than an angry vampire, especially one as powerful and old as Brynleigh's Maker.

Brynleigh shifted on the desk. Maybe this was a bad idea. Maybe her Maker didn't want her to check in.

It was too late now, though. She'd already called.

She kept her gaze locked on the door and whispered, "It's me."

Jelisette sucked in a breath. "Brynleigh?" Her voice was slightly less venomous, but the icy tone remained. "Where are you?"

"I don't know." Brynleigh shook her head before she realized her Maker couldn't see her. "There was an attack, and—"

"I know about that. It's all over the news," the older vampire snapped. "Rebels attacked the Chancellor's residence, triggering riots throughout Golden City. They're still being contained. Zanri and I evacuated to the Western Region."

Brynleigh's eyes widened. This was worse than she'd imagined. "Did a lot of people die?"

"They aren't reporting casualty numbers yet. What happened to you? The feeds to the Choosing went black when the first bomb went off, and they haven't come back online."

Brynleigh made a split-second decision not to tell Jelisette about almost falling into bloodlust. She'd never lied to her Maker before, but she didn't want a lecture about being more careful. Besides, guilt was already a blade jabbing her conscience. She didn't need Jelisette to tell her it was wrong, too.

"They moved us," Brynleigh whispered, cognizant of the guard outside. "I'm in a cabin, and the air is colder. If I had to guess, I'd say we're in the Northern Region."

"Find out," Jelisette ordered, her tone one Brynleigh had heard many times before.

"Hold on."

Holding the phone to her ear, Brynleigh hopped off the desk. The nearest window was behind her. The phone cord stretched as Brynleigh reached for the thick, black curtain. She inched back the fabric. If it was daytime, the tiniest touch of sunlight on her skin would be like burning alive.

Luckily, the moon glowed in the night sky.

Brynleigh exhaled and peeked out the window. Snow-covered pines were all around, and fresh snow fell from the starry sky.

"Yes, it seems we're in the north," she confirmed.

The Northern Region, previously known as the Kingdom of Eleyta, was the ancestral home of the vampires in the Republic of Balance. It struck Brynleigh as odd. How could a stunningly beautiful land be home to beings as deadly and cold as vampires?

The faint outlines of more buildings through the trees were cast in silver moonlight. Brynleigh described them as best she could until her Maker was satisfied.

"How is your relationship?" the older vampire asked next.

Brynleigh's stomach twisted, and despite her earlier vow, a

pulse of pure want ran through her. She couldn't help it. The memory of Ryker's skilled fingers was so fresh.

"It's progressing well." She forced the words out of a dry mouth.

"Good girl," her Maker said. "You remember the rules?"

The ones that Brynleigh had obliterated? Yes. She remembered them far too well. If anything, she wished she could forget them. Anything so she could feel better about the dream she'd had.

How could something that felt so good be so bad?

"Brynleigh, answer me!" Cold steel edged Jelisette's voice. "Do you remember the rules, daughter of my blood?"

"Yes, ma'am," Brynleigh replied automatically. "I won't get attached, and I'll kill him on our wedding night the moment we're alone."

It didn't matter that the captain seemed like a good fae, or that he was kind to Brynleigh, or that he made her feel safe.

None of that mattered because he'd murdered her entire family in cold blood.

Brynleigh would do well to remember that. The captain had a nice exterior, but inside, he was still a bad man. She just... hadn't met that side of him yet. She was certain it was there, though. It had to be there. What other explanation could there be?

A branch snapped outside, and Brynleigh jolted.

"I have to go," she hissed.

Brynleigh hung up without waiting for a response. Drawing on her shadows, she sped across the room and climbed in bed. Ripping open the first bag of blood, she downed the crimson liquid. She was almost at the bottom of the bag when the door opened.

This time, the door remained ajar long enough to give Brynleigh a good look around.

A pair of guards dressed in black stood in front of the cabin. Their stances were wide, and guns hung off their belts. They meant business as they stared straight ahead into the wintery forest. Wherever they were, it must have been far in the north. Snow wouldn't hit Golden City until right before Winter Solstice, which was still several months away.

Doctor Carin strode inside, kicking the snow off her boots before shutting the door. She spoke quietly into a cell phone, barely glancing at Brynleigh as she grabbed a sheet of paper off the desk. The doctor dropped into the office chair with an audible sigh and spun it around so her back was to Brynleigh.

The doctor's murmurs filled the cabin as exhaustion slammed into Brynleigh. It was sudden and all-consuming. Keeping her eyes open was a struggle. She fought to remain alert long enough to finish the bag of blood before letting her head fall back on the lumpy pillow.

Sleep. That's what she needed. Quiet, peaceful, rule-following sleep. There would be no dreams of troublesome, dangerous captains this time. Brynleigh wouldn't allow it.

One day, she would be old enough for sleep to be part of her past. Some vampires were so ancient that they felt no aches and pains and no longer required rest like mortals. A few vampires who had lived several thousand years no longer needed blood.

Right now, Brynleigh felt so mortal that she couldn't imagine living for that long. She would take this one day at a time.

This time, nightmares of deadly storms and watery screams plagued her all night long.

CHAPTER 14
Breaking Rules and Guilty Consciences

"Where. Is. She?" Ryker bit out the words and crossed his arms. He channeled his mother and sent a withering glare at the soldier at the door, hoping it would loosen the man's tongue.

The guard shook his head. "I told you, Captain, I can't share that information with you. She's safe; that's all I'm authorized to say."

Safe, but not here in the library with the rest of them.

Ryker barely contained the growl rising in his throat. The past few days had been an absolute shit show, the likes of which he hadn't seen for several years.

After the rebels' attack, Matron Cassandra briefed the men. Her information had been minimal, at best. There was an attack. No, she didn't know if there were casualties. Yes, they were safe. No, she couldn't tell them anything else.

Frustrating.

After the meeting, they were given thirty minutes to gather their belongings. A dozen guards shuffled them onto an enormous blacked-out bus. The women were transported in another vehicle, and armed guards had made up the rest of their entourage. They'd driven through the night, crossing from the Central Region into the Northern one.

When the driver had pulled through looming stone gates and driven up a long circular driveway, red streaked the sky. They'd stopped in front of a brick three-story home that was nothing short of palatial. The estate was large, and at least one other building, barely visible through the pines, was tucked behind the main one.

When the bus had stopped, Matron Cassandra had explained that for security reasons, the Choosing would continue in this more secluded location. Representative Therald, one of the werewolf Alphas, had kindly donated his pack house for the remainder of the Choosing. A team had flown up a few hours earlier and prepared the house for them. They had installed the necessary technology to stream the remainder of the Choosing to the world and covered all the windows with blackout blinds to accommodate the vampires in their group.

"Chancellor Rose is adamant that the Choosing continue," Cassandra had said. "After all, it's more important than ever to remind the Republic that we are a united country."

After the Matron's speech had concluded, Ryker disembarked the bus with the others. He'd found his room, showered, and then collapsed on the bed. It had been an extremely long night. He had slept most of the day, emerging long enough to eat before returning to the comfort of his sheets.

That was yesterday, though.

This morning, he'd woken up with a strong desire to talk to Brynleigh. He needed to make sure she was alright.

Following the Matron's directions, he'd located the two-story library, where a hastily erected wall bisected the room.

Everything had been going as expected until he'd slipped on his headphones. The morning had rapidly deteriorated from there.

First, Celeste had connected him with Valentina. He'd

explained, in no uncertain terms, that although he had enjoyed their conversations, he would pursue another option.

She hadn't taken it well.

At.

All.

Ryker endured Valentina's wrath for the better part of an hour. It was the longest sixty minutes of his life. She yelled, and he spoke to her calmly. She berated him, insisting he would regret this. He knew she was wrong. She swore. He sighed.

At least she confirmed he'd made the right decision.

When Celeste had informed him the meeting was over, relief had coursed through his veins. He couldn't wait to speak with Brynleigh and tell her he'd broken things off with Valentina.

However, after Celeste had disconnected him from Valentina, the AI informed him that Brynleigh was unavailable. Not talking to someone else.

Unavailable.

The word had echoed around in Ryker's mind, a battering ram against his senses. If Brynleigh wasn't there, where was she?

Worry had gnawed at his gut, which led him to this tense conversation with the guard at the entrance.

"Why can't I speak with her?" He waved the white headphones at the man. "What happened to her? Is she still in Golden City?"

"As I previously stated, all Choosing participants have journeyed to this new location," the guard said evasively.

Ryker's worry twisted and grew. What wasn't the guard telling him? Brynleigh was strong, but even vampires weren't infallible. He couldn't shake the idea that the guard was keeping something from him.

The other men's conversations were the quiet backdrop to the pounding of Ryker's heart.

"I have to see her," he insisted.

Ryker's muscles were rigid, and his jaw was tense from being clenched for so long. Some might say he was overreacting, but after the events of the past few days, a little overreaction might not be entirely out of place.

A vein feathered in the guard's jaw, and his eyes flashed. "Sir, you cannot see the women. It goes against the very structure of the Choosing. You must know we cannot allow it."

Ryker's fists curled. The urge to acquaint this soldier with his fist was close to overwhelming.

The only thing that stopped him was the red light on the bookshelf behind the guard's head. They were being recorded, and Ryker had no desire to deal with the aftermath of his actions if he punched the unhelpful soldier.

Footsteps clicked in the hall, and Ryker glanced over the soldier's shoulder. Wearing white from head to toe, Matron Cassandra approached the library. She touched the guard on the arm and whispered in his ear.

When they broke apart, the guard turned back to Ryker. "You're in luck. Miss de la Point is indisposed, but Matron Cassandra will deliver a note if you want to send her a message."

"What the fuck does that mean?" Ryker bit out.

"She's indisposed," the guard repeated unhelpfully.

Ryker growled. He had even more questions than before. He'd learned his lesson, though. There would be no getting information out of this soldier.

Instead, Ryker shifted and met the Matron's gaze. "You'll personally deliver the note?"

Cassandra pulled a black pen and a small notebook out of her pocket. "I will."

Ryker took them, rolling the pen between his fingers as a plan formed in his mind. It was risky, but he couldn't sit around and wait for someone to decide to update him on what was happening. He needed to take matters into his own hands.

"Very well. I'll write one up, and then I'd like to rest." Not a lie. He would like to rest. He just didn't plan on doing it right now. "If Brynleigh isn't here, I don't want to talk to anyone else."

Truth.

The Matron frowned. "There is no one else? It's highly irregular—"

"No." His voice was firm. "She's mine."

Even though Brynleigh didn't know it yet, it was true.

Both the Matron and the guard widened their eyes as if the claiming words caught them off guard. They didn't surprise Ryker, though. They'd slipped off his tongue as easily as his own name. Now that he'd parted ways with Valentina, he was ready to make it official with his vampire.

A smile tugged on the Matron's lips, and her eyes twinkled. "I see. Of course, Captain. You may return to your room."

"Thank you." He had no intention of doing such a thing, but he kept that to himself.

Instead, he took the offered pen and paper with a smile. He slipped into a wooden chair that creaked as he put his full weight on it. Hints of the ruby theme of the Choosing were scattered throughout the library—mugs, pillows, and a few red armchairs—but the room was a study in woodwork.

Everything from the bookshelves to the high ceiling and the polished planks on the floor were made of wood. It reminded him of the hunting cabin he kept outside Golden City. He'd bought it a decade ago, and after the Incident six years ago, it had become a refuge for him. He'd spent nearly as much time at the cabin as he did at his home in the city.

He hoped Brynleigh would enjoy it as much as he did.

Ryker penned the note with the speed of a man desperate for answers. He wasn't a youngling and was well aware that writing something in a letter didn't guarantee it would remain private. He purposefully kept his message vague. Folding it in half, he scrawled his vampire's name on the front before handing it to the Matron.

"I'll deliver this as soon as I'm done here," Cassandra promised.

"Thank you." Ryker dipped his head and made a show of

departing. Nodding at the guard, Ryker slipped his hands in his pockets and nonchalantly strolled down the empty hall.

Instead of returning to his room, he ducked inside the first doorway and watched the library entrance.

He didn't have to wait long. The Matron exited a few minutes later, humming a tune as she walked away from Ryker. She clutched his note, her hips swaying as she made her way to the end of the hall and turned left.

Keeping his distance, Ryker trailed her. It wasn't difficult. She was a human, and he was a trained fae. Tracking her movements without being seen required minimal energy. They strolled past the guards stationed throughout the house, and none of them noticed him. He supposed he couldn't hold it against them. They were searching for external threats, not internal ones.

Still, if these were Ryker's men, he'd have a few words with them. Evidently, this "secure" location had more than a few security issues. However, their lackluster guarding was playing into Ryker's favor at the moment.

He kept pace with the Matron through the house. She stopped at the kitchen and picked up a pear tart before descending two flights of stairs. She went down a plain, small corridor, lifting a knitted shawl off a hook on the wall. She wrapped it around herself and slipped out the door without a backward glance.

That was unexpected. Ryker had assumed the Matron would deliver his note somewhere within this house.

"What the hell?" he muttered, his eyes narrowing. "Where are you going?"

As the questions piled up and the lack of answers became even more glaring, Ryker took the stairs three at a time. He scanned the door, searching for an alarm, but he didn't see anything.

At this point, all plausible deniability on his part was gone. If he were caught, he'd have some serious explaining to do as to why he was sneaking about the pack house.

He couldn't be caught. It was that simple.

Ryker didn't want to go outside without any sort of weapon. He didn't know what was waiting for him on the other side of the door. Opening his palm, he reached within himself and summoned his magic. The water was always there, waiting for him. It came eagerly, and he pulled it from his veins, forming a dagger of ice.

Armed and ready to go, he gingerly touched the door handle. It was cool. He held his hand there, waiting to see if there was an alarm, but nothing happened.

He opened the door, and once he was certain the coast was clear, he stepped outside.

A bitter, icy gale slammed into him like a wall of bricks. The sun shone on a blanket of white that covered everything in sight. The snow was beautiful when observed from inside, but outside, it was unpleasant at best.

He swore, rubbing his arms. His black t-shirt, jeans, and sneakers were not weather-appropriate. The ice dagger in his hand was a part of him, and the cold emanating from it didn't bother him. It was his magic, and it sang to him. But although he could hold his dagger for hours without his hand hurting, he wasn't impervious to weather conditions.

Still, there was no time to wait. He would have to put up with the cold. Picking up a rock from the side of the house, he jammed it inside the lock. Hopefully, the Matron wouldn't notice that the door didn't fully close if she returned before him.

The Matron's shawl flapped as she hurried through the trees, a flag leading him in the right direction. Ignoring the goosebumps crawling over his arms, he was a shadow as he trailed her.

A voice in Ryker's head chided him for breaking the rules as he prowled through the trees. This kind of behavior was wholly unlike him. He couldn't remember the last time he'd disregarded a regulation.

But it wasn't for him. It was for Brynleigh. It didn't matter that he'd only known the vampire for a month or that he'd never seen her. Ryker cared about her and would do anything to keep her safe, including going where he wasn't supposed to. Technically, they had never *said* the participants of the Choosing had to remain within the confines of the mansion, but it felt like an unspoken rule.

Birds chirped, and a squirrel hopped across branches, but he kept his eyes on the human ahead of him.

Several minutes passed before a small log cabin appeared through the trees. It wasn't very big, and midnight curtains were drawn shut. This small building was guarded, unlike the mansion side door he'd slipped out of. Two armed soldiers stood on a wooden covered porch. The Republic's insignia was on their chests, and they each held large guns as they scanned the forest for threats.

Ryker swore and ducked behind a tree, flattening his palms on the rough bark. Of course, there were guards here who seemed to be doing their jobs. Were they here because of Brynleigh? Perhaps more importantly, were they keeping her safe or holding her against her will?

He wasn't sure, but he would find out.

He would have to be patient. Years of military service had drilled into him the benefit of forbearance. He would discover what happened to Brynleigh, but he had to be smart about it.

Ryker studied the cabin, ignoring how the icy wind burned the skin on his bare arms. Although they were armed and seemed to be paying attention, the guards' relaxed aura boded well for Ryker.

Using the trees for cover, he slowly circled the building on silent, trained feet. There were six windows and two doors, one at the front and one at the back.

The latter was unguarded. A spark of hope came to life within him. He circled the cabin twice more, taking in all the details through analytic eyes.

Adjusting his grip on his ice dagger, he snuck towards the

back door. The knob was cold, and it didn't budge as he wiggled it. Locked.

He huffed, and his nostrils flared. That would've been too easy.

In case the guards were in the habit of walking the perimeter, Ryker hurried back to the trees and crept around to the front to keep watch.

A few minutes later, Matron Cassandra re-emerged. She stepped outside, nodding to the guards before returning to the mansion. Her hands were empty, and his note was nowhere to be seen.

Confident that his vampire was inside the building, Ryker exhaled and quickly formulated a plan. It was risky but the best way to get eyes inside.

Now, he had to wait. Leaning against a tree, he allowed the forest to conceal him until the right opportunity arose.

Minutes went by.

The temperature dropped. He rubbed his arms in an effort to conserve heat, although the action didn't do much good. His teeth chattered, and his skin prickled.

He refused to let the temperature bother him. He could warm up later. Something as trivial as being cold could not force him to abandon his post. He would wait as long as necessary.

Finally, after an hour, Ryker saw his chance.

"Mind if I grab a smoke and make a call?" The shorter guard stretched his arms above his head and cracked his back. "I should check on Marie. You know how pregnant women get when they don't hear from us."

The other man snorted. "Yes, I remember my sister's pregnancy. Thank all the gods, Justinian and I don't have to worry about that."

"Thanks, man. Be back soon." The first guard jumped off the porch and strode into the woods away from Ryker.

As soon as his companion was gone, the second guard relaxed and leaned against the wall.

This was Ryker's moment. He hurried to the back of the cabin and placed his dagger on the ground next to him. Though far more vigilant than the ones in the house, the guards hadn't bothered to check the back door in the time he'd been here.

Drawing another stream of water from his palms, Ryker froze it into a pick and angled it into the lock. If this were a regular icicle, it would have snapped as soon as he put pressure on it. Thank the gods; Ryker was one of the strongest water fae in the entire Republic of Balance. His powerful magic was malleable and would serve him well in this task.

Feeding strengthening magic into his improvised tool, Ryker jiggled the pick around in the lock. They didn't teach these kinds of tricks in the military academy, but he'd picked up a few things hanging around with Atlas.

The earth fae grew up in the streets and had several less-than-reputable, but helpful, skills. Ryker made a mental note to thank Atlas for teaching him how to pick locks when the Choosing ended.

Pressing his pointed ear against the frigid door, Ryker slowly moved his pick until the tell-tale *click* of locks tumbling filled his ears. "I owe you a beer, Atlas," he murmured.

Exhaling a sigh of relief, he allowed the pick to melt back into liquid form. He rose to his feet, keeping a small sphere of water in his palm in case something awaited him on the other side.

Ryker slid the door open.

It was...

A supply closet.

"Damn." He slipped inside, careful not to jostle the broom and mop that were haphazardly placed near the door. The confined space was dark except for the artificial yellow glow of fluorescent lighting running along the gap between the door and the floor.

Ryker dropped to his knees and ran his hands carefully down the walls. Then he felt it. A grate, roughly the size of his head, intended to allow air to flow through the cabin, was on the left side of the door. He felt his way to the edges and worked on the exposed screws with his fingers.

Thank the gods, whoever had installed the grate had done so in a lackadaisical manner. The screws were already loose, and it only took a few minutes to remove all four of them. Ryker held his breath as he pried the grate off the wall and placed it beside him.

Drawing in his shoulders, which was a feat in this small space, he contorted himself and peered through the opening.

His breath caught. Resting on a cot not far from him was a woman. She faced the door, her back to him. Like shards of sunlight, long, wavy blonde hair fell over her pillow. A brown blanket was tucked under her chin. He wasn't certain whether she was sleeping or glaring at the front door, but she wasn't moving.

On the other side of the room was a desk. A woman in a medical coat and pink scrubs typed on a laptop, her fingers flying over the keys. Ryker studied her briefly before determining she wasn't an immediate threat.

Ryker's gaze returned to the cot. Something about this woman drew him like a moth to a flame. An unexpected, pulsing need burned within him. He wanted to go to her, draw her into his arms, and never release her.

Beyond the shadow of a doubt, Ryker knew this was her.

Brynleigh de la Point.

His vampire.

They'd only known each other for a month, but it felt like a lifetime. They'd spent hours talking about everything and nothing, but this was the first time he was putting a body to her voice.

And gods, what a body it was. Ryker would be lying if he said he hadn't frequently dreamed of Brynleigh since their first date. He'd fantasized about being alone with her. He'd thought about how he'd make her his. He would taste her mouth, then have her writhing beneath him as he licked and suckled every sensitive part of her until she shattered. Then he would claim her.

Before, they'd been nothing but dreams. But now...

Now he *knew*.

In the same way that Ryker knew the sky was blue, the grass was green, and his magic was strong, he knew she was meant to be his. They would be partners in every single way. Not just in marriage but also in life. She was the other half that would complete him.

His soul recognized hers.

He'd heard of this happening—not between fae and vampires, but fae with other fae. Unbreakable bonds forged between two beings were blessed by the gods and extremely rare. Ryker didn't think that was happening to him—he didn't know if a fae could form a mating bond with a vampire—but he was sure she was meant to be his. He wanted to shout, to reach through the grate and pull her towards him, to pick her up and embrace her until the end of time.

But he wasn't supposed to be here.

Ryker's gut twisted. What the fuck was he doing? Participants of the Choosing weren't supposed to see each other until the Masked Ball. If Brynleigh knew he was here, would she report him for breaking the rules? Would she leave?

He gasped, his stomach contorting in on itself at the thought. Fucking hell. He couldn't let that happen. He couldn't risk it.

Brynleigh rolled onto her back, and he could see the steady rise and fall of her chest. Not only that, but the doctor didn't seem concerned with the vampire's health. Maybe they were keeping her here until the sun set, and it would be safe for her to join the others?

He hoped that was the case. If she weren't back tomorrow, then Ryker would return. He'd raise hell to see this woman again. For now, he would retreat to the mansion and act like everything was normal.

He slid the grate back and replaced the screws. Pressing his palm against the wall, he breathed in deeply. Beneath the clinical, bleach-like quality in the air were traces of the night, shadows, and... something that he couldn't quite put his finger on. Whatever it was, he wanted more.

Soon, he promised himself.

Ryker slipped out of the cabin and discreetly returned to the main house. This time, he didn't notice the cold at all. He returned to his room and cranked the shower as hot as possible. As the hot water rained down on him, he dreamed of that silky blonde hair and how she would feel in his arms.

He promised himself this wasn't the only time he would see her. He wouldn't allow it.

CHAPTER 15
Young Love

Thunderstorms and bergamot.

At first, the scent was faint. Barely there. Brynleigh had caught a whiff of the unique fragrance on the note when the Matron delivered it. After that, she'd fallen asleep, holding the paper to her chest.

And when she woke?

The smell was everywhere. It had infiltrated the air, seeping into the particles themselves.

It was him.

Ryker had been here. His scent lingered even now, growing fainter but still present. She wanted to bathe in it. It was the best thing she'd ever smelled.

She'd looked around for him, but nothing was out of place.

He'd left.

What had he been doing here? Had he somehow discovered her secret and come to kill her, too?

Brynleigh ran her fingers over her pendant, mulling over the possibility that she'd been found out. It was unlikely that he knew who she was. After all, she'd taken on Jelisette's surname after the storm. Not only that, but the destruction of Chavin hadn't exactly been plastered all over the news.

Like everything else related to Brynleigh's family's demise, the untimely flood and the resulting deaths had been buried by the Waterborn's political influence. A fluke of nature, the few people who reported on it had said. Others speculated it was an act of Nontia, the goddess of the sea. No one cared. Not really.

A week after the flood, another event stole the spotlight, and the media forgot about Chavin.

Not Brynleigh, though.

She was the sole survivor from that night. Although, technically, she hadn't survived either. Vampires, in the truest sense of the word, had to die to become their immortal selves. Had she not been Made, she would not be here.

No, there was no way he knew. If he did, he would kill her on the spot.

Why had he come?

She unfolded his note and read it again. It was simple and to the point.

I missed talking to you today, sweetheart. I hope we can chat tomorrow.

Ryker's writing was atrocious, like that of a child. But... he'd written her a note. Even though it wasn't a declaration of love or a proposal, it had to mean she was making headway. Right?

Yes.

The note, combined with the fact that he'd broken the rules to see her, was a good sign. A fucking fantastic one, actually.

A luminous grin spread across Brynleigh's face. She knew how much the captain cared about rules from their countless conversations. It was evident in the way he spoke and carried himself. For him to throw them aside for her was... everything. This was the confirmation she needed that her efforts hadn't been in vain.

A month in the real world wasn't that long, but in the Choosing, every day was like a week.

The more she thought about it, the more Brynleigh was convinced she was right. This was good. Better than good, in fact. The rebels had done her a favor because now she had tangible proof of her mark's affections. He'd been here. For so long, she had hunted the reclusive captain. Now, *he* sought *her*.

Everything was on track.

She could still accomplish her mission despite all the complications she'd encountered. Wedding bells chimed in her head, declaring their union to the world. They sounded awfully similar to the music she imagined would play at Ryker's funeral after she got her revenge.

He had no idea he was courting the instrument of his impending death.

Maybe she should've felt bad about that, but she didn't. The people of Chavin hadn't had any warning when he called a deadly hurricane upon them, drowning them while they slept.

Brynleigh would be a silent assassin. She would play the role of doting bride until the life drained from the captain's eyes. She couldn't wait to see his face when he realized it was all a charade, that he'd been betrayed by the one person he thought he could trust.

Revenge would be sweet, indeed.

She focused on vengeance and nothing else. Those were the rules; this was her game, and she would be the victor.

Hours passed.

Brynleigh remained in bed with her thoughts as her only company. She had many of them. They were all of the deadly variety... or at least, that's what she told herself.

When a smile came to her lips, she convinced herself it was because she was excited by the thought of avenging her family, not from Ryker's lingering scent tickling her nose.

When her mind wandered to the dream and her core tightened, she shoved those feelings deep down. She was only happy because Ryker would be dead soon, not because of the way he had touched her and brought her comfort.

And when she wondered what it would be like to plunge her fangs into Ryker's neck and taste his blood, it was purely for the purpose of killing him and not for other more... pleasant activities.

Yes, all she thought about was revenge.

Nothing else.

Around seven, Doctor Carin's phone rang. The crisp sound shattered the silence. Brynleigh jolted.

Carin picked up the phone. "Hello?"

The voice on the other end of the line was too quiet for Brynleigh to hear.

"Yes, she looks much better." Carin's eyes swept over the vampire. "Mhmm." She paused, listening. "Understood."

After another minute, the doctor hung up and faced Brynleigh. "Are you ready to rejoin the Choosing?"

A flutter of delight ran through Brynleigh, and she grinned, displaying her sharp fangs. "Absolutely."

Chuckling, the doctor reached behind her desk and pulled out a spare pair of boots and clean socks. She handed them to Brynleigh with a smile. Carin's eye had a distinctive twinkle as she asked, "Looking forward to talking to your captain?"

"Oh, yes." Brynleigh sat up, swung her legs off the cot, and pulled on the socks and footwear. "I certainly am."

The events of the past few days confirmed that Brynleigh needed to concentrate. The dream was the perfect example. She'd momentarily lost sight of her goals and wandered down a path of simple pleasure.

That wouldn't happen again.

Killing the captain on their wedding night would be poetic justice, sure to inflict maximal pain on his family.

It was fitting.

Once Ryker was dead, Brynleigh would escape to the Rose Ocean and watch everything unfold from afar.

Jelisette promised to get Brynleigh to safety as soon as she accomplished her mission. The older vampire would protect her progeny from the long arm of the law.

The door swung open, and Matron Lilith entered. She stomped her boots and shook off the snow. Complaining about the cold, she frowned as she clapped her mittens together before turning to Brynleigh. "Are you ready?"

"Yes," Brynleigh exclaimed, perhaps a bit too eagerly. "I mean... I am." She tried to tone down the excitement in her voice as she stood. "I missed talking to Ryker today."

That was it, right? She just wanted to talk to him to make sure he would fall in love with her so she could kill him. No other reason.

"Ah, young love," Matron Lilith chuckled as she led Brynleigh out the door. "It's a beautiful thing."

Brynleigh didn't bother correcting the older woman, but she knew the Matron was wrong. She didn't love Ryker. She hated him with every fiber of her being.

Right?

Thanking the doctor, Brynleigh nodded at the guards and went outside. Snowflakes fell leisurely from the night sky.

Matron Lilith led Brynleigh through the trees towards a beautiful, snow-covered mansion. As they walked, Lilith explained that the remainder of the Choosing would take place here until the Masked Ball, thanks to the rebel attack.

Brynleigh nodded her understanding. Relocating them made sense. So did their isolated northern location.

It wasn't until they'd climbed steps to enter through large double doors that looked like they belonged in an ancient castle that the Matron's words shocked the vampire.

"The timeline has been condensed."

"Condensed?" Brynleigh echoed. Her mind raced. What, exactly, did that mean? How would this affect her plans?

Matron Lilith placed her hand on Brynleigh's and squeezed. "The Masked Ball will take place two weeks from today."

Two weeks.

That was... not long. Not long at all.

Fuck.

All that earlier confidence fled.

Brynleigh was supposed to have two more months to make Ryker fall in love and propose. Two weeks?

That was... incredibly short.

Her heart boomed in her chest, and a headache started to form.

Isvana have mercy on her. Brynleigh couldn't catch a fucking break. First, the rebel attack, then her dream, and now this?

"I know it seems quick," Matron Lilith added compassionately. "But trust me, you'll be fine."

Fine? Brynleigh wasn't sure that was the case. She nibbled on her lip. "I—"

"Someone was very worried about you yesterday." The Matron waggled her brows suggestively. "I can't say much more, but suffice it to say, I would be willing to bet a large sum of money that a certain captain will happily be on one knee in two weeks."

Brynleigh hoped Lilith was correct. She'd have to be even more compelling to ensure she received Ryker's proposal.

Fourteen days to make Ryker fall completely, irrevocably, mindlessly in love with her.

And then she'd destroy him.

LILITH GAVE Brynleigh a tour of the mansion, showing her the room where she would be sleeping before bringing her to a home theater on the first floor. The other women were gathering for a movie.

"This is where I leave you," the Matron said. "You ladies enjoy your evening."

"Thank you, Matron." Brynleigh pushed open the doors, stepping into the darkened room. A white screen stretched across one wall, and three rows of comfortable seating were spread in front of the screen. The mansion's owner must have been wealthy beyond measure because Brynleigh had never seen a private cinema before.

"Brynleigh!"

At the sound of her name, the vampire looked up. Hallie came barreling towards her, her translucent wings fluttering.

"Thank Kydona, you're alright!" the Fortune Elf exclaimed as she hugged Brynleigh tightly. "They wouldn't tell us where you were, and when I walked the silver planes to See you, I couldn't find your future."

A pit yawned in Brynleigh's stomach at the dire prediction. What did that mean? Probably nothing good. However, the more rational part of Brynleigh's mind reminded her that Fortune Elves had a flair for both the cryptic and the dramatic. Maybe Hallie just misinterpreted the future.

Hoping that was the case—because, to be honest, Brynleigh couldn't deal with any other problems right now—she shoved her worry aside and smiled at the elf. "You searched for me? That was so kind of you."

Hallie grinned. "Of course I did. You're my friend. I was worried about you."

An unfamiliar emotion sprung to life inside Brynleigh. It was nice—and a little strange, if she was honest—to know someone had been worrying about her. The vampire had never expected to make a friend, yet it seemed she had.

"Thank you." Brynleigh smiled. "I'm here, and I'm safe."

A pointed cough came from behind them.

Brynleigh turned around.

"Well, if it isn't the vile bloodsucking creature that nearly killed us all." Valentina's horrible, grating voice was almost as unpleasant as the sneer carved onto her face.

The fire fae wore a skin-tight white sweater and jeans that looked like they cost thousands. Her blue-black hair was swept into a high ponytail, and a dusting of makeup decorated her features. Valentina looked perfectly put together, whereas Brynleigh knew the last few days had taken their toll on her appearance.

Still, she held her head up high. "I had it under control."

"Liar." A promise of violence flickered in Valentina's violet eyes, and she stepped towards the vampire. "You were going to tear everyone to shreds because of a bit of blood. You shouldn't be here. This competition isn't meant for people like you." She scowled. "Return to the cemetery where you came from."

"Fuck. You." Brynleigh balled her fists. Shadows flooded out of her, and her wings burst from her back. Her sweater shredded, leaving her in her violet t-shirt, which had slits for wings. She didn't care about the ruined clothes. It was time to teach this fae a lesson.

"Oh, the vampire bitch wants to play," Valentina snarled. A flame flickered to life above her outstretched hand. "Let's see how well you do around a little fire."

Despite the pounding of her heart, Brynleigh didn't move. She refused to give in to this bully. "You want to fight? Fine. I'll fucking fight you."

She could use the outlet for all the emotions she'd been shoving deep within her.

Valentina lifted a manicured brow and looked down on Brynleigh. "There is nothing I'd love more than to teach you a lesson, little leech."

The other women stepped back amid a flurry of gasps and rude remarks. The tension was so thick that the air practically crackled.

This wouldn't be the first fight Brynleigh had gotten into. At ten years old, she had tackled Diana Laurent on the playground after school when she'd learned the older girl was bullying Brynleigh's little sister Sarai.

Displeased with the situation, the principal had threatened to suspend both girls, but Brynleigh didn't care. She'd made her point. That day, Diana went home with two black eyes and never bothered Sarai again.

It was time Valentina learned precisely who she was dealing with.

Brynleigh was a heartbeat away from throwing her shadows at the fire fae when Hallie screamed at the top of her lungs, "Stop!"

The sound was so sudden that for a moment, it felt like time halted.

Then, both Brynleigh and Valentina turned to the Fortune Elf. "What the hell?" they said at the same time.

"You can't fight here." Hallie took Brynleigh's hand and yanked her towards the door. "They'll kick you out. Is that what you want?"

Brynleigh's eyes widened, and she glanced back at the fae.

Valentina stood there with fire flickering in her outstretched palm. "They could try to kick me out," she said haughtily, "but Mother would never stand for it. I can do whatever I want."

Lips curled, Brynleigh snarled. That was precisely why she was here. "You are a horrible, awful—"

With a strength Brynleigh didn't know the other woman possessed, Hallie jerked her out of the room and slammed the door behind them.

Hallie's eyes flashed with silver, and she looked fierce. "Ryker was looking for you today," she hissed. "Therian told me he refused to stop asking about you. Think about him, not that rich fae bitch."

Brynleigh drew in breath to too-tight lungs. Wisps of shadows slipped from her hands. Her nostrils flared. She tried to do what Hallie suggested but couldn't get Valentina's sneer out of her mind. "She's awful."

"She is," Hallie agreed. "But she's also right."

"What?" That was the last thing Brynleigh expected to hear, and it caught her off guard.

The Fortune Elf's wings flared. "Valentina probably won't get kicked out, but you definitely will. You were Selected, just like me. You know we're not the same as them."

When the words sank in, they were like cement around Brynleigh's feet, holding her in place. Her friend was right. Brynleigh had to get her head on straight. She had to focus on Ryker and nothing else. She couldn't fight Valentina, no matter how horrible the woman was. She couldn't afford to leave after all she'd been through to get here.

Closing her eyes, Brynleigh inhaled deeply. She focused on the rhythmic throb of her heart, letting it ground her. Once she was certain she wouldn't bolt back into the cinema and rip out Valentina's throat, she exhaled.

Retracting her shadows and wings, she opened her eyes. "Thank you, Hallie."

Without a backward glance, needing to put as much space between her and the fire fae as possible, Brynleigh stepped into the Void.

The complete and utter darkness of the space in between consumed her, and for a moment, she was utterly at peace.

In her room, Brynleigh showered away any lingering desire to fight Valentina. She wasn't here for her.

Her vengeance was so close; she could taste it.

CHAPTER 16
Pen Pals and Nicknames

"Greetings and salutations, Captain Waterborn." Celeste's voice seemed more chipper today than normal, or maybe it was Ryker who was different.

Last night, he'd slept better than he had in years. The memory of Brynleigh's wavy blonde hair and luscious scent kept him company through his dreams.

It surprised Ryker to realize that he did not regret visiting her yesterday. He'd broken the rules, but it was for a good reason.

He would do it again in a heartbeat.

"Morning," he replied. Adjusting the headphones with one hand, he accepted a coffee from the Light Elf manning the temporary bar near the door. Thanking the elf, he moved towards the wall.

The library was significantly smaller than the ballroom in the Hall of Choice, and even with the headphones, he could hear the faint murmurs of the other men speaking as he situated himself in a cozy armchair.

"Your date is incoming, Captain," Celeste said pleasantly. "Please, stand by."

A languid cello concerto trilled through the headset. Clearly, they were getting right to it. He probably had the condensed timeline to thank for that. Some of the other men were concerned about the new timeframe, but not Ryker. He didn't need the two weeks.

He was ready to propose now.

Some might have said he was moving too fast, but Ryker had already decided. He wanted Brynleigh de la Point. She might not be the kind of wife his mother desired for him, but she was the woman *he* wanted.

Ryker would cherish the next two weeks. He would use the time to familiarize himself with his future bride and learn everything about her. Besides, Brynleigh might still need the time to make her decision. He wasn't so full of himself that he thought Brynleigh would fall over herself in a rush to the altar to meet him.

Love took work on both sides, and he intended to prove to the vampire that he would be the best possible partner for her. Ryker would provide for Brynleigh in every way, keep her safe, and give her a home full of love. He could see it now—their life would be filled with laughter, games, intelligent comments, and hours of conversation.

He couldn't wait.

The music quieted until all Ryker could hear was his thundering heart.

A soft inhale came through the headphones, barely more than a breath.

"Brynleigh?" he murmured, his coffee cup frozen midway to his mouth. "Is that you?"

What a stupid question. Of course, it was. After his final, disastrous conversation with Valentina yesterday, he'd requested that Brynleigh be his only date from now on. Still, he had to know.

The silence seemed to stretch for an eternity as he waited and waited for a response.

Was she there?

When a lifetime—or a few seconds, it was hard to tell—

passed, a serene, feminine exhale caressed his ears. It was like a refreshing breeze whispering on his skin on a hot day. That voice that was becoming as familiar as his own breathed, "Ryker."

At the sound of his name on Brynleigh's lips, Ryker groaned. His cock stirred, and he adjusted himself as he let his eyes fall shut.

No one else said his name like that. It was half-prayer, half-plea, and all... her. The lilt of her voice, the specific way she pulled out each syllable, was everything he ever needed. Tension left his shoulders, and he relaxed.

"Hey there, sweetheart. I missed you." Truth.

"I missed you, too."

He'd never heard better words. Leaning forward in his seat, he opened his eyes once more. "Did you get my note?"

A wooden wall was all that separated them. He stared at the striations in the wood and waited.

Ryker used to be patient—his mother often described him as imperturbable—but he was so eager to hear his vampire's words that every second she was silent was too long.

"Yes, the Matron delivered it." A breathy laugh filled the air. "You know, no one's ever written me a note before. It was very sweet."

A smile stretched from ear to ear as he settled into the chair. If everything went well, this would be a long, comforting conversation. "Does that make me your first pen pal?"

He *really* liked the sound of that. He was greedy and wanted as many of her firsts as she would give him.

First proposal, first time seeing each other, first dance, first kiss when they were alone...

His mind ran wild with everything they would do once they were away from the public's watchful eye.

She chuckled. "I suppose it does."

"And did you like the note?" By the Obsidian Sands, he sounded like a schoolboy. Still, he had to know.

"I did." Brynleigh laughed.

"Good," he breathed.

There was a pause, and he imagined her twirling those long golden strands through her fingers. "Although, I do have a few critiques I'd like to submit."

"Oh?" Ryker tilted his head. "I'm all ears."

He would welcome any topic of conversation as long as it meant they were talking.

"Well, first of all, your handwriting leaves something to be desired."

Ryker snorted. "Yes, that's true."

His mother and the headmasters at the academy had always encouraged him to work on his penmanship, but as far as he was concerned, it was a lost cause. Ryker was left-handed; no matter how hard he tried, he couldn't achieve the nice, neat loops his mother desired.

"Quite frankly, I'm surprised they let you in the army with chicken scratch like that, Captain," Brynleigh teased.

"Is that so? Is yours much better?"

"It is." She sounded smug. "I was always first in my class for handwriting, which qualifies me to make such a statement."

A low laugh bubbled out of Ryker. "It's a good thing my job doesn't require a lot of writing. You'll be happy to know most of my correspondence is electronic these days."

"Oh, good. We wouldn't want anyone to misunderstand your orders because they couldn't read them."

"No, we certainly wouldn't." Ryker rested his chin on his fist. "What were your other critiques? I'm dying to hear them."

She huffed a laugh, and the sound warmed Ryker from the inside out. He wanted to hear that sound a million times over. "My goodness, Captain. I had no idea you were so eager to be criticized."

"I'm eager to speak with you." The words slipped off his tongue before he could even think about them. "It doesn't matter what we're talking about because hearing your voice is like listening to my favorite music. I could do it all day long. Like an enchantress, you enthralled me with your voice."

A hitched breath came through the headphones, and for a prolonged moment, Brynleigh didn't say anything. Every beat of his heart was long and drawn out. Every pulse of his magic in his veins was louder than before. Had he spoken out of turn? Was this too fast? Too much?

Ryker was a statue, unable to blink or move as he waited. Had he scared her off? Gods, he hoped that wasn't the case. He didn't want anyone else, and he needed a bride.

Then, the most beautiful sound came through his headphones. Brynleigh *laughed*.

His soul drank in each drop of her delight. He didn't move or speak. He just... listened.

"I'm no enchantress and I can't Persuade anyone, but I like you, too," she murmured. "Although I will say, your note was a little short."

Ryker's lips twitched. He never thought he'd enjoy receiving criticism, yet she was proving him wrong. "Is that so?" He arched a brow. "Would you have preferred a novel? A poem? A song?"

Ryker wasn't much of a writer, but for her, he'd try. It turned out that breaking a rule was the first of many things he was willing to do for this vampire stealing his heart.

"Maybe one day. I'll let you know."

The conversation between them didn't require any thought. "You do that, sweetheart."

She chuckled, the sound warming him through. "That's not my last critique, though."

He canted his head. "No?"

"You didn't sign or initial it. How was I supposed to know it came from you?"

Ryker's eyes widened. He hadn't even considered that she might think it came from someone else. A low growl rumbled through him. "Brynleigh, *I* sent the note."

The mere thought of one of these other men sending *his* vampire anything made him want to roar his frustrations skyward. She was his and no one else's.

Fuck. This was a level of possessiveness that Ryker had never experienced. Part of him knew it was irrational, but he still wanted to rip off his headphones and yell at the other men to stay away from Brynleigh.

"Hmm. Maybe you don't know how to sign your name."

"I know how to write my name," he growled, still trying to get himself under control.

"So, it must be a problem of length," she postulated, a hint of mirth in her voice. "Is that it? Ryker has far fewer letters than Brynleigh, but still..."

She paused, and he imagined she was chewing on her lip. Was it full? Plump and kissable? Waiting for him to lay claim to it? Probably. His fingers itched with the urge to tear down the wall between them and see for himself.

Two weeks, he reminded himself. *That's all.*

He could wait two weeks, right? Fourteen days wasn't that long, especially for long-lived beings like the fae.

The thought, though rational, did not ease his frustrations.

"Ry," she said suddenly.

His brows creased, and his mind raced to catch up. "Excuse me?"

There was a definite smile in Brynleigh's voice as she said, "You could've signed it, 'Ry.' I get that you were busy and all, but—"

"Ry?" he repeated. The name sounded foreign on his tongue, but he didn't mind it at all.

And when Brynleigh said it, it felt... right.

"Yes, Ry. It's a nickname." She snorted, and gods help him, but that sound made him fall for her even more. "Typically, something people choose as a term of endearment for someone they spent a lot of time with."

"I know what a nickname is, sweetheart." He couldn't sit any longer. Abandoning his coffee, he stood, stretched his arms above his head, and cracked his back. He strode over to the bookshelves and studied the spines. "I *am* a Mature fae."

A soft, barely there chuckle filled his ears. "Ah. I see what the problem is. Captain, has no one ever given you one before?"

The playful intonation of her voice warmed him from the inside out. Who could have known such a simple interaction could bring someone so much joy?

"No one whose company I enjoy as much as yours," was his murmured response.

She sucked in a breath, and Ryker's fingers stilled on the leather binding of the *History of Coral City*. He wracked his brain, trying to pinpoint whether he'd said something wrong.

By the Black Sands, Ryker was never usually like this. He didn't question his words. He was self-assured and confident, a leader in his own right.

"Do you enjoy my company, Ry?" Her question was quiet, almost... hesitant.

Enjoy was too simple of a word for how he felt around her. He'd spend every minute of every day with her if he could. In fact, that was exactly what he planned to do.

When this was over, he would be with her when he woke and come home to her after a long day. He would find refuge in her arms after inevitable hardships. She would rest her head in his bed at night. He could see it all now. Even the most mundane tasks, like walking the dog, would be more pleasurable with her.

Ryker inhaled deeply. "I enjoy coffee. Pastries, also. There's nothing like the thrill of playing a game of chess and winning against a worthy opponent. Those are all things I *enjoy*."

Turning from the bookshelf, he strode toward the wall and placed his palm flat on the surface. His eyes fell shut. "To say that I enjoy your company, sweetheart, would be a vast underestimation of how much I look forward to hearing your voice and spending time with you. I do not enjoy it because that is too simple of a word. Rather, I am quickly finding that I am desperate for your company. For you. I thought I proved that yesterday."

Resting his forehead against the wall, he curled his fingers against the wood. His heart raced in his chest as he waited for her to say something. Anything.

Every moment that passed in silence was longer than the last.

Right then, as he waited for her response, Ryker realized he was falling in love with Brynleigh de la Point. They had only known each other for a month, but his heart beat for her.

He'd promised his father he would enter the Choosing to find a wife, but he'd never imagined he'd find this kind of soul-completing, mind-bending, world-altering love.

And she...

Was still silent.

Ryker's heart seized, and he whispered, "Brynleigh—"

"I'm here," she murmured. "I just... I'm here."

The wooden divider was rough against his fingers as he dug his hand into the wall. "Tell me what you're thinking."

He couldn't stand the silence anymore.

"Do you... what you said... is it..."

"It's true," he whispered.

She blew out a long breath. "Because you can't lie."

"That's right." He exhaled, his heart still thundering. "I'm standing at the wall." He needed to tell her.

A silken chuckle that would follow him into his dreams came from her. "Me too."

He slid down the barrier until he sat on the floor. Resting his head against it, he breathed in deeply. They were close, separated only by this wall. How thick was it? Two or three inches? That was nothing. It would be easy to rip it down and see his vampire for the first time.

He wouldn't. Not yet.

But soon.

"I wish I could see you right now," he admitted. "I want to know everything about you."

That glimpse of golden hair hadn't been nearly enough for him. He was beginning to realize nothing would ever be enough. Not until she was fully his in every way.

His headphones echoed with the rustling of fabric. "I'm not going anywhere, Ry." She sounded almost... sad about that. But he had to be mishearing her. "Not today, not tomorrow. I'll be here every day. There's no one else I'd rather speak with."

"I love speaking with you, too," Ryker said.

Another pause, then she whispered, "I'm not as eloquent as you, but it seems I've taken a liking to you, too. It's... I didn't... It took me by surprise."

"Just a liking?" His voice was teasing, but he couldn't hide the undercurrent in his words as he pushed deeper. "Is that all you feel for me?"

He hadn't planned to ask the question today, but suddenly, hearing her answer was the only thing that mattered.

Waiting with bated breath, he rubbed his hands down his jeans. He straightened an invisible crease in the denim as time slipped on. He was a powerful water fae, the son of a Representative, and yet he was riddled with anxiety. Did she know she could crush him? That her words meant the world to him?

Even so, he wouldn't push her. He never would. Sometimes, time was the best gift one person could give to another. He would give her as much as she needed, and he wouldn't go anywhere.

Brynleigh sucked in a deep breath. "Maybe... I think... Maybe it's more." Her voice shook as if she was afraid to admit it. "I think..."

"Yes?" Hope sparked in his stomach, and his fingernails dug into his palms. His arms were empty, waiting for her.

"It's really scary to admit this," she breathed. "I don't... I'm not suppo... but..." A shuddering breath escaped her. "I think I could fall in love with you, Ryker."

Those last words were barely more than a breath, but he heard them as if she'd screamed them in his ear. That spark of hope exploded into a burning flame. He would cherish it for the rest of his life.

A long moment passed as her words settled into his heart.

He pressed his forehead against the wall. "Me too, Brynleigh."

"You could fall in love with yourself?" The teasing tone in her voice was back. "I had no idea you thought so highly of yourself."

He chuckled. "You know what I mean."

Her voice was a soft caress in his ears. "Yes, I do." She sighed wistfully. "I wish I could see you."

He groaned. "I know. Soon."

Maybe if he kept reminding himself that it wouldn't be long, the next two weeks wouldn't feel like an eternity. At the moment, he doubted it.

"Soon," she echoed softly.

Ryker didn't want their date to end. He could stay here for hours, talking with his vampire. "Did I ever tell you about my dad?"

She hummed. "No, I don't think so."

That didn't surprise him. "I thought so. I don't talk about him much," he admitted.

"Oh," she murmured. "Is he..."

"Both my parents are alive," Ryker answered, sensing where she was going with the question. "My parents both love me, but my father..." He raked a hand through his hair. "He's everything to me."

Memories flashed through Ryker's mind.

Riding with his father, galloping through the fields of the family's country house in the Western Region. The plains stretched for miles, a sea of grain in all directions. Watching sports together. Learning to read. Listening to music. Hunting. Playing chess.

Everything Ryker enjoyed doing linked him to his father in one way or another.

"Tell me about him?" The request was soft, as if Brynleigh was afraid to pull him out of his memories.

"Dad and I were close," Ryker said. "He taught me to ride a horse and was always my biggest champion."

Another memory, a much more recent one, flashed through Ryker's mind.

"How is he?" Ryker asked the nurse quietly.

She shook her head, her soft smile tinged with pity. "I'm afraid it's not a good day, Captain."

Ryker's mouth pinched. "I was worried that might be the case."

Still, he would see his father. Tomorrow, he was entering the Hall of Choice. He needed his dad to know.

Thanking the nurse, Ryker entered the room quietly. Once, it had served as one of the three studies in Waterborn House. Now, it was his father's sick room. Machines beeped, disinfectant covered the underlying scent of illness, and a hospital bed with crisp white sheets sat in the middle of the room.

"Dad." Ryker strode towards the bed.

His heart nearly stopped in his chest as he took in his father's sickly state. His father's condition had deteriorated since Ryker's last visit.

Unseeing eyes stared at the ceiling, and even after Ryker picked up his father's hand, they didn't even blink.

Ryker's cheeks were damp as he squeezed his father's hand. "I'm going to find a wife in the Choosing, Dad," he promised. "Like I told you I would."

There was no response.

"I'm going tomorrow," he said. "I won't be able to visit while I'm gone, but Mom and River will take good care of you."

Cyrus' fingers tightened ever so slightly around Ryker's. It was more than Ryker expected, and it stole his breath.

"I love you," Ryker said gruffly.

There was no response.

A tear slipped from the corner of Ryker's eye, and he quickly wiped it away. No matter what, he would keep his promise.

"Was?" Brynleigh's quiet question drew Ryker out of his thoughts.

He ran a finger under his eyes, surprised when it came away wet. He was crying again. "My father's been sick for a long time."

"Oh no."

Ryker's chest burned, and he rubbed his heart. "A few years after my sister was born, Dad was infected with the Stillness. He's alive, but..."

A lump rose in Ryker's throat, and his voice trailed off. His unspoken words hung in the air between them. *Not for long.*

The Stillness was a deadly, incurable sickness. It only affected fae, and no one knew where it came from. There was no surviving it. The Stillness ate away at the victim's body, slowly stealing their ability to move. The best medical care on the continent could not stop its deadly advance.

Ryker had been watching his father slowly die for the better part of two decades.

"I'm so sorry, Ryker." Brynleigh's voice cracked, and silence stretched between them for several minutes. "Losing your family is an indescribable kind of pain. Mine... They passed away."

His heart squeezed. They both knew grief intimately. It was a thread weaving them together, drawing them closer than before.

He hated that she understood where he was coming from. Hated that they had this in common. Hated that she, too, had probably had sleepless nights and exhausting days filled with tears. He remembered their date when they had remained silent, sitting in grief.

By the Sands, he wished he could remove that pain from Brynleigh. There were no words that could describe the absolute, soul-shattering agony that was grief. No real way to explain the emptiness that sometimes settled within him when he remembered his father's illness. He knew words were often empty, and platitudes didn't get people far.

Ryker understood all this about grief, so he didn't offer Brynleigh meaningless words. Instead, he shook his head. "I'm sorry for your loss, Brynleigh."

Truer words had never been spoken. He would never wish the kind of melancholy sorrow that grief cultivated on anyone, let alone the woman he was falling in love with.

Minutes passed in heavy silence.

Ryker mourned. Not only for his father and the man he used to be but for the relationship they'd once shared. The ever-present pain throbbed in his chest, but today, something was different. Maybe it was because he'd shared with Brynleigh, or maybe it was something else, but it wasn't as acute as normal.

And so, when Brynleigh quietly asked him to tell her about his family, he did. He closed his eyes and shared stories he'd never spoken aloud.

He talked for hours, and Brynleigh listened. It meant more to him than he could ever put into words.

That day, they didn't play chess or laugh again, but when Celeste announced their date was ending, Ryker had made up his mind.

Brynleigh de la Point would be his bride because there was no way he was letting this vampire go.

She was his, even if she didn't know it yet.

CHAPTER 17
Rule Number Eight

Three days later, Brynleigh stepped out of the shower and wrapped a towel around herself before applying a fresh face of makeup. She was getting ready for a date, and she felt...

Nothing.

Brynleigh felt nothing because she refused to let herself experience emotions right now.

Rule number eight: emotions are for mortals, not vampires.

The day she'd returned from the library when Ryker had shared about his father, she had shoved all her feelings deep in her soul and locked them tightly away. She would never let them out.

It was easier this way.

If she were emotionless, then Ryker's words wouldn't affect her. His kindness wouldn't affect her. His grief over his father's illness wouldn't touch her heart. It couldn't. After all, the Choosing was almost over.

She was so close. Today, they weren't meeting in the library. Following an old tradition, the men had planned blind one-on-one dates with a partner of their choice.

If Brynleigh had allowed herself to feel emotions, her stomach would have been in knots. But it wasn't because she was numb. A blank slate. A weapon of death, nothing more.

Brynleigh was confident Ryker would invite her on his date. After all, he was enamored with her.

And Brynleigh?

She was definitely not falling in love with Ryker. That would be impossible because there was no way she would ever love the man who'd killed her family.

Anytime Brynleigh felt any emotions around Ryker, she shoved them down. Ignorance was bliss, after all.

When her fangs ached in his presence, she refused to acknowledge the desire blooming within her. Whenever his laugh made her feel a certain way, she bundled up those feelings and stuffed them deep inside. Every time he haunted her dreams, she woke up and refused to fall back asleep lest she think of him again.

She was the master of her emotions, not the other way around.

Fishing out cherry red lipstick from her makeup bag, Brynleigh applied it carefully to her lips. She needed the armor her makeup provided today more than ever before.

"You fucking hate him," she told her reflection sternly. "You hate him, you hate him, you hate him."

Why did the word hate sound suspiciously like another four-letter word? Something banned that she absolutely could not be feeling.

No.

This was not alright.

She hated Ryker Waterborn because that was the only acceptable response. Her mother, the gods be with her soul, had always said that love and hate were two sides to the same coin.

Brynleigh couldn't love Ryker. Her hate was just... different now that she knew him.

That was it.

She would keep reminding herself of that fact, over and over and over again until it was true.

A knock came on the door, pulling her out of her thoughts.

"One minute." Brynleigh placed the lid on her lipstick and wrapped her hair in a second towel before heading over and opening the door. "Yes?"

Matron Lilith stood in the hallway and grinned up at Brynleigh. "Mail delivery." Giggling like a schoolgirl, she handed the vampire an envelope. "You're in for a treat, my dear. Of all the dates planned for today, yours is the most intriguing."

Brynleigh's stomach fucking *flipped*. It somersaulted within her as though she was a teenager, not a fully grown woman, and a deadly vampire.

She grabbed that nervous excitement and forced it deep inside herself. There was no reason for her to be excited about going on a date with Ryker. No reason to wonder what they were doing or whether she'd enjoy it.

This was nothing but a means to a bloody end.

Closing her eyes, Brynleigh inhaled and forced herself to pull up memories she rarely thought of. She remembered the screaming, the burning of her lungs, the deluge of water pouring from the sky. Her heart raced at the recollection of seeing a tall man cloaked in shadows standing next to a smaller form at the edge of the forest.

That memory had haunted Brynleigh for months after her Making.

Jelisette had filled in the blanks for her progeny. The man wasn't a man at all but a water fae. A captain in the army. He wouldn't be prosecuted for the deaths he'd caused. Nothing would happen to him at all because his mother was a Representative.

That was why Jelisette was helping Brynleigh. As a new vampire, no one would see her coming, making her the perfect weapon to teach the Representatives a lesson.

A hand landed on Brynleigh's arm, pulling her out of her thoughts. The Matron must have mistaken the vampire's pause for excitement because her smile was kind. "I'm sure you'll have a wonderful time with the captain. Go ahead and finish getting ready. I'll return to escort you in an hour."

Brynleigh thanked her and slipped the door shut. Letting the towel fall, she strode to the chair where her duffle bag sat. Tossing the envelope on the bed, she fished through her bag until she found the folded-up picture she sought.

Silver lined Brynleigh's eyes as she gently unfolded the paper and ran a finger down the creases.

A beautiful, smiling face with dirty blonde hair stared up at Brynleigh. A moment captured in time, a memory lost in a torrent of water.

Brynleigh wiped away a tear and sniffled. "I miss you," she whispered. "I'm getting closer, and I promise you, he's going to pay for what he did."

There was no answer. Of course not. Sarai's voice had been stolen that night, along with her life. This picture had been taken days before the hurricane. Sarai's blue eyes sparkled with joy, and her mouth was wide open, caught in a candid moment as she laughed at someone off-camera. She wore denim shorts and a red crop top. It had been her favorite outfit that summer.

Brynleigh had taken this picture, along with several others, but this was the only one that survived the tempest. It had been in her pocket when the storm struck.

The longer Brynleigh looked at the image, the angrier she got. Her shadows vibrated in her veins, red seeped into her vision, and she clenched her fists.

This emotion, this bone-deep anger, she kept. It was safe. Good, even. It wouldn't hurt her or break her heart.

Brynleigh let the anger grow until it was all she felt. She would not fail. She hated Ryker Waterborn for what he did, and he deserved what was coming to him.

Eventually, Brynleigh glanced at the clock. Over half an hour had passed, and she needed to finish getting dressed. She carefully refolded the picture and slipped it into her bag.

Rummaging through her things, she found the perfect dress.

It was tight and hugged her curves in all the right ways. The sleeves were long, and the scoop neckline allowed her pendant to settle freely between her breasts. The hem fell midway down her thighs. She slipped on black heels and stepped into the bathroom to admire her handiwork.

Brynleigh tilted her head, her gaze assessing. A beautiful, deadly vampire smiled back at her. Her hair tumbled over her left shoulder. Black eyes stared back at her. Red lips highlighted her fangs.

All vampires were almost painfully beautiful—it was one of their gifts from the goddess of the moon—but the spark in Brynleigh's eyes had nothing to do with her beauty and everything to do with her impending revenge.

CROSSING HER LEGS, Brynleigh tapped the air with her foot. When it was time for Brynleigh's date, Matron Lilith had been waiting for her with Harper, one of the guards. He'd blindfolded Brynleigh before leading her to this room.

That was ten minutes ago.

Most vampires were patient, but that wasn't a skill Brynleigh excelled at. As a human, she'd never been good at waiting. That trait had carried over into her vampiric life.

Matron Lilith had handed Brynleigh a glass of blood wine before she left. Brynleigh sipped it now, letting the stillness of the room settle around her. She wasn't sure what their date would be, but she was certain Ryker had put a lot of thought into it.

If there was one thing Brynleigh knew for certain after a month of nearly daily conversations with the captain, the fae didn't do anything halfway.

Neither did she.

It was fitting. He truly was a worthy opponent in the game she was playing. Too bad he would have to lose.

Two heavy sets of footsteps came from the hallway.

Brynleigh tilted her head in the direction of the sound. The blindfold amplified her other already strong senses. Their heartbeats were steady, rhythmic drums in their chests as they approached, beating nearly twice as fast as hers.

The door creaked open, the hinges proclaiming their need for oil to the world.

Brynleigh moved gingerly, feeling for a space on the table for her wine before letting go. When it didn't spill, she exhaled and turned her head towards the entrance.

"Right this way, Captain." She recognized Harper's voice.

Her spine tingled, and her shadows flared within her. Ryker was here.

If his scent had been a mighty river on the day he sneaked into the infirmary, tonight, it was an Isvana-damned tsunami. There was no barrier between them. No wall to protect her from him. No AI to filter his voice.

The flimsy black blindfold was the only thing keeping her from experiencing all of him. It was hardly anything at all.

Her heart pounded in her chest, and she flushed.

An adverse reaction to his presence. That's what that was.

More emotions had the gall to rise within Brynleigh. She struggled to rein them in. She didn't give herself time to think about what they were or what they meant before she pushed them down. It was far more difficult than before. Nearly impossible.

Ryker smelled so fucking good. So right. So *delicious*.

There wasn't a single part of Brynleigh that didn't light up at the familiar aroma. Her skin prickled. Her shadows sang. Her eyes widened beneath the blindfold. And her fangs.

Her goddess-damned *fangs*.

Had she thought they ached when she first heard his voice? This was a hundred times worse than that. Now they were twin flames, burning in her gums. An overwhelming urge to leap from her seat and sink her fangs into his neck coursed through her. She gripped the table, the wood cracking beneath her touch.

Under no circumstances could Brynleigh ever taste Ryker.

Fuck, this was bad.

She shoved those illicit emotions and that awful desire she had no business feeling deep, deep, deep within her soul.

Brynleigh could do this. She'd once called herself a master of compartmentalization. She could keep everything separate and make it to their wedding night.

This was all an act. Like a masterful fisherwoman, Brynleigh was luring Ryker in. She was the predator and the bait. That must be why she felt like this. She was just very good fucking bait. Too good, if the twisting in her core and the dampness between her thighs were any sign.

Brynleigh's body was just... reacting to Ryker's. That was to be expected, right? She was a vampire, and he was a fae with a delectable scent, so naturally, she wanted to devour him.

It didn't mean anything.

Saying the words was one thing. Convincing herself they were true was another matter entirely.

Brynleigh pictured her sister in her mind and held her there as she drew a series of deep breaths. By the third exhale, she felt more normal. Or at least, less... drawn to Ryker.

She could do this.

For her family.

For her revenge.

For herself.

The guard was still in the room. Brynleigh sensed the man behind her, but his masculine scent did nothing for her. Unlike Ryker's.

You can end this now, a voice niggled at the back of Brynleigh's mind. *Get it over with.*

She could do it. She was certainly strong enough to overpower two men. But that wasn't the plan. If she acted now, she'd have no chance of escaping. No shot at freedom. Brynleigh was certain Jelisette would be displeased if she acted out of line.

Patience was key. She couldn't throw away years of planning because the captain smelled good.

That would be completely and utterly ridiculous.

Killing Ryker on their wedding night would send a message to his family and all Representatives: the way they flaunted the Republic's laws and acted without consequence had gone on long enough.

She had to stick to the plan, meaning she had to get out of her head and focus on the fae in front of her. Her mark.

Brynleigh reached out, intent on grabbing her glass of blood wine when her index finger grazed something warm.

She froze. Her heart stopped beating. Her lungs seized. Her shadows became ice in her veins.

They were touching.

And it...

Gods damn it all, but it did not feel bad. It did not feel like she was touching the man who murdered her family.

It felt like...

Home.

Brynleigh's head swam as lightheadedness threatened to pull her under.

This was...

It was...

Too much.

It wasn't enough.

Fuck.

She could barely think.

Then, instead of pulling away and giving her the space she desperately needed, Ryker's fingers traced up her hand. He clasped her wrist, wrapping his much larger fingers around her.

Brynleigh's heart chose that moment to remember it was supposed to be beating. Now, it tried to escape her chest.

How was it possible that in all her planning, she'd never accounted for the fact that he might touch her? Here she was, playing the game of her lifetime, and somehow, she had completely overlooked this possibility.

Butterflies fluttered in her stomach, having exploded within her at the point of contact. She scrambled to gather them all, shoving each one deep inside. How many could it hold? How many emotions could she suppress before they ruined her?

She wasn't certain.

All Brynleigh knew was that Ryker was touching her, and it felt like they were stepping onto a new game board. One where she didn't know the rules.

She was more frightened than she'd been since the night her family died.

CHAPTER 18
Universes Collide

One single touch was all it took to shift Ryker's world on its axis.

He hadn't even done it on purpose.

As soon as he'd entered the room, Brynleigh's scent had nearly bowled him over. Other aromas had diluted her fragrance in the infirmary, but that was no longer true.

Fae might not have the senses of vampires, but he could pick her out of a crowd, regardless. She smelled like a crisp evening and night-blooming roses. He'd never been one for flowers before, but now, he wanted to be surrounded by them daily for the rest of his life.

Her scent was as intoxicating as the strongest glass of Faerie Wine.

Ryker barely noticed the guard leading him to the table, barely heard him say the server would be around with dinner in a few minutes.

The entirety of his focus was on *her*.

Finally, the barriers between them were gone. Nothing was keeping him from her but a flimsy table and a pair of blindfolds.

Even sightless, he'd sensed her. His magic had bubbled within him, his water eager to play with her darkness. This had never happened before. Usually, his magic was calm, waiting for him to draw upon it, but not today.

He'd been reaching across the table for a glass of wine, careful not to knock it over, when it happened.

He *touched* her.

Her skin, soft and cool, had intercepted his. It was just a graze, barely more than a feather's brush against his hand, but it was *everything*. The moment they touched, his magic leaped in his veins. He sucked in a breath. His heart pounded.

Universes collided.

He'd dreamed of this moment, but the reality of their touch was far more than he'd ever imagined. Ryker wasn't a youngling, and he'd had his fair share of partners, but none of those moments had ever felt like this.

And it was a *touch*.

Brynleigh was soft, whereas he was hard and calloused. Her skin was smooth and unblemished. That, at least, he'd expected. All vampires were like that—polished versions of their previous mortal selves.

Fascinatingly, she was cold. Not freezing, but not warm. It should have worried him or made him want to pull back. Instead, all he wanted to do was cover her with his warmth.

She sucked in a breath, and her hand froze beneath his. Pulling away would be the right, gentlemanly thing to do, but he didn't. At that moment, Ryker wasn't feeling like much of a gentleman. Removing this one point of contact would be like taking a knife to his gut.

He'd rather die.

Instead of releasing Brynleigh, his fingers crawled up her wrist. He encircled her, noting the hitch of her breath as his fingers wrapped around her.

He was a starving man, and every touch she allowed gave him life.

Seconds ticked by. Minutes? Hours? He couldn't be sure. His entire existence was focused on this one gentle caress.

It was at once too much and not at all enough.

"Ry." The nickname was a whispered supplication as it slipped from her lips.

It sent a bolt of desire through him. He shifted in his seat, subtly adjusting himself. Had he wanted her before? Now, he needed her.

Ryker's dreams had not done her justice. He'd never been one for hand-holding, but he never wanted to let her go. His thumb brushed gentle circles over the slow beating pulse on the inside of her wrist.

"Hi," was all he could manage. It wasn't eloquent, but there was no room for that right now.

Several long seconds went by in silence. Was this simple touch shaking the core of her foundation as much as it was his? He'd never imagined something so small could be so life-changing.

She breathed, "I—"

The door opened with a bang, shattering the moment between them.

Brynleigh jerked her hand away from Ryker as though she'd been burned.

Barely holding in a groan, Ryker turned his head towards whoever had interrupted them. "Yes?" His voice was curt. He couldn't help it. He was finally in the same room as Brynleigh. He didn't want to waste a single moment of their time together.

Wheels creaked as something moved along the floor.

"I've brought your dinner, sir," said a small, meek voice. He hadn't heard it before and assumed it belonged to one of the many humans employed to keep the mansion running.

Their food. Of course. He'd forgotten all about it.

Ryker sighed and raked his hand through his hair. "Thank you."

Porcelain chinked as the server placed several items on the table, working silently.

"Chef has prepared several dishes for you this evening," the server said. "He recommends eating with your hands and discovering the food as you go."

"Oh, no," Brynleigh whispered. The words, though short, were filled with horror.

Ryker's eyes widened beneath his blindfold. What was wrong?

"Miss?" the server asked.

She cleared her throat, and her chair creaked. "I just... I don't exactly eat... food."

Blood rushed to Ryker's cheeks. By the Black Sands, how could he have made such a monumental mistake? He'd somehow forgotten this crucial fact about vampires.

He was a fucking idiot.

Thank the gods, it seemed the chef wasn't as obtuse as Ryker.

"Not to worry," said the server. "Chef has whipped up several vampire-friendly dishes. He took the liberty of lacing them with blood for you, and they're the ones I placed closest to you."

At least someone had their head on straight around here.

"That's so thoughtful," Brynleigh replied after a moment. "Honestly, I didn't expect this. Thank you."

"Of course, miss." The server explained that the chef believed the meal was best explored without further directions. According to him, it would increase their ability to taste individual, unique flavors. The server would be in the hall if they had any questions.

Kydona, the mother goddess the fae had adopted when they crossed the Indigo Ocean, must have been watching over Ryker because the server took his leave after that.

They were alone once again.

The moment the door slipped shut, Ryker turned back to Brynleigh. His fingers clenched and unclenched, and he wished he could see her. "I'm sorry," he blurted. "About the food... I wasn't thinking when I planned this."

That was a mistake he wouldn't be making again. Right after this date, he would find Jacques and Horatio, the two male vampires in the Choosing, and ask them what he could do to make Brynleigh's life more comfortable with him.

No more guesses, no more mistakes.

"No need to apologize," Brynleigh said.

"On the contrary, there is a need." He cleared his throat. "I made a mistake, and I will endeavor to do better by you."

"That's very sweet." The vampire hummed. "You know, we *can* eat. It's just that when we put food in our mouths, it tastes like ash. Not coffee, though. Thank Isvana, because I love it."

"I love coffee, too." He palmed the back of his neck. "So you're not angry with me? It's alright if you are. I should've thought ahead, and I didn't."

"No, I'm not. No one has ever prepared me food laced with blood before. Honestly, I'm intrigued."

"By me or the food?" he asked, unable to help himself.

Brynleigh chuckled, "Both."

Somehow, that was exactly what he needed to hear.

They dug in, trying a little bit of everything.

Once in a while, they touched. Each time was as explosive as the first, leaving Ryker wanting more.

Time slipped by. The meal was delicious, and they spoke about nothing in particular as they ate.

Ryker loved every single minute of it.

"Gods, that was good." Brynleigh sighed.

"Yeah?" Ryker chuckled. "You enjoyed it?" He'd quickly adapted to the blindfold, and it wasn't impeding his experience at all.

"It was amazing. I never would've guessed chocolate and blood paired so well together." She smacked her lips and sighed in delight. "I'm going to have to find this chef and get the recipe."

Ryker leaned back in his seat, his stomach full. The chef was undeniably skilled. The plates had varied from a spiced, roasted venison to a shaved, raw salad. Everything he'd tasted had been delicious. "The cake was that good?"

"The best," she gushed. "Thank you, Ryker. Truly. I didn't even realize I missed food until tonight."

The happiness in Brynleigh's voice sent a rush of heat through Ryker. Talking to her was always enjoyable, but tonight felt even better than normal. He wasn't sure whether it was the small, stolen touches or something else. Either way, his heart soared.

Ryker slowly navigated his way around the obstacles of empty dishes and cups strewn across the table until his hand found Brynleigh's once again. This time, nothing was unintentional about how his fingers laced through hers.

She inhaled deeply but didn't pull away. If anything, her grip tightened around his. "Ryker, I don't know if we should—"

"Dance with me?" he asked before she could finish that thought.

He was all too aware that their time together in the Choosing was slowly slipping away. He didn't want to waste a single second of their remaining time.

A tinkling laugh tinged with darkness slipped from Brynleigh's lips. "What? There's no music."

"We can make our own." Ryker rose to his feet, grateful he'd chosen to wear comfortable shoes tonight. "I want to feel your body against mine."

This date was probably being streamed to the Republic, but Ryker didn't care. He would do almost anything to have this fantastic, intriguing woman in his arms.

He stood beside the table, but she still hadn't responded. He squeezed her fingers. "Please?"

Brynleigh hitched a breath, and he sensed she was still unsure. "I have two left feet," she warned him. "I know most vampires are graceful, but not me. I'm likely to step on your feet."

"Sweetheart, if you think a little clumsiness is going to turn me away from you, you're wrong." He gently tugged on her hand and drew her to her feet. She was taller than most women in his life, and her head rested under his chin. She didn't fight as he brought her closer to him. "I'm all in."

She froze. "You mean—"

"I want you, Brynleigh." His hand slipped around her hip, settling on the small of her back. "Only you."

"What about the other women?" she asked breathlessly.

"They don't haunt my dreams the way you do." He only wanted her.

"There's still a week and a half," she reminded him.

He held Brynleigh to him as he navigated them away from the table. "I don't need it. I've already made up my mind."

The moment he'd followed Matron Cassandra into the snow, he'd decided. His conversation with Brynleigh about his dad proved he made the right decision.

Brynleigh sucked in a breath. "Does that mean—"

He bent his head, finding the curve of her ear and brushing his lips over it in the gentlest of kisses. "I want you to marry me, Brynleigh de la Point," he breathed. "I'll ask you formally on the night of the Masked Ball, but there's no point pretending I haven't decided. If you'll have me, I'm yours."

Her heart thundered between them, and he held her close as they danced. Several minutes passed, but he didn't push her for an answer.

"Yes, I will." She rested her head on his shoulder and relaxed against him. "After all, you're what I came here for."

Ryker's heart soared at her words. They were exactly what he wanted to hear.

His body was airy, his feet light, his heart worry-free as he held Brynleigh close. Ryker led them around the room in dance after dance, humming tunes he'd heard hundreds of times before.

Ryker didn't kiss her. Not yet.

It wasn't that he didn't want to—on the contrary, his mouth yearned to be on hers and taste how—but he wanted to save their first kiss for the moment they saw each other face to face.

He was certain she was worth waiting for.

CHAPTER 19
Losing Was Not an Option

Frigid water poured from the shower head, pelting Brynleigh from above like tiny needles made of ice. She hadn't even stripped off her tank top and pyjama shorts before getting under the water, having sought refuge in the bathroom after several hours of sleepless tossing and turning.

She had hoped the cold would instill some sense into her, but it didn't seem to be working. She was freezing, which was a feat in and of itself for a vampire, but her mind was a wiring hub of activity.

This entire situation had become a gods-damned mess. Her date with Ryker had been a week ago, and she had been unable to get the fae out of her mind since then. She kept replaying his touch, the memory driving her mad with want. She had so many suppressed emotions. No matter how many she shoved down, there were still more.

Brynleigh needed to talk to Zanri. None of their contingency plans accounted for something like this.

"Fuck." She banged her head against the soaked wall.

Regrettably, other than making her head ring, the action was pointless. She couldn't hide from the truth anymore—she was in a world of trouble.

Brynleigh had feelings for Ryker. Actual, tangible, heart-twisting feelings. She swore again, the curses slipping from her mouth and being swallowed by the water.

The emotions grew stronger every single day. It was getting harder and harder to separate herself from them, and she didn't know how long she could last.

Every day, Ryker did something new to endear himself to her. She hadn't glimpsed the monster once, nor had she seen or heard anything that would lead her to believe an evil man resided in his skin. That was a problem.

An enormous, horrifying problem.

Brynleigh released her shadows. They darkened the bathroom but did nothing to ease the anger and doubt running through her.

The Masked Ball was in two days. Tomorrow, they were returning to Golden City. Apparently, the Hall of Choice had been repaired after the attack. Brynleigh wasn't worried about the journey or the rebels. The participants would be well-guarded, and she was strong enough to care for herself.

No, the problem lay entirely with Ryker. The more time she spent with the water fae, the more she learned about him and the more conflicted she became about her purpose.

He had killed her family in cold blood. By definition, that made him a monster. As someone with blood on her hands—blood of criminals, but still blood—she recognized when someone was evil.

But Ryker hadn't shown her the monster. She hadn't even glimpsed him. Where the fuck was he?

The captain was a sore loser—which secretly delighted Brynleigh, because one would think that a military man would be able to lose gracefully—but he was also kind, caring, and had a slight hint of possessiveness that Brynleigh enjoyed more than she dared admit.

Brynleigh groaned and shut off the water. She stepped out of the shower, toweling off. This would be so much easier if Ryker were evil.

Hanging up her towel, she strode back into the small bedroom. Sarai's picture was on the nightstand, but even that didn't spark the usual fire of revenge. She needed answers, and if she weren't going to sleep, she'd focus on finding out what was going on.

Stepping into a pair of black leggings, Brynleigh pulled them up before drawing on a matching sweater. She threw her hair in a messy bun and drew the hood over her golden locks before sliding her sister's picture into her pocket.

This was risky. The participants weren't supposed to leave their rooms at night. The men and women were staying in different wings of the mansion, and the Matrons had made it very clear that although they were not currently in the Hall of Choice, the structure of the Choosing was still to be respected. These included following archaic laws such as remaining apart during the dating process and abstaining from sexual relations until the wedding night.

Brynleigh wasn't sure what the recourse would be if she were caught, and she didn't plan to find out. She had something the other women didn't: shadows.

Darkness was a deep, powerful song in Brynleigh's veins. Her shadows were always there, waiting to be used. Her wings were an equally powerful form of magic, but unlike the shadows that were her birthright, they didn't itch to be set free if she didn't use them enough. On the other hand, her shadows were an intrinsic part of Brynleigh, an extension of her limbs, and needed to be used.

The vampire exhaled, opened her palms, and released the wisps of night. They flowed from her until the darkness swallowed everything, even the glowing light of the clock. She didn't have time to appreciate her dark magic's effectiveness because she had places to be.

Pulling on her shadows, Brynleigh stepped into the Void. The black, empty place allowed vampires to move from one location to another. Uncertain of whether there were wards that would keep her from journeying far from the mansion, Brynleigh decided the easiest and safest course of action would be to return to the small infirmary.

Traveling to the moonlit woods was a matter of seconds. She stepped out of the Void and wrapped her darkness around her like a cloak. The arctic wind bit at her exposed flesh, but she ignored it to study the cabin.

A burly guard dressed in black gear, gloves, and boots was stationed out front. The curtains were pulled back, and the light of a single desk lamp sliced through the night.

Damn. Brynleigh hoped Doctor Carin would be asleep, but apparently, she was a night owl.

Still, the vampire had made it this far. Giving up on her plan was not an option. Brynleigh was far too aware that she may not have another chance. She surveyed the door. She would knock out the guard if she had to, but she'd rather not leave any trace of her presence.

A quarter of an hour passed before the light flickered off. Isvana must have been smiling down on Brynleigh, because moments later, the doctor stepped out of the cabin. Wrapped in a thick fur coat, Carin carried a stack of files.

Brynleigh smiled at the sudden stroke of luck.

"Done for the night, Doctor?" the guard asked.

"I am, Lucas." She locked the cabin door. "Thank you. You didn't have to stay. I would've been fine."

Lucas shook his head and offered the doctor his arm. "I couldn't leave you alone. There are reports of increased rebel activity all through the Republic. Besides, I've met your wife. No one wants to piss her off."

"True, she's fierce." Carin chuckled and placed her hand on Luca's extended limb. "Thank you for waiting."

Brynleigh added more shadows around herself as the pair walked past, careful not to let her cloak slip. She waited until they had disappeared through the trees before running to the cabin door in a blur. She pressed her ear against the wall and listened intently.

When she was confident the cabin was empty, Brynleigh stepped into the Void again. The lock on the door might prevent most people from entering, but it wouldn't stop her.

Brynleigh's shadows dropped her into the middle of the cabin. She moved with stealth towards the desk and picked up the phone. She couldn't waste any time—what if Lucas planned on returning?

Her fingers dialed Zanri's number from memory.

Her handler picked up on the first ring. "Hello?" He sounded groggy, and for a moment, Brynleigh felt bad. She probably woke him up.

"It's me, Z," she whispered.

"Brynleigh, what the hell?" Someone grumbled in the background, and it sounded like Zanri stumbled into another room. A door closed. "You shouldn't be calling me. The risk—"

"Fuck the risk," she bit out. It didn't matter that she interrupted him. She didn't have time for his rambling. The guard could come back at any moment. "I had to call. It's important."

A sigh that could level cities slipped from Zanri's mouth. Leather creaked, and she imagined him dropping into his favorite red, worn armchair. "Jelisette isn't here."

"I figured," said Brynleigh.

As long as Brynleigh had known Jelisette, the older vampire had kept a standing appointment once a week. She'd never missed it.

"What's going on?"

"I called to talk to you, Z. I need your advice, not Jelisette's."

Brynleigh already knew what her Maker would say. Jelisette would remind her of all ten rules and reassure her she was on the right track. The problem was that Brynleigh wasn't so sure about that anymore.

"What do you need, B?"

She palmed her neck. "You've been watching the Choosing?"

"Of course. We all have."

Her eyes fell shut, and she groaned. "I'm having trouble."

That was an understatement.

"What kind of trouble?" Zanri sounded like he didn't want to know.

That made two of them. These feelings were wrong. These questions were wrong. And yet, she couldn't stop the next words from pouring from her lips. "Ryker is nothing like what I expected."

"Brynleigh," the shifter growled in warning. "The fae is your mark."

As if she needed the reminder. The truth of what happened to Chavin haunted her every waking moment.

"I know what he is," she hissed into the receiver, clutching the phone. "You think I've somehow forgotten that? Every day, I remember."

"Then what's the problem?"

She pressed the phone against her ear and picked at her pendant with her free hand. "I know what he did. I was there. But maybe..." She chewed on her lip. "Maybe he's changed? Maybe the reason he was in hiding, the reason we couldn't find him, was because he was turning his life around."

Six years was a long time. People changed, learned, and became better all the time. Or worse. Brynleigh was the perfect example. In six years, she'd become a cold-hearted killer. It was plausible that Ryker was no longer the same man as before. Right?

A long silence came through the line. A thousand-pound weight bore down on her shoulders. The sound of Zanri's breath was heavy in her ears.

Several minutes went by. Brynleigh's heart rapped an unsteady beat. Her hands slickened, and she passed the receiver from one hand to the other.

"Captain Ryker Waterborn is your mark." Zanri's voice was ice, altogether void of emotion.

"I know," Brynleigh replied.

"You entered the Choosing with one goal in mind. What was it?"

"Make him fall in love with me, marry him, and kill him on our wedding night," Brynleigh automatically whispered the words that had been drilled into her over years of practice.

A rumble of approval. "That's correct. And what is rule number ten?"

The hand gripping the phone trembled, and a cold sweat broke out on Brynleigh's forehead. *This* was why she had risked breaking the rules to call Zanri. This was the reminder she needed. She'd expected the words, but the pain...

She hadn't expected it to feel like a wooden stake piercing her heart.

"Focus, Brynleigh!" Zanri barked. "Rule number ten?"

Brynleigh closed her eyes and ran her tongue over her fangs. She took a deep breath and forced the words out of her dry mouth. "Once the game has begun, losing is not an option. The only alternative to winning is death."

Her voice trembled. Brynleigh knew the rules. She had agreed to them, having never even considered the consequences of losing. Her victory had been assumed... until she met her mark.

But now?

Now, doubt was an ember in her belly. It was warm and glowing, growing brighter by the day.

"Again," her handler demanded. "What is rule ten?"

Brynleigh briefly wondered why Jelisette and Zanri insisted on this course of action. Why were they pushing her so hard to kill Ryker?

But then Zanri barked her name, and she forgot those doubts. "Once the game has begun, losing is not an option," she repeated. Her voice was harder this time, and the doubt was further away. "The only alternative to losing is death."

Each word was crisp as it settled in her soul.

"Again," Zanri ordered for the third time.

She complied. Ten times, she repeated the rule. Soon, her

voice was bolder. Firmer. That ember of doubt flickered and dimmed until it was nearly extinguished altogether.

Zanri was right. Losing wasn't an option. Ryker killed her family. He was responsible for their deaths. It didn't matter that the man wasn't what she expected. He was still a murderer.

Finishing the game was Brynleigh's only option.

"One more time," Zanri demanded coldly. The harshness in his voice was good. It reminded her of the realities she would face outside of the Choosing.

The box holding Brynleigh's emotions was fortified. She drew in a deep breath. "Losing is not an option. The only alternative to winning is death."

The ominous tenth rule rang through her head long after she'd hung up the phone and returned to her room.

Zanri was right, and rule ten was clear: Ryker Waterborn had to die.

CHAPTER 20
Retribution Would Be Hers

Ever since her phone call with Zanri two days ago, Brynleigh had replayed rule number ten through her mind until it was the only thing she heard. He was right. Losing was not an option.

Last night, under the cover of darkness, the participants of the Choosing had returned to Golden City. During the journey, Matron Lilith had explained that while they'd been in the north, the unrest in the Central Region had continued. As a result, the guard around the participants would be doubled. Other measures were being put in place, precautions to ensure everyone's safety.

Even now, a soldier was stationed outside Brynleigh's room. The vampire sat on her bed, brushing her hair and wondering what would happen if she dismissed him. It wasn't that she didn't appreciate his effort—she did. She'd be lying if she said the rebel activities weren't worrisome.

It was just that Brynleigh was antsy. Between everything going on with Ryker and the soldiers' presence, she couldn't find peace. Her fangs ached, and despite having imbibed in multiple pints of blood since returning to Golden City, she was starving.

Something was missing from her life, and she couldn't figure out what it was.

She wanted the guard to leave because she was itching for a fight. She would find Valentina, except getting kicked out of the Choosing hours before the Masked Ball seemed ridiculous. She'd done all the work to get here. Fighting that fiery bitch wasn't in the cards, but if a rebel showed up, Brynleigh would gladly take them on.

Someone knocked on the door.

Brynleigh's brow arched. What were the chances a rebel stood on the other side, serving themselves up on a silver platter? Slim, probably, but a vampire could hope.

Placing the hairbrush on the bed, she strode to the door and cracked it open. "Yes?"

Unless the rebels were in the habit of recruiting young elves with bright red hair and luminescent smiles, this wasn't one of them. The girl looked like she was in her late teens, not yet Mature, and she extended a long black garment bag in Brynleigh's direction. In her other hand, she held a smaller gift bag. "I've brought your gown, Miss de la Point."

Traditionally, in the Choosing, a woman's parents picked out her gown for the Masked Ball. Since Brynleigh's family was dead, she assumed her Maker had filled the role for her.

Thanking the elf, Brynleigh took both bags and let the door slip shut behind her. She returned to the bed and began unpacking her Maker's gift.

When Brynleigh saw the dress, she let out a low whistle of appreciation. This was, without a doubt, the finest gown Brynleigh had ever worn. This was the kind of dress most women admired from afar, and very few had the chance to wear.

It was stunning, perfect for a proposal, and...

Her family wasn't here tonight.

A tear lined the bottom of Brynleigh's eye. Her sister would have loved this dress. Sarai had always been interested in clothes and sewing in particular. A few months before the storm, Sarai had been accepted to the Western School of Design and Fashion to study fashion history. She would have attended in the fall.

Even without Sarai's sense of style, Brynleigh recognized a masterpiece when she saw one. Changing out of her leggings and t-shirt, she drew the gown over her head. Several well-placed zippers allowed her to get the garment on without help.

It fit her like a glove.

Once the zippers were closed, Brynleigh made her way to the floor-length mirror in the bathroom. After all, what was the point of wearing a beautiful gown if one didn't spend at least a few minutes admiring it? And this dress was meant to be admired.

It *screamed* vampire.

The scarlet garment was perfectly tailored to her body. It matched the theme of the Choosing beautifully. The ruby fabric shimmered and sparkled, making Brynleigh feel like she was wearing a jewel. The neckline was a low V that dipped almost to her navel. Long, slim sleeves ran to her wrists, and the dress pooled at her feet. A slit ran dangerously high up her leg, cutting off mid-thigh. She turned around and looked over her shoulder.

The back scooped low, barely covering her bottom. Perfect for wings. There was no doubt in Brynleigh's mind that her Maker had selected this dress for that very reason.

In the second bag was a pair of ruby heels, a crimson rose for her hair, a mask, and a piece of paper. Leaning against the dresser, Brynleigh carefully unfolded the note. Her Maker's handwriting looped across the page, and a splotch of ink on the top confirmed that Jelisette had used a quilled fountain pen to write the missive.

My youngest progeny,

May the goddess of the moon and the god of blood bless your Choice tonight. I know you will Choose correctly.

Remember what you've been taught.

- Jelisette

Brynleigh read the note twice before sighing and dropping the paper on the bed. A wave of disappointment washed over her, which was rather unexpected.

After six years, she thought Jelisette would have something a little more sentimental. Though her Maker wasn't exactly kind, Jelisette had filled a motherly role for Brynleigh over the past few years. This note lacked all sense of kindness though. There were only cold, regimented words meant to remind Brynleigh of her purpose.

If Brynleigh's parents were still alive, they would have words of wisdom for her. They would probably be excited for her—she was getting engaged, after all.

But her parents were dead. Sarai was dead. And Brynleigh? She was a vampire, and now, she was alone. Tonight, she would get engaged, but just like all the feelings she was ignoring, it was a lie. An act. A series of falsehoods.

Brynleigh's heart burned as dark fury ran through her veins. Maybe Jelisette knew exactly what she was doing when she penned that note. There was no room for emotions. No room for sentimentality. No room for anything at all except cold-blooded revenge.

Brynleigh was playing to win, and no one would deter her from her goal.

Not even the man who smelled like thunderstorms and bergamot.

The rules started playing through her head as she put in her earrings.

Rule number one: you cannot trust anyone.

Rule number two: doubly blessed vampires do not hide behind jewels or makeup. They let their gifts speak for themselves.

Her ears glistened, and she bent, sliding her feet into heels.

Rule number three: vampires are weapons. They must always look their best, ready to use their every gods-given gift to their deadly advantage.

Rule number four: vampires must always remain calm, even in the face of difficulty.
Rule number five: always trust your instincts.
She applied her makeup, the crimson lipstick reminding her of blood as she swiped it across her lips.
Rule number six: let nothing distract you from your goal.
Rule number seven: your Maker always knows best.
Rule number eight: emotions are for mortals, not vampires.
Gathering her hair, Brynleigh allowed some curls to fall halfway down her back before tying the rest in elaborate knots on top of her head.
Rule number nine: never turn your back on your enemy.
Rule number ten: once the game has begun, losing is not an option. The only alternative to winning is death.
Brynleigh stuck one last hairpin in her locks, then grabbed the rose. It was heavy, weighted like a tiara, and she pinned it behind her right ear. Other than that, the only jewelry she wore was the golden necklace. Last of all was the mask. It was crimson, like the gown and rose, and she tied it behind her head.
She stepped back, taking herself in critically before nodding approvingly. There was a certain lethal edge to her appearance that she enjoyed immensely.
Two things were missing.
Brynleigh reached within, drawing on her shadows and wings. The first pooled around her feet, the dark wisps giving her strength. The second hung on her back, the wings symbolizing her vampiric strength and power.
Now, she was ready.

ARMED GUARDS WERE STATIONED in front of the closed ballroom doors. Their faces were tight, and their eyes dark as they surveyed the hallway.

Brynleigh's gown swished as she strode towards them. She kept her wings tight against her back and held her head high.

"Miss de la Point," the guard on the left said. "Welcome."

Brynleigh smiled demurely, keeping her gaze locked on the closed double doors. Faint musical overtures trickled from the ballroom. "Is it my turn?"

Earlier, the Matron had explained how the Masked Ball would work. Each participant would enter separately so they could be announced. There would be drinks and small bites during the cocktail hour, but the real party would start after the proposals.

"Soon," he replied.

Heels clicked behind Brynleigh. An aura of wrongness settled around her. It was a warning, a pause before a storm, a moment of peace before danger. The vampire stiffened and turned around as a tall woman drew near.

Even in a mask, Brynleigh recognized Valentina. The fire fae's floor-length ballgown was so wide that it would barely make it through the door. Pale pink, almost white roses covered the dress from the top of the bodice down to her feet. Valentina's blue-black hair was in a tight bun, and tendrils floated around her face. Cruel violet eyes peered out from behind a cream mask and narrowed when they landed on the vampire. Red lips twisted into a wicked sneer.

"Well, if it isn't the fucking leech who stole my fae." Valentina stalked towards Brynleigh, her eyes flickering with an undisguised threat of violence. "If it weren't for you, he'd be Choosing *me* tonight."

Shadows frothed in Brynleigh's veins, and her fangs tightened in her gums. Her fists wanted nothing more than to connect with Valentina's ugly face, but she couldn't give in to her desire.

The fourth rule played in Brynleigh's mind. She amended it, adding a clause for awful fire fae with hateful vendettas. Gods, why couldn't Hallie have been here instead?

Brynleigh had the worst luck.

"Your fae?" Brynleigh tilted her head, forcing her face into a mask of calmness she did not feel inside. "I'm certain I don't know who you're talking about."

Valentina snarled, baring her elongated canines. They were nothing like the fangs within Brynleigh's mouth, but they were sharp... for a fae. "You undead, whoreish, night-walking grave dweller. You know exactly who I'm talking about."

Was Valentina so unintelligent that she could not come up with insults unrelated to Brynleigh's species? How incredibly unoriginal.

"Do I?" Brynleigh picked at non-existent dirt beneath her nails. "Hmm. I'm not sure."

An unladylike growl rumbled through Valentina. "Captain Ryker Waterborn, that's who. He was supposed to be mine."

Brynleigh's wings fanned out behind her, and her head snapped up. She dropped her hands and curled into fists. "What the fuck did you say?"

She knew he and Valentina had been seeing each other early on during the Choosing—they were a small group, after all—but she'd never heard the fire fae lay a claim on Ryker.

And Brynleigh did not like it. Not one bit.

"You heard me." Valentina had the gods-damned audacity to take another step closer to her. "The captain is the most prestigious fae here. He would've made the best husband for me. And you had to come in with your dirty blonde hair and sharp fangs and ruin everything."

Anger was burning lava as it ran through Brynleigh's cold veins. Shadows flooded out of her, and she snarled.

"Fuck you." Brynleigh's fangs burned. Her nails sliced through her palms and drew blood. Stepping closer to Valentina, she met those violet orbs and hissed, "He's *mine*."

Her claiming words rang through the hall. Somewhere deep within Brynleigh, something shifted.

Valentina's eyes widened, and her mouth opened and closed. Was she in shock that Brynleigh would claim her man so openly? She wasn't the only one.

Brynleigh hadn't meant to speak the claiming words. At least, not with so much passion and truth. Of course, Ryker was hers... to kill. She refused to acknowledge that there might be any other reason she had claimed him.

The guard cleared his throat. "Miss de la Point, it's time."

Thank all the gods. Shooting Valentina one last glare for good measure, Brynleigh moved towards the doors. She ran her fingers down her gown and straightened an invisible wrinkle before drawing in a deep breath.

Once again, rule ten ran through her mind.

"I'm ready," she said confidently.

The guard nodded and opened the door. The music slowly died as hundreds of eyes turned towards Brynleigh at once.

She refused to feel nervous beneath the weight of their attention. Instead, she held her chin up high and kept her wings tight behind her as she stood in the doorway, taking in the ballroom.

It had undergone yet another transformation. There were no signs of the rebels' attack. Now, the ballroom was a grand space meant to house the party of the decade. Six diamond chandeliers glistened. Ruby tapestries adorned the walls, bearing the Republic's crest. Servers wearing black milled about handing out flutes of sparkling wine and small finger foods.

And the people.

Gods, there were so many of them. There had to be close to five hundred, if not more. The scent of their blood was enticing, but Brynleigh had already drunk plenty tonight in preparation for being in front of so many people.

Horned and winged elves stood among fae. Werewolves chatted with witches. Shifters interacted with vampires. There were even a few humans among the crowd. The clothes were a testament to the beauty and expansiveness of the rainbow, each outfit slightly different from the last. Everyone was masked, like her.

Despite the face coverings, Brynleigh noted many familiar faces in the crowd. Guards she'd come to recognize over the past few weeks intermingled with guests. They wore suits and gowns, attempting to blend in, but nothing could hide the glint of awareness in their eyes. Weapons bulged under black jackets, and she pitied anyone who tried to attack tonight.

A ten-piece orchestra sat on the stage, their stringed instruments poised mid-air.

A herald dressed in crimson-edged black stepped out from the shadows on her right. "Ladies and gentlemen." His voice boomed through the now-silent hall. "It is my honor to present the ninth participant in this year's Choosing, Miss Brynleigh de la Point."

Her heart pounded in her chest as she waited for someone to move. It felt like every second stretched longer than the last until finally, someone in the crowd clapped. They triggered the others, and a roar of applause soon filled the ballroom.

Blood rushed to Brynleigh's cheeks, and she fought the urge to look down at the floor. It wasn't that she minded the attention, per se, but simply that she wanted to get this evening started.

The sooner she got in there, the sooner they could get to the proposals and the sooner the evening would be over. She'd be engaged and one step closer to her goal.

And yet... those claiming words echoed in her mind. What was she thinking, saying them out loud?

He's mine.

Her heart thrashed in her chest, a wild animal. Emotions threatened to rise. Her lungs burned. She closed her eyes, inhaling deeply. Those watching her probably mistook her actions for nerves.

They were wrong.

Brynleigh was grounding herself in the one thing she knew—pain. Pulling forth memories of the past, the vampire did something she rarely allowed herself to do.

She remembered the night her family died.

"I saw Mrs. Caldwell at the store yesterday." Isolde Larkspur, Brynleigh's mother, scrubbed at a pot in the sink while Brynleigh dried the dishes by hand.

"Oh?" Brynleigh's fingers tightened around the pale blue dinner plate.

Her mother didn't notice. "Yes. She mentioned Jonah will be returning home next month. He'll be staying with his parents until the new year." She smiled at her daughter, a twinkle in her blue eyes. "He's going to be here for the Winter Solstice."

Isolde was not subtle.

Brynleigh stared out the window. The cloudless sky was tinged with orange as the evening slowly gave way to night. "That's nice, Mama."

Please drop this, she silently added. Brynleigh knew where this was going. She and Jonah had known each other since they were children. He was a few years older than her, but she hadn't seen him since her return from university last year.

"And he's single." Isolde bumped her hip against Brynleigh's. "Maybe you should see if he's interested in being your date to the family holiday party?"

There was no way Brynleigh could miss the note of hopefulness in her mother's voice. She groaned. "We're just friends, Mama."

"But you could be more!"

That was unlikely. When Brynleigh was six and Jonah was nine, she'd witnessed the unfortunate event of Jonah eating a worm. There wasn't enough time to make her forget that. "I don't think so."

The neighbors probably heard Isolde's responding sigh. In the beginning, Brynleigh had found Isolde's not-so-subtle approaches to matchmaking amusing, but now they were becoming dreary. She wasn't even sure she wanted a relationship. She'd enjoyed her time at the University of Balance, experimenting with men and women as one did, but for now, she was happy to focus on her life.

She'd returned home to work in her parents' general store, unsure of what she wanted to do with her life. Chavin was a small town filled with hardworking humans. It wasn't a big city, but it was home, and Brynleigh liked it here. If her parents could make a life here, she could, too.

Isolde handed the pot to Brynleigh, and her gaze swept over her daughter as she leaned on the counter. "I want you to be happy, Brynny. That's all."

"I know." And she did. She'd never doubted her parents' love.

"We love you," her mother added. "It's important that we see you settled."

Isolde meant well. Her actions, though overbearing, were filled with love. Brynleigh knew her parents meant well. They had a good family life, and she couldn't complain about her childhood.

Setting the pot on the drying rack, Brynleigh sat at the round kitchen table and picked up the navy skein of yarn she was working on. Wrapping it around the knitting needle, she purled three stitches. "I am happy."

Her mother sat across from her and picked up her own project. "But you could be happier."

Brynleigh chuckled and shook her head. "Let it go, Mama, please."

Soon, the steady clicking of knitting needles filled the kitchen as the two women silently worked. This was the fourth time she and Isolde had this conversation this summer. Brynleigh was starting to understand why many of her friends hadn't moved back home after school.

"What the hell?" Isolde swore.

Brynleigh dropped a stitch, her mother's harsh language so out of place from her usual calm demeanor. She jerked up her head and turned around. The moment Brynleigh looked out the window, a slew of curses slipped from her own tongue.

The sky was an ominous dark gray edged with green. Lightning bolts shot above the endless plains of the Western Region. The wind swirled, and shouts came from outside.

Isolde didn't scold Brynleigh for using foul language. Instead, she ran as quickly as she could out of the kitchen. "Gavin! Sarai!" Her voice was frantic. "Come quickly!"

Abandoning her knitting, Brynleigh raced after her mother.

Footsteps pounded down the stairs of the modest two-story home as Gavin raced towards them. "What's wrong, love?"

"Look!" Isolde raised a shaking finger to the bay window in the living room.

Seconds later, Gavin was barking into his phone, calling the police.

The air crackled, and the scent of ozone surrounded them.

Isolde turned to Brynleigh, her eyes darting frantically between the staircase and the storm outside. "Where's your sister?"

Brynleigh frowned, and her stomach twisted. "I thought she was upstairs."

Sarai should have come down with all the yelling, though. She was nothing if not attentive.

"Get her," Isolde commanded.

"Of course." Brynleigh took the stairs two at a time. She shoved open her little sister's door, not bothering to knock. "Sarai, what's going on? There's a random storm—"

The room was empty. Where was she? A quick search of the closet and upstairs bathroom revealed Sarai wasn't there.

Thunder boomed, and Brynleigh hurried back into her sister's room. A calendar hung above Sarai's desk.

Today's date was circled, and scrawled underneath was "Fairgrounds."

"Fuck." Brynleigh whipped out her phone and speed-dialed her sister as she ran downstairs.

There was no answer.

Brynleigh pulled on her raincoat, tucked the necklace her

parents had given her for her eighteenth birthday beneath her collar, and shot her sister a series of texts.

She stared at the screen, waiting for the telltale checkmarks to show them as read. The notifications never came.

Of all the days for Sarai to be unreachable, why did she pick today?

Rain pelted the windows, each drop sounding like a gunshot. The wind wailed like a screaming woman. Thunder roared its fury through the heavens.

Brynleigh had never seen a storm of this magnitude in her twenty-three years.

She shoved her feet in indigo rain boots.

"Where are you going?" Isolde ran up behind Brynleigh and grabbed her arm.

"To get Sarai." Brynleigh pulled her hood over her hair. "Stay inside. I'll be back as soon as I can."

Wide, horror-filled eyes met hers. "You're going out in this? You can't! It's dangerous."

"I'll be fine, Mama," Brynleigh said placatingly. It was a rainstorm. What was the worst thing that could happen? "Someone needs to get Sarai. She's not answering her phone, and I want to ensure she gets home safely."

It was Brynleigh's job as the older sister to look after Sarai. She'd always felt that way, even when Sarai was a baby. This was no different. Besides, the fairgrounds weren't far from their house. The massive clearing was a frequent gathering spot for young adults. Brynleigh had spent many a late night there in the past.

Gavin thrust an umbrella at his eldest daughter. "Be safe. This storm came out of nowhere. Get your sister and come home as quickly as you can. I'll check on Mrs. Cooper. She must be scared."

As if emphasizing his point, the power flickered and went out. Darkness surrounded them. A faint scream came from next door. Mrs. Cooper was an elderly widow, almost ninety years old, and as long as Brynleigh could remember, she'd lived alone.

"Good idea, Gavin," Isolde said. "I'll stay here in case Sarai comes back."

"Call me if she does." Brynleigh kissed Isolde on the cheek before hugging her father. She tucked her phone into her pocket and opened the door. "I love you both," she said over her shoulder. "Be back soon."

Streams of water fell from the heavens.

Brynleigh pressed the button on the side of the umbrella, and the waterproof fabric fanned out over her head. It did little to stop the deluge of water pouring over her. The storm was escalating. Where had it come from? She could ponder the origins of the storm after she found Sarai.

Brynleigh ran down the street, her feet pounding against the cement. She moved swiftly, barely seeing the other people running in the opposite direction. Everyone was soaked and confused, staring skyward as water pelted them from above.

She turned towards the fairground.

The sky was a swirling, furious mass of black and gray. There were no stars. No moon. The only light came from the flashes of lightning crashing through the midsummer night at regular intervals.

The closer she came to the field, the more worried Brynleigh became. She had expected to see Sarai on her way here, but there was no sign of her sister. Where was she? Sarai was smart. She would've started running home as soon as the storm hit.

The water rose far too quickly to be normal. First, it reached her ankles. Then, her knees.

Thunder bellowed its anger.

In the distance, someone screamed.

Dropping the useless umbrella, Brynleigh cupped her hands around her mouth and yelled, "Sarai! Where are you?"

The wind swallowed her words.

She ran to the fairgrounds, calling for her sister.

The water rose and rose. She half-waded, half-sprinted through the torrential storm. Soon, it was up to her thighs.

The fairgrounds were in sight.

"Sarai!"

Nothing.

Trees bowed in her direction, the wind pulling them nearly in half. Debris floated on top of the water. Branches the size of her arm flew through the air.

She swore, her stomach dropped as she scanned the area. No one was here. Even the stands, usually occupied by at least two or three couples enjoying each other's company, stood empty.

A chasmic, numbing panic settled in Brynleigh's stomach. She couldn't go home without Sarai. Her imagination ran wild as she imagined the look of horror on her parents' faces if she returned alone. She couldn't do that to them. Sarai was the youngest member of their family. She was kind and good and never caused any trouble.

Brynleigh had to find her.

The water was up to Brynleigh's hips when she turned and started back home. She swiped her hands over her eyes, trying to clear her vision. She waded, shivering and rubbing her arms as she searched left and right for Sarai.

The storm still raged. Chavin descended into watery chaos. Trees split. Glass shattered. People screamed. Wood creaked. The rain kept coming.

Brynleigh's heart pounded as she headed in the direction she thought Sarai would take to go home. Maybe she'd see her on the way. They could laugh about how silly this was as they found refuge inside. They would sit and watch the lightning from the living room, like when they were little girls. Isolde would—

There!

Sarai was down half a block, standing in hip-deep water at the street corner with her back to Brynleigh.

Hope surged in Brynleigh's chest, and she pumped her arms and legs as she hurried towards her sister. "Sarai! We need to go!"

Sarai wasn't moving. She was just... staring off into the distance.

What was she looking at?

"Hey!" Brynleigh screamed. "Turn around! We have to go home. This isn't safe!"

A boom of thunder that was like a stack of bricks being thrown crashed through the sky.

It felt like it took an eternity of pushing through water to reach Sarai. Brynleigh fought against the current, the water from below nearly as powerful as the storm rushing from above, but she kept moving.

She'd never give up.

Her lungs burned, and her muscles ached as she grabbed Sarai's arm. "Let's go!"

Sarai lifted a trembling finger at the horizon. "L-l-look."

Brynleigh turned, her eyes widening as a scream ripped from her throat.

A wave taller than all the houses in their village crested over the roofs. It was a harbinger of doom, a bringer of death, and it was coming straight for them.

"Fucking run!" Brynleigh shouted, yanking Sarai behind her.

The unnatural storm chased them through the streets. No matter how fast they ran, they couldn't escape the screaming, the crashing of water against wood, and the destruction of one house after another.

And in the end, they weren't fast enough.

The water was a hungry, ruthless beast as it devoured them whole.

BRYNLEIGH OPENED HER EYES.

Time seemed to slow as she grounded herself in the present once more. She was in the ballroom, not in the midst of a deadly storm. Her heart thudded from a memory, not from being chased by an enormous wave.

Her shadows throbbed in her veins.

Death had reigned in Chavin that midsummer's evening. The entire town had flooded and been destroyed. Their prairie homes weren't built to withstand the force of nature that had been Ryker's storm.

It had raged for hours, killing everyone and destroying everything within ten miles of the town before abruptly ending. By then, Brynleigh was an orphan, and Jelisette had Made her.

Brynleigh took a deep breath and scanned the crowd. She wasn't certain what she was looking for, but she kept searching until she met a pair of chocolate-brown eyes across the room.

The moment their eyes locked, her heart ceased beating in her chest. Shadows spun around her feet.

Time froze.

They stared at each other, the crowd between them meaningless. It didn't matter that she'd never seen him before. It didn't matter that he wore a mask. She knew it was him. Ryker Waterborn. Holding his gaze, she stepped towards him.

It was time.

CHAPTER 21
A Meeting for the Ages

Ryker was standing at the far end of the ballroom discussing military maneuvers with Therian when the doors opened.

"Ladies and gentlemen," the herald announced, the microphone pinned to his lapel projecting his voice, "it is my honor to present the ninth participant in this year's Choosing, Miss Brynleigh de la Point."

Ryker's eyes flew to the ballroom doors. His height afforded him the ability to see over the heads of most of those gathered, giving him the perfect view of his intended bride. Like most of the men here, he was dressed to the nines. His suit and shoes were black, but he'd picked his tie for Brynleigh.

The moment she stepped into the ballroom, he knew he'd made a good choice. The crimson tie matched her stunning gown perfectly.

By the Sands, she was gorgeous.

Brynleigh paused on the threshold. Ryker's lungs tightened as he drank in the sight of his intended. The crimson mask hid her features, but the beautiful black bat wings and the shadows curling around her legs marked her as a creature of the night.

His creature of the night.

Ryker unabashedly studied his vampire. Immortal grace and poise emanated from her, and she was impeccably put together. Silken gold hair framed her face. A crimson gown hugged her body.

And her curves. His imagination hadn't done her justice. She was a dark goddess. The low V of her dress highlighted full breasts that were begging to be held and loved and admired. Her hips were rounded. A muscular thigh peeked through the slit in her dress.

Fucking perfection.

Ryker's entire body tightened as pure, hot, primal need ran through him. He couldn't wait to get her alone, to run his hands over her and claim her as his.

She stepped forward, poised and graceful. Her mouth tilted into a small smile, and her black eyes swept over the assembled group. Searching.

Kydona help him, but he'd waited so long for this moment. Tracing the outline of the box in his pocket, he turned to Therian.

"I've got to go." He clapped his friend on the back.

If the dragon shifter replied, Ryker didn't hear it. He was already moving across the ballroom, pushing past curious onlookers drawn towards her. The closer he got, the stronger her scent became.

Soon, night-blooming roses were all he could smell.

Nothing could keep him from going to her. Why were there so many people here?

Ryker was halfway across the ballroom when those beautiful obsidian orbs met his gaze. Though they were masked, it was like she stared directly into his soul.

He froze mid-step as if something had slammed into him. His heart was a drum in his ears. Shivers ran down his spine. The world stopped spinning, his magic thrummed in his veins, and deep within him, something he hadn't known he was missing settled into place.

A sea of people separated them, but it didn't matter. It turned out nothing mattered but her.

Time unfroze.

They both moved as if pulled by the same cord. He kept his eyes on her, pushing through the crowd until nothing but a few feet separated them.

Finally. Together at last. No barriers. Nothing keeping them apart. Not anymore.

Her lips parted, and he glimpsed two fangs nestled in her gums.

Hi, she mouthed.

He returned the silent greeting, vaguely aware that other things were happening around them.

The remaining participants of the Choosing were announced, and they entered the ballroom in turn.

He held Brynleigh's gaze.

Chancellor Rose took the stage, speaking into the microphone.

Brynleigh raised a brow as if saying, *Can you believe we have to listen to another speech?*

He smirked.

Ignatia Rose applauded the members of this year's Choosing for their "flexibility." A fucking understatement, but Ryker didn't even care. His vampire was here.

Ryker took another step towards Brynleigh. He committed her to memory.

Mine.

Soon, the entire world would know this gorgeous vampire was his, and his alone.

Earlier, Ryker had volunteered to propose first. Stepping up wasn't difficult—he was already certain of his decision and couldn't wait to see Brynleigh. His fingers twitched at his sides. He itched to rip the mask off her face.

He wanted to see her, touch her, kiss her.

It felt like the Chancellor's speech stretched on for hours, although it was likely mere minutes.

The entire time, Ryker's gaze didn't slip from his vampire's. Not when Chancellor Rose announced it was time for the first proposal. Not when the crowd moved back, lining the walls, until only the couples remained in the middle of the ballroom. Not when a spotlight shone down on them, illuminating them for the cameras that were certainly watching.

He was ready for this.

Ryker stepped forward, finally closing the distance between him and his vampire. Silence fell upon the ballroom as hundreds of eyes landed on them. They didn't bother him. As far as he was concerned, it was just him and Brynleigh.

No one else, not even the Chancellor, mattered.

Holding Brynleigh's gaze, Ryker reached out and took his vampire's hand in his. She hitched a breath at the contact, this touch as powerful as their first. Sparks coursed through him, and her fingers curled against his.

Once again, he marveled at the softness of her flesh. Her long, slender fingers fit perfectly within his hand. His thumb rubbed slow circles against her as he drew her closer.

When there was a mere foot between them, the corner of his lips twitched upwards. "You're beautiful." His hushed words were meant for her ears only.

Her red lips slanted up, giving him another peek of fang. She blushed, her cheeks turning a dusty rose that accented her beauty.

He would endeavor to make her blush every day.

"Thank you, Ry," she murmured. "You don't look so bad yourself."

The way her lips formed his name would forever be seared on his heart. He yearned to hear her say it a thousand times over, and he would cherish each instance.

His thumb swept across the back of her hand. "Ready, sweetheart?"

She drew in a deep breath and dipped her head. "It feels like I've been waiting for years for this moment."

In a way, so had he. When he'd agreed to enter the Choosing, Ryker had never imagined it would feel like this. So perfect. So right.

His entire body was on edge as Brynleigh stepped back and withdrew her hand from his. He let her go, his gaze glued to her willowy movements as she reached for the black silk strands securing the mask to her face.

His breath caught in his throat, and his eyes focused solely on the pull of her fingers. She tugged, and the silk knot behind her head came loose. The mask tumbled to the floor like an autumnal leaf.

Brynleigh was *stunning*. Beautiful in an unusual way that spoke to the deepest parts of him. Wide black eyes met his. Her cheekbones were strong. Her red lips were plump and kissable. She was everything he'd ever dreamed of, and yet, nothing like he'd ever imagined.

It took everything he had not to surge forward and wrap her in his arms.

Holding her gaze, his fingers rose and found the ribbons of his mask. He undid the knot and let the mask go.

His hands dropped, and his heart hammered as her gaze swept over his face. He would give anything for the ability to read minds right now. He wanted to know each of her thoughts.

After what felt like an eternity, Brynleigh stepped towards him. She reached up, her fingers grazing his cheek. "You're real," she murmured as if she couldn't believe it. "I'm touching you."

He felt the same way. This was like a dream.

Over the past six weeks, he'd learned to interpret every influx of Brynleigh's voice, every hitch of her breath, and every laugh. They'd shared some of their deepest secrets, talked about everything and nothing, and played chess for hours, and he was finally putting a face to the person behind it all.

And this was more than he'd ever imagined.

Seeing Brynleigh for the first time was like having lived his life in darkness and then stepping into the sunshine. Their connection was deep, powerful, overwhelming, and *right*.

"I'm real." Capturing her hand in his, he brought it to his mouth and grazed a feather-light kiss over her knuckles. "So are you."

Brynleigh sucked in a breath, and her wings flared out behind her. Someone in the crowd murmured, but he couldn't make out their words over the slamming of his heart against his ribs.

Threading their fingers together, Ryker held Brynleigh's hand as he dropped to one knee. The floor was cold beneath him, but the temperature didn't bother him.

Her mouth opened, and her tongue flicked against her bottom lip, wetting it.

Ryker reached into his suit pocket and closed his fingers around the black velvet box he'd tucked in there earlier. He drew it out slowly, prolonging the moment.

Silence enveloped the ballroom. It was so quiet that every sound, every hitched breath, was amplified a hundred times over. Nerves were tiny butterflies dancing in his stomach, and beads of sweat broke out on his forehead.

Ryker had practiced what he would say, but now the words didn't seem like enough. What if she said no? What if he was about to make a fool of himself?

His lungs squeezed, and for a moment, he thought he would pass out. Black spots appeared before his eyes, and he struggled to breathe. Right now, he wasn't a military captain or a powerful fae. He was a man hoping the woman he loved would accept his proposal.

Brynleigh gripped his hand, and her mouth curved up. *It's okay*, she seemed to be telling him. *We're in this together*.

Just like that, the nerves were banished. The butterflies found a new home, far, far away from him.

Ryker held Brynleigh's hand and stared deeply into those black eyes. "Sweetheart, getting to know you over the past six weeks has been the greatest honor of my life." His voice was steady and as unwavering as his grip as he spoke. "The day I walked through the doors of the Hall of Choice, I hoped to find a bride. I wanted someone smart, fierce, and loyal who could love someone like me."

He kissed the back of her hand. "I was hoping for you, even if I didn't know it yet."

Someone in the crowd gasped.

Another murmured, "This is so romantic."

Ryker tuned them out, focusing solely on the vampire before him. "Brynleigh Elise de la Point, I love you."

This was the first time the water fae had said those words aloud, but it wouldn't be the last. He would proclaim them every single day from now until he Faded.

"You are the moon, shining your brilliant light into my life," Ryker murmured, his voice deepening. "I lived in darkness before I met you and didn't even know it. You complete me. I wake daily thinking of you, and you've already taught me so much."

Brynleigh's gaze softened, and she whispered his name. "You've taught me a lot, too."

"I can't wait to see where the rest of our life goes." Ryker's grip tightened on her hand. Though his next words were quieter, their impact reverberated throughout his entire being. "Will you marry me?"

Brynleigh inhaled deeply, and her fingers twitched in his.

He silently begged her, *Please say yes.*

The entirety of Ryker's world revolved around the beautiful vampire before him. Every breath, every heartbeat, every second felt like an eternity as he waited for her response.

She opened her mouth and whispered, "Yes."

Ryker rose to his feet in one smooth movement. "Yes?"

His vampire—his fiancée—laughed. The beautiful, familiar sound washed over him like springtime rain. "Of course, I'll marry you." Her smile could have lit up the darkest room. "I've been waiting for this day since we first met."

Elation, unlike anything he'd ever felt, washed through Ryker. He grinned and picked Brynleigh up, twirling her in a circle. Her crimson gown trailed behind her, and she giggled.

"She said yes!" he shouted. He wanted everyone to hear their good news.

Cheers and claps filled the ballroom as Ryker returned Brynleigh to her feet. Remembering the box he held, he popped open the lid. Smaller onyx jewels encircled the sole diamond, and the ring sparkled in the light.

Brynleigh gasped. She reached for the ring, only to pull back at the last moment. "Ryker, this... it's too much."

She was wrong. Nothing was too much for her. She was his, and she would soon learn what it meant to be loved by him. Ryker always looked after those closest to him.

He shook his head. "No. It's perfect, like you."

She opened her mouth, but nothing came out.

Ryker was delighted that he'd rendered her speechless. He'd chosen this ring with her in mind. Lifting her left hand, he asked, "May I?"

She nodded slowly. "Of course."

Sliding the ring onto the appropriate finger with care, Ryker admired the fit. "Do you like it?"

Glistening black eyes met his, making him feel like the most important man in the world. "I love it."

The look on Brynleigh's face made Ryker forget they had an audience. She looked at him like he was the reason the world turned; she was there for him and only for him.

He felt the same way.

Threading their fingers together, he drew Brynleigh closer to him. He bent his head, his arm wrapping around her waist and settling beneath her wings.

She hitched a breath as his lips brushed the shell of her ear, and he whispered, "I love you."

She shivered beneath his touch, and he kissed her cheek before he could stop himself. The responding frisson that ran through her delighted him. He wanted to kiss her more thoroughly, but he would wait until they were alone.

While he was willing to share the beginning of their relationship with the world, their first kiss and everything that came after would be just for them.

He couldn't wait.

CHAPTER 22
Death is the Only Alternative

Brynleigh's container of emotions was dangerously close to overflowing. Everything had been going well until she locked eyes with Ryker and tumbled headfirst into a spiral of feelings. No matter how much she shoved them down, they insisted on making a reappearance.

After Ryker's proposal, seven more couples got engaged. That was a record number for the Choosing, and the air in the ballroom was one of absolute delight. Chancellor Rose took the stage and spoke for a few minutes about how pleased she was with the outcome of the Two-Hundredth Choosing. According to her, it was a sign of prosperity and good things to come for the Republic of Balance.

Brynleigh wasn't so sure. She noticed the guards lining the walls behind the Chancellor, their presence a reminder of the unrest outside these walls. No one else seemed to mind them, though. Maybe Brynleigh was wrong, and the worst had passed.

The stringed orchestra picked up their instruments before Brynleigh could delve too far into those thoughts. They began to play, their lyrical music stunningly beautiful.

Ryker turned to Brynleigh. A radiant smile shone on the water fae's face.

Guilt stabbed Brynleigh in the gut.

Ryker was so happy, and she was a terrible person for stringing him along. He had no idea about her true intentions. How could he? She was supposed to be marrying him for love, or at least the potential for love.

Instead, she was playing him.

"Dance with me?" Ryker dipped into a low, old-fashioned, courtly bow and held out his hand. A lock of his hair—a brown several shades darker than his chocolate eyes—fell forward, but he made no effort to brush it away.

Brynleigh stared at his hand, the inviting gesture drawing her towards him. She shouldn't dance with the handsome water fae. It was a very bad idea. The offer alone made yet another pesky feeling that she refused to acknowledge sprout up within her, and she shoved it deep down.

But it would be rude if she ignored him... right?

All around them, other couples danced. The muscular dragon shifter, Therian, spun Hallie in a circle. Her wings fluttered behind her, and they both laughed as he lifted her off the ground. They were a cute couple, especially with the way the dragon shifter towered over the smaller woman.

Less delightful was the couple dancing beside them. The second-to-last proposal had been from Edward, a fae, to Valentina. Brynleigh didn't know his affinity, but seeing as the fire fae had accepted his hand, she assumed he was powerful. Brynleigh would be watching them both carefully. Whoever put up with Valentina was either a saint or as horrible as she was.

Ryker was still waiting patiently for Brynleigh to accept his offer to dance.

For a long moment, she stared at his hand while her internal debate raged. She was moments away from declining when she felt a heavy gaze bore into her. She glanced up, and a familiar pair of black eyes met hers.

Brynleigh swallowed at the sight of her Maker.

Jelisette's gown matched her progeny's, except hers was a blue so dark it was almost black. She wore a matching mask that covered the top half of her face, but Brynleigh recognized her Maker on sight.

Standing next to Jelisette, wearing a crisp black suit, was Zanri. The shifter wore a tiger mask, his eyes sharp as he gazed through it. His red hair hung loosely around him, giving him a wild edge in this room full of polished people.

Jelisette's black eyes narrowed and locked onto Brynleigh's. The message hidden within them was clear: *don't mess this up.*

Brynleigh didn't intend to. Calling Zanri for a helpful reminder of why she was doing this was one thing, but being faced with her Maker was another. If Brynleigh admitted she was struggling with emotions, Jelisette wouldn't hesitate to punish her. She'd made that abundantly clear several months ago.

"Never forget, Brynleigh, death is the only alternative to winning." Jelisette's piercing gaze met Brynleigh's from across the chess board. Like Brynleigh, she wore a thick sweater as snow fell lazily outside.

Bobbing her head, Brynleigh picked up the black queen and twisted it in her hands before placing it across the board. "Of course."

Her Maker smiled, but there wasn't a drop of warmth in the gesture. Instead, the sight of Jelisette's sharp fangs sent a shiver down Brynleigh's back. Had Brynleigh been mortal, she would've screamed at the sight. This was a woman who killed without compunction, and she had no problem handing out punishments as she saw fit.

"Wonderful." Jelisette picked up her knight and took Brynleigh's rook.

Fuck. How had she missed that?

Brynleigh stared at the board, trying to think of a way out of the inevitable checkmate as Jelisette added, "Never forget, you must always be planning several steps ahead."

"I won't fail you."

Those words echoed in Brynleigh's head as she broke eye

contact with Jelisette. Hoping her Maker couldn't sense the turmoil churning beneath her skin, Brynleigh dipped her head and forced a smile on her face as she retracted her wings. "I'd be delighted to dance, Ry."

She would just make sure there were no emotions involved.

Ryker smiled and took Brynleigh's hand in his. She ignored the way it felt good to be touched by him, ignored those sparks running up her arm as he led her onto the dance floor.

The first song wasn't too bad. The orchestra played a slow waltz, and she mostly succeeded in hiding her two left feet *and* keeping emotions out of this.

That wasn't the end of it, though.

The songs kept coming. She thought that after the first, they'd be done, but no. They danced and danced.

Damn it all, but this activity with Ryker was far more enjoyable than Brynleigh would ever admit. He moved with grace and ease, unencumbered by his tailored black suit.

Each wave of music, each dance, each moment Brynleigh spent in Ryker's arms chipped away at her resolve to keep emotions out of this situation.

It wasn't her fault. Not really. From a purely physical standpoint, Captain Ryker Waterborn was a well-built, muscular, tall fae. His jaw was chiseled, his ears were pointed, and a fire in his eyes burned brighter every time he looked at her.

"Do you trust me?" Ryker whispered into her ear, his hand splayed across her lower back as they danced their fifth song in a row.

There was a multitude of reasons why she shouldn't. And yet, as Brynleigh stared into Ryker's eyes, she nodded. "Yes."

Her eyes widened at the admission and the truth behind it. What did that mean? She couldn't trust him. She knew what he'd done.

And yet...

She didn't take back her statement.

Ryker's grip tightened on Brynleigh's hand. His eyes sparkled, and he spun her away from him before twirling her back. Brynleigh couldn't help it. She giggled like a love-sick schoolgirl. Ryker brought something out in her that she couldn't label.

It had to be his handsomeness. That was the only logical reason for this kind of reaction.

After all, Brynleigh wasn't the only one who noticed how good-looking her fiancé was. As they spun across the dance floor, she caught sight of several other women and even a few men eyeing Ryker with unmasked lust.

Brynleigh wanted to snarl at each of them to keep their eyes to themselves. This man, with his sharp jaw and lips made for kissing, was hers.

At least for now.

Was jealousy a bad emotion? Should she shove it down like the others? She wasn't sure if it was dangerous or not. It certainly wasn't as awful as the feeling that had welled up within her when he proposed.

That one, she refused to name. If she didn't label it, it wasn't real.

Except it felt far too fucking real. All of this did.

Ryker's gaze never wavered from Brynleigh's. His hand was a brand against her back. Even as he led them across the dance floor, he made her feel seen in a way that no one else ever had. It was like he peeled away all the layers of her identity and peered into her soul beneath.

It was extremely unnerving and made it difficult to remember this was all an act. He made her feel like...

No.

She wouldn't even acknowledge that feeling. Whatever it was, she would ignore it until after the life drained from those chocolate brown eyes.

Two more songs went by, and Brynleigh... enjoyed them. Each chord, each note, affected her more than the last.

Thank Isvana, eventually, a hand landed on Brynleigh's arm when they were near the edge of the dance floor.

"Excuse me, mind if I cut in?" Zanri smiled, his eyes twinkling behind his mask.

Ryker turned to the shifter, his face hardening. "Who are you?"

There was a gruffness in Ryker's voice that caused Brynleigh's core to tighten in wholly inappropriate ways. She squeezed her thighs together and turned to the masked shifter. "This is Zanri. I... work with him."

In as much as working meant that Zanri found criminals for Brynleigh to kill. Semantics.

"Ah." Tension slipped from Ryker's shoulders. "Would you like to dance with him?"

Honestly, the only thing Brynleigh wanted was for this entire evening to end. However, since that didn't seem possible, this was a close second. If she danced with Zanri, she could keep those frustrating emotions in check.

"I do," said Brynleigh.

Ryker reluctantly released her before leaning over and kissing her cheek. "I'll be right over there," he whispered. His voice was much firmer when he told Zanri, "One song."

The shifter nodded and led Brynleigh silently onto the dance floor. He drew her close—but not too close—and started swaying. "I hear congratulations are in order."

Brynleigh smiled. "They are."

Zanri spun her. It was nice but didn't compare to Ryker's impressive dance skills.

"And how are you doing?" he asked when he drew her back in.

That was a loaded question. There were many ways she could answer. Confused. Antsy. Emotional. Torn up inside. In the end, she asked for clarification. "You mean with rule number ten?" Her voice was low, meant only for Zanri.

He nodded. "Yes."

"I'm... alright." Lie. Her box was filled to the brim with illicit emotions. But what else could she say?

Twice now, Ryker had declared his love for her. Both times, she hadn't said anything. Lying to him was one thing, but proclaiming false love was another. It was a step too far, even for her.

Brynleigh had never said those words to anyone, and she wouldn't start now.

"You must stay strong, B." Zanri's soft voice was firm and grounding, as if he knew the inner turmoil she was experiencing.

"I will." Brynleigh nodded, trying to convince herself of the fact.

Somehow, her voice was unwavering despite the storm churning within her.

The shifter squeezed her hands. "You must."

Again, Brynleigh wondered at the forcefulness in Zanri's voice. Maybe it was just her time away from the safe house, but he seemed so... insistent. It struck Brynleigh as odd. Why was he pushing this? He didn't have anything at stake.

But then the song ended. Zanri stepped aside, and Ryker took his place.

The fae's hand settled on the small of her back again, and he pulled her close. His eyes searched hers. "Are you okay?"

No. She was so far from okay that she couldn't even remember what that felt like.

She couldn't say that, so instead, she said, "Yes."

His gaze searched hers, and his thumb rubbed circles on her exposed back. All night, he'd been touching her. It was gods-damned distracting and made it hard for her to think.

"You can tell me the truth, Brynleigh," he murmured, just loud enough to be heard over the music.

That was the last thing she could do.

If Ryker knew the truth of who she was and what she was doing there, this would all be for naught. He would either throw her in prison or finish the job he started six years ago. She imagined he'd be pissed if he learned about her true intentions.

Remaining silent didn't seem like it would work, though, so

she looked out to the crowd. Several people were still watching her fae. Their gazes followed him, the lust evident as they blatantly checked him out. It was as good of an excuse as any. "People are looking at you."

Ryker's brown eyes twinkled at the tone of Brynleigh's voice. His lips twisted up into a devilish smirk, revealing...

Fucking great. Of course, the incredibly handsome water fae she was supposed to kill had dimples.

Why not?

He sported a pair of them, one on each cheek, and they only added to his attractiveness. It wasn't fair for one person to be blessed with such good looks. Couldn't the gods have thrown a wart on his face, or perhaps given him a crooked nose? *Something* to make him be not so... so... beautiful.

And fuck, he was perfect. Brynleigh felt like she had done a pretty good job of ignoring that fact until now, but it was becoming impossible.

"Why, sweetheart, are you jealous?" Ryker's deep, smoky voice was low as he spun her across the dance floor in a move she could never have done on her own.

Her cheeks heated. "No, I'm not."

Ryker whirled her through the air, the crimson fabric swirling around her. He settled her back on her feet, his gaze darkening as he looked her over.

"You lie so beautifully, little vampire." He held her so close that she could feel his heart beating in his chest.

Brynleigh had no words. She *was* lying... just not about what he thought. Her entire persona was nothing more than a facade. At least, that's what she kept telling herself. The problem was that the longer she remained in close contact with Ryker, the more difficult it was to remember what, exactly, she was lying about.

Thank Isvana, Ryker didn't seem to mind her silence. A baritone chuckle rumbled through him, and they continued dancing as the music picked up.

Several songs later, Brynleigh's throat was dry. She slowed, lifting her hand off Ryker's arm and rubbing the base of her throat absentmindedly.

Instantly, Ryker's gaze darkened and locked on her hand. "Thirsty?"

Was she? Many desires pulsed through her, most of them illicit. There was only one she could give into right now.

She nodded, and he led her towards the bar.

A masked Death Elf with red markings crawling up his right hand put down the glass he was polishing as they approached. "Good evening, and congratulations on your engagement."

"Thank you." Brynleigh smiled at the bartender.

Ryker's hand never left Brynleigh's as he ordered a glass of blood wine for her and a beer for himself. Brynleigh usually took offense to men ordering for her. It was demeaning since she was more than capable of placing her own requests. But something was endearing about the way Ryker seamlessly took charge. To her eternal chagrin, Brynleigh liked it.

The bartender returned with their drinks in short order. Ryker thanked the man and took the glasses before tilting his head towards a shadowy alcove near the back of the ballroom.

"Come with me?" he asked in that rough voice of his.

A shiver ran down Brynleigh's spine, and her breath caught in her throat. She shouldn't be alone with Ryker. That could only lead to bad things. She knew that, and yet, she didn't say no. Not yet.

The prudent choice—the right choice, the rule-following choice—would be to stay with the crowd. She shouldn't be alone with him, couldn't afford for more emotions to try and get the better of her.

Rules six and eight popped into Brynleigh's head, reminding her of all the reasons this was a terrible idea. But just one time, she didn't want to follow the rules. She wanted to go with Ryker. Besides, they weren't *truly* alone. Others were here. They would be secluded but not isolated.

What harm could come from bending the rules this one time? Probably nothing.

"I'd love to," she said before she could stop herself.

Those damned dimples decorated Ryker's cheeks once again. Handing her the goblet of wine, he laced their fingers together and led her away from the crowd. They garnered a few curious glances, but no one stopped them.

The alcove was dark, hidden behind some large speakers, and it was quieter. Tension left Brynleigh's shoulders, and she exhaled. This was nice. Maybe it wasn't such a bad idea.

For a single moment, she relaxed.

And then she looked up.

Ryker stood right in front of her. Barely a foot separated the two of them. He was all fae, his gaze dark and hungry as it swept over her.

Brynleigh could barely think. Breathing was practically impossible, and speaking was definitely out of the question. He was close. Far too close.

Fuck, this was a bad idea. Maybe the worst one Brynleigh had ever had. That said a lot, because once she'd challenged Zanri to a drinking game involving Faerie Wine and a trashy reality dating show that followed merfolk and sailors as they tried to bridge the divide between their lives and make love work. The next morning, the two of them had been in so much pain that they'd both sworn off the beverage for eternity.

This was worse than that.

Ryker came even closer. His knuckles brushed her cheek, and she practically melted right then and there.

Brynleigh tried to remember the rules, to ground herself in them, but it wasn't working. Her mind was blank, empty of everything except for an awareness of the fae before her.

She closed her eyes, which amplified Ryker's scent until it was all she could smell. Her fangs ached. She wanted to draw nearer. She wanted to leave. Isvana help her, but she had no idea what to do.

She froze.

A finger landed under her chin, and Ryker rumbled, "Look at me, Brynleigh."

The commanding tone of his voice was entirely too pleasing. Brynleigh wasn't ready to dissect that, though. She'd never be ready. She grabbed those feelings and shoved them down, down, down.

When she was certain she wouldn't spontaneously combust, she opened her eyes. "Yes?"

"You were jealous earlier." Not a question. "I liked that."

Her breath caught. Fuck, she had no business enjoying the deep rumble of his words so much. Before she could reply, Ryker bent, slanting his lips over hers. It couldn't be called a kiss because it was barely more than a graze of their mouths. Still, it reverberated in the depth of Brynleigh's soul.

Her heart fluttered, which was a strange experience. A feeling rose. She snatched it, forcing it into away. Whatever it was, if she didn't acknowledge it, she couldn't let it affect her.

"I don't like them looking at us," she said honestly, though she didn't quite know why she was telling Ryker this. "I've never enjoyed being the center of attention. When I was young, I did almost everything to stay out of the spotlight. I never answered questions in school, nor did I speak up. It was easier to blend into the shadows, even then."

Sarai had been loud enough for both of them. She had been vibrant and full of life. Watching her sister bloom like a flower in spring had been a highlight of Brynleigh's life. It was a cruel joke that now, Brynleigh was still alive and in front of the cameras.

"Let them look. I'm drawn to you and no one else." Ryker's voice deepened. "My attentions are firmly where I desire them to be."

He lowered his head, his eyes never leaving hers. Brynleigh's heart pounded in her chest. She stared at his lips, her stomach twisting in what she told herself was dread.

She was a gods-damned liar.

Would he kiss her now? Really, truly kiss her? Would she let him? She had no idea.

Brynleigh watched Ryker's mouth descend upon hers like it was the most interesting thing she'd ever seen. Half of her wanted to dart back into the crowd, but the other half held her still, eagerly waiting for that first touch of his mouth against hers.

Anticipation thickened the air between them.

At the last moment, Ryker turned his head and skimmed her lips, kissing the corner of her mouth. She exhaled a breathy moan as his mouth landed on the side of her neck. Against her better judgment—which, to be honest, was hanging on by an Ithiar-damned threat—her eyes fluttered shut.

A thousand curses flew through her head, but not a single one made it to her lips. No was a simple, two-letter word. She should say it. She should stop him. This was wrong on so many levels.

Brynleigh knew all these things, but none of them stopped her from inching towards Ryker. She tilted her head, giving him better access to her neck.

His large, warm hand landed on her hip, pulling her closer. His sharp canines grazed her skin, not biting but sending enough pressure that the space between her thighs dampened. Her heart raced as he kissed a trail down her neck.

Control was careening out of Brynleigh's fingers. Some part of her still possessed enough common sense to realize she needed to maintain some power in their relationship.

Recalling their previous conversation was difficult with his mouth on her, but Brynleigh murmured, "And what if I don't want them looking?"

Truth. She didn't want anyone watching her with Ryker. Not anymore. They'd shared so much with the world already. She wanted to be alone with him and let him kiss her all over. She would let him remove all the barriers between them and take her however he wanted.

Wait.

What?

No.

That was wrong. *This* was wrong.

She wanted...

Ryker's fingers curled around her hip, and he *nipped* her. Oh gods. One simple action had no business feeling so good. A tremor ran through Brynleigh, starting at her toes and making its way up her legs and to her core. Her head fell back on a groan. Her glass of wine dangled from her fingers. She forgot everything else. This fae could do whatever he wanted to her.

"Then I'll get rid of them," he growled. "I'll do anything for you."

Darkness was laced in his words, an unveiled threat directed towards anyone that might come between them that Brynleigh liked far too much. She'd never been one to enjoy overt acts of possessiveness, especially not from fae males, but that seemed to be rapidly changing.

Brynleigh could get used to having someone willing to fight for her. She'd been alone for so long.

Except...

No.

What the fuck was she doing? This was incredibly wrong. She couldn't get used to this or let the captain talk to her in this fashion. She wasn't just bending the rules but breaking them all together.

Gods-damn it, what was she thinking? This was a game. She wasn't supposed to let him touch her like this. She wasn't allowed to have any emotions. They were far too dangerous.

Brynleigh's blood chilled, and her fingers spasmed.

The crystal glass tumbled from her hand in slow motion, the liquid spilling out in a red arc and staining the ground in a pool of blood moments before the glass shattered.

Her head ached. A buzzing filled her ears. She needed to get out of here right now. Shadows bubbled in her veins. Control was a foreign concept as her head spun.

There was no losing. Not in this game.

Ryker shouted her name, but she could barely hear him over the roaring. She blinked, trying to clear her head.

His hands landed on her forearms, and his grip was firm but gentle. "What's wrong?"

Mistake, mistake, mistake.

She needed to leave, but the panic...

Tighter and tighter, a fist squeezed her lungs. Air. She sipped it, but it didn't help. She gasped, "I—"

The power flickered, and then the overhead lights went out.

Someone screamed.

A man yelled, "Take cover!"

Another shouted, "Get the Chancellor!"

"For freedom!" a woman cried out.

Brynleigh's brows furrowed. The hairs on her neck stood on end. Her shadows pulsed in warning. "What—"

Her next words never came. The ground shook like the gods were throwing furniture around. An explosion.

Something slammed into Brynleigh's neck. Pain bloomed, drawing her into its agonizing embrace.

Someone roared. Arms wrapped around her.

Cold. So fucking cold.

She moaned.

Someone yelled her name.

Everything went black.

CHAPTER 23
Protective Measures and Perfect Control

"Sit down, son. If you keep that up, you'll wear a hole in the floor." Tertia Waterborn, Representative of the Fae, raised a chestnut brown manicured brow from where she sat at the dining room table and frowned.

Somehow, Ryker's mother looked put together despite the hell they'd endured over the past twenty-four hours. Her hair was perfectly coiffed in her traditional chignon, pulled away from her face.

Ryker didn't look so good. He raked a hand through his hair for the twentieth time that hour and groaned. Last night, he'd been kissing Brynleigh—a thoroughly enjoyable activity that he planned on resuming as soon as possible—when chaos had erupted.

"I can't do that, Mother," Ryker growled. How could his mother sit there having a coffee as if they hadn't left the Hall of Choice covered in blood?

"And why not?" Again, with the pleasant tone. It was driving Ryker up the walls. He loved his mother, but sometimes, she did not seem connected to reality.

Although Tertia Waterborn appeared like a human in their

third decade of life, she was almost three centuries old. Fae aged slowly, and of all the species that lived on the Continent, they Faded the slowest... when they weren't hit with the Stillness. There was a chance Ryker's mother could live for another thousand years or more.

Ryker pointed to the closed door, his finger shaking with pent-up frustration. "I should be out there right now."

Tertia shook her head and slid her attention to the tablet before her. "Let the army handle the rebel situation," she said calmly, tapping the screen. "That's why we're here."

After the bomb had gone off last night, the Chancellor had ordered that all the Choosing Participants, the attending Representatives, and their families be brought to The Lily to be guarded. It was the most expensive hotel in the entire Central Region, and as such, it already boasted strong security measures. Chancellor Rose had pulled some strings and ensured there were enough rooms for everyone. Once they'd been transported here, soldiers were stationed at every hotel entrance and in front of every room.

Ryker hated places like this. Everything, from the floor to the ceiling, was gilded, expensive, and lacking in life. He'd much rather be at home or his cabin curled up with Brynleigh on the couch.

That wasn't possible right now, though. He was locked in this room, separated from his vampire. Fuck, he hated this.

He balled his fists. "I'm in the fucking army, Mother," he snapped. "It's my job."

One he wasn't allowed to do because he was trapped inside this gilded room like a prisoner.

"Excuse me?" Tertia's brown eyes, a mirror of his own, widened. She placed a hand flat on the table and power rippled through the room. A reminder. A warning. Tread lightly.

Ryker had seen what his mother could do. Witnessed her power. There was a reason her children were such strong fae.

He dipped his head ever so slightly, the message clear: *I understand.*

It wasn't enough for Tertia, apparently, because she said, "You may be going through a lot right now, son, but that doesn't give you the right to speak to me in such a vulgar manner."

Ryker's nostrils flared as he breathed heavily through his nose. Damn it all. His mother was right, but he had nothing left. Manners were something civilized people used, and at the moment, he felt anything but that. How had everything turned out so badly?

The Masked Ball had been going without a hitch right up until the moment Brynleigh dropped her glass. She'd seemed shaken, but before he could find out what was wrong, the bomb went off.

"I shouldn't be here right now, Mother." Ryker tried to keep his voice flat, even though every single part of him shook with the urge to roar. "I need to be with her."

The Chancellor had decreed that all the participants needed to be kept apart while the soldiers contained the threat.

This separation was driving Ryker mad.

"The vampire?" Tertia sipped her coffee. "She'll be fine. They got to her in time."

He shook, his vision clouding, as his control slipped. His own magic thrummed, eager to help him feel better. But nothing would help. Not right now. Not after last night.

"Barely!" Ryker shouted. "Her blood covered me from head to toe!"

Last night, when he'd finally stumbled into the shower, the water had run red. When the bomb exploded, a piece of silver shrapnel grazed the side of Brynleigh's neck. If she'd been human, she would have died. As it was, she'd lost copious amounts of blood.

One moment, his vampire had been staring at him. The next, a crimson river spurted from her neck like a fountain.

Ryker would have nightmares about how Brynleigh's face

went from pale to snow white for the rest of his life. Her blood had poured out of her so fast that he'd barely had time to comprehend what was happening. Vampires were immune to many things, but silver was one of the few that could kill them.

Thank the Blessed Obsidian Sands, Jelisette de la Point had been present at the Masked Ball. She'd swooped in, bitten her own wrist, and fed her progeny her blood. It was only because of her quick thinking that Brynleigh was still alive and in a different suite, receiving intravenous blood transfusions.

"I know you're worried, son," Tertia said in a business-like voice. "But your vampire has the best medical care in the entire Republic. She'll be fine. Calm you."

Calm was not a word in Ryker's vocabulary. He wasn't meant to sit around and do nothing. He should be out there, searching for the bastards that built the fucking bomb. If they knew what was good for them, they'd fall to their knees and beg whatever deities they believed in that Ryker would not be the one to find them. When he did, he would tear them limb from limb for what they'd done.

Brynleigh wasn't the only one injured in the blast. Countless people were hurt, and several lives were lost altogether, including Luca, one of the Choosing participants. The young werewolf had been a good man and hadn't deserved to die so young.

"I need to see Brynleigh." Ryker had already tried to leave the suite, but a guard had stopped him at the door.

He pulled his hair, hating the helplessness churning in his gut.

Ryker understood the purpose of rules and knew they were in place for a reason, but right now, he didn't care. All he cared about was his vampire. Nothing else. Not right now. Once he saw Brynleigh with his own two eyes and confirmed she was healing, he would feel better.

Gods–damn it all. A growl rumbled through him, and he palmed the back of his neck. What were the chances he could sneak out of this suite and find the one where they were keeping her? He didn't know the guards stationed at his door, which was likely a conscious choice on the Chancellor's behalf, so he couldn't talk his way out of the suite.

But maybe...

A plan started forming in his head as he mulled over the possibility of getting hold of either Atlas or Nikhail. They might be working, but if they weren't, he was certain either would do as he asked.

Except Atlas was watching Marlowe. As much as Ryker loved Marlie, his dog wouldn't be much help in an operation like this. That left Nikhail as the more logical choice. Ryker nodded to himself, feeling incrementally better now that he had the semblance of a plan.

He turned on his heel, intent on heading back to his room and calling the air fae.

"I hope you're not planning on doing anything foolish, my son." Tertia didn't even lift her eyes from the tablet where she was typing a message. "Remember—"

"Everything I do reflects on you," he finished for her, biting back the urge to roll his eyes. He stopped in his tracks, though. "Yes, I know."

He'd heard the refrain a thousand times over.

That was the burden of being a Representative's son. His mother lived in the spotlight, and even though Ryker had spent the past six years living as a recluse, sometimes he still got caught in those bright rays.

"Are you certain?" This time, Tertia looked up. Her piercing gaze met his. "Need I remind you—"

Thank all the gods, a door slammed shut on the other side of the suite. It saved Ryker from his mother's impending lecture.

A slender fae jogged into the main room, her brown hair pulled into a high ponytail. Diamond studs glittered in her pierced, delicate, pointed ears, and a black ring sat in the middle of her bottom lip. She wore a neon pink t-shirt that was cropped high enough to show off her pierced navel and ripped jean shorts. The outfit was a bright contrast to Tertia's refined apparel.

"Ryker! I'm so glad you're safe." River slammed into him, and he hugged her. "I wish I could have seen you last night before everything went down. It was so horrible."

"Perhaps if you hadn't been tardy, you could've seen your brother before he proposed," Tertia remarked from the table, her voice icy.

Both Ryker and River sighed at the same time.

River's inability to arrive anywhere on time had been a topic of countless conversations in the past. It wasn't that his sister liked being late. She just never seemed to get anywhere when she was supposed to. Ryker had thought she would grow out of it, but that didn't seem to be the case.

"I'm sorry, Mother." River rubbed her temples. "I got stuck at the university studying and lost track of time. But I made it! That's the most important thing, right?"

Tertia's face made it clear that it was, in fact, not the most important thing.

Ryker wasn't in the mood to referee a fight between his mother and sister. Instead, he put his hands on River's shoulders and angled her away from their mother. "How's school going, Shortie?"

River was in her fourth year of pre-med at the University of Balance. The oldest of the five universities on the continent, the school had been founded by the High Ladies of Life and Death soon after the Battle of Balance. It was the most prestigious academic institution on this side of the Obsidian Coast.

"Good." River smiled tightly. "I'm acing all my classes."

"Your sister is on track to graduate at the top of her class, as she should be," their mother added. "She wouldn't be a Waterborn if she didn't perform to the best of her abilities."

They'd heard the same refrain their entire lives. Waterborns did not fail. Waterborns did not cause scenes. Waterborns were chosen by the gods to lead the fae, and as such, they had to keep their heads on their shoulders at all times.

Being a Waterborn was fucking exhausting.

"Of course, Mother," Ryker and River said simultaneously.

Tertia studied them both for another moment before dipping her head. She returned to her work, but the air remained tense.

"I've been watching you, Ryker." His sister returned her attention to him. "Every day, whenever I'm not in class or studying. You're a star."

He chuckled. "I'm still your brother, River."

"I know you are." She punched his arm, and he faked being hurt.

River laughed and called him a baby.

"Well, children, I think that's my cue to leave." Tertia stood, tucking her tablet under her arm. "I have to call the Council." She glared at them both. "Behave, young ones. I'll return soon."

"Of course, Mother," the siblings said in unison.

Tertia was a good parent, and she wanted the best for her children, but the only person Ryker had ever seen his mother be affectionate with was his father. She wasn't built like the rest of them. Luckily, their father had enough love for them all.

Tertia smiled at them, the expression verging on cold, before gliding into the third bedroom in the suite. She moved with a grace that spoke of her age and power.

Once the door closed behind her, Ryker turned to his sister.

"How are you doing?" he asked seriously. He hadn't wanted to bring this up in front of their mother, but now that they were alone, the question pressed on his mind. "Have there been any more incidents while I was gone?"

River's face paled, making her piercings stand out even more. "No, none."

"You've been doing your exercises? Is it under control?"

"I haven't missed a single day, like I promised." River's brows rose and nearly touched her forehead. "You know, Ryker, I am twenty-one. Just because I haven't hit my Maturation doesn't mean I can't manage it."

All fae Matured around twenty-five years old. Maturation brought them to their full power and slowed their aging until they were practically immortal. Having undergone his own Maturation thirteen years ago, Ryker knew this, but he still worried about his sister. She was the most important person in his world. Well. Now, she was the second most important person.

He needed to make sure she was alright. "If it starts to get too bad—"

"I'll go to Isolation Lake and let the magic out," River finished his sentence, repeating the words he'd said to her each time they spoke over the past six years. "I know. Under no circumstances am I to go near any inhabited towns or villages, especially if I haven't released my magic recently."

Ryker exhaled. "Good. And if something does happen—"

"It won't," she said firmly. "Not again."

Ryker placed a hand on River's shoulder and waited until her gaze met his. "If it does, you tell me."

"So, you can fix it again?"

"Yes," he said gravely.

"I can take care of myself," she protested. "I won't lose control again, I promise. Gabriel and Carson have been teaching me, just like you asked them."

The pair of water fae were some of the best, but they weren't Ryker. He'd asked them to step in and take over his sister's magical education while he was in the Choosing. If Ryker could have been in two places at once, he would've done it. But the rules had been clear.

He couldn't allow River's training to lapse, though. The last thing they needed was another incident. The last one had been bad enough and with their father's health failing...

Ryker would do whatever it took to keep his sister safe.

"Show me," he said.

Instead of doing as he asked, River crossed her arms and glowered. "You know, sometimes you can be an overbearing ass."

The hairs on Ryker's neck bristled. Was it overbearing to want to ensure his sister's safety? All he wanted to do was make sure she didn't accidentally harm herself or anyone else ever again. That wasn't overbearing in his books. It was his job as her older brother.

Ryker did what he always did in challenging moments like these. He fell back on his training. His back straightened, and he looked down at River. Right now, she wasn't his little sister. She was simply a fae who had previously lost control of her magic.

"Do it," he requested again, his voice hard.

She scowled. "Seriously?"

He held her gaze. "Yes. Show me what those two fae taught you while I was gone."

With a groan that spoke to exactly how deep her frustration ran, River held out her hand in the space between them. Her lips pinched together, and she frowned, focusing on her outstretched limb. Her brows furrowed, and water pooled in her palm. It started as a few drops but quickly grew.

The air hummed as River pulled on her extensive power. The clear liquid surrounded her hand, crawling up her wrist and forearm like a glove. The water twisted, and tiny currents ran through the translucent liquid.

Ryker had to admit that he was impressed with his sister's control. Her magic completely contained the water, and not a single drop fell on the floor.

River spread her fingers and twisted them in the air. The water spun and danced above her hand, coiling into a tube several feet long.

She murmured an ancient fae prayer beneath her breath and stared at the tube. Her eyes flashed, the color momentarily shifting from brown to stark blue, and the temperature in the room plummeted.

Goosebumps pebbled on Ryker's arms as the water turned into solid, opaque ice.

River grabbed the new creation out of the air. Her lips twitched into a smirk, and she sketched a bow. "See?" She handed the ice to her brother. "Perfect control."

Reluctantly, Ryker had to admit that Gabriel and Carson had

done a good job with her training. He'd chosen well—and thank all the gods for that. Ryker constantly worried about River. Her power exceeded both his and their mother's. It was both extraordinary and deadly.

"Good job, Shortie," Ryker said proudly. Rather than putting the ice in the sink—the suite was equipped with a fully stocked kitchen—he twisted his fingers.

Channeling his water magic had always been as easy as breathing.

The ice melted in a heartbeat, returning to liquid form. Before it could splash the absurdly expensive carpet, Ryker ordered the liquid to make a sphere. He sent it sailing through the air and out the open window before releasing it.

"Show off," River muttered, frowning.

He laughed, ruffling her hair. "I'm your big brother. I have to show off. It's in the handbook."

"Sure, it is." River turned and strolled towards the kitchen. "Want a coffee?"

Ryker's gaze darted between his sister and the door. A large part of him wanted to leave right now and call Nikhail, but the rest of him wanted to spend time with River. Their schedules were both so full, and he would be married soon. Who knew when they'd get to see each other except to train?

He could wait a little while longer.

"Sure," he called out. "Pour me a cup."

Reaching into his back pocket, Ryker drew out his phone. Thank all the gods, the guards had returned the contestants' technology on the way to the hotel. Typing up a quick message to Nikhail asking him to investigate the security at The Lily, Ryker followed his sister into the kitchen.

"How's school really going?" he asked, knowing his mother wasn't within earshot.

River groaned. "The classes are fine. The people? Not so great. Last week, I was at…"

Sipping his coffee, Ryker listened to his sister share the woes of life as a twenty-one-year-old in her fourth year of college. Apparently, there were many of them. It was nice to be with his family, but Ryker's mind kept returning to Brynleigh.

After this, he promised himself, he'd see her.

No matter what.

CHAPTER 24
Nothing But a Physical Reaction

Brynleigh was living in a cloud. Her head was light, her eyes were exceedingly heavy, and something soft and cushiony was beneath her. The air smelled strangely crisp, almost void of scents entirely. That would have struck her as odd, except her mind was having trouble focusing. Everything was foggy.

She frowned and tried to shove past the dark mist. She was missing something vital, but she couldn't remember what it was. That wouldn't do. She pushed and shoved against the fog. It hurt, but she didn't give up.

It was an unmovable wall. That wouldn't do.

She slammed against the fog. Harder and harder, until she was certain that if she were hitting a real wall, she would have dislocated her shoulder.

Eventually, her perseverance paid off.

A crack broke through the darkness, a sliver that soon let light flood in.

Events flashed through her mind, slowly at first but picking up speed like a snowball rolling down a hill. She'd entered the Hall of Choice and met Ryker. They dated. Then, he'd proposed.

The next thing Brynleigh remembered was the feeling of Ryker's lips on her neck, and then…

Oh gods.

Something had hit her. *Hard*. Pain, that strange mortal sensation that she'd rarely felt since her Making, had swallowed her. Demolished her.

And then she'd tumbled into blackness.

She'd been hurt. Maybe even killed? Brynleigh wasn't certain. She didn't feel dead, but then again, it was hard to tell. Vampires weren't truly alive in the first place, so perhaps true death was simply... peace? But that didn't make sense because when vampires touched silver or were staked, they screamed.

That was the mystery at hand.

Brynleigh was certain of one thing: when Ryker touched her, she felt alive. They had taken a leisurely stroll down a dangerous, forbidden path the night of the Masked Ball. Would she have let him go further if they hadn't been interrupted?

Before, Brynleigh would have said no. But now...

Maybe.

There was no denying the fact that her body desired Ryker's. She'd practically melted against him when they danced. But that was nothing but a physical reaction to his physique, right?

Good, old-fashioned lust. That's all it was. Lust was a completely normal, absolutely valid response when presented with someone as handsome as Ryker. There was nothing wrong with that.

Yes, there is, a small voice in the back of her mind reminded her. *He murdered your family. How could you forget that?*

The voice was right. Ryker wasn't hers to lust after. How could Brynleigh have forgotten who Ryker was, even for a moment?

She was definitely going to hell for this. Then again, it wasn't like she was perfect.

Brynleigh had done many bad things in her life, especially after Jelisette Made her. Why not add one more sin on top of it? Especially when the other person looked like Ryker Waterborn.

Maybe it wouldn't be so bad. Maybe she could—

"It's time to wake up, B," a familiar masculine voice said near her ear.

Zanri. She would recognize the shifter's voice anywhere. That had to mean she wasn't dead, right? They were friends, but she'd never dreamed about the shifter.

A hand gripped her shoulder, the touch just on this side of pain. "Wake up. We don't have long."

Brynleigh hitched a breath. It felt like fiery needles were being jabbed into her.

Well, at least now she knew this was real.

"Fuck, that hurts." Brynleigh opened her eyes, wincing at the bright light right above her. Her vision was blurry, which was an unusual event that hadn't occurred since her Making, and she blinked several times to clear it. "What happened?"

The shifter canted his head. Auburn scruff covered his face, and shadows hung beneath his eyes. "A bomb went off, and you were hit with a shard of prohiberis-lined silver. You don't remember?"

Another curse slipped from Brynleigh's lips. If her mother were still alive, she'd be shocked at how her daughter spoke. But she wasn't, so it didn't matter.

"Yeah, that was the same way Jelisette reacted." Zanri crossed his arms and looked down at Brynleigh. "You know, B, you're supposed to be getting ready to kill him, not get yourself killed."

"I know," she said through gritted teeth. "You think I planned to get blown up?" These gods-damned rebels were throwing a wrench in everything.

"Of course not." Zanri met her eyes, and a disapproving frown marred his features. "But I saw you with him, B. In the shadows."

When Ryker was kissing her neck...

Brynleigh's blood ran cold, and she gripped the sheets. The look in Zanri's eyes, the warning in his voice...

She whispered, "Did she see?"

Neither of them needed to clarify who Brynleigh was talking about.

Zanri held Brynleigh's gaze for a long moment before he sighed and shook his head. "No, she was talking with Representative DuBois at the time."

"Thank Isvana." Brynleigh blew out a sigh of relief and pushed herself up onto her elbows to take in the room. Even with the beeping equipment and screens surrounding the bed, this place was far fancier than the safe house. "Where are we?"

She should probably spend more time reassuring Zanri that she felt nothing for Ryker, but she was too tired to talk much right now. Words were hard to come by.

The longer Brynleigh was awake, the more she realized everything was muted. Dimmer than normal. Even her shadows were a gentle hum in her veins instead of the typical thrum they usually sang. If she hadn't just spent far too long battling against the fog to access her memories, she'd be concerned about that.

"The Lily." Zanri perched on the side of the bed. "Chancellor's orders. She moved everyone here after the bomb went off."

Brynleigh was surprised by that. "Even Jelisette?" The old vampire had an unusual attachment to the safe house. Brynleigh had never seen her stay anywhere else.

Whatever drew Jelisette there, she never spoke of it. Just like she never spoke of the reason she always wore long sleeves or she sometimes had a far-away, dead look in her eyes.

"No," Zanri chuckled. "Not even Ignatia Rose could make Jelisette do something she didn't want to. She and I are staying at the safe house."

That made sense.

Brynleigh took another look around. "It's... shiny."

She'd heard of this hotel, but she'd never been here before. It was far too expensive, and besides, vampires were rarely invited to establishments like this. To say the room was gilded would be a vast understatement. It was like someone had taken all the makings of a regular hotel room, dumped them in a pot of liquid money, and called it a day.

The bed frames were gold. The television stand was gold. The doorknobs? Gold. The entire space was luxury personified, and it was extremely obnoxious. The windowsills, the picture frames, even the gods-damned comforter shimmered when the light hit them.

This show of wealth was made even more disgusting by the fact that people were literally starving in the streets of Golden City. Little wonder she'd felt like she was in a cloud. It was a rich, golden one.

She understood why the rebels were attacking.

"Yes, it is. But focus, B." Zanri shook her shoulders roughly. "The medicine they're giving you makes you sleepy. The doctor said you'd only be awake for a few minutes."

Medicine? What medicine? She lifted her hand to grab his arm when she noticed the needle sticking out of her.

Brynleigh's gaze followed the tubing to a bag hanging beside the bed. There was no label on it, but the clear liquid was going into her body. All she knew was it wasn't blood. What were they giving her?

Ice filled her veins at the thought of something foreign being injected into her. She wanted to yank out the needle, but she was unsure of what would happen if she did.

"The rebels are getting bolder." Brynleigh's head felt like it weighed a thousand pounds. Her tongue was heavy.

Zanri nodded. "They are. They've been gaining traction over the past year or so, but this is…"

"More." She shifted to look at him, and her neck ached. She lifted a hand, feeling for an injury. Although her skin was sore, there weren't any wounds.

"Yes. Focus, Brynleigh."

"It's hard."

"I know. Jelisette gave you her blood at the party," Zanri explained. "After that, they brought you here to transfuse more. Even with all that, you almost died."

That black mist was returning. Paying attention was a monumental feat.

Brynleigh blinked, and now there were two Zanri's sitting beside her.

"I met him." She yawned, unable to hold it in.

Zanri's red brows furrowed. "The captain? I know you did. You're going to marry him in two weeks."

Her eyes shuttered. She fought to keep them open, but they weren't listening to her. "He seems so... nice."

"Fuck, Brynleigh. You can't talk like that. You don't know... you haven't seen the worst."

She wasn't listening to Zanri. Her cloud was so comfortable, and she was going to return to its fluffy embrace. "I think... I think I like him."

She might even more than like him.

Was this the medicine talking or something else? Brynleigh wasn't sure. But either way, it seemed like Zanri should know. Maybe he was her friend. He was here while she was sick, after all. That's what friends did, right?

Zanri grabbed Brynleigh's hand, and he gripped it so hard that she was certain it would bruise. "Listen to me. You can say that kind of stuff to me but don't ever let Jelisette hear you. Since you've been gone, she's been even more volatile than ever. You don't want to end up like me, B. Owing her..." His voice grew even more distant as Brynleigh fought to stay awake. "She's setting something up. Even if you..."

Darkness was a beast drawing Brynleigh into its black embrace once more.

THE NEXT TIME SHE WOKE, golden curtains were pulled back. The shimmering silver moon cast its light into the gilded room. Opening her eyes was easier this time, and the mist was gone from her head. Thank Isvana, the song of her shadows had returned and was as loud as ever. Their dark tune was a welcome symphony.

Brynleigh felt like herself.

Reaching over, she yanked the needle out of her arm. Whatever the medicine was, she no longer needed it. No, what she needed was to center herself. To do that, she needed more specifics about The Lily. What was the layout? Who was here? And perhaps most importantly, where was Ryker?

An urgent need pulsed within her, pushing her to find him. Because he was her mark. After all, it was good business practice for vampires to keep track of the people they intended to kill.

She glanced at the nightstand, searching for her phone, before remembering that she still didn't have it. She'd have to ask someone about that.

Step one: get a layout of the land.

Step two: find Ryker.

Step three: make a new, better plan. Probably something along the lines of adapting to her environment and grounding herself.

Zanri had said the weddings were in two weeks. That didn't give her long.

Step one would involve getting out of bed. That seemed like a good place to start.

Brynleigh glanced down and frowned as she took in her outfit. Her ballgown from earlier was gone—not surprising, based on how much blood she must've lost—and in its place was a black spaghetti-strap tank top and a pair of gray sleep shorts.

Comfortable, yes. Great for clandestine activities? Not so much. That didn't matter. While she preferred to wear leggings and hoodies when sneaking about, they weren't prerequisites for the endeavor.

A hairbrush sat on the gilded nightstand. She grabbed it and ran it through her knotted hair, trying to remove as many tangles as possible. When it became apparent that a shower would be required to return her hair to its prior silky state, she gave up and threw her hair into a messy bun on top of her head.

Then Brynleigh stood. She wobbled, her feet displaced with the task of bearing her weight once again, but she quickly righted herself. She released her shadows, letting them pour out of her. They were eager to play, crawling over her like a second skin until she was covered in darkness.

Brynleigh briefly considered the merits of shadowing to the safe house to talk with Jelisette before deciding that her initial plan was better. Besides, if The Lily was warded, there was a chance she would set off alarms by shadowing in and out. The last thing she wanted to do was bring attention to herself. Not only that, but there wasn't a guarantee that Jelisette would be at the safe house. The older vampire had a lively social life, and she had many contacts that even Brynleigh wasn't privy to.

Having decided, Brynleigh walked to the door on bare feet. The shadows absorbed the sound of her movements. She was as silent as the night itself.

The doorknob was cold in her hand as she curled her fingers around it and peered through the peephole.

Three figures cast in shadows stood in front of her door. This was a potential problem. She needed to leave the room the old-fashioned, mortal way: on foot. She couldn't shadow to another part of The Lily because she had never been here before. Traveling through the Void was a valuable skill, but it only allowed vampires to return to locations they'd previously been.

Silently cursing, Brynleigh assessed the obstacle in front of her. Two of them were clearly guards. They wore the same black uniforms as the soldiers who'd guarded them during the Choosing. The Republic's insignia was on their chests. Black guns were at their sides.

But the third...

Brynleigh inhaled deeply. Thunderstorms and bergamot flooded her nostrils.

At the same time, the last man took a step closer to the other two.

Ryker.

Her stomach somersaulted. That was a problem. So was the way her heart sped up at the sight of him. Inwardly, she groaned. To say that these bodily reactions were quickly getting frustrating would be an understatement of epic proportions.

Brynleigh had never experienced anything like this before. Why was it happening now, around the captain? It was utterly inconvenient and had to come to a quick end.

Forcing those ridiculous, out-of-place emotions aside—desire had no place here, only revenge—Brynleigh focused on the scene unfolding outside her room. Usually, she was able to hear through doors without any issue, but there must have been some protective barriers over this one to muffle sound.

Still, she picked out her fae's voice. Wait. No. Not her fae. *The* fae. Despite what Brynleigh had said to Valentina, she had no real claim to the captain except that she wanted to kill him.

"Let me in. I need to see her," Ryker said.

The guard with auburn scruff shook his head. "... orders... needs to rest... her Maker."

Ryker crossed his arms, his muscles bulging under his black t-shirt. Fuck, that shouldn't look so attractive. "I'm... superior officer..."

The guards glanced at each other and whispered.

Isvana must have been smiling on Brynleigh tonight. This obstacle wouldn't be difficult to overcome, after all.

Tuning out the guards, she dropped her cloak of shadows and retracted the darkness. She reached over and unlocked the door.

"Good evening, gentlemen," she said primly, as though she weren't dressed in nightclothes.

The guards straightened and turned towards her. Their hands

fell to their sides, and they dipped their heads, murmuring greetings beneath their breath.

"I didn't realize you were awake, miss," Auburn Scruff said.

"I just woke up," Brynleigh replied. Then, there were no more words because her gaze drifted over the guards and landed on Ryker's.

The moment their eyes met, it was like worlds smashed together. Intensity and longing filled his chocolate orbs and stole her breath. Her core twisted as he devoured her with a single look. His eyes shone brightly as if he were a dying man, and looking at her was the only cure to his ailment.

Brynleigh's heart slammed violently against her chest. For several long seconds, she forgot to breathe. She moved to step towards him before she realized what she was doing. *Who* she was moving toward.

Gods-damn it.

She swallowed and grabbed the doorframe, forcing her eyes away from his. Breaking his stare was physically painful, but it had to be done.

It's just a physical reaction, she reminded herself. *That's all.*

Brynleigh would keep telling herself that until she believed it... or until he was dead beneath her, his lifeless eyes staring into hers one last time.

She refused to allow this to be anything but a physical response.

Those urges she felt? The desire to move towards him and let him hold her? The deepest need to seek refuge in his embrace? Just impulses that she wouldn't act on.

How hard could it be? Brynleigh would erect a few barriers and set some boundaries, and she'd be good to go.

Yes. Boundaries were a good, solid amendment to her plan.

Hand holding? Fine, she'd have to allow it. Ryker would probably be suspicious of her if she didn't.

Touching, though? Nope.

Kissing? Not a fucking chance.

This was a game, and these boundaries would help her get her act together. She desperately needed them to work.

Brynleigh forced a smile on her face. "Hi."

In her mind, she chanted, *Boundaries,* repeatedly, until it was all she could hear.

Ryker's lips tilted up, and the stern expression he'd been wearing moments ago melted away. He pushed past the guards and took Brynleigh's hands in his.

She leaned into his warm touch before she remembered that it went against her newly created boundaries. She straightened her back so fast; she was surprised it didn't crack.

"Hello, sweetheart." Ryker's gaze searched hers, those swirling depths of emotions still present. His fingers swept over the back of her knuckles, and he drew her towards him. "How are you feeling?"

Honestly?

She was fucked.

That was the first thing that came to mind. All the boundaries, all the rules, and all the reinforcements she'd rebuilt dissipated the moment his hand touched hers.

How could something so simple be so incredibly powerful? What was it about this fae that made her entire world turn upside down? She wasn't sure, but it was dangerous.

If Brynleigh were being honest with Ryker, she'd confess that he confused her. She didn't understand him at all. He was a powerful fae—proven not only by his rank in the army and the storms he commanded but also by the deference these guards showed him—but he was kind to her. A vampire.

Even though she knew better, what had begun as a kernel of doubt grew each time she interacted with Ryker.

Was there a bigger picture she wasn't seeing?

There were the facts: a storm hit Chavin. That was indisputable. Brynleigh had been there, seen the water and death and destruction. She'd also seen two shadowy figures, one tall and dark, the other slender and much shorter, standing on the edge of the forest as she floated, dying as her lungs drank in more and more water.

But what if...

Actually, no.

Brynleigh couldn't do this right now. She stomped on that kernel of doubt, smashing it to smithereens. It was Ryker. Who else could it be? It wasn't as if the Republic of Balance was overrun by water fae. Very few of them were powerful enough to summon a hurricane like that, especially so far inland.

It. Was. Him.

There was no other option.

Seeing as how she couldn't confess all that to Ryker, she tilted her head and smiled softly at him. "I'm a little worn out."

It was true. It must've been the emotions. They plagued her, draining her unlike anything else she'd ever experienced. She gathered them up and shoved them down. Like all the others, these would have to wait their turn.

She could unpack them after he was dead.

Maybe it was normal to feel some level of doubt. Maybe it was good. A sign she hadn't lost all traces of her humanity. She could not forget that this was an act. None of this was real, except for the fact that he'd killed her family.

Yes. That was a good, boundary-strengthening thought. Brynleigh latched onto it.

Ryker reached up and cupped her cheek. It took everything she had to remain rigid.

Boundaries. See? They worked.

"Do you need more blood? Sleep? What can I do for you?" he asked.

Her fangs ached at the suggestion. She didn't think he was offering to let her bite him—and even if he was, it was definitely off the table because biting was an inherently sexual act reserved only for lovers in this modern age—but it was sweet that he recognized her hunger.

Brynleigh paused. What? She never thought anything was

sweet. Maybe she wasn't feeling so great after all. Maybe the medicine from earlier was addling her senses.

Actually, now that she thought about it, that seemed plausible. Could drugs make vampires doubt everything and forget their murderous purposes? Probably.

She latched onto the thought like it was a lifeline, and she was drowing. That's all this was. Just the drugs. She needed to sleep them off.

"More sleep." Abandoning her plan to explore The Lily, because now it seemed monumentally stupid, Brynleigh moved backward until she felt the reassuring curved doorknob behind the small of her back. She grabbed it, thankful the door hadn't slipped shut. "You're right, I'm... tired."

Ryker leaned forward, and despite their audience, he brushed his lips over hers.

It wasn't a kiss, she reasoned. Not really. It was a peck. It didn't count.

Her boundaries were still in place.

No kissing, starting *now*.

"Maybe tomorrow, we can find Hallie and Therian?" Brynleigh asked.

Group settings were good. They should avoid being alone as much as possible. She could respect her boundaries and see her friend. It was a win-win situation.

"I'd like that," Ryker said. "I'll see what I can do."

They finished making plans, and he scribbled his phone number down on a piece of paper for her to program into her phone when she found it before they said goodbye. Thank the gods, her boundaries remained intact.

Brynleigh slipped back into the room and turned all the locks. She leaned against the door, breathing heavily. Damn her body. Damn the pull she felt towards Ryker. Damn it all.

Several minutes went by before her heart rate returned to normal, and her lips stopped tingling from Ryker's non-kiss.

Two weeks.

She could do this.

First step: sleep.

Drawing the curtains closed, because the last thing she needed was to be burned by the sun when it rose, she stumbled back to bed and collapsed on the cloud-like mattress.

Even as her eyes fluttered shut, the unwelcome memory of Ryker's lips on hers haunted her.

CHAPTER 25
Welcome Home

"You'll be at the big house for dinner tonight, right?" River gripped Ryker's hand with surprising force, and her painted black nails dug into his skin.

A week had passed since the bombing. Today, Ryker's sister wore an all-black ensemble with as many cut-outs as fabric. It was... a choice, to be certain. One that Ryker didn't necessarily approve of.

"We'll be there." He squeezed his sister's hand reassuringly. "Is being alone with Mom and Dad so bad?"

River frowned. "Yes, it is. If you're not there, Mom will yell at me about my piercings. Again."

Ryker's sister and mother had a tumultuous relationship, at best. He'd seen more than a few of their fights, which usually lasted for hours.

This morning, things had been quiet. Not because the women had worked out their differences but because the Chancellor had finally given them the go-ahead to leave The Lily.

"You know, if you stopped provoking her, things would be easier." It wasn't a secret that Tertia hated the way her daughter marked up her body. Ryker was fairly certain River did it to anger their mother. "Can't you get through a single dinner without fighting?"

"No." River shook her head. "We cannot. We clash at every turn. You know this."

River's aptitude for lateness was only overshadowed by her desire to argue with their mother. Her first word had been no, and she hadn't stopped since then. Cyrus had been the buffer, and now, the duty fell to Ryker.

"I do. I promise we will be there on time." He embraced his sister. "Have I ever let you down?"

River shook her head. "Never, not once."

"Exactly." Ryker kissed her forehead. "I'm taking Brynleigh to the apartment to meet Marlowe, and then we'll head over for dinner."

Ryker was completely done with hotel life. During the past seven days, the participants had been under constant guard—for their own safety, according to Chancellor Rose—so he and Brynleigh hadn't even had a moment alone together.

She had gotten her phone back from the guards, though, and they'd been texting daily. The messages had been short, but they were the highlights of his day... other than when they were together.

Being near his vampire and keeping his hands to himself was slowly killing Ryker. When he signed up for the Choosing, he knew about the laws that kept couples out of the bedroom until their wedding night—some archaic purity bullshit that had no real ramifications in this modern time—but he hadn't considered the effects it would have on him.

Delayed gratification was one thing, but this was pure torture. The sooner Brynleigh was his, the better.

"Good," River said sternly. "Don't be late."

Ryker bellowed a laugh. "That's rich, coming from you."

His sister's reputation for lateness was renowned. She'd have to figure out a way around that before she graduated and started working as a doctor. He couldn't imagine hospitals were very forgiving of tardiness, especially from their staff.

"I live with Mom and Dad," she said primly. "I can't be late to my own house."

"Debatable." If anyone could do it, it was River.

She wisely ignored his comment. "When I video-called Dad yesterday, I told him you were coming. He's going to be so happy to see you."

Ryker hoped so. He had held off introducing Brynleigh to his mother and sister because he wanted his fiancée to meet his entire family at once. He hoped they would love her as much as he did. She was his perfect match in every way.

"How is Dad? Are the new meds working?" Gods, he wanted that more than anything. The Stillness had been around for so long that it was practically the fifth member of the Waterborn family while it slowly stole their father's life. He fucking despised it.

River nodded slowly. "It seems that way." Her voice shifted, taking on an academic quality he was familiar with. For all her rebellious streaks, River excelled at science and medicine. "This new study is groundbreaking, and the treatment combines several drugs."

"Gods, if this works—"

"It would be incredible," River finished, a small smile creeping on her face. "I agree."

Ryker took his sister's hand and drew her close. "Did you release some magic this morning?"

The last thing he wanted to do was bring Brynleigh into a potentially dangerous situation.

River sighed. "Yes, Ryker." She drew out his name, just like she had when she was younger. "I did it today like I have every single morning since... you know."

He knew exactly what she was talking about. "Good. Don't let it build up."

"I won't." A flash of pain went through her eyes before they shuttered. "I'll never forget, Ryker. Even if you don't remind me, I'll always remember. I live with it every day. All those people..."

She looked up at him with wide brown eyes, her unspoken words echoing in the air. *It won't happen again.*

Watching his sister wrestle with the burden of her magic pained Ryker. He helped as much as he could, but he knew River struggled with the weight of her gods-given gifts. Her piercings, her fashion choices, and even her attitude towards their mother were all ways of coping with the hand she'd been dealt.

River's phone rang, the upbeat, boisterous pop tune shattering the silence. Ryker didn't recognize the song. Moments like these reminded him that nearly two decades separated the two of them.

River glanced at the screen before shoving her phone in her pocket. The heaviness from a few moments ago dissolved as River stood on her tiptoes and kissed Ryker's cheek. "Got to go; my ride's here. See you at dinner."

She bent to pick up her suitcases, but Ryker grabbed them before she could. What kind of man would he be if he let his little sister carry her own bags out of the hotel? "Go on, I've got them."

River grinned and grabbed her purse—black, like the rest of her outfit—before holding the door for him. She chattered as they rode the elevator to the main floor, explaining more about the new drug their father was on.

The captain helped his sister into the taxi and loaded the suitcases in the back. She smiled as she closed the door, opening the window to shout one final reminder to come to dinner tonight.

Slipping his hands into his pockets, Ryker strolled into The Lily. He felt lighter than he had in years. His sister was happy and safe; her magic wasn't causing any problems, and tonight, he would introduce Brynleigh to the family.

What could go wrong?

One of the first lessons Ryker had learned as a youngling was that staring was rude, but he couldn't seem to stop. Brynleigh sat beside him in the car, silently gazing out the window, and his eyes were locked on her.

His bride-to-be was stunning. Like him, she was dressed casually. Unlike him, she looked like she'd walked off the pages of a magazine.

She wore an oversized maroon sweater that fell to mid-thigh and black leggings that hugged her legs. There were two slits in her sweater, which he assumed was an accommodation for her wings, although they weren't visible. Her chin rested on her hand as she looked out the blackened car window. Her blonde hair hung over her shoulders, and she wore a minimal amount of makeup.

He couldn't believe she was marrying him. She was a goddess of the night, and he was... himself. Barely worthy of being in her presence. Gods, he loved this woman. Now that he had said the words, he couldn't seem to stop.

Ryker held Brynleigh's other hand, and he rubbed his thumb over the back of her palm. She hadn't spoken much since he'd helped her into the darkened vehicle half an hour ago. The silence didn't bother him. He was at ease in Brynleigh's presence, and the quiet lacked all traces of awkwardness. It was companionable, peaceful, and everything he had hoped for.

Davis, the driver Ryker's mother insisted on paying for, had picked the couple up in The Lily's underground parking garage to avoid the sun. Admittedly, it would take time for Ryker to get used to staying out of the sun, but he was willing to do whatever it took to keep Brynleigh in his life. If she asked him to become fully nocturnal, he would do it. He certainly wouldn't be the first person in history to alter his lifestyle for vampires.

Besides, what was a bit of change when the person you were changing for was your whole world?

And Brynleigh was Ryker's entire world. In the six weeks since they met, she'd catapulted into the first-place position in his life. He couldn't imagine living without her. Watching her bleeding out on the ballroom floor had solidified how important she was to him.

Brynleigh was meant to be Ryker's. There was something so profoundly *right* about the two of them. Their connection was deep and wasn't built on superficial things like appearances. He had the Choosing to thank for that.

He felt like he knew everything about Brynleigh. Her likes and dislikes. Things she missed (the sun, no surprise there) and things she enjoyed doing (playing chess.) He knew her birth family was dead, although she never spoke of what happened to them, and her Maker was her only real connection to the world.

He hoped she would come to see his family as her own.

Ryker had many dreams for the future, and they all revolved around the blonde vampire beside him.

The car slowed, and the familiar sights of Ryker's neighbourhood came into view. He tugged Brynleigh's hand. "We're here, sweetheart."

The car stopped in front of a ten-story apartment building complex surrounded by flourishing gardens.

Brynleigh looked out the window, then back at Ryker. "This is your home?"

"Our home," he corrected softly, squeezing her hand. "Or at least, it can be if you like it. If not, I'm sure we can find something else. It's just... this is a good location. We're halfway to the base and halfway to my family home. But if you want to move, we'll move. We can do whatever you want after we're married."

Something dark flickered in Brynleigh's eyes. It was too quick for Ryker to be certain, but he could have sworn he glimpsed intense longing and regret in her black gaze. But that couldn't be right. It was gone before he could decipher it.

"How long have you lived here?" She looked back at the apartment complex, but her grip tightened on his hand.

"Just over a decade."

He'd moved here after his Maturation, eager to have his own

place. Tertia had protested, of course. She wasn't delighted by the idea of her son, a future Representative of the Fae, living in such "downtrodden" conditions. He hadn't given in. He needed his privacy.

Besides, it wasn't like Ryker lived in a shack. His one-bedroom apartment was nice and clean, and he could afford it on his military salary without dipping into the family coffers. It was in a good part of Golden City but not in the luxurious neighborhood where his parents lived.

Even though Tertia was born with a silver spoon in her mouth and believed everyone in her family should live in a mansion filled with servants, Ryker disagreed. He didn't hate how he grew up—on the contrary, he'd had a good childhood—but he loved his apartment. This, and his hunting cabin, were his safe spaces.

This apartment was his. Maybe, with some work, it could be *theirs.*

That idea made Ryker smile. Raising his fist, he rapped on the roof. Davis would understand his signal. The car started moving again, and they rolled into the underground parking lot, where the sun's deadly rays couldn't touch Brynleigh.

The vehicle stopped, and the door slammed, signifying Davis's departure. Ryker reached over and unbuckled Brynleigh's seatbelt. Earlier, he'd told Davis they would be here for several hours. The driver was meeting a friend nearby for lunch and would return to take them to Waterborn House.

But for now, they were alone.

Ryker tugged Brynleigh across the seat and over to him. She didn't protest as he cupped her cheeks, his gaze searching hers.

"I love you," he murmured. "And I'm so glad you agreed to marry me."

Brynleigh seemed to wrestle over her words for a minute before her fingers tightened around his. "Me too," she breathed, licking her lips. "I... I'm looking forward to our wedding."

Her voice cracked on the last word, but he assumed she was as anxious for their marriage as him. He just wanted to get it over with, to finally claim her as his in every way.

"So am I," he whispered.

Her fingers gripped his as if she never wanted to let him go.

Ryker would gladly remain with her. He laid a hand over hers and inched closer. "I want to kiss you, Brynleigh."

This was the moment he'd been waiting for. The cameras were gone, and for the first time, they were truly alone.

She hitched a breath, and her mouth opened, giving him a peek at her fangs. Gods, the sight of those sharp teeth sent a bolt of want through him. He had always noticed the unnatural beauty of vampires, but none of them had ever affected him the way Brynleigh did.

"You do?" Brynleigh's cheeks heated, which only added to her beauty.

He loved that she was flustered because of him.

"Yes," he breathed. He moved closer but still gave her room. "Is that okay?"

Her eyes searched his for the longest moment until she dipped her head in the briefest of nods.

Ryker had dreamed of this moment. Some nights, he had barely slept because his desire to taste her was so strong. And now, he finally could. Holding her gaze, his hand slipped behind her neck as he drew her close. His heart sped up and his entire being focused on Brynleigh.

He slanted his mouth over hers. Their lips met in an embrace that was at once gentle but powerful.

But it was... one-sided.

This wasn't the kiss he'd dreamed about. Brynleigh was a frozen statue next to him. She didn't move, let alone breathe.

His heart stalled in his chest. Had he done something wrong? Had he misread her consent?

Those beautiful eyes stared at him, unblinking. There was something in the depth of her gaze that he didn't understand. Dark. Strange. A flicker of... fear? Was she scared of him? Gods, he hoped that wasn't the case. He would never do anything to hurt her.

She was his.

Again, Ryker moved his lips tentatively over hers.

She still didn't react.

This was not how he thought this would go.

Ryker was about to pull away, to apologize and ask what was wrong, when Brynleigh muttered something that sounded awfully similar to "Fuck it" under her breath.

He had no time to be confused because whatever decision she reached meant she was no longer frozen beneath him. She transformed in the blink of an eye. No longer a stone sculpture, now she was a living flame, destined to burn him from the inside out. She returned his kiss with an urgent, fiery passion they had yet to explore.

By the fucking Sands, yes. *This* was the kiss he'd dreamed of. Brynleigh slid onto Ryker's lap, straddling him. She threaded her fingers through his hair and moaned his name against his lips.

Fuck, that sound went straight to Ryker's cock. He abandoned his confusion and held her close. He needed her now more than ever.

Evidently, Brynleigh felt the same. Their mouths fused in an ardent embrace. She kissed him like he was the air she needed to breathe; like she was dying and he was the only way she'd survive; like he was a bad decision that she couldn't keep herself from making.

He couldn't tell where his mouth ended and hers began. Their kiss deepened. She embraced him in a way that no one else ever had, and by the Obsidian Sands, he loved each and every moment.

Ryker would never get enough of this—of her.

His hand slipped from her neck to her hip, and he wrapped his other arm around her and held her close. She moaned, rubbing herself against his hardening length.

"Gods, Brynleigh," he groaned against her lips.

Their clothes were an unwanted barrier between them. He wanted to rip off each offending piece of fabric and lay her bare before him.

"I want you," she breathed against his mouth. "I know we shouldn't, but…"

"I want you, too." He could barely remember how to form words; her scent was so intoxicating. "Fucking archaic laws."

Whose damned idiotic idea was it to keep couples apart until their wedding night? It was completely moronic.

And Ryker *liked* rules. A lot. It pained him to acknowledge how ridiculous this one was.

Still, even without the law, Ryker knew their first time together wouldn't be in the back of a car. He had far bigger plans for them than that.

"It's horrible." She embraced him again, and they both lost themselves to the passion burning between them.

They kissed and kissed. Hands wandered. Their bodies rubbed against each other. Lust was a blazing fire between them.

Ryker gave Brynleigh control for a few minutes, even though letting someone else lead wasn't in his nature. Eventually, though, he needed more. He swept his tongue over the seam of her lips, and a groan ran through him as she parted them, granting him access.

At his first taste of her, his hand on her hip tightened. The rightness of the moment flooded him. Brynleigh tasted like shadows, the night, and the subtlest hint of oranges.

She tasted like she was always meant to be his.

His tongue swept through her mouth and grazed her fangs. The sound that left her lips was utterly delectable, and she ground herself against him wantonly.

At that moment, Ryker knew he would never kiss another woman again. How could he?

This was it for him—*she* was it for him.

Any control he might have had snapped when she nipped his

bottom lip. It wasn't strong enough to draw blood, but it didn't matter.

His fingers slipped beneath the waistband of her leggings, seeking the warmth hidden between her legs. She moaned, her head arching and exposing the column of her neck as he ran the back of his knuckles against her sensitive flesh.

"Ry, don't tease me." She shifted in his lap.

He kissed her. "What do you want?"

He knew what he wanted but wouldn't do anything without her consent.

Her eyes darkened as they met his. "Touch me."

Those words. He'd fantasized about hearing her say them since their very first date. How could he deny her?

Capturing her lips with his once more, Ryker swept aside her underwear and ran his fingers over her. Touching. Teasing. He went everywhere except that warm heat that beckoned to him.

Brynleigh bucked. "Please, Ryker."

It was all the encouragement he needed. He slid one finger into her inviting warmth, letting the heat from her core envelope him. He groaned against her lips. She was so tight and wet and fucking perfect.

Gods, she would feel so good against his cock. It was that thought that had him adding another finger. He crooked them in a beckoning motion, and she gasped.

He kissed her mouth, her jaw, and her neck as his fingers thrust in and out of her heat. She writhed against him, begging him for more.

Each time his name fell from her lips, each moment she asked for more, his love for her deepened. The sounds Brynleigh made would forever be imprinted on his mind.

His thumb found her clit, and he rubbed it. She screamed.

He captured the sound with his mouth, swallowing her cries as he brought her closer and closer to the edge. Her fingers dug into his hair as if she was afraid that he would disappear on her and leave her wanting.

Never. He wouldn't leave her.

He added another finger, and she moaned. Her walls fluttered against him.

"I'm so close," she gasped, her words little more than air.

"Let go," he told her. "I've got you."

He held her, his fingers bringing her closer and closer to the precipice of oblivion until she shattered with a final scream. Still, he didn't move, letting her ride out of the waves of pleasure on his hand.

Brynleigh gripped his shoulders, panting as she came down from the high of what they'd just done. Only then did he remove his fingers from her warmth, sliding her leggings back into place.

Brynleigh's beautiful black gaze watched him as he lifted his hand. He opened his mouth and licked his fingers.

"By the Sands, you taste so good," he groaned, nearly losing the last strands of his restraint.

He licked every last bit of her off him. This was but an appetizer, he reminded himself. She was his, and this was their first moment of many to come.

Ryker couldn't wait to have Brynleigh spread out on the bed in front of him, naked and glistening. He would spend an eternity between her legs, feasting on her. She would be all he needed.

The only thing stopping Ryker from carrying Brynleigh upstairs to have his way with her, rules be damned, was that Atlas and Marlowe were waiting for them.

With a groan that reverberated through his entire body, Ryker lifted Brynleigh off him. Their chests heaved, and the air was thick with the scent of desire as they stared at each other.

Long, endless seconds went by.

"We should go inside." He didn't want to.

She studied him, running her tongue over her bottom lip, before nodding slowly. "Alright."

There was a rasp to her voice that made him feel alive. *He* did that to her. No one else. This moment was theirs and theirs alone.

It took every ounce of strength Ryker had to get out of the

car. He held the door for Brynleigh and extended his hand. She adjusted her leggings and took his hand, their fingers sliding together as he helped her out of the vehicle.

"Who knew you were such a gentleman, Ry?" she teased, letting go of his hand to straighten her sweater.

He grinned, closing the car door behind her. Davis would bring up his suitcases later. "Perhaps I'm a man of many secrets."

Not a lie. Between his job and looking after his family, Ryker was the caretaker of more secrets than he'd like. Hopefully, in the future, he could share those with Brynleigh. He wanted his wife to be his partner in every way, someone who could help carry his burdens and share every aspect of his life.

"Is that so?"

"It is."

"It so happens I like secrets." She brushed her hair over her shoulder and slid her hand into his. "Take me home, Captain Waterborn."

Gods, he loved the sound of that. "With pleasure, sweetheart."

CHAPTER 26
Tendrils of Doubt

What the hell was wrong with Brynleigh? She'd worked so hard to build up her boundaries, only to let Ryker completely demolish them in a single moment. A very good, pleasurable moment, but still a moment.

Many things could happen in a moment. People were born. Others died. Lovers declared their affection. Killers took their final blows.

And Brynleigh?

She gave Ryker control over her body. She let him bring her to immense pleasure.

A thousand curses ran through her mind. She barely paid attention as Ryker led her into the elevator, barely noticed that he still held her hand. All she could do was think about what they'd done in the car. She needed to rebuild the wall between them, and this time, she would respect them.

It didn't matter that Ryker made her feel better than anyone else or that she'd come harder on his fingers than she'd ever been able to do alone.

It didn't matter that when they'd kissed—really, truly kissed for the first time—it was like the world exploded behind her eyes.

And it really didn't matter that his touch sparked things within her that she had absolutely no business feeling.

This was a game. She had one purpose. One reason for being here.

Brynleigh was just having a gods-damned difficult time remembering what that was.

Get through today. The thought churned through her mind. She could do this. In less than twelve hours, after dinner with Ryker's family tonight, Brynleigh would return to the safe house.

That was good. Once she was on familiar ground, she would have an easier time remembering her purpose. It would ground her. And after spending the past week in The Lily and what they'd done in the car, she needed that more than ever.

By the time the elevator dinged, Brynleigh was ready.

In an action that was becoming as familiar as tying her shoes, she collected all her emotions—there were more every gods-damned time she was around the captain—and got rid of them.

Just in time, too.

Ryker's thumb brushed against the back of her hand as they stepped out of the elevator. He led her down the hallway, pointing at several doors and naming the neighbors who lived in each space.

It looked like a clean, comfortable building, although the designer didn't seem to realize there were other colors besides brown and beige. Everything, from the carpet beneath their feet to the ceiling above their heads, was a dull, muted shade. It wasn't Brynleigh's favorite, but since she had no actual plans to reside here—Ryker would be dead before she officially moved in—it didn't matter.

They were halfway down the hall when a loud bark came from further down. Brynleigh tensed, but Ryker didn't seem concerned. In fact, he seemed... happier. They rounded the corner as a door opened at the end of the corridor.

An enormous inky lump of fur the size of a bear cub barreled towards them. It woofed, and then, two massive paws landed on

Brynleigh's chest. She stumbled back at the impact, her back slamming into the wall. A slobbery tongue ran up her face, and the black furry monster nuzzled her cheek.

"Down, Marlowe." Ryker's stern voice left no room for discussion. "Let your new mom say hello."

Brynleigh's eyes widened as the bear—no, the dog—listened immediately. Marlowe sat in front of her, his tail thumping against the ground in obvious delight. His pink tongue lolled out of his mouth, and he looked up at Brynleigh with big, brown eyes.

"This is Marlowe?" She peeled herself off the wall. "You said he was a dog, not a bear."

Fae couldn't lie, but this animal was... enormous. Far bigger than she had expected.

A booming laugh left Ryker's lips and echoed around the hallway. "Marlie is an Eleytan Mountain Dog. They're..."

"Gigantic," Brynleigh finished for him. She hadn't known they made canines this huge.

A tall, red-headed fae with tattoos on his neck and arms jogged out of the open doorway, holding an empty blue leash in his hands. "Sorry, Ryker. I tried to keep him in, but you know how he is."

"No worries, Atlas, no harm done," said Ryker.

Pieces clicked into place. Ryker had spoken about the earth fae several times, and now she could put a face to the name.

Ryker slung an arm over Brynleigh's shoulder and kissed her cheek. "Atlas, this is my beautiful fiancée."

She waved awkwardly. "Hi."

"Atlas is a pain in the ass, dog-watcher extraordinaire, and he's also one of my oldest friends." Ryker nodded in the earth fae's direction.

"Nice to meet you." Atlas put out his hand, and Brynleigh shook it.

Even though Atlas was objectively handsome, with his tattoos and muscles for days, Brynleigh didn't feel a single twinge of attraction toward him. Not like she did for Ryker. When the water fae touched her, it was like she was burning up from the inside out.

Damn it all to hell. That probably meant something, but like everything else lately, Brynleigh shoved all those emotions down, down, down until she was somewhat numb.

No matter what, Ryker was still her family's murderer, and she would still kill him.

"Here, Marlowe," Atlas called.

The dog trotted after to the fae, his tail wagging. Smiling, Ryker put his hand on Brynleigh's back and led her into a small mudroom. Shoes sat on racks, and several jackets hung on hooks. A picture of Ryker and Marlowe was on the wall. The two of them were posing together, surrounded by pine trees. A shining blue lake was behind them. It seemed impossible, but between the relaxed posture and the grin on Ryker's face, he looked even more handsome than before.

More emotions went away. The box threatened to burst open right then and there.

That wouldn't do.

Desperate and in need of a new solution so she could survive this, Brynleigh decided she would try being numb. If she didn't acknowledge the emotions, they couldn't bother her.

That was good.

Numbness was the answer. She needed it to work.

If Brynleigh weren't numb, watching Ryker love on Marlowe and shower him with hugs and slobbery kisses would've tugged on her heartstrings. If she weren't numb, her smile and laugh would've been genuine when Ryker and Atlas shared stories about how they met in high school. And if she weren't numb, her insides would've warmed when Atlas pulled out his phone and showed her a picture of the two gangly fae as teenagers with big glasses and stacks of books in their arms. Ryker had certainly grown up since then.

But since she was numb, they didn't affect her. Nope. Not at all.

She was numb. Empty. A void. That's what she told herself.

Her heart certainly didn't grow three sizes when Ryker crouched down and hugged Marlowe, letting the dog give him a series of wet embraces before Atlas took him out.

That didn't happen.

She was ice. Emotionless. She focused on rebuilding her boundaries, brick by fucking brick.

A crack appeared in the cold, numb veneer when the door closed, and Ryker's hand landed on the small of her back. "Ready for your tour of the apartment?"

They were still in the mudroom.

"Yes." A blatant lie. Brynleigh was not ready for this. She should turn and run.

Was it too much to pray for a sudden illness? Something to stop this from happening. If she were mortal, she could claim food poisoning. Alas, she hadn't eaten anything.

Brynleigh supposed she could kill Ryker now, but there were witnesses. They'd seen her come up, and it was unlikely she'd get out of the apartment complex before being caught. It was daytime, which severely limited her escape routes.

And then there was the added complication that Brynleigh didn't want to kill Ryker. *Yet*. Following the plan was the best course of action. No need to act irrationally.

There was definitely no other reason she was hesitating.

"Welcome home, sweetheart." Ryker opened the door to the main apartment and held it for her.

One step was all it took for the ice around Brynleigh's heart to melt. Her boundaries? Smashed into smithereens. Her resolve to stay numb? Gone.

She stood in the doorway, unable to move. Her heart slammed against her chest, and she stared at the windows.

Ryker had assured Brynleigh that she would be safe in his apartment. She had believed him, expecting to see blackout curtains stretched across the windows to block the sun's deadly rays. That's what most people did.

This, though? This was far more than that.

Every single windowpane had been replaced with high-quality black glass. Specialty material that she'd heard of but never seen. And it wasn't like there was only one window. No. The corner apartment had an entire wall that looked out onto the balcony, and another large set of windows was over the sink in the kitchen.

Having this done on short notice must have cost Ryker an Isvana-damned fortune.

Brynleigh's feet were approaching the windows before she realized what was happening. She navigated around the leather couch and placed her palm on the tinted glass. Her breath caught in her throat, and she looked outside. She couldn't have torn away her gaze, even if she tried.

For the first time in six years, she saw the sun. It was muted and had grayish tones, but there was no doubting what it was. She fixated on that yellow orb. Gods help her, but she'd missed it so damn much. Her vision blurred.

"Fuck," she muttered, wiping a finger under her eyes.

She wasn't supposed to feel anything. This wasn't supposed to be real.

Except… Ryker had given her the sun. The one thing she missed most since her Making. How was she supposed to ignore that?

This unexpected gift was the single most thoughtful thing anyone had ever done for her.

Several minutes passed in silence. Ryker walked up behind her, his footsteps quiet as if they were in a temple. Neither of them spoke.

Brynleigh drank in the view. The sun. From this vantage point, the golden arches that gave Golden City its name were visible in the distance.

Eventually, Ryker moved. His chest pressed against her back, and his hands landed on her hips as he rested his chin on her shoulder. He didn't disturb her, didn't try to talk. He let her look at the sun for as long as she needed.

Minutes passed.

Heat bloomed in Brynleigh, and a feeling that she had absolutely no business experiencing came to life within her. She didn't even bother identifying it. She bundled it up along with everything else and shoved it down, down, down.

At this rate, Brynleigh would be a cold, numb, emotionless vampire when she married Ryker. Maybe that was for the best. Her emotions and her body were both clearly confused, having forgotten why this was the best course—the only course—for her vengeance.

Even now, Jelisette's voice echoed in Brynleigh's head.

Not only will killing the reclusive captain on your wedding night be poetic vengeance for the death of your family, but it will teach all the Representatives a lesson. From that moment until the end of time, they will always be watching, always waiting for the next hit. Because of you.

Brynleigh had heard the rhetoric a hundred times. She knew it by heart. It used to sound so good, so right. She used almost to feel giddy when she thought of her plan. But now?

Tendrils of doubt were weaving their way through her soul, taking root, and growing like hungry weeds. Every time she ripped one up, two more grew in its place.

"Let's take a look at the apartment." Ryker's hand landed on the small of her back.

Gods help her but she didn't pull away. She couldn't.

He added, "We can change whatever you want, sweetheart. Say the word, and it's done."

Great. Now he was being fucking considerate, too? How in the hell was she supposed to deal with this?

Cold-blooded killers weren't supposed to act like Ryker. They weren't supposed to give you the sun or be amenable to making alterations for your comfort. They were supposed to be horrible, awful people who didn't give a damn about you.

Turning around—and pointedly ignoring the fact that Ryker was touching her—Brynleigh took in the space. It was a nice apartment, a little masculine for her taste if she were being honest, but well-built. The large kitchen was clean, and it opened into the living area. There was a sturdy dining table with four matching chairs. A chess set sat on the coffee table in front of the TV. Down the hall were two doors that led to what she assumed were the bedroom and bathroom.

"Maybe a few coats of paint?" After all, she was supposed to be playing the part of the excited bride. Besides, she'd always been partial to springtime colors. "Or we could get a few throw pillows to liven it up."

"We can buy as many as you want." He wrapped his arms around her from behind and rested his chin on her head. "Anything you can think of, it's yours. I barely have any expenses, and I've been saving money since I started working."

See? Considerate. Why couldn't Ryker have been an alpha fae asshole who bossed her around and didn't have a trace of kindness in him? It would've made her life a hell of a lot easier. But no, she had to get stuck with the one fae who seemed to care about her thoughts and feelings.

This was... a lot. The longer they looked around the living room, the worse she felt. Her lungs squeezed, and old sweat broke out on her neck.

"Is there a bathroom?" Brynleigh extricated herself from Ryker's grip and stepped back, trying to put some room between them.

Space. That's what she needed. Space to breathe. To recover. To just... be away from all *this*.

"Of course." He smiled and pointed down the hall. "First door on the right."

Brynleigh thanked him and hurried down the corridor. She didn't slow down to look at the pictures on the walls. She slipped into the bathroom and shut the door behind her.

Gods, there was even a blacked-out window in here, right above the tub. Was there no escaping Ryker's kindness?

Closing her eyes, Brynleigh leaned against the bathroom

door and released her shadows. They'd been thrumming incessantly in her veins since the incident in the car. As soon as she permitted them to slip from her hands, they whipped out of her violently, darkening the room until the night surrounded her.

Breathe. She forced her lungs to take in air.

Inhale. Exhale.

So, Ryker had a huge, cuddly dog that he seemed to love. That didn't inherently mean he wasn't evil. Even bad men could care about dogs. She'd probably be more concerned if he *didn't* like animals. What kind of psychopath didn't care about pets?

And the windows. Admittedly, the unexpected gesture was nice, but Ryker was still the same man who'd called down a tempest and drowned everyone she knew. He was still a cold-blooded killer.

Brynleigh twisted the necklace her parents had given her on her eighteenth birthday. It was a constant reminder of their loss. Right now, she desperately needed that reminder.

Opening her eyes, she met her reflection's gaze in the mirror. "They're gone because of him," she hissed, careful to keep her voice low. "Pull yourself together."

Captain Ryker Waterborn put on a good show, but he was still the cause of all her heartbreak. He still deserved to die.

The front door clicked open, and two male voices murmured. Claws scratched on the floor. A bark.

Atlas was back with Marlowe.

Turning on the tap, Brynleigh splashed her face with cold water. The frigid temperature was good for her. It helped snap her back to reality.

She was a doubly blessed vampire, for Isvana's sake. She thrived on blood and darkness and shadows. She wouldn't let something as trivial as a few considerate, kind gestures deter her from her goal. Gripping the countertop, Brynleigh hardened her eyes and glared at herself.

"You are strong and will not crack," she told herself sternly.

"Remember why you're here. Respect your boundaries, and you'll be fine."

Confident in her renewed ability to keep emotions out of this, Brynleigh rejoined the others.

She could do this.

Fuck.

She couldn't do this.

By the time the clock struck four in the afternoon, and they were set to leave Marlowe behind in Atlas's capable hands, Brynleigh was a ball of nerves.

At least *those* emotions, she could keep. There was nothing wrong with nerves. Thank the gods they were safe because she had many of them. Apprehension gnawed at her stomach, eating her up from the inside out. It was those damned tendrils of doubt. They had exploded within her and were now a tangle of knots.

Brynleigh had always assumed that the Ryker she got to know during the Choosing was an act. A show he put on to attract a wife.

No one could actually be that good of a guy, right?

Except it didn't seem to be an act. Atlas shared story after story about his friend, even after Ryker asked him to stop, and though the words varied, the theme was the same. Ryker had saved Atlas from a life on the streets, giving him a home when he had none. Ryker had backed Atlas up when someone from his past came calling for blood.

Ryker did this. Ryker did that. Story after story painted the captain in the same light: he didn't seem to have a bad bone in his body.

And that was just... not fair.

Not fair at all.

And Marlowe? The big dog had leaped on Brynleigh the moment she'd left the bathroom, and he'd been glued to her side ever since. He was the sweetest animal, cuddling beside her on the couch and placing his head in her lap as she absentmindedly petted him.

Even worse than all that, Ryker kept checking in on Brynleigh. He brought her a mug of warmed blood from the stash he'd had shipped to the apartment, and he stayed beside her the entire afternoon.

And they weren't just sitting together. No. The water fae was always touching her. A hand on her shoulder. A thigh pressed against hers. His thumb on her hip, rubbing circles.

If their date had ended here and she'd been returning to the safe house right away, Brynleigh would have been fine. She could have handled that.

But no.

That had just been the beginning. Now, the real test was underway. Ryker's hand was a brand on Brynleigh's back as he led her to the underground parking garage. The same man who'd driven them there stood outside the car.

"Captain, Miss." The driver dipped his head. "I hope you had a pleasant afternoon."

Unfortunately, yes, Brynleigh thought to herself. She had the common sense not to say that, though. It would open a can of worms she had no intention of dealing with.

"We did, thank you, Davis," Ryker said.

Davis moved towards the door as though to open it, but Ryker got there first. In yet another considerate gesture—really, this was becoming overwhelming—he held it open for Brynleigh and waited for her to enter the vehicle.

Once Brynleigh was inside, Ryker slid in after her. The air still smelled of sex, and Brynleigh blushed as she buckled in. Gods, this day couldn't be over fast enough.

"How far is your parents' house?" Brynleigh tapped her pocket to make sure she hadn't forgotten her phone. She needed to be available in case her Maker called.

"Thirty minutes without traffic." Ryker slung his arm over her shoulder and drew her flush against him. "How do you feel?"

"I'm... nervous." And for good reason. She had no idea what she'd say to his parents.

Hi, it's nice to meet you. My name's Brynleigh de la Point. I'm twenty-nine, and six years ago, your son killed my entire family and almost killed me. I'm going to marry and then murder him to get my revenge in the most dramatic and emotionally damaging way possible.

She hadn't participated in many family gatherings in the past six years, but she was fairly certain that wouldn't go over well.

"They're going to love you as much as I do." Ryker kissed her forehead, and his lips lingered on her skin for several seconds before he added, "You're amazing, and they'll see that."

"I hope so," she murmured.

"They'd be stupid not to." He rapped on the roof, and then, they were off.

As Golden City passed them by, Brynleigh stared out the darkened window. Everything she'd learned about Ryker's mother scrolled through Brynleigh's mind. Although Ryker himself had become somewhat of a recluse since the flood, plenty of information was available about Representative Waterborn.

Born almost three centuries ago, Tertia was a direct descendant of the very first fae who'd crossed the Indigo Ocean and settled into what used to be known as the Four Kingdoms. Her great-grandfather, seven times over, was part of the initial council that had abolished the kingdoms' borders and created the Republic of Balance after the High Ladies of Life and Death and their mates Faded.

None of that research had told Brynleigh what Tertia was like as a mother, though. Was she kind, as Isolde had been? Or perhaps Tertia was distant, cruel, and preoccupied. Brynleigh wasn't sure. All she knew for certain was that the Waterborns were made of money.

That begged the question of why Ryker lived in a one-bedroom apartment in the middle of Golden City. Surely, he could afford to reside wherever he chose.

It was a question for another time. Or not. Ryker would be dead in a week. He could bring the answer with him to the grave. Brynleigh should be focusing on asking less questions, not more. She was already confused, and feeding that doubt was unwise.

The view slowly changed as they left the central city behind. Tall, looming glass buildings gave way to short, sprawling homes made of red brick. Shining offices became long one-story malls and individual shops. Packed neighborhoods became rambling estates with pristine gardens and emerald-green lawns.

Ryker sat beside Brynleigh, his quiet presence grounding her as they drew nearer to his childhood home. He didn't try to engage her in conversation, seeming to realize she needed the silence.

Because, of course, he did.

The car slowed as they entered a gated community. Brynleigh's palms slickened.

They drove up a long, paved driveway. Her heart slammed violently against her ribs. It hadn't beat this quickly since before she was Made.

No one had ever brought Brynleigh to meet their parents before. She wasn't a nice girl—even before she'd taken up vigilante killing and revenge plots, she hadn't been sweet. That was her sister's role in life.

This isn't real, she reminded herself for the hundredth time. *Remember your boundaries.*

But the problem was, it felt real. Far too fucking real.

It felt as if she'd fallen madly in love with Ryker during the Choosing, and now, she was preparing to meet her future in-laws.

Her feelings were wrong, though. She wasn't in love with Ryker. She hated him. After this, she should take up acting. She would excel at it.

A voice crackled over the in-car speaker. "We're pulling up to Waterborn House, sir," said the driver.

"Thank you, Davis. Please proceed into the garage." Ryker lifted his arm, ran his hands down his jeans, and rolled his shoulders. His face hardened almost imperceptibly, and his jaw feathered.

Within seconds, Ryker transformed from a relaxed fae into one who looked ready for a fight.

There he is.

For the first time, Brynleigh saw the warrior fae.

Other people might have been frightened by how quickly he changed, but her? Fear had no place here. Relief ran through her, coating her insides. She'd been beginning to think this part of him didn't exist.

This was the fae who'd murdered her family. It had just taken him longer than expected to rip off the mask.

This was good.

Davis drove into a luxurious garage that resembled an airplane hangar before cutting off the engine. The door closed as the driver exited, leaving them alone.

Ryker turned to Brynleigh, his countenance pinched as he palmed the back of his neck. "Before we go in, there's something I should warn you about."

CHAPTER 27
I Made My Choice

"Warn me?" Brynleigh echoed Ryker's words. "What do you want to warn me about?"

Ryker had spent the car ride debating whether or not he should have this conversation, but in the end, he decided he wanted Brynleigh to be prepared. Still, he picked his words carefully.

"My mother can be... difficult, at times." Most of the time, if he was being honest.

Ryker loved his mother, but she'd never exactly been soft. She wanted her children to be perfect in every way. After the Incident, she'd been colder and harder than before.

Usually, Tertia directed her ire at River, but this week, she had turned her sights off her rebellious daughter and onto her son. She'd made frequent passive-aggressive comments about Brynleigh whenever they spoke. She never expressed her displeasure directly, but it wasn't necessary.

Ryker understood his mother far better than most, and he knew she was disappointed he hadn't picked a more "appropriate" bride like Valentina Rose.

No matter how plainly Ryker put it, Tertia refused to understand that he wasn't interested in the fire fae. He didn't want someone who enjoyed throwing lavish parties and attending all the social events. He'd done these things for years, fulfilling the duties that came along with being the son of a Representative, and he hated them. He didn't want a party planner. He wanted someone who made him laugh, challenged him, and was godsdamned amazing in every way.

That someone was Brynleigh.

Ryker had explained as much to his mother multiple times during their stay at The Lily, but he still had a niggling fear that she might try something tonight. He needed to prepare Brynleigh for the fact that his mother might be... abrasive.

All fae knew how to watch their words—it was one of the first things they learned because lying wasn't an option—but they could also speak cutting jabs like no one else. Just because Tertia might not outright insult Brynleigh—he hoped his mother would exhibit more class than that—didn't mean she would be kind. She was the only one he was worried about. River and Cyrus would fall in love with Brynleigh as soon as they met her, just like Ryker had.

Two lines creased Brynleigh's forehead, temporarily marring her unblemished skin. "What do you mean?"

Ryker took her hand in his and kissed the back of her palm. "I love you."

She frowned, and he felt he was messing up all of this. "I know you do."

It hadn't escaped Ryker's notice that Brynleigh had yet to return those three words. He'd be lying if he said he didn't want to hear them, but he wouldn't pry them out of her lips before she was ready. Waiting would make hearing them all the sweeter.

Ryker forced his lips to form a smile. "My sister's going to love you, too. Dad will, too. Of that, I'm certain."

"Oh." Brynleigh ran the tip of her tongue over one of her fangs. That minuscule movement had no business being so attractive. "But your mother..."

"By the Obsidian Sands, I hope I'm wrong." If Ryker thought

it would help, he'd travel to the nearest fae temple and pray upon the vials of sand themselves, begging the deities to hear his pleas. Unfortunately, he was a realist. He didn't think that anything, even the black grains that had been brought across the Indigo Ocean with the fae, could change Tertia's opinion about her son's bride.

Brynleigh was attentive, and she picked up what he wasn't outright saying. "Your mother won't like me, will she?"

His heart twisted at the doubt in her voice.

Ryker cupped Brynleigh's cheek, and she leaned into his touch. He loved that she relaxed around him and trusted him enough to let him touch her like this. "I hope she does," he said. "You are incredible. She'd be a fool not to see that."

"I understand." Disappointment flashed through Brynleigh's eyes.

The sight was a knife to Ryker's gut.

"Listen to me, sweetheart," he said gruffly. "No matter what she says in there, I picked you. I *Chose* you. I will continue to do so until the end of time."

Nothing would ever tear them apart. No person could destroy the relationship they'd built. It was steadfast, built on a stronger foundation than simply physical attraction. Their souls were linked.

Ryker's heart boomed as he waited for Brynleigh's response. Each moment stretched on and on until she finally nodded. "Alright, I understand."

He prayed to the gods that she did. Or that his gut was wrong, and he was worried for no reason. He hoped this dinner wouldn't be a disaster.

Only time would tell.

Ryker had been to his family home hundreds of times since he moved out, but this was the first time he felt strange about it. Almost like he didn't fully belong here.

It was because of the vampire at his side. He'd given Brynleigh his heart, and now, his life belonged with her. Where she went, he would always follow.

Two hours later, Ryker knew he'd been right to worry. His mother had been kind enough to Brynleigh when she greeted them in the garage, but he'd caught the clench in Tertia's jaw and the hardness in her eyes.

Tertia was incredibly overdressed for the occasion. She wore a floor-length cerulean ballgown with three-inch heels as if she was about to attend a formal engagement and not have dinner with her two children and soon-to-be daughter-in-law. That was Tertia, though. She was the definition of dramatic.

Unlike Ryker, who'd had arranged for contractors to swap out the windows in his apartment to accommodate Brynleigh's inability to be in the sun, his parents hadn't changed their windows. However, they had installed blackout blinds since he had made it a condition of their visit. He wouldn't take Brynleigh anywhere that might endanger her.

It wasn't Tertia's words that had Ryker on edge. For the most part, his mother was kind enough as she played tour guide and showed Brynleigh through the mansion. It was what she wasn't saying that had Ryker ready to bolt far earlier than he had planned.

Whenever Tertia thought Brynleigh wasn't looking, she shot Ryker searing looks. When she spoke, she used the sickly-sweet tone she reserved for people she considered beneath her. Disapproval radiated from her pores.

Anger frothed and bubbled in Ryker's veins, worsening by the minute. Brynleigh was to be his bride, and he wouldn't allow his mother to continue treating her in such a fashion.

"This is Cyrus's study." Tertia pointed at the closed door, which hid the space that had sat empty for the past decade and a half. "It doesn't get much use anymore."

"Oh, I'm sorry," Brynleigh said softly.

So was Ryker. He waited for his mother to say something kind. To acknowledge Brynleigh's comment.

Instead, Tertia said, "Hmm," turned, and walked away. Her heels clicked on the marble flooring, and Ryker stared at her retreating back.

"I'm sorry," he whispered, squeezing Brynleigh's hand. "She's not usually... I'll talk to her."

"Thank you," Brynleigh murmured. "It's okay, though. She doesn't like me. I understand."

No, it wasn't okay. Not with Ryker. The sooner this tour was over, the better. He would be talking to his mother *tonight* about her attitude. This was inappropriate, and he would not stand for it.

They followed his mother.

As a child, Ryker used to love running down these halls. Waterborn House had over forty rooms and three floors. When his mother wasn't home, he had free rein. Ryker had many memories of racing through the house, roaring with laughter, and sliding down the floors in his socks as his father chased him, imitating a dragon.

Those shrieks of joy were long gone. Now, Waterborn House was simply a ghost of times long gone. A holder of memories. A keeper of the past.

Ryker tried to see his childhood home through Brynleigh's eyes. It was massive. Paintings of his ancestors adorned the walls. Centuries-old statues perched on tables. Gold trimmed the baseboards. A hundred other little touches screamed "old money." It was less of a home and more of a museum.

They finally reached the engraved library doors. Tertia stopped in front of them and turned. The Representative was nearly a foot shorter than Ryker, but there was no denying the authority with which she carried herself.

Tertia looked past Ryker to the vampire at his side.

"Tell me, Miss de la Point." His mother had yet to call

Brynleigh by her first name, which was grating on Ryker's last nerve. He would be addressing that issue with his mother tonight as well. "Have you ever read the *Ballad of the Light Elves?*"

Ryker stared at Tertia. What the hell was going through her mind? The ballad predated the Battle of Balance, a pivotal turning point in their country's history, and it was written in an ancient dialect of the Common Tongue that very few people still spoke. He had only read the ballad because it was compulsory for his twelfth-grade literature class. The epic tale of good and evil took place during the Fall of the Rose Empire and had no ramifications on their current lives.

"Unfortunately, I haven't had the privilege," Brynleigh said sweetly. She hadn't stooped to Tertia's level, speaking kindly despite his mother's uncouth behavior.

"Hmm." Tertia lifted her shoulder and frowned. "Such a pity. All the girls attending Highmountain's School for Young Fae study the ballad during their fourth year."

Ryker slid Brynleigh behind him. It was a subtle movement, but he knew Tertia noticed. "Enough, Mother," he growled in warning, clenching his fists at his sides.

The Representative's eyes widened in mock shock, and her hand flew to her heart. Did his mother think him a fool? He knew she was doing this purposefully, and he understood precisely what kind of game she was playing.

"What?" Tertia had the gall to sound innocent. "I'm just curious about what kind of education my son's girlfriend received. What's wrong with that?"

"She's not my girlfriend; she's my fiancée," Ryker corrected, not bothering to mask the ire in his voice. "We're getting married in a week." He growled. "You know that."

As far as Ryker was concerned, the week couldn't go fast enough. He never thought he'd be one to look forward to a wedding, but he was eager to marry his vampire. The weddings promised to be extravagant affairs. When one had as much money as the organizers of the Choosing had at their disposal, lavish events could be thrown together in less than a month.

Tertia sighed. "You know I'm concerned for your well-being, Ryker. If the vampire doesn't even know the *Ballad of the Light Elves*, who knows what else is lacking from her education?"

"I—" Brynleigh started to say.

Apparently, Ryker's mother had lost her mind because she spoke right over Brynleigh. "I'm just saying that you need to be careful, my son. That's all."

Ryker growled, "Mother—"

"It's not too late, you know. I talked to Ignatia, and the Rose girl would be willing to break her engagement to Edward. I watched the Choosing with the rest of the world and saw you two together. Valentina would be a marvelous wife for you, Ryker, dear. She's powerful, strong, and well-educated."

Had Ryker been angry before? That was nothing compared to the fury churning in him now.

The air in the hallway practically crackled. His water magic thrummed steadily in his veins, itching to be released. There was a storm within him, needing to protect what was his. His nostrils flared. Red tinged his vision.

He stepped towards his mother, looming over her, and yelled, "Enough!"

Tertia gasped, pressing a hand against her heart once more. "Ryker Elias Waterborn, do not raise your voice to me!"

Power rippled from her.

Goosebumps broke out on Ryker's arms. So much for waiting until after dinner. Their conversation would be happening right fucking now.

"I will do whatever it takes to protect my fiancée, Mother." He held Brynleigh at his side. "I will not allow you to disrespect my Chosen bride in such a manner. Do not speak to me of Valentina Rose or any other woman again. I will not stand for it. I have made my Choice, and I will not go back on my word. I *love* Brynleigh."

His chest heaved as his words echoed around them. He had meant every single one and wouldn't take them back.

His mother's bottom lip wobbled. For a single moment, Ryker wondered if he'd been too harsh. But then Tertia opened her mouth. Her voice lacked all traces of maternal warmth, and she stared daggers at her firstborn.

"You dare speak to me about your Choice?" Her eyes narrowed, and the temperature in the hallway dropped as she moved closer to Ryker. "You've Chosen an undead bloodsucker who has no lineage, proper education, or finances to speak of. You don't want my advice? Fine. Don't come crying to Mommy when it all falls apart. I won't give a damn."

Ryker snarled, the sound feral as it ripped through him.

How fucking dare she? In all his years, he'd heard his mother be cold but never cruel in this fashion. He'd brought Brynleigh for a nice, civilized family dinner, but his mother was destroying it before it even began with her poisonous, barbed words.

"This won't fall apart. I love her," Ryker seethed. His fingers curled around Brynleigh's, and he stepped back from his mother. "This was a bad idea. We should—"

Footsteps came from behind them, and River hurried down the hall. She'd changed and now wore a knee-length black pencil skirt and a flowing purple blouse. It softened her look but did nothing to temper the rebellious spark in her eyes.

"Ah, my daughter. Late as usual," Tertia remarked caustically.

Yeah, this wasn't going well at all.

"Am I late? It looks like I'm right on time for the fight." River crossed her arms.

Mother and daughter glared at each other, and the tension rose and rose. Gods damn it all.

Ryker clenched his jaw and inhaled deeply. If this evening could be saved, he would have to do it now. He pinned Tertia with a glare that would have sent soldiers scurrying to do his bidding. His mother glared right back.

"We're not fighting," Ryker ground out. "I was telling

Mother how much I love Brynleigh and would do anything for her."

Ryker held his mother's gaze. He let her see everything on his face. His anger, his willingness to turn and walk out of this house with his bride, and his resolve to put Brynleigh first, always.

Tertia might have given birth to him, but it didn't give her the right to treat his Chosen partner with anything less than the utmost respect. Of all the things Ryker held dear, his family was at the top of his list. He respected his mother, but in a week, Brynleigh would be his wife. That put her above everyone else. He would not hesitate to remove them from this situation if it became toxic.

"That's so sweet, Ryker." River walked up behind her brother. She wrapped one arm around his waist and the other around Brynleigh's. Resting her head between them, River grinned first at him and then at his vampire. "Hi. I'm River. It seems my brother has forgotten to introduce us."

He hadn't forgotten. He'd been preoccupied with other things, like making sure his mother knew he wouldn't tolerate disrespect toward his bride.

Brynleigh disentangled herself from his arms and turned around. "It's nice to meet you, River. You know, I've heard quite a bit about you. Your brother is rather proud of you."

Proud was an understatement. River was the most powerful water fae of their generation, and with some training, she would be unstoppable. Not only that, but she was kindhearted and caring. Ryker would do anything for his sister. He'd proven that six years ago.

Memories that he usually kept under wraps pulsed through his mind. Water, pouring from the sky. His hands, outstretched. His well of magic, rapidly draining as he reeled it all in. Utter exhaustion that had kept him down for days.

"I'm proud of him, too." River smiled up at Ryker and touched his arm. "I came to let you all know dinner's ready. Dad's waiting for us." She bit her lip, making the ring in the middle stand. "He was... tired today."

Ryker heard the unspoken words as though she'd shouted them at him. *We don't have long.*

He turned and hurried to the dining room.

DINNER WAS a formal affair in more ways than one.

Instead of eating in the smaller dining room near the family's living quarters like they usually did for their family dinners, they sat in the massive one that could hold fifty people. The table was enormous, and the five of them looked comical sitting at it. A classical concerto dating back to the time of the High Ladies of Life and Death streamed from hidden speakers, adding to the ceremonious air of tonight's dinner.

Tertia sat at the head of the table, glaring icy daggers at Brynleigh. The Representative hadn't said anything to the vampire since the library, which was good. If she did, Ryker would either lash out with his magic, words, or both. He wasn't sure which he would choose if push came to shove, but he would defend Brynleigh to his last breath.

Either way, he knew his mother would not appreciate his actions.

He and Brynleigh sat together in the middle of the table. The pristine white tablecloth was long and hid their joined hands. River was across from them, and Cyrus sat beside his daughter.

No one spoke, as was the norm. For as long as Ryker could remember, Tertia always had one rule at family dinner: no one was allowed to talk until the food was served. Even though her children were grown, the rule still stood.

Ryker picked up his glass of red wine, curling his fingers around the stem. Beside him, Brynleigh had a similar beverage, although hers was spiked with blood. River stared at her empty plate, twisting a lock of hair through her fingers, but Ryker studied his father.

Cyrus's gaze was clear as he looked around the room from his wheelchair. Though the bags beneath his eyes spoke to the tiredness River had mentioned, it seemed like today was a good day.

Those were rare. The Stillness was a silent thief, stealing their father day by day. Soon, Cyrus would Fade to nothing but dust, his body returning to the black sands where the fae first came from. When the illness first hit, Ryker's father lost feeling in his toes. Less than a year after that, he'd woken unable to move his feet. Then, his legs.

Every year, it got worse and worse.

The Stillness varied from fae to fae. It struck some like a lightning bolt, stealing their ability to live in one day, while it drained others of life over several years or decades. There was no cure, only methods to make the end of life more manageable.

One day, Cyrus's heart would stop beating, and his lungs would no longer be able to draw air.

Ryker dreaded that day. All children were meant to see their parents Fade—it was a natural part of life. But this was different. Cyrus hadn't lived the thousand years his father had before him. He was young for a fae, only four centuries old.

Cyrus Waterborn was everything Tertia was not. Where she was cold, he was warm. Where she was focused on her work, he made sure their children knew they were cared for and loved. Ryker had never doubted his parents loved him because his father showed him affection daily.

And now, he was dying.

Everyone had their ways of dealing with the Stillness. Tertia threw herself into work. Ryker took over the patriarchal role in their family, ensuring everyone's well-being. And River? She spent hours praying to Dyna, the fae goddess of life and healing. When she wasn't at the temples, River was at school learning to be a doctor. She hoped to try and find a cure before it was too late.

Ryker wasn't sure his sister's prayers would do any good. It wasn't that he didn't believe in the gods and goddesses worshiped throughout the Republic of Balance. They were as real to him as the Obsidian Sands the fae revered.

He just didn't believe the deities were watching their every move. If the gods cared as much as River or the priests would have them believe, how could they let the world fall apart around them? How could they let people starve in the streets? How could they let his father die of the Stillness?

No, Ryker was reasonably certain the gods didn't care about what was happening in the Republic of Balance.

The dining room door slid open, and three servants entered the room. They were all Light Elves employed by his mother to keep the house and serve meals. There had been help around the house for as long as Ryker could remember.

Mr. Cobalt, the oldest of the three servants, cleared his throat. "The first course is served, Representative Waterborn."

"Wonderful, thank you." Tertia smiled, but the gesture was frigid. Evidently, she hadn't gotten over the incident at the library earlier, either.

The servants stepped forward, serving a chilled tomato gazpacho to the four fae. Another glass was brought for Brynleigh. This one was filled to the brim with dark, crimson blood.

"Thank you." She took a sip and hummed. "It's perfect."

The servants slipped out of the dining room as quickly as they'd appeared, closing the door behind them.

For a moment, no one spoke. The silence stretched on and on.

Then, Tertia picked up her spoon. "Well, let's eat." She sent a withering glare in Brynleigh's direction. "Or drink, I suppose, since you can't do anything else."

Ryker bristled, the spoon curling in his fist as he glared at his mother. This was going down in history as their worst family dinner, which was a feat.

Every part of Ryker's body was tense like he was moments away from shattering.

Seconds went by, long and endless and painful.

Then, the strangest thing happened.

A cough came from across the table. It was weak but so unexpected that it sounded like a gong.

"Be... kind, Tertia." The admonition was a murmur slipping from Cyrus's mouth.

The entire room seemed to take a breath.

Ryker's heart stopped beating momentarily as he lifted his gaze to his father's.

What he saw there stunned him. Cyrus's eyes were alert and lacked the glassiness that often ran through them. There was *life* in his eyes, a vividness that had been missing for many years.

At that moment, nothing outside this room mattered. Even if the rebels attacked, Ryker wouldn't notice.

His dad was *alert*.

"Daddy?" River's lip quivered, and tears lined her eyes.

The hope in River's voice made Ryker's heart lurch in his chest. This was real, right? It had to be real.

Cyrus turned his head slowly—so gods-damned slowly that it felt like an eternity passed—towards his daughter. His trembling, nearly translucent hand rose in the air, and he placed his fingers on her healthy, sun-kissed skin.

"Yes, Princess." His chapped lips formed the words with the utmost care. "I'm... here."

Ryker's heart remembered that it had stopped beating. It picked up, the rhythm a staccato in his chest. The spoon was a twisted piece of metal as he dropped it to the table, forgotten.

Everyone stared at Cyrus, whose gaze crawled from River to Ryker to Tertia.

The moment the patriarch looked at his wife, the Representative's composure shattered. She cried out, and her chair tumbled to the ground. She practically flew around the table.

"Dyna, have mercy on us," Tertia sobbed as she kissed her husband. "You're here."

CHAPTER 28
Complications Abound

What had begun as a formal dinner quickly evolved into something that made Brynleigh uncomfortable in more ways than one.

Earlier, Tertia's abhorrent, bitchy behavior had been one thing. It was fine. More than fine, if Brynleigh was being honest. If that was how his mother acted, maybe Brynleigh was doing the right thing by killing Ryker. Maybe that mask she'd seen in the car, the one he'd worn when they first entered the house, was really who he was, and he was just like his mother.

Brynleigh had been feeling more confident in her plan and boundaries right up until Ryker's father coughed. When Tertia's chair crashed to the ground, Brynleigh saw an entirely new side of the family.

It was wholly unwelcome.

Now, she felt like an intruder in the most intimate of moments. Brynleigh was a spectator, sitting back and trying to shrink against the wall as the family hugged their patriarch and cried.

The cold Representative had transformed into a warm, loving wife as she peppered her husband with kisses. She took his hand gently and spoke to him in soft tones.

The way River looked at her father—like he had personally hung the moon and stars in the sky—reminded Brynleigh of the love she'd had for her parents.

And Ryker.

Captain Ryker Waterborn of the Army's Fae Division fucking *cried*. Not just a tear or two. He openly wept, tears rolling down his cheeks as he kneeled at his father's side.

Gods damn it all, witnessing Ryker cry made Brynleigh feel all sorts of things that she had no business feeling.

She couldn't ignore the truth any longer: she was in trouble. Things were getting far too complicated for her liking. She had come to this dinner hoping to find more reasons to kill Ryker.

And now? This wasn't what Brynleigh had signed up for. This game was about death, brutality, and heartless revenge. She knew that, yet her heart insisted on breaking at the joy and sadness in this room. Damned tears lined her eyes.

This was too much. There were too many emotions. Too much going on in this room.

She must have made a sound because Ryker glanced at her as though asking if she was alright. She wasn't, but she still nodded. Ryker returned to his father, murmuring.

At some point, the servants brought in more food. There was a veritable feast on the table, which Brynleigh could not eat.

Avoiding the emotional scene still unfolding before her, Brynleigh studied the paintings on the wall. Some were landscapes, a few were portraits, and all looked expensive. Usually, displays of wealth like this turned her stomach, but she had bigger things to worry about right now. Tertia slowly spooned her husband some gazpacho while River and Ryker spoke to him through watery smiles.

The four of them seemed happy, and it was...

Horrible.

She needed to get out of here.

Brynleigh refilled her blood wine from the nearest decanter

and pushed her chair back from the table. "Where's the ladies' room?"

Ryker met her gaze from across the table. "Down the hall and three doors to the left. Do you need me to come with you?"

So gods-damned considerate.

Another emotion arose. Brynleigh didn't analyze it before grabbing it and pushing it down. It barely fit. She shook her head. "No, I'm fine, thank you."

"She's nice," Cyrus whispered. "You Chose well, Ryker."

No, he didn't. He Chose a woman intent on killing him.

Panic was churning mass, threatening to spill the contents of Brynleigh's stomach. Fuck, she had to get out of here.

Ryker's attention returned to his father. "Brynleigh's wonderful. You're going to love..."

Brynleigh hurried from the room, and Ryker's words faded. She clutched her wine like it was a lifeboat and counted the doors. Thank the gods, the bathroom was precisely where Ryker said it would be.

It was luxurious, reminiscent of what she expected to see in The Lily's lobby, not a home. A long marble counter with three sunken sinks spanned one wall. A mirror ran above it. Soft lighting was embedded in the ceiling, casting a warm glow on the interior. Three stalls were behind her. The navy blue doors matched the striations running through the counter.

Opening each door to ensure she was alone—although really, who would be here?—she leaned against the counter and gulped the rest of her wine. Her head tingled and felt lightheaded, but it wouldn't last long.

Alcohol never had a lasting effect on vampires. Only Faerie Wine had any real influences on children of the moon, and this was not that.

Slowly, the panic dwindled, and she could draw deep breaths once more.

Her phone buzzed, and she pulled it out of her pocket.

> Z: See you tonight. Safe house.

Short and to the point, exactly what she expected from the shifter. Brynleigh tapped back a brief reply confirming she understood, hitting "send" before sliding her phone away and staring at herself in the mirror.

Black, shining eyes. Silky blonde hair. Fangs. She was a vampire through and through. There wasn't a hint of the human she'd once been.

Why couldn't she follow the rules? Why was she so overcome with emotion tonight?

Quite frankly, Brynleigh's behavior was unbecoming of a vampire who'd killed more people than she could count.

"Get a grip," she told herself firmly. "His dad is alert and spoke for the first time in a while. So what? It doesn't mean anything."

Her harsh, callous tone didn't help her feel better. If anything, it made her feel worse. Odd.

She tried another tactic. Fingers digging into the counter, she glared at herself. "Remember the game. Rule number one: you cannot trust anyone." Okay, that was working. Her spine straightened. "Rule number two: doubly blessed vampires do not hide behind—"

The door swung open.

Brynleigh clamped her mouth shut and spun on her heels as River entered the washroom. Even red-eyed and puffy-cheeked, the slender water fae was beautiful. Her long brown hair hung to her waist, and there was an elegance about her that probably came from years in the same type of school that Valentina had attended.

River was leaner than Ryker and less battle-worn. However, she had enough piercings for both of them. Brynleigh counted three in each ear, one on River's lip and another in her nose. Beyond the piercings, though, there was a depth in River's brown eyes that Brynleigh recognized.

Grief called to grief.

And behind that, strength hid in River's gaze. It was the kind that could only come from surviving something difficult. Whatever the young water fae had been through, it hadn't been easy.

"Sorry about that scene in the dining room." River moved towards the sink closest to the door and turned on the tap. She splashed water on her face and rubbed her cheeks before drying her hands on a nearby towel. Her eyes were still red, and her cheeks still puffy as she smiled softly. "It's just, Dad isn't often..."

"You don't need to explain." In fact, Brynleigh would strongly prefer if River didn't. "Ryker told me about the Stillness."

A tear ran down River's cheek. "Yes. Dad's been sick for so long. Practically my whole life."

Apparently, they were going to talk about this. Great. What was it with people confiding in Brynleigh? First Hallie, now River. Brynleigh thought she did an excellent job of giving off a "leave me alone" vibe. Clearly, she was wrong. She'd have to work on that when all this was done.

"I'm sorry." Brynleigh truly was. No matter what she thought about Ryker, she couldn't deny that Cyrus Waterborn appeared to be a beloved member of his family.

"Thank you." River chewed on her lip, drawing her piercing into her mouth before popping it back out.

An awkward silence stretched between them. Brynleigh was reaching for her empty wineglass, intent on leaving when River's hand landed on hers.

"My brother is a good fae," River murmured.

Brynleigh blinked. Where did that come from? Had River deduced Brynleigh's true intentions?

A thousand curses ran through her mind, each worse than the last. She searched River's face, trying to see what the fae meant. That panic was back, a fist constricting her heart. "I—"

River shook her head and squeezed Brynleigh's fingers. "Ryker doesn't know I'm here. I mean, he knows that I came to the bathroom, but..."

He didn't know she'd come to talk to Brynleigh.

Against Brynleigh's good sense, intrigue unfurled within her. She canted her head and studied the fae. "Oh?"

River chewed on her lip, which seemed to be a habit. Probably not a great one, considering the placement of her piercing. "Ryker is... protective."

Brynleigh snorted. "I've gathered as much."

That was one of the first things she had noticed about the captain. She'd expected him to have some protective tendencies—most fae did—but Ryker exceeded her expectations.

He was protective and considerate. And kind. And...

Nope. She wasn't going down that road. She shoved those feelings down and concentrated on the conversation at hand.

"Anyways," River continued, "I wanted to talk to you alone. I know Mom can be... a lot."

That was an understatement.

"She's kind of... mean." Her meanness wasn't like Jelisette's, whose version of cruelty was deadly, but Tertia was unpleasant.

River's mouth twitched. "Yeah, she can be cold. When I was young, and Dad was healthy, she was different. But now..." She shrugged. "Grief changes people, you know?"

Yes, Brynleigh knew exactly what the water fae was talking about. She was far too familiar with the depth of grief. It was a blanket that shrouded one's life, coloring everything in shades of gray. Brynleigh and grief were old friends, whether she liked it or not.

"I do," Brynleigh whispered.

River's gaze searched hers for several long moments. "Yes, I see that. Come with me."

That intrigue remained as the water fae took Brynleigh's hand and tugged her into a small study next door.

They sat on a red couch. River folded her hands in her lap. "You're good for my brother, Brynleigh."

The vampire reared back. That was the last thing she needed or wanted to hear. She wasn't good for Ryker. She wasn't good for anyone, because she wasn't *good*. She was a vampire. A killer. A creature of the night. Created for darkness and destruction.

"I'm... No, I'm not..." She stumbled on her words and shook her head.

"Yes, you are. And that's why I'm going to tell you something I don't think Ryker will share with you."

Brynleigh's heart flung itself around her chest. What was River talking about?

The water fae smiled kindly. "You're about to be family, and if you're going to tie yourself to him... to us... you need to know everything."

Brynleigh's stomach was a tangle of knots. What was River talking about? Was she pulling back her brother's mask for her? Brynleigh would be eternally grateful to the pierced water fae if so.

She waited for River's next words with bated breath. Little did she know, no amount of time could have prepared her for what the fae was about to reveal.

CHAPTER 29
Mistakes Were Made

"Fuck!" Brynleigh screamed, her voice echoing across the night. Droves of shadows poured out of her, hiding the moon and stars as her powerful wings beat against the darkness. The wind swallowed her screams, stealing them away before anyone else could hear them.

It didn't matter. *She* heard them. Over and over again, she cried out into the darkness. Every second, every moment felt longer than the last. Anger, bitterness, and confusion were a twisted, acerbic trio pounding through her veins.

Hours had passed since she'd spoken to River in the study, yet it felt like mere moments ago.

The water fae's words would forever be seared in Brynleigh's mind. She had never seen this coming.

After River had finished turning Brynleigh's world upside down, Brynleigh walked back to the dining hall in a daze. She told Ryker she wasn't feeling well and needed to go home.

It was the truth.

She couldn't breathe. Couldn't think. Couldn't fucking do anything at all.

The moment the sun set, Brynleigh left the Waterborns in

their mansion and launched into the sky. Shadows streamed from her, covering her as she flew aimlessly through the night.

She couldn't get River's words out of her head.

"Six years ago, I made a mistake."

A rushing, roaring sound had started in Brynleigh's ears, and it hadn't let up since.

"My magic was too powerful. I didn't know... it slammed into me. I was out with some friends, and it just... poured from me. I... tried to stop it, but I couldn't. I lost control." She shuddered. *"It's my curse. My burden."*

Lost. Control.

How could such small words be used to describe the death and destruction of that night?

River had looked at Brynleigh with tears in her eyes.

Gods-damned, fucking tears.

As if she cared. As if she was pained by it. As if she was the one who had lost everything that night.

"The storm was too big. I tried to reel it in, to make the rain cease, but I couldn't. It wouldn't listen to me."

Shadows had slipped from Brynleigh's fingers. She hadn't even noticed they left her until the light was nearly gone from the study.

No.

Brynleigh had wanted to stand, scream, and tell River to stop, but her mouth had been incapable of forming words. She was a statue, rendered immobile by the confession she'd never expected to hear.

"It poured out of me like water from a broken dam."

"No!" Brynleigh yelled again, her wings carrying her across the darkened sky.

How could this be happening? Brynleigh had done the math quickly, sitting on that blood-red couch. River had been fifteen at the time. Not even Mature. Not even an adult.

How could someone so young be responsible for such devastation?

Brynleigh had so many questions, so much to say, but in the end, she'd stared at River.

"Ryker came. He saved me and stopped the storm before even more people could be hurt, but the destruction..." More tears had slipped down River's cheek, and she buried her face in her hands. *"He's so good, and I'm so fucking dangerous."*

How could Brynleigh have missed this? Moreover, how could *Jelisette* have missed this?

Brynleigh yelled into the night, letting the shadows devour the sound of her anguish. It didn't help. No matter how often she cried out, it didn't alter the reality of what she'd learned.

Wrong. It was all fucking *wrong*. Nothing made sense anymore. Not a single thing.

Brynleigh had left without hurting a hair on River's head. She'd been frozen by disbelief but couldn't have done anything even if she hadn't been.

Not really.

Killing Ryker was one thing. He was a decorated officer in the army and a fully grown, Mature fae.

River was twenty-one. Barely a legal adult. Even by her own admission, she'd lost control of her magic and made a mistake. One that had cost Brynleigh everything... but it was a *mistake*.

All these years, Brynleigh had operated under the assumption that Ryker had a reason—a twisted, wicked one, but still a reason—for what he'd done.

But no.

This was infinitely worse than that.

It was a gods-damned accident.

She flew and flew and flew.

Brynleigh's phone buzzed in her pocket, but she ignored it. She knew who was calling. She should have been at the safe house hours ago. She hadn't even texted Zanri or Jelisette before flying off. She should have responded, but she just... wasn't ready yet.

Maybe she never would be ready.

There were no rules for this. This wasn't a change in the game. Fuck, this wasn't even a game. Not anymore.

This was a new situation, and Brynleigh had no idea what to do. The ring on her finger was a thousand-pound weight, reminding her that she'd almost killed an innocent man.

The worst part of this entire thing was that it all made sense.

The moment River had started talking, pieces fell into place. It was little wonder that Brynleigh had been so confused by Ryker's behavior.

Everything she thought she knew was a lie.

Now, when Brynleigh thought back to that night when her world changed, she knew the much smaller person she'd seen standing next to Ryker had been River.

It was all River.

At some point during her flight, the box holding Brynleigh's emotions shattered. It didn't just break—it exploded into a million pieces.

All the feelings she'd shoved deep down inside came rushing out at once.

Tears flooded her eyes, pouring down her cheeks as she yelled her frustrations to the world.

No wonder Ryker seemed like a good man. No wonder she couldn't see the evil in him. She wasn't insane. She hadn't given her heart to the fae who had killed her family.

She'd been given the wrong information.

Did Jelisette *know*? Had she planned this whole thing? Did she have an ulterior motive, or was it like River had said?

"Ryker and my mother helped cover it up. I... I didn't mean to do it. I'm so sorry. I carry the weight of what I did every day."

Brynleigh could've had her revenge right then. She could've ripped out River's throat on that crimson couch and been done with it.

Something had stopped her. She didn't want River's blood on her hands.

Brynleigh killed people who deserved it. Bad people.

But River? Despite the water fae's confession, Brynleigh didn't sense any evil in her. She was hurting, like Brynleigh.

And now, Brynleigh had no idea what to do.

Hours passed.

She flew until the first rays of sunlight stretched through the darkness. The impending day clawed back the night. Her heart galloped as the dawn approached, the sun's deadly fingers drawing nearer.

One touch from them, and she'd be burned from the inside out. Dead. Forever. There was no surviving sunlight. Not for vampires.

She waited and waited and waited until she had mere seconds left.

It was only when the sun made its final stretch across the sky, its golden claws reaching for her, that Brynleigh called on her shadows and allowed them to draw her into their safe embrace. The dark magic enveloped her. She grabbed onto it and allowed it to pull her into the Void.

Keeping her wings out, Brynleigh moved through the shadows until she reached her destination. The safe house wards rippled as she passed through them. She landed in the living room.

As soon as Brynleigh stepped out of the Void, her Maker's eyes landed on her. Jelisette's gaze was as cold as ice, sending skitters running down Brynleigh's spine. "You're late, daughter of my blood."

Brynleigh had suspected this would be the reception upon her arrival. "I know."

There was no point in denying it. Besides, Jelisette disapproved of lying. A fact that Brynleigh was now realizing was rather laughable. But she wouldn't laugh. She had to tread carefully.

Over the past few hours, Brynleigh arrived at three conclusions. The first was that she absolutely would not kill Captain Ryker Waterborn. She had already been having doubts. This was the nail in the coffin. He was innocent, and Brynleigh did not murder people who didn't deserve it.

The moment she'd reached that conclusion, a powerful wave of relief had washed over her. Brynleigh's wings had faltered for a moment before she continued flying.

If her first realization had brought her immense relief, the second had brought worry. The rules had changed. In Brynleigh's mind, they no longer applied. But there was no way in hell that her Maker would understand or care about her sudden change of heart. The old vampire did not see things like most people did. Telling Jelisette of her change of plans would result in a swift execution for Brynleigh.

Instead, she'd come up with a new plan.

Brynleigh would marry Ryker in a week, and then, she'd strive to become exactly what River had called her: good.

She wasn't exactly sure how forgiveness worked—it wasn't something she'd engaged in particularly often—but it seemed like the better course of action. She couldn't kill River. The water fae had been little more than a child when she lost control of her magic. Brynleigh might be a vampire, but she wasn't heartless.

Brynleigh would protect Ryker and his family, including his icy bitch of a mother, for as long as she could.

If she survived this.

"I was with Ryker and his family," Brynleigh said calmly, careful not to let any emotion show in her eyes. "Things ran a little long."

"So long that you couldn't send me a message?" Jelisette snapped as shadows slithered from her palms. "I've been waiting for you."

"My apologies." Brynleigh bowed her head in deference, lowering her gaze to the floor. Her wings were snapped tight against her back, and her shadows were within reach, just in case.

Brynleigh may have looked the picture of the perfect, apologetic progeny, but inside, she was anything but.

Thankful that Jelisette hadn't inherited their bloodline's gift of reading minds, Brynleigh focused on keeping her face blank despite the barrage of questions swirling through her.

Did Jelisette know it was River, not Ryker, who'd destroyed Chavin? Did she care? What other lies and half-truths had she fed Brynleigh?

Fae couldn't lie, but vampires had no such trouble. Brynleigh had proven that time and again. Doubt caused her to reconsider everything she'd been told from the moment of her Making.

The clock ticked, echoing the hammering of Brynleigh's heart, as Jelisette glared at her. Brynleigh studied the striations in the wooden planks beneath her feet, waiting for her Maker's next words.

Survival was the only thing on her mind.

Eventually, Jelisette exhaled. "Alright. I believe you. Tell me what you learned."

Brynleigh lifted her head and met her Maker's gaze. Anything less than perfection would be viewed as an act of weakness. Brynleigh couldn't afford to be weak, especially if she was going to lie her way through this. She assumed Jelisette would have questions for her when Ryker was still alive the day after her wedding.

She had already thought about that. She would tell her Maker the water fae fought back, and she'd have to try again. Hopefully, after a few variations on the lie, Jelisette would back down. The plan was shaky at best, but it was the only one Brynleigh had.

She needed it to work because she had no other options.

The third and final conclusion Brynleigh had reached was one that she'd never expected.

After the box containing her emotions exploded, she'd had to deal with everything she'd ignored for weeks.

Of all the feelings, only one had slammed into her like a freight train, leaving her breathless.

She *liked* Ryker more than anyone else she'd ever met. Maybe even more than that if she was being completely honest with herself. She wanted him, not because he was her mark, but because he was hers.

And that frightened her more than anything else.

CHAPTER 30
A Visit to the Obsidian Palace

The ground shook beneath Ryker's feet as the pulsing, low base beat echoed through The Obsidian Palace. A renowned fae club in Golden City, this was *the* place to gather in the capital. White flashing lights burst from the ceiling like erupting stars. Music blared from massive speakers that stretched from floor to ceiling. Everything was black, from the thick columns supporting the roof to the tables and chairs.

The club mimicked a fae temple in the most debauched fashion possible. The men who worked at this establishment wore cropped black priestly robes that cut off at mid-thigh, while the women wore priestess garments that covered their breasts, asses, and little else.

This was a place where bad decisions were made, and Ryker was already on edge. Frowning, he glanced between his watch and the front door for the fifth time in as many minutes.

"Relax, Ryker, she'll be here," River shouted over the booming pop music pulsing through the club.

That was ironic, coming from his sister. He'd purposefully given River the wrong time, knowing her tendency to ignore all social parameters when it came to being on time, and she'd still been ten minutes late when he drove over to pick her up from Waterborn House.

River wore a tight pink dress that was far too short, with a cut-out along the midriff highlighting her new belly-button ring. When Ryker had pointed out the lack of material on his sister's dress when he'd picked her up, she reminded him that she was an adult and could do what she wanted.

This night out was River's suggestion. She wanted to get to know Brynleigh better since they'd be sisters-in-law in three days.

"I hope so." He pulled out his phone, hoping there was a message from Brynleigh.

Still nothing. The blank screen taunted him.

Brynleigh wasn't late yet, but it was getting close.

Two long days had passed since Ryker last saw his fiancée, and he was getting antsy. He wanted to have Brynleigh in his arms again, and this time, he wouldn't let her go.

The bartender, a tall fae with half her black hair shaved and the other half in a high pony, walked over. "Can I get you a drink?"

"That would be great." Ryker opened a tab and ordered a beer while his sister asked for a fruity cocktail that sounded sugary and disgusting.

The bartender went to work, and Ryker's gaze returned to the door. Still no sign of his vampire.

River jabbed him in the side. "Come on, Ryker. Don't you know how to relax?" she teased.

His frown deepened. "No."

Relaxing wasn't high on Ryker's priority list. He had too many things to worry about, too many different obligations pulling at him.

His sister chuckled as the bartender returned with their drinks. Thanking the fae, River took a sip of the drink that was the same color as her dress. "It's not good for you to be so uptight."

"I'll relax when Brynleigh's here," Ryker grumbled.

He wished he had insisted he pick her up.

Unfortunately, Brynleigh's Maker had kept her busy all week. Apparently, Jelisette de la Point cared little that her progeny was getting married in a few days. Even though Ryker had asked about the project occupying Brynleigh's time. She hadn't been able to tell him much about it.

"You worry too much," River said.

"Debatable." As far as Ryker was concerned, not worrying about the important people in his life was an impossible request. It was his job. He'd done it for years, ever since his father fell ill. Right now, when reports of rebel activities were at an all-time high, he had more reasons to be worried than usual.

River snorted and shook her head. Finishing her drink, she placed the empty glass on the counter and grabbed her brother's hand.

"You need to be patient." She tilted her head at the dark dance floor a few feet away, where fae were losing themselves to the music. "Come dance with me. Get your mind off everything else."

Ryker would rather jump off a cliff. It wasn't that he didn't occasionally enjoy dancing, but he had other things on his mind. Before he could decline, someone clapped him on the shoulder.

He stiffened and turned around, ready to yell at whoever touched him, but all tension left his body as he caught sight of his two friends behind him.

"Hey, man." Nikhail grinned. "Thanks for the invitation."

Even though this was a casual club, the air fae was dressed like he was attending a business meeting with high-ranking Representatives. That was normal for him. Ryker had never seen this friend in anything less than slacks and a dress shirt, even when they got together to watch a game of laser. Nikhail worked in intelligence for the government, and his position was so classified that even Ryker didn't know what he did.

"Of course." Ryker gave a one-armed hug to Nikhil, then Atlas. He was glad they came since he wanted them to get to know Brynleigh. After all, they'd be spending a lot of time together in the future.

Like Ryker, Atlas wore jeans and a black sweater. The earth fae waved his hand, getting the bartender's attention. "Two beers, please."

"Sure thing. One minute," she replied.

Atlas leaned against the bar top, and Nikhail moved to Ryker's other side. "You're looking beautiful tonight, River."

River's cheeks reddened, and she sucked on her lip ring before smiling. "Thank you, Nik." Her gaze crawled over the air fae's suit appreciatively. "You look good, too."

Ryker's mouth pinched in a line, and his gaze darkened as it darted between them. What the hell was going on here? He didn't like it at all. The last thing Ryker needed was for his little sister to get involved with one of his best friends.

Especially Nikhail.

The man was like Ryker's brother, but he was known for his dalliances and one-night stands. That was not the kind of fae River should be interested in, especially not so close to graduation.

Before Ryker could do something stupid, like punch a certain air fae in the face, the club doors opened once more. His gaze slipped to the entrance, and he exhaled as a blonde with black wings entered.

"I'll talk to you guys later." Ryker walked away from the bar, shooting Nikhail a look that he hoped conveyed, *Stay the fuck away from my sister, or else.*

To Ryker's relief, the air fae nodded and stepped back from River, taking a swig of his beer. The problem, at least for now, was solved. Still, Ryker would be keeping a closer eye on Nikhail. He was a good man, but he wasn't right for River.

No one was.

Ryker pushed his way through the crowded club, moving past hordes of fae grinding against each other to the sensual beat of the music. Most of the dancers' clothes were severely lacking in the fabric department, but he barely noticed. He only had eyes for the vampire making her way towards him.

Brynleigh was a vision of death in her figure-hugging knee-length crimson halter dress and black wings. Her blonde hair flowed around her. As always, her only jewelry was her necklace and the engagement ring he'd given her.

The moment she was within arm's reach, Ryker took her hand and pulled her towards him.

"I missed you, beautiful," he breathed, his eyes sweeping over her before he claimed a kiss.

Their mouths fused, and Brynleigh melted against him. Instantly, none of his other worries existed. Not his sister and the looks she was exchanging with Nikhail, who was definitely off limits. Not the rebel activities or the report he'd received this morning about yet another riot that had resulted in three deaths in the Southern Region.

The only thing that mattered was Brynleigh and how she felt in his arms. It was like they'd been made for each other.

Eventually, he broke off their kiss and slid their fingers together.

She smiled up at him, her fangs peeking out. "I missed you too. Three more days."

"Three days," he echoed. Somehow, it felt like the longest and shortest seventy-two hours of his life. Pecking her cheek, he asked, "Are you thirsty?"

"I am." She leaned against him. "I'm glad we get to spend time together tonight, Ryker."

"Me too." Already, he felt better than he had in two days. Her presence was a balm to his soul.

Ryker led Brynleigh to the bar, never letting go of her hand. The trio he'd left behind was engaged in a heated discussion, which grew more animated as they approached.

Atlas crossed his arms and frowned. "I'm telling you both, the Vlarone Raiders will wipe the floor with the Drahanian Dragons.

No one can beat them. They're the best laser team on the continent."

"You're wrong." River glared up at the earth fae, who was more than a foot taller than her. "The Dragons have won every single game this year."

"Only because the Southern Region hasn't come against the Western one yet this season," Atlas argued.

"Ugh!" River threw up her hands and huffed, "You'll see. They'll win, and you'll eat your words."

This scene was familiar. Comfortable, even. Ryker had mediated more than a few disagreements between River and Atlas. Both were enthusiastic about sports and willing to talk to anyone who would listen.

Ryker chuckled, pulling Brynleigh up next to him. "Atlas, did you make the mistake of asking River about sports?"

"Apparently," he grumbled, raking a hand through his hair.

"You know how seriously she takes them," Ryker said. "Dad and River have watched laser games together ever since she was a toddler, right, Shortie?"

"Right." River crossed her arms. "That's what makes me qualified to speak on the expertise of the Drahanian Dragons."

Tension simmered between Atlas and River.

Nikhail, in an apparent effort to relieve it, swigged his beer and walked between them. "Personally, I don't understand what you're fighting about. There's little appeal to the game."

River's eyes widened, and she sputtered as she turned on her heels and faced the well-dressed fae. "What? Inconceivable. Everyone loves sports." She looked at Brynleigh. "Right, Bryn? Which team is your favorite? It's the Dragons, isn't it?"

The hand Ryker held stiffened. "I... uh, don't know." Brynleigh pressed herself against Ryker's side, her wing brushing against his other arm. "I've never watched a game of laser."

In a dramatic move that proved River was Tertia Waterborn's daughter, she gasped and pressed her hand against her heart.

"What? We'll have to rectify that immediately. This is an absolute travesty."

Ryker could think of other things that were actual travesties: the poverty crisis in the Republic of Balance, the rebels, the stack of papers piling up on his desk waiting for him to return after his honeymoon. This didn't exactly fit the bill. Still, his sister meant well.

"If Brynleigh agrees, sure." Ryker would never force his bride to do something she didn't want to.

River turned her eager gaze back to the vampire. "Will you come over and watch a game with me after the wedding?"

Brynleigh drew her bottom lip through her teeth before nodding slowly. "Sure, I guess."

That seemed to be the correct answer.

"You will *love* it." River bounced on the balls of her feet. "I promise. It's the best."

"It's—" Ryker's phone buzzed in his back pocket. He pulled it out, wincing. "Shit."

The number flashing across the screen was reserved for emergencies.

"What's wrong?" Brynleigh asked.

"It's work. I have to take this." He kissed his vampire's forehead. "Do you mind?"

Brynleigh shook her head and retracted her wings. "No, go ahead. I'll order a drink."

Promising that he'd be back as soon as possible, Ryker slid his credit card to the bartender before accepting the call. Pressing the phone against his ear, he yelled, "Hello?"

"Captain Waterborn, this is Major Ulysses. There's been a situation, and..."

CHAPTER 31
No More Rules

A low, steady beat hammered Brynleigh's ears. The Obsidian Palace was an assault on her senses. The lights were low, the music was loud, and the air pulsed with the heady scents of desire and lowered inhibitions.

Ryker's call had come in nearly half an hour ago. River had chatted with Brynleigh for a few minutes, but now she danced in the crowd. She had invited Brynleigh to join her, but the vampire had declined, wanting to finish her drink.

"Here you go, miss." The bartender handed Brynleigh another glass of blood wine. "Enjoy."

"Thank you, I will." Accepting the beverage, the vampire studied the throng of dancers.

River was easy to spot on the edge of the crowd, her bright dress standing out among all the black. Her partner was an elf with long, curling horns that reached for the sky. She seemed to be enjoying herself.

Nikhail, Ryker's black-haired friend, danced a few feet away with a redheaded fae. River and Nikhail hadn't spoken much, but Brynleigh had noticed them glancing at each other throughout the evening. That was interesting.

The Obsidian Palace wasn't Brynleigh's scene, a fact which

became more apparent the longer she was here. She'd much rather be curled up in front of a movie right now, but she didn't want to pass up an opportunity to be with Ryker, especially after the day she'd had.

This morning, Jelisette had sent Brynleigh to an underground club in the Western Region to deal with a problem. Complications had risen, her mark had fought back, and the bloody task had taken her far longer than normal.

Brynleigh had showered for nearly an hour to scrub all the blood from her body before getting ready for tonight. Not only had her job been a lot, but Zanri had been hanging out at the safe house all day. Brynleigh itched to tell him the truth about River. Not so her handler could hurt the young fae but so someone else would know the truth.

Ultimately, she had decided it wasn't safe to share the information. Holding her tongue had been painful.

After the wedding, things would be easier. Surely, Brynleigh could make Jelisette understand why she couldn't kill Ryker. Besides, by then, they would be married.

Brynleigh planned to move out of the safe house and into Ryker's apartment when they returned from their honeymoon. With a few coats of paint and a couple of throw pillows, it would feel like home. Marlowe seemed to like her, giving her confidence that she'd fit right in.

As for work, Brynleigh would tackle that issue later. She assumed the law-abiding captain would probably take an issue with his wife killing criminals in her spare time, so she'd have to find something to do that was above the law.

But they would be happy, and that was all Brynleigh wanted.

Losing herself in daydreams about what their married life would look like, Brynleigh didn't notice Ryker's return until he stood in front of her.

"All done. Thank you for waiting, sweetheart." Ryker slanted his lips over hers, his kiss claiming and possessive.

Heat went straight to Brynleigh's core, and she clenched her legs together. Isvana help her, but she wanted him so badly. Waiting until the wedding night was torture. She replayed their stolen moments in the car over and over again. She reminded herself of the way his fingers felt deep within her and wondered what it would feel like when it was his cock.

"No problem," she murmured when their kiss broke apart. "Is everything alright?"

A shadow flickered across Ryker's face before he nodded. "Yes, just some trouble in the Northern Region. The rebels are being... difficult."

And the heat was gone.

Brynleigh frowned. "Are the rebels always this bad?"

She didn't remember them causing as many problems as they had over the past two months. Not that they weren't justified in their actions because the inequality in the Republic of Balance was impossible to hide, but their timing felt strange.

"No, usually..." Ryker sighed and palmed the back of his neck. "I'm sorry, love. I can't really talk about it. It's classified."

"I understand." And she did.

After all, Brynleigh had a world of secrets that she couldn't share with Ryker. She didn't even want to think of his reaction if he ever learned her true intentions in joining the Choosing. She'd be taking that truth to her grave.

Ryker smiled, and his eyes twinkled. "Thank you." His thumb brushed her chin. "Did I tell you how beautiful you look tonight?"

She chuckled. "You might have mentioned it."

Brynleigh didn't always enjoy wearing dresses, but this one was a favorite. It was comfortable, had pockets, and highlighted all her best assets. She had chosen it tonight specifically with Ryker in mind.

"You're absolutely fucking stunning." His hands landed on her hips, and he drew her against him for a kiss.

His hard length pressed into her, and she gasped against his mouth.

Ryker groaned, and he kissed the shell of her rounded ear. "If we weren't in a room full of other people," he whispered, "I'd show you exactly what this dress does to me."

Gods, the mouth on this man.

Brynleigh blinked at him, trying to think of a clever response, but a hand wrapped around her wrist and tugged before she could.

"Come dance with me, Bryn!" River's cheeks were flushed, her hair mussed, and she wore a grin that spoke to her having enjoyed several alcoholic beverages in quick succession. "Just because Ryker has a stick up his ass doesn't mean we can't have fun."

River didn't give Brynleigh a chance to refuse her offer. The younger water fae pulled her towards the crowd of moving bodies.

"I'm not a great dancer," Brynleigh admitted, shouting to be heard over the blaring music.

"You don't have to be!" River threw back her head and laughed. "Let the music speak to you."

Brynleigh was pretty certain that wasn't how it worked. However, she didn't want to say no to River. Not when the water fae reminded Brynleigh of her sister. Sarai would've spent all night on the dance floor, shaking her hips and letting the music move her.

For her sister, Brynleigh would dance. "Alright, I'll give it a try."

And she did.

The music blared, the beats were low, and the lights dim as they danced. Neither Brynleigh nor River spoke, letting the music guide their movements.

It surprised Brynleigh to realize she started enjoying herself sometime around the third song. Dancing to the pop music was a far cry from when she and Ryker had spun around the ballroom. It was easy. No one was looking at her.

For the first time in years, Brynleigh felt free. She was clumsy, but that didn't seem prohibitive with this style of music. Soon, she swayed her hips, her eyes hooded as she let the rhythm run through her. Her shadows danced in her veins, echoing the song.

This was... nice.

Several songs later, River looked behind Brynleigh and smiled. She nodded, then slipped away into the crowd of bodies.

Confused, Brynleigh went to turn around. Before she could, a pair of large, warm hands settled on her hips. The vampire tilted up her head, and a grin stretched across her features.

Ryker stood behind her, all broody and beautiful in his fae way.

"River said you didn't want to dance," Brynleigh murmured.

Ryker drew her against him, her back lining up with his front. He held her hips, and they swayed to the music as it slowed.

The captain's breath ghosted over Brynleigh's ear. "Sweetheart, it seems I'm breaking all my rules for you."

The shiver running through Brynleigh had nothing to do with the chill in the air and everything to do with the hardness pressed against the swell of her ass.

"Oh?" She twisted in his arms and gazed up at him.

Strobing lights cast Ryker in alternating blue and white, giving him an ethereal aura. His hands slipped around her and pressed against her bottom. "Yes." His head dipped, and he kissed the corner of her mouth. "I would do anything for you, Brynleigh de la Point."

Her heart pounded at his concession. Gods, how was it possible to care so much about someone in such a short period of time? Now that she knew the truth, Brynleigh could admit her true feelings to herself. She *really* liked Ryker, and there was nothing wrong with that.

Maybe she more than liked him. She would explore that thought when she was on her own. Either way, emboldened by her feelings, Brynleigh didn't wait for Ryker to kiss her properly. She threaded her hands behind his neck and pulled him towards her.

Their mouths slammed together in a passionate embrace.

They remained like that for several minutes. Kissing. Swaying. Touching. Being together.

This was a moment Brynleigh would never forget. Right now, there were no more rules or games. No one watching or judging them. They were alone, and she allowed all the emotions rising within her to remain. She was... happy, and she loved it.

Eventually, the music shifted. The beat picked up, and the new song demanded they move their bodies.

So, they did.

Ryker's grip tightened around her hips.

Brynleigh ground herself against him, wishing there were no more barriers between them.

They kissed again and again and again. Hands explored. Her fangs ached. Her shadows throbbed.

They moved as one, dancing the night away until the sun was about to rise.

There were no rules, and it was good.

CHAPTER 32
Wedding Bells and Blessings

"Ready for this?" Nikhail clapped Ryker on the back.

Ryker straightened his black suit jacket, adjusted his crimson tie, and nodded. "More than ready."

After a short deliberation, Ryker and Brynleigh decided to hold their ceremony in Isvana's temple. It was packed to the brim. Black curtains covered the windows, but the darkness did not detract from the beauty of the space. Glittering lights hung from the columns. Through a trick of technology, stars danced on the ceiling. Rows upon rows of chairs were laid out before them, filled with an eager crowd.

Cameras were already in place. One pointed at Ryker on the dais and another at the back of the temple where Brynleigh would arrive.

Although the timeline to assemble the weddings had been quick, no expenses were spared. Everything, from the decorations to the clothes to the following reception, was expertly put together.

Cyrus and Tertia sat in the front row, and although Ryker's father wasn't as alert as he had been the other night, he smiled at his son. Their presence meant the world to Ryker. Along with his parents, several other familiar faces were at the wedding, including other Choosing participants. Numerous armed guards were hidden among the wedding guests, and more were stationed throughout the temple.

Although Ryker hadn't heard of any new threats, Chancellor Rose wasn't taking any chances. After all, the weddings were the most anticipated portion of the blind love competition.

Ryker straightened an invisible wrinkle on his black suit. He'd barely slept last night, thanks to the excitement of the day. Yesterday, they'd gone to a winery with Hallie and Therian, the evening a nice, quiet lead-up to today's wedding.

He would be lying if he said he wasn't eager to get this over with. He couldn't wait to get Brynleigh alone tonight. Her unique scent of a crisp evening and night-blooming roses had followed him into his sleep, and she'd starred in his dreams all week.

The doors opened, and a tall vampire with stark white hair entered the space. The priestess, who'd introduced herself as Plyana during their rehearsal yesterday, wore a long white robe edged in crimson thread. It trailed behind her as she strode into the temple. The crowd hushed, sensing that the ceremony was about to begin.

Ascending the steps to the stage, the priestess smiled at Ryker. "Are you nervous?"

"No." He stood tall, his shoulders back and head held high "Not at all."

Ryker was destined to marry Brynleigh de la Point. He wouldn't have been surprised if the gods had written their union in the stars.

"Good." Plyana made a religious gesture in front of her chest. "I pray that Isvana and Ithiar will bless your union."

"Thank you. That's my hope as well." They would journey to the fae temple during their journey north to receive a blessing from the priests and make an offering to the Black Sands.

Then, the time for nerves was over. The classical violin

concerto, which had been playing quietly through speakers, switched to a traditional wedding march.

That was the signal. The ceremony was about to begin.

Keeping his hands flat at his sides, Ryker turned his attention to the large double doors across the temple. His heart, which had been doing an excellent job of keeping him alive since he was born, thundered. His hands grew clammy. His water magic pulsed a steady beat.

Anticipation was thick in the air, a sweet and slightly bitter taste at the back of his mouth. His back straightened, and he inhaled deeply as the doors swung open with a resounding bang.

River entered first, resplendent in a blue gown. After their night at the Obsidian Palace, Brynleigh had asked Ryker's sister to be her maid of honor. River had been shocked, but she had readily agreed. River's long brown hair was styled in delicate waves, and she'd exchanged all her flashy piercings for diamond studs. She looked like a star walking down the aisle.

It thrilled Ryker that his sister and his partner got along so well. This was a glimpse into their future, and he loved what he saw. This past week proved he had Chosen well. Brynleigh was a strong woman who could hold her own, and she made Ryker a better man.

River confidently strode towards her brother.

"Happy wedding day," she whispered as she stood across him.

A corner of Ryker's mouth twitched upward. "Thank you, River."

She smirked. "Before you ask, I already released my magic today, so you don't need to worry about it."

She might joke about it, but Ryker would always worry about River. Even after she Matured, he would watch over her. He didn't say that, though. He didn't say anything because there was a flurry of movement at the temple entrance.

Time crashed to a stop as Ryker's gaze landed on his vampire. The sight of her stole the breath from his lungs. He couldn't pull his eyes away from her, even if he tried.

His bride was exquisite.

In the place of a veil, she wore a white lace fascinator that fell over her eyes. Her gown was strapless and hugged all her curves. It glistened like fresh snow as the light fell upon it, as though thousands of snowflakes were embedded in it. Onyx earrings hung from her lobes. Her arms were bare, and she wore no jewelry except for her necklace and the ring he'd given her. Her blonde hair was elegantly styled in a complicated, twisted knot.

By the Black Sands, Brynleigh was the most beautiful being he'd ever seen in his entire life. Two large, jet-black bat wings extended from her back. They hung on either side of her, a symbol of her power. The shadows pooling at her feet were a direct contrast to the bridal ensemble she wore.

Then her gaze rose and met his.

The breath returned to his lungs in a whoosh. They stared at each other, the rest of the room disappearing into nothingness. Everything that had ever gone wrong in Ryker's world righted itself at that moment. She was his other half, his partner in all things, the woman he was destined to love forever.

There was a subtle movement as the cameras panned to the doors. He knew the world was staring at his bride. It didn't matter, though. They could look because Brynleigh wasn't looking at the cameras, the crowd, or the priestess.

Her eyes were locked on him. The distance didn't matter. Her searing gaze made him feel like he was the only man in the world.

"Please stand," Plyana commanded.

The crowd shuffled as they all stood, save for Ryker's father.

Music crescendoed. Brynleigh glided across the marble floor towards Ryker, holding his gaze.

Following vampiric tradition, Jelisette met her progeny at the end of the aisle. The older vampire wore a black ball gown that seemed better suited for a funeral than a wedding. Long black gloves went to her elbows, and glistening black diamonds sparkled in her ears. Strange.

Brynleigh never moved her eyes from Ryker's, even as she slipped her hand onto Jelisette's outstretched arm.

Priestess Plyana began speaking, regaling the crowd and cameras alike with the history of the Choosing like Chancellor Rose had done during the Opening Ceremony. The priestess reiterated the importance of the practice that unified the Republic of Balance, her voice echoing through the large temple.

Ryker barely heard any of her words. To be fair, he wasn't attempting to pay attention.

Brynleigh smiled at him, and he smiled back.

Hi, he mouthed.

His vampire's lips twitched. She mouthed back, *Hey*. Her eyes widened as if saying, *Can you believe this?*

He knew instantly what she meant. The grandeur, the temple, the crowd, the cameras, everything. They were all here to watch them get married. It was overwhelming, even for someone like him who'd grown up around wealth and the press.

He'd done everything he could to remain out of sight for the past six years, but the reporters didn't bother him today.

This was not about him—it was about *them*.

Plyana turned to Jelisette. Her voice boomed across the now-silent temple. "Do you give your progeny over to this fae to be married?"

Brynleigh visibly bristled at the priestess's words. Ryker could almost hear his vampire's voice in his head, railing against the injustice of being spoken about as though she was not a person but a belonging to be bought and sold. She didn't say anything, though, probably because she was as eager as Ryker to get this ceremony over with.

Jelisette's ancient obsidian gaze swung to Ryker's. It took everything the water fae had not to shudder. Something about this woman put him on edge.

She didn't break his stare, even as she said, "I do. After all, this is the moment we've been waiting for."

Had the words come from anyone else, they would've

sounded kind. Coming from Jelisette, they made Ryker's skin pebble. No, he did not like Brynleigh's Maker. Hopefully, they wouldn't have to deal with her much in the future.

Ryker descended the steps and stood before the vampires, extending his right hand. Brynleigh held his gaze as she lifted her hand from Jelisette's and took his.

The moment they touched, fiery sparks ran through him. He raised her hand to his lips and held her gaze as he pressed his mouth against her pale flesh.

"You look beautiful," he murmured.

His vampire blushed, and the crowd made sounds of delight as he led her onto the stage.

Brynleigh retracted her wings into her back as they took their place before Plyana, but she kept her shadows around her feet.

Such a stunning vision of power.

Ryker was utterly enamored by the woman he was marrying. His fingers ran over the back of her hands, rubbing gentle circles, as the ceremony passed in a blur.

They exchanged rings—Ryker's was a thicker version of the delicate onyx band he slid onto Brynleigh's finger—and they signed the legal documents officially binding them as husband and wife.

Then came the moment Ryker had been waiting for.

The pair stood before Plyana; their hands joined in the space between them.

"You may kiss the bride," the priestess declared.

She may have said more after that, but Ryker stopped paying attention. He was utterly focused on his gorgeous vampire.

Ryker stepped towards Brynleigh, closing the space between them as he tightened his grip on her fingers. Their eyes met once again, and the crowd faded away.

Brynleigh breathed his name as he lowered his head. His lips descended on hers, anxious and eager to taste what was his.

The moment their mouths met, Ryker groaned. Slipping one

hand behind Brynleigh's neck, he gently cupped the back of her head. With the other hand, he held her close.

Every single inch that separated them was far too much.

Ryker had gone six weeks without seeing, touching, or holding Brynleigh.

Never again.

She was his, and he was hers.

Brynleigh's lips were soft beneath his as they kissed. He'd intended for this to be a peck, a promise of what would come, but now that they were in the moment, he couldn't stop.

A soft moan slipped from her, and he tightened his grip on her neck. He held her close, angling her head as they embraced. His tongue swept the seam of her lips, intent on tasting her.

She was his everything.

His other half.

His Chosen partner.

His wife.

CHAPTER 33
Chocolate Cake, Happiness, and Suspicions

Brynleigh should've known that her new husband's kiss would blow her mind. After all, everything else about the fae had thrown her world off its axis, so why not this, too?

And this was far more than she'd ever expected.

Ryker's mouth fused to hers. It wasn't just a kiss. It was a claiming. A declaration to the entire world that he had Chosen her, and now, she belonged to him.

Brynleigh always thought something like that would bother her. After all, she wasn't a possession but a person. It turned out it didn't bother her at all. There was something about Ryker that had made her feel safe and loved, even as he asserted that she was his.

She let him kiss her like he owned her because maybe he did.

Her heart was his.

Tomorrow, she would finally tell Ryker she loved him. The time was right.

Gods, it felt good to be married to this man. He was intelligent, kindhearted, and protective in a way that she hadn't known she wanted in a partner. Yesterday at the winery, Ryker was attentive but not overbearing while she and Hallie chatted like schoolgirls about their upcoming nuptials. It was sweet, the way he kept checking on her, and Brynleigh couldn't believe she'd gotten so lucky.

Ryker's tongue probed her lips, and she opened her mouth. He tasted her. With each powerful sweep of his tongue against hers, she melted more into him. She gripped his suit jacket, holding on as they passionately embraced. Heat flooded her core, and she lost herself in him.

This was the only thing that mattered.

Over the past week, Brynleigh had perfected her acting skills. In front of Jelisette and Zanri, she'd worn a mask of indifference as they finalized their plans to murder Ryker. She hadn't revealed River's confession, even though it pained her to hide things from Zanri. He was her handler, and she'd come to realize over the last week, her friend. But Brynleigh couldn't risk him telling Jelisette that she'd changed her mind. She'd gone through all the actions, pretending that tonight, after the reception, she still planned on killing the captain.

But that's all it was.

An act.

This kiss, though? Isvana help her, Brynleigh was not acting now. This embrace was real. The emotions coursing through her were real. The vows she'd spoken were real. Their relationship was real.

Well... as real as something could be when it was built on a foundation of lies.

But she and Ryker could get past their rocky beginnings. They had to. Brynleigh wouldn't accept any other alternative.

Brynleigh would fight for this relationship because she was meant to be with Ryker. She knew it in the depths of her soul. Even though she'd entered the Choosing with dishonorable intentions, she still wanted Ryker to be hers.

His tongue flicked against her fangs, and she moaned his name. His hardness pressed against her, sending a surge of want through her.

Brynleigh couldn't wait until Ryker saw the surprise she had waiting for him under her dress.

Someone coughed in the audience, and Brynleigh's eyes snapped open.

Oh, gods.

She had completely forgotten they weren't alone. Judging by the sheepish look in Ryker's eyes, so had he. They split apart, their mouths plump and cheeks flushed, but he kept hold of her hand.

Priestess Plyana looked amused as she studied the newly married couple. Her cheeks were flushed, and her fangs were fully displayed and she smiled warmly. "Well, I suppose we have additional proof the Choosing works."

A smattering of laughter rolled through the crowd, and even Ryker chuckled. Brynleigh's chest warmed, but before she could crack a smile, the hairs on her neck stood on end. She turned her head ever so slightly, and sure enough, Jelisette's black eyes drilled into her.

Worry churned in Brynleigh's stomach. Had she gone too far? Did her Maker know she felt more for Ryker than she'd been letting on? What if—

Actually, fuck that. It didn't matter.

When the sun crested the horizon tomorrow and Ryker still breathed, Jelisette would know Brynleigh had broken all the rules. She would have to deal with it.

Brynleigh was an adult, not a puppet that her Maker could boss around and make do whatever she wanted. She had married this fae, and he was hers. They'd vowed to be with each other, for better or for worse. They were bound together beneath the eyes of the law. They'd Chosen each other, and no one, not even Jelisette, could break them apart.

Plyana rested a black cloth across Brynleigh and Ryker's joined hands. The ceremony was almost over. "In the name of Isvana, the goddess of the moon, it is my greatest honor to declare you husband and wife. May your union be Blessed from this day until your last."

She lifted the cloth, and the crowd roared their approval.

It was done. They were married.

Brynleigh thought she'd be nervous or frightened, but instead, a warm, fuzzy feeling filled her stomach. When she entered the Choosing, she'd never expected to feel like this on her wedding day.

She was happy.

A PLEASANT LIGHTHEADEDNESS floated around in Brynleigh's head as she nursed her glass of Faerie Wine. She'd already had two servings of blood while Ryker and the other non-vampiric guests had their appetizers, and she'd moved on to the pink wine while the guests enjoyed their dinner.

The grand reception hall reminded her of an elegant, five-star restaurant. Low-hanging chandeliers cast a light over the space. Off-white tablecloths covered round tables. Classical music trilled from hidden speakers. Servers dressed in black delivered copious amounts of food and beverages. The windows were bare, and the moonlight provided a romantic ambiance for their joyous occasion.

Brynleigh and Ryker sat together at a high table, just the two of them. Their family and friends, along with guests and several undercover guards, were scattered throughout the hall.

Jelisette stood at the back of the reception space, talking to a man cast in shadows, but Brynleigh had yet to see Zanri. It was strange since she'd ensured her friend was issued an invitation. After all, it wasn't like she had any family to invite to the wedding. It stung that he wasn't here.

What could be more important than this?

A warm hand landed on Brynleigh's thigh, drawing her attention to Ryker. His eyes crinkled at the corners, and he brushed a lock of hair behind her ear. "Are you alright, sweetheart?"

Gods, this man was so considerate. She loved that he was checking in on her.

"Yes," she replied honestly as she sipped her wine.

It bothered her that Zanri wasn't here, but she wouldn't let his absence ruin her night. This wonderful man beside her was her husband, and she would enjoy every second of their wedding.

"More than alright." Brynleigh *giggled,* which was wholly unlike her. It was, quite frankly, disconcerting. "I'm very happy. Delighted, even."

Clamping her mouth shut, Brynleigh eyed the glass she clutched. Maybe she'd had enough to drink. Everyone knew Faerie Wine loosened the tongues of even the most tight-lipped vampires.

A deep, warming chuckle ran through her husband. "Me too."

A familiar pair of white wings caught Brynleigh's attention. Hallie hurried towards their table. She wore a beautiful ruby cocktail dress, reminiscent of the Choosing's theme, and matching heels. Therian followed behind, his hands in his pockets as he trailed his fiancée. The much larger dragon shifter dwarfed his partner, but they fit together perfectly. Just like Brynleigh and Ryker. Matches made in the heavens.

Brynleigh stood, wobbling slightly thanks to the Faerie Wine, and hugged Hallie. "I'm so glad you could make it. It's nice to have a friend here."

The Fortune Elf smiled. "Your wedding was beautiful."

"Are you excited for yours?" It would take place three days from now. Brynleigh looked forward to attending before she and Ryker went on their honeymoon.

A brilliant grin lit up Hallie's face. "Yes, I am." She glanced behind her at Therian. "We can't wait to get married, right?"

Therian bent and kissed Hallie's cheek. "Right, love." He looked up and smiled. "The wedding was very well done."

"Thank you," said Brynleigh. Even though she and Ryker didn't have a lot to do with the actual planning, the wedding planner supplied by the Chancellor had listened to their suggestions. Brynleigh would forever remember this day.

"Of course." Therian glanced at Ryker. "Captain, can we talk?"

Ryker stood and glanced at Brynleigh, an unspoken question in his eyes. *Do you mind?*

"It's fine," she assured him.

He slanted his mouth over hers, stealing a kiss. "I'll be right back." He trailed a finger down her collarbone, sending sparks running through her. "Wait for me?"

A smile danced on her lips. "There's nowhere else I'd rather be."

Ryker returned her smile as he and Therian moved away from the table. He whispered, "What's going on?"

Therian rubbed his neck. "I got a message from my squad. There's news about the rebels. They've..."

His voice dipped into a low whisper, too quiet even for Brynleigh to hear. Not that she tried. She'd ask Ryker about the conversation later. She was certain he'd tell her what he could.

She turned back to her friend. "I'm so glad you were able to come, Hallie."

Unlike Zanri. She tried not to think about her friend's absence because it was making her angry.

"You make a beautiful bride." Hallie ran a hand down Brynleigh's gown appreciatively. "This is absolutely stunning."

It was. The moment Brynleigh had seen the dress on the rack, she'd known it was hers.

"Thank you." Brynleigh moved her hips, the gown swishing around her. Yes, the wine was definitely getting to her head. "Isvana Blessed my Choice. Sometimes, I feel like this is a dream, you know?"

She never would've predicted this outcome.

Hallie's head bobbed, and she shifted from one foot to the other. "I know exactly what you mean. Looking at Therian, I can't believe we're getting married. It's insane how well we work. Does that make sense?"

Absolutely. Brynleigh couldn't imagine her life without Ryker now.

"It's like you're two halves of the same whole."

"Yes," Hallie breathed. "Exactly. I tried to explain it to my parents, but they looked at me like I was crazy. But they weren't in the Choosing. They don't understand the connections that we made."

Brynleigh glanced over her shoulder to where her new husband clapped Therian on the back.

"I completely understand." She took Hallie's hand in hers and stepped towards her friend. "It's like you were missing something, but you didn't know what it was until they were right before you."

"Yes, that's it!" Hallie beamed, and her wings fluttered.

The pair chatted for a few more minutes, the air between them light, before a server stopped by and slid an enormous slice of chocolate cake on the table next to them.

Brynleigh stared at it. Of all the foods she missed from her human days—and there were many—cake was the biggest one. She loved cake in all forms, but chocolate was her favorite.

Maybe it had been a mistake to ask for it because this one looked delicious. The lush, dark chocolate sponge was covered in thick swirls of brown icing, and it was the most inviting food she'd seen in years.

Her mouth watered at the sight. Logically, she knew that if she took a bite, it would taste like ash, but it looked *so* good. If only she'd requested the recipe from the chef who'd made the scrumptious blood-laced food she'd enjoyed on her date with Ryker.

Ryker slid his hand around Brynleigh's waist and held her to his side. "I'm back," he murmured.

Immediately, she relaxed and leaned against him. It was insane that she felt so comfortable in his presence, considering that she had been planning to kill him for the majority of their relationship, but his soul called to hers.

"Is everything okay?" she asked.

"Yes." He kissed her forehead. "It's nothing to worry about. I promise, I'm yours for the rest of the night."

Those words delighted her in a way that nothing else ever did. *He* delighted her. How could she have ever thought he was a monster?

Therian took Hallie's hand. "Dance with me?"

The Fortune Elf grinned. "I'd love to." Hallie looked back at the newly married couple, a knowing twinkle in her eye. "Enjoy your evening."

Brynleigh winked at her friend. "Oh, we will."

To say that Brynleigh was eager to leave this reception and be alone with her husband would be a vast understatement.

Like a gentleman, Ryker pulled out Brynleigh's seat for her. She sat and picked up her glass of blood wine. "What was that about?" she whispered.

Drawing over the plate, Ryker speared a piece of cake. "The rebels are on the move again," he murmured. "I might get called into work early."

Brynleigh had suspected that might be the case. She hadn't anticipated the resulting pang of disappointment that twisted in her stomach. It was a strange emotion she hadn't felt since before her Making. "Oh. Okay. I understand. You'll be careful, right?"

Ryker's job was dangerous, but he was powerful. Surely nothing would happen to him.

His hand curled around hers. "Look at me, sweetheart." He waited until her eyes were on him. "I'll be safe. I always am. My soldiers are the best because my squad is a family. No one is ever unguarded. I have their backs, and they have mine."

Logically, she knew that. The reason she entered the Choosing in the first place was to catch Ryker alone. Illogically, she didn't want him to go because they wouldn't be together.

That was ridiculous.

What was wrong with her? Brynleigh didn't need to be by her husband's side every minute of every day. That was actually impossible. They weren't Tethered together, and besides, she enjoyed her privacy.

It must be the Faerie Wine. She pushed the glass away, determined not to have another sip. It was making her delusional.

A knife tapped against a glass in the reception hall. "Kiss!" a woman shouted.

A distraction from all these nonsensical emotions. Thank Isvana.

Brynleigh's lips twitched as more people picked up the chant, calling for them to embrace. She'd never enjoyed wedding traditions much in the past, but she had to admit this particular one was no hardship.

Ryker turned to Brynleigh, his eyes sparkling as he squeezed her hand. His gaze caught on her lips, and a heady scent of desire flooded from them both. Sometimes, being a vampire with heightened senses was nice since she knew without a doubt that he wanted her as much as she wanted him.

He asked, "Do you want to?"

She wanted to do so much more than that, but she'd settle for this... for now. "I mean, the crowd is demanding it, Ry. We don't want to let them down."

He smirked, "Then I suppose we must."

His mouth lowered to hers. Their kiss wasn't soft or gentle, but little about her new husband was. It was filled with lips and tongues and teeth. His mouth worked hers as if he'd spent years researching how to kiss her in the most effective and passionate manner possible.

It was the small moments like these that made it seem impossible that she and Ryker had only known each other for a couple of months. They fit together so well; it was like they were always meant to be this way.

When they finally broke apart, Ryker's mouth went to her ear. His warm breath brushed her skin, and he whispered, "Soon."

One word. A promise of what was coming. And gods, Brynleigh couldn't wait. Before she could reply—or yank her new husband with her through the Void in haste to get to their hotel room—a swarm of black shadows pooled on the ground beside her.

That was all the warning Brynleigh had before her Maker appeared beside her. Jelisette's black dress clung to her frame, a deathly dichotomy to Brynleigh's bridal gown.

Jelisette met her progeny's gaze and raised her brow in silent question.

Brynleigh dipped her head, the movement subtle enough that only the most perceptive vampire would notice it. She had anticipated this moment, and yet her stomach still tied itself up in knots.

Leaning over, Brynleigh brushed her lips over Ryker's cheek and whispered, "I'll be back soon."

She had to pretend one last time. For both their sakes.

Ryker's thumb brushed the back of her hand. "I'll miss you."

Bubbles rose in her stomach that had nothing to do with the Faerie Wine.

A week ago, Brynleigh would've shoved those emotions down, but no longer. Now, she simply let the truth in those words wash over her. He would miss her, and she would miss him.

Tomorrow, when the sun rose and she'd officially failed at her task, she would unpack this emotion and give it a name.

Taking one last fortifying sip of good, old-fashioned blood wine—it was more of a gulp, if she was being honest—Brynleigh stood.

She glided on steady legs away from the head table to a shadowy alcove near the back of the reception hall. Jelisette's heels clicked as she strode alongside her.

Neither woman spoke.

When they were alone, Jelisette twisted her hand. Shadows slipped from her palms, and the familiar crawl of her Maker's magic swept over Brynleigh as the older vampire erected a privacy ward around them. Others could see them, but they would be unable to hear their words.

Brynleigh had been inside countless wards with Jelisette, but for the first time, she felt a tingle of unease twisting in her stomach at being in such a confined space with her Maker. She always knew Jelisette was dangerous, but ever since she learned the truth about the storm, she wondered what else her Maker was hiding.

But this wasn't the time for questions. This was the final test before Brynleigh could leave with her husband and spend the night in peace.

She had to pass with flying colors. Jelisette was a dangerous, ancient vampire, and if she knew what her progeny was planning...

Well, she couldn't know.

Brynleigh had decided to keep her husband alive, and she would deal with the consequences tomorrow. Maybe Zanri could help her develop a good story as repayment for missing her wedding.

"Are you ready?" Jelisette's icy tone matched the frozen, dark expression on her face.

Inside, Brynleigh screamed that she would never be ready. She asked a dozen questions, wondering why Jelisette was insistent about this course of action. Why was she pushing for Brynleigh to kill Ryker when River had been the one to destroy Chavin? What did Jelisette know that Brynleigh didn't?

Outside, Brynleigh wore a blank mask. She nodded briskly. "Yes, ma'am. I am."

The cousin of a smile, although it was bereft of all kindness, spread across Jelisette's face. "Does he suspect anything?"

Brynleigh dared to glance back at Ryker. Atlas was in her seat, and the two men were chatting amicably. The water fae must have felt Brynleigh's gaze on him because he looked over his shoulder. He caught her eye and waved. She smiled back.

"Not a thing. I've played my role perfectly."

Jelisette studied Brynleigh like the younger vampire was an interesting insect, and she was deciding whether or not to squash her. Brynleigh held her breath and remained statue-still, unwilling to give her Maker any reason to suspect she was lying. Steadying her breath, she stared straight ahead and kept her face impassive as she waited.

It felt like hours passed as Jelisette's steely gaze ran over every inch of Brynleigh before the older vampire nodded curtly. "I see."

Brynleigh exhaled, and her shoulders relaxed. She'd done it. She'd fooled her Maker. "Everything is in order."

"Good." Jelisette's red lips curled, showing a glimpse of a fang. "Make it painful."

That was, apparently, her goodbye. Jelisette twisted her fingers again and drew the shadows back into herself. A heartbeat later, she disappeared into a plume of shadows. She left so fast that Brynleigh didn't have a chance to ask about Zanri. Maybe the shifter was ill.

Brynleigh had half a mind to find her phone and call her friend before she decided it could wait until tomorrow. After all, tonight was for her and her husband. She was certain they could find plenty of ways to occupy themselves until the morning.

And then, Brynleigh would deal with the aftermath of her actions... or lack thereof. But she wouldn't worry about that right now.

Why borrow tomorrow's problems today?

CHAPTER 34
They Were a Pair

The party was still underway when Ryker and his wife danced one last time. Hours had passed since the servers cleared the last plate, and many of the older fae and other party guests had already departed.

It amused Ryker to no end that his vampire had two left feet. He'd never danced with anyone as clumsy as his wife. She'd stepped on him multiple times, but he didn't care. The flush of her cheeks was adorable, and he'd stolen dozens of kisses throughout the night.

Now, it was over. Thank the Obsidian Sands, they could leave without causing a scene.

Ryker pulled his bride off the dance floor as the music switched to a more upbeat tune. A guard stood against a column nearby, failing at blending in with the party guests. He averted his eyes as Ryker led his wife away from the dance floor.

Brynleigh was always beautiful, but tonight, she was something else entirely. Ryker hadn't thought it was possible to fall even more in love with her, but he was certain he loved her more tonight than he had yesterday. Her pale cheeks were flushed, several golden locks of hair framed her face, and her black eyes created a stunning contrast to the white gown. She was exquisite, this wife of his.

Ryker bracketed his arms above Brynleigh's head, boxing her in against the wall. He leaned over, using his body to hide her from view, and brushed his lips over hers. "How are you feeling, Mrs. Waterborn?"

Gods, those words caused his stomach to jump and a grin to stretch across his face. She was finally his.

"I don't know." Brynleigh's black eyes twinkled, and he sensed she knew what he was saying. "Are you asking whether I'm tired?"

He chuckled, kissing her jaw, then nibbled on her earlobe. "Maybe."

She sighed dramatically. "Alas, I regret to inform you that I'm not the tiniest bit tired."

"Pity," he murmured before kissing her neck. She gasped, arching her head back to give him more room. He asked, "Could I convince you to be tired?"

She clutched at the front of his jacket, holding him there as he kissed her. "I'm fairly certain you could convince me to do anything, Ry."

That name. It snapped the last bit of his restraint—not that there was much of it left.

"Good, then we're leaving." With one final brush of Ryker's mouth against his wife's throat, he straightened and scooped her into his arms in a bridal hold. She laughed, her heels kicking in the air as she settled into his hold.

"I *can* walk," was her weak protest.

"I know." He slanted his lips over hers. "I want to carry you."

She didn't argue after that.

Leaving was a quick, painless affair. First, Ryker said goodbye to Nikhail and Atlas. The two men were flirting with a trio of brunette fae he didn't recognize. Then he searched for his sister. River sat alone at a table, nursing a glass of wine. She met his gaze and waved.

Ryker was grateful he'd had the foresight to book a room for him and Brynleigh in the hotel where the reception was taking place. Marlowe was staying in a kennel, so they didn't need to rush home. The five minutes it took for them to pass the giggling couples in the hallway and wait for the elevator felt like a lifetime.

The ride up wasn't much better since Brynleigh had taken it upon herself to start kissing his neck the moment he stepped into the steel box, much like he'd done to hers earlier. Every time her lips met his skin, his vision clouded, and his legs trembled.

Gods above, he needed her.

Finally, the elevator dinged, and the doors opened on the penthouse floor. The honeymoon suite, one of two on this floor, was a wedding gift from his parents, as was the month-long trip to the Northern Region he and his wife would depart on after attending Therian and Hallie's wedding.

"We're here," he said gruffly.

In response, Brynleigh ran her fangs over his neck. Good gods. Tremors ran through him. Shifting her in his arms, Ryker reached into his pocket and felt around for the small key card he'd been given earlier.

"Keep that up, and we won't make it inside the room," he warned her hoarsely.

"Is this... bothering you?" She nibbled on his neck again.

He groaned, stumbling down the hallway and fumbling with the card. "It's... not bad," he managed to force out the words in a somewhat respectable voice.

Laughing to herself, his vampire continued her pleasant torture until he finally got the key to work. The door beeped, and then it unlocked.

Ryker carried Brynleigh over the threshold and kicked the door shut behind them. He listened for the tell-tale click of the lock before he set her on her feet. "One moment, sweetheart. I need to look around."

Even now, his military training remained with him.

Brynleigh watched him with an amused look in her eyes as he

inspected every inch of the hotel suite, guided by the light of the moon shining in through the open window. He looked under the king-sized bed with its mountain of pillows, red comforter, and scattered rose petals. Then, he checked the closets and the balcony. Once he'd ensured those were empty, he went through the bathroom. There was a massive tub and a shower big enough for two, which he fully planned on taking advantage of later. The room was empty.

He strode to the door and flipped the deadbolt. "All clear."

He was about to turn around when a delicate hand trailed down his back.

"You are aware that I'm a vampire, right?" Brynleigh kissed the other side of his neck, and he shivered as her fangs scraped his skin. What would it be like if she bit him? "I'm capable of taking care of myself if there's a threat."

Something primal inside him roared at the thought of her being in a dangerous situation.

Ryker captured her hand with his, turning her around to face him. "I know you're strong." He met her dark gaze, loving how she caught her bottom lip between her teeth as she studied him. "But I want to take care of you. It's part of my nature. Will you let me do that?"

Looking after those he loved wasn't burdensome for Ryker. It was how he showed affection. He'd done it for River her entire life and planned to do the same for Brynleigh.

A long moment passed as she studied him. His vampire was strong—he had Chosen her in part because of that—but it didn't mean he would stop needing to protect her.

"You can take care of me. It's not... I'm not great at letting other people in, let alone letting them help take care of me. But for you, I'll try." A shy smile crept on Brynleigh's face. "I'll do just about anything for you."

"Thank you, sweetheart." He kissed her softly. "How can I help you tonight?"

"There actually is something." Tugging his hand, she led him to the middle of the room before releasing him and turning around so her back was to him. Tiny pearl buttons, half the size of a fingernail, ran up her spine.

She looked over her shoulder. "Care to help me out of this?"

"With pleasure," Ryker practically growled.

He'd wanted to get this dress off her from the moment he first saw it. The garment was beautiful, but she could have been wearing a paper bag, and he would not have cared. It was not what she wore or the way she styled her hair that he loved, but the woman beneath it all.

"Thank you." Brynleigh crossed her arms in front of her. "It took River half an hour to do up the buttons. They're fiddly."

Ryker snorted, accepting the unspoken challenge. "I assure you I will get this dress off you in less time than that."

He'd rip it off if he had to. He wouldn't resort to such measures yet, though. Working steadfastly and swiftly, he undid the buttons one by one. Excitement bubbled in his veins, and he felt like a youngling on Winter Solstice morning, ripping open his presents.

The buttons slowly fell away, revealing Brynleigh's skin.

Flawless. Every inch, every freckle, every part of her was gods-damned perfection.

She chuckled, glancing at him over her shoulder. "Thank you, Ryker."

He hadn't realized he'd spoken out loud. Smiling sheepishly, he continued. When he was halfway down the row of pearls, he sat on the edge of the bed. Brynleigh shifted with him, remaining silent as he worked.

Anticipation thickened the air, growing stronger with each flick of a button. *Soon*, his every heartbeat seemed to say. *Soon, soon, soon.*

Eagerness made his fingers move even faster until, finally, the last button fell away. The dress yawned, exposing Brynleigh's back from her neck to the swell of her ass.

Ryker didn't have time to appreciate the beauty before him

because Brynleigh lifted her arms. The dress fell to the floor like snow falling from a tree.

Ryker's jaw dropped open, and he breathed, "Fuck."

His wife was completely bare, her beautiful body on display for him to see.

Ryker had been with his fair share of women, and he appreciated beauty as much as the next person, but he'd never seen anyone as incredible as Brynleigh. Her figure was curvy, her body superbly proportioned as if it were made for him.

He groaned at the striking sight of her, unable to believe this was real.

His vampire wasn't shy. She barely gave him a minute to adjust to the sight of her before she glanced over her shoulder and raised a knowing brow. "Oh no," she said coyly. "Did I forget to mention that I wasn't wearing anything underneath my dress?"

Ryker scrubbed a hand over his face. No, he would've remembered if she told him that. He wouldn't have been able to concentrate on anything else.

"All day?" he asked, apparently incapable of uttering anything but the simplest words. His brain was short-circuiting.

"All day." She studied him for a moment longer over her shoulder. "Will you pass out if I turn around?"

Possibly. At this point, he wasn't entirely sure he could feel his fingers. All his blood was rushing to his center.

"I'll try not to." He didn't want to miss a single moment of their first night together.

Brynleigh stepped out of the dress. Shadows slipped from her hands, lifting the garment and placing it over the back of the armchair in the corner.

"Nice trick," he said, still struggling to find his words.

"It's not my only one." Even with her back to him, he heard the smile in her voice. She deftly pulled pins from her hair, one by one, until her golden locks tumbled down her back. She raked her fingers through them, shaking her hair out.

Then, Brynleigh slowly turned around.

Ryker couldn't help it—he stared at his wife. For one thing, her breasts were level with his face because he was sitting on the bed. It wasn't like he was actively *trying* to look at them. They were inviting his gaze. For another, he didn't want to stop.

His fingers curled around the comforter as he drank in the beautiful sight before him. She was captivatingly alluring in a way that was meant solely for him. He wouldn't change a single part of her.

After a few minutes passed in silence, Brynleigh whispered, "Say something."

He pushed himself to his feet, cutting the distance between them in half. Taking her hands in his, he lowered his mouth until it hovered above hers.

"You're utterly fucking perfect," Ryker growled.

Brynleigh hitched a breath, her gaze searching his. "Really?"

Maybe his vampire *was* a bit shy. Interesting. That wouldn't do at all. The woman Ryker had come to love over the past two months was anything but timid. He wanted to draw her out to play with him.

"Really." Ryker's breath skated over Brynleigh's mouth teasingly. "Can I kiss you?"

She murmured her assent, and then, his mouth was on hers. Like the earlier kiss in the temple, this one was claiming, powerful, and filled with intense longing. Unlike that kiss, Ryker had no intention of stopping.

He poured everything he'd felt since he first heard Brynleigh's voice into this embrace, letting her know precisely how much he wanted her. One of his hands tangled in her hair, and he pulled her close. The tips of her breasts brushed against his still-clothed chest and hardened.

Fuck, she was so responsive. Continuing to kiss her, he slipped his other hand between them and gently rolled her nipple through his fingers.

She gasped.

"Beautiful." He broke their kiss long enough to murmur the

word over her mouth before claiming her lips again. The next time he took a breath, he added, "Fucking incredible."

She loosened in his arms, but he wasn't done with her yet. She moaned. He swept his tongue into her mouth.

Their mouths fused together.

Emboldened by the way Brynleigh melted against him, Ryker brushed his tongue against the sharp tip of a fang.

She shivered.

Oh, he wanted her to do that while he was inside her.

Brynleigh tugged on his shirt. She lifted her lips from his long enough to demand, "Take this off."

There she was.

"Gladly." Ryker stepped away, his body instantly mourning the distance between them, as he slipped off his suit jacket. "Anything else?"

Brynleigh took his place on the edge of the bed. "The pants, too."

He happily divested himself of those, as well. Within minutes, he wore nothing but black boxers.

His fingers were in the waistband when she said, "Wait."

Ryker stilled instantly, his gaze returning to hers. "Yes?"

She stood and reached for him. "May I?"

He swallowed, suddenly feeling like he was fifteen again. "Of course," he rasped. "You can touch me however you want."

It would be the sweetest torture, and he would willingly submit to her. For now.

Brynleigh smiled and hooked two fingers in the elastic. Her black eyes smoldered as she tugged down his undergarments.

He stood there, letting her see all of him.

"Oh, gods." She licked her lips and stared at his hardened length.

The sight of that alone was enough to bring Ryker close to the edge. He stepped out of the clothes, kicking them at the wall as he approached his vampire. "Brynleigh, I want you."

This wasn't the time for coyness. They had spent more than

enough time waiting. His heart drummed, and need to be coursed through his veins.

She murmured, "I want you, too. More than I ever thought I would."

Warmth sparked in his chest as he kissed her. They became a tangle of tongues, teeth, and wandering hands as they explored what had so long been hidden.

She groaned.

He moaned.

She nibbled on his lips, her fangs grazing him teasingly but never biting.

He palmed her breast, rolling her nipple between his fingers.

Her hand slipped between them. Her fingers grazed his cock, and any blood that he had left in his brain officially departed.

Ryker broke away from the kiss as he stared at Brynleigh through hooded eyes.

"Do you like this?" she asked softly.

Did he require air to breathe? Did water run through his veins? Was he completely in love with this woman?

"Fucking yes," he groaned, both wanting her to continue forever and needing her to stop before he made an utter fool of himself.

She chuckled as if she knew where his mind had gone.

"Enough." Ryker couldn't take it anymore. He grabbed her hips and, with a swift maneuver, landed them both in the middle of the bed.

Brynleigh blinked innocently as if she hadn't just had his cock in her hands. "What's wrong?"

This vampire would be the death of him. He could feel it now. But he would gladly die a happy man if it meant he got to be with her.

She reached across the bed as if to touch him again, and he growled. Capturing both her wrists with one hand, he lifted them above her head and held them there. She looked positively beddable, stretched out before him.

He wanted to lick and suck and taste every single part of her.

"If you keep touching me like that, this will be over before it starts," he warned.

"Oh?" A brow rose, and Ryker could've sworn a glint of amusement entered Brynleigh's eyes. "Is that so?"

He nipped her lip for her impish reply. Settling his hips against hers, he pinned her to the mattress. "It is, and it's not how I intend this evening to go."

She wiggled, bringing her core dangerously close to him. "Oh? How did you think it would go?"

His wife was such a tease. Did she think she was in control here? That was not the case.

Keeping Brynleigh's wrists up high, Ryker slipped his hand between them, finding her clit and pressing gently. She gasped, arching her back into his touch.

"Something like this." There was no hiding the masculine pride in his voice.

She moaned beneath him, her words a mess of gibberish as he circled his thumb. Every soft moan, every gasp, sent a thrill through him. Yes, this was what he'd imagined. He'd dreamed about how she'd come on his fingers since their stolen moments in the car.

He wouldn't stop there tonight, though.

Ryker bent his head and kissed his bride as he slid a finger into her heat. She was so wet and tight. He groaned, moving his hand slowly. She gasped. He added another finger, loving how she cried out against his lips as he curled them just so.

Brynleigh moaned his name, and his cock became almost unbearably hard. Had his name ever sounded as perfect as it did at that very moment? He thought not.

He added more pressure on her clit and sucked her bottom lip.

She panted, "So close."

"That's it, love. Come for me. Scream. Let them all hear how I make you feel." He punctuated each word with a kiss as she writhed beneath him, desperately seeking her release.

Brynleigh's words were a steady stream of nearly incoherent babble as he drew her closer and closer to the edge.

More.

Please.

Don't stop.

Fuck me.

Ry.

That last one was his favorite. And when she yelled his name as she came, her tight walls clenching around his fingers, he knew there was nowhere else he'd rather be.

Lifting his fingers from her soaking core, he licked them clean as she watched with wide eyes. "You taste incredible," he told her smugly.

In response, she arched her hips and spread her legs. "I want you."

That was all she had to say. He released her wrists, settling between her like he belonged there because he did. His tip brushed her core, and he nearly lost himself there.

Her fingers found his shoulders, and she clung to him as he brought his hips forward. Dipping his head, he kissed her. "I love you," he murmured.

He lowered himself into her, one inch at a time, as she stretched to accommodate him. He moved as slowly as he could, letting her get used to him.

Gods, it took every ounce of patience Ryker possessed.

A vampiric purr rumbled through Brynleigh's chest as he filled her to the hilt. Shadows slipped from her hands, and she moaned beneath him, rolling her hips. "You feel so good, Ryker."

His forehead fell on hers, and he panted, "You feel better than all my dreams."

He allowed her to take the lead at first, to move slowly while she got used to him. To them.

That's what they were now. A pair. Partners in every way.

Brought together by the Choosing and forever bound to each other in love.

Nothing could ever tear them apart. No one could break them. He wouldn't allow it.

Eventually, Brynleigh's nails raked down his back. "More, Ry," she demanded. "Harder."

She didn't need to ask him twice. Withdrawing almost all the way, he thrust into her with all his strength. He wasn't worried about breaking this vampire of his. She was even stronger than him and could take anything he gave her.

Brynleigh moaned, her legs wrapping around him. She met each of his movements with her own. Their sweat-slicked skin moved together as they each climbed towards their release. Her nails dug into his back. He slammed into her. She cried out. He groaned.

They drew closer, closer, closer to oblivion.

"I want you to come on my cock, Brynleigh." His hand slid between them and found her clit. "Now."

She obeyed beautifully, shattering with a scream that he would never forget. She broke apart beneath him, and his own release quickly followed. He came so hard that stars appeared behind his eyes.

Later, after they'd tested out the shower—it did indeed have enough room for the two of them, especially when he pinned Brynleigh against the wall and took her standing up—they cleaned up. He locked the balcony doors and shut the curtains before climbing into bed behind his wife. The only light came from the dim glow of the alarm clock on the nightstand.

Brynleigh's head rested on his chest, and her eyes were closed as she drew circles on his skin. "I'm glad I entered the Choosing," she murmured. "This is... far more than I could've ever imagined."

He kissed her. "Me too, Mrs. Waterborn. Me, too."

Ryker couldn't imagine having Chosen anyone else.

Brynleigh was his.

Forever.

CHAPTER 35
New Game, New Rules

Brynleigh's shadows slammed through her veins, urging her to wake up. They swam into her dreams, pulling her out of her fantasies.

What was happening?

She blinked, staring at the glowing red numbers on the clock. It was barely four in the morning. She should've slept for a few more hours after the way Ryker had tired her out. An arm pressed her into the mattress, and a heavy thigh was pinned between hers. She was naked, as was he, but that wasn't what had woken her.

Something was terribly wrong. Brynleigh's stomach twisted, and her shadows writhed, warning her to pay attention.

Her eyes swept through the room, searching for trouble. Their clothes were where they'd left them. Their suitcases, which had been delivered sometime during the reception, were in the open closet. Her eyes lifted to the curtains covering the windows.

Wait. The curtains.

She could've sworn that Ryker had locked the balcony door and closed the curtains before they went to sleep, but now the fabric was cracked open.

That was odd. Maybe the air conditioning blew them apart? They didn't appear to be secured by any fabric.

Frowning, Brynleigh extricated herself from her husband's grip. She slipped off the bed and moved towards the window. Grabbing the curtains, she shut them tight. She was about to turn around when the hairs on her neck prickled.

Releasing shadows from her palms, her spine stiffened as she spun on her heels.

A large tabby cat, nearly twice the size of a house cat, sat on the TV stand. A bag dangled from its front paw, and it stared at her. The animal was unfamiliar, except...

Those eyes. She knew them.

Brynleigh swallowed the scream rising in her throat as a flash of white light erupted from the cat. Her heart pounded violently against her ribs, and she stumbled back a step.

The feline disappeared, and Zanri took its place. He was naked, and the bag that had looked so big against the cat's paw appeared much smaller now.

"What the actual fuck?" Brynleigh whisper-yelled, her gaze darting between her handler and the bed where Ryker slept soundly. "Why are you here?"

Panic caused her thoughts to run at a million miles an hour. She was supposed to have until the morning. They'd all agreed on the plan. It was still early, and the sun hadn't yet risen. How did they know? What had she done to give herself away?

Zanri looked at Brynleigh with something akin to pity in his eyes. "The fae is still alive."

Not a question. Was there... sadness in his voice?

Maybe Brynleigh could lie her way out of this. Maybe it wasn't too late. "Yes, for now." Zanri opened his mouth, but she continued, "I'll still do it, Z. The timing just... wasn't right."

It would never be right.

"Because you were fucking him." The shifter's knowing gaze swept over her.

Now, Brynleigh wished she wasn't naked. The way Zanri looked at her made her feel dirty, like she'd done something to be ashamed of. But she hadn't.

"No. Well. Yes. I..."

I wasn't ready.

I think I might love him, which scares me.

I'm not going to kill him because his sister is really the one who caused the flood, and I can't bring myself to hurt her.

I want him.

He's mine.

The words were on the tip of her tongue, but she didn't say any of them in the end.

Instead, she stepped towards the bed, trying to get between Zanri and Ryker. She didn't think Zanri would hurt the fae, but she wanted to be sure.

The shifter watched her carefully. "Jelisette knows."

She furrowed her brows, and her confusion wasn't faked. "What?"

"Love makes us do stupid things." Zanri reached into the bag, and there was a snapping sound. "I should know."

Brynleigh's eyes widened, and she reached for the shifter. "What? Don't—"

"I'm sorry, B."

"No—"

He pulled something out of the bag. There was a flash of silver, then a pop.

Pain exploded in Brynleigh's chest. A mangled scream slipped from her lips. She called for her shadows, but they were gone.

As she fell to the floor, darkness edging her vision, she could've sworn she heard Zanri say, "Jelisette said to remind you that rules are rules."

Brynleigh went to cry out, but nothing worked anymore. Not her shadows or her wings or her magic or her voice.

And then she tumbled into blackness.

Drip, drip, drip.

The sound of something wet smacking rhythmically against the floor pulled Brynleigh out of the emptiness that had become her entire existence.

How long had she been unconscious? A minute? An hour? A day or longer? She wasn't certain. But Isvana help her, she hurt all over. From her head to her toes, her body felt like it had endured the beating of a lifetime. There was a mortality to her pain that didn't make sense.

Brynleigh frowned as she struggled to understand what was happening to her. Once again, a thick, heavy fog blanketed her mind. This was becoming an exhausting reoccurrence. She pushed through it, struggling to get back to herself. It was like she was swimming through the Black Sea, the inky waters clouding her vision.

What the fuck was going on?

Instinctively, she reached within herself and searched for her shadows. But they weren't there.

Gone.

Next, she searched for her magic.

Gone.

Her ability to summon her wings.

Gone.

Stripped away as though they'd never existed.

Had the past six years been a dream? Maybe she would open her eyes and see Sarai leaning over her bed, grinning. Maybe the storm had all been a nightmare. Maybe her family was still alive, and—

Her tongue brushed against a tooth. A very sharp, very pointed tooth.

A fang.

None of it was a dream. All of it had been real. Which meant...

Her family was dead. Sarai was dead. She was a vampire. And Ryker...

Oh, gods help her. Ryker.

Every single memory smashed through the fog and collided with Brynleigh at once. The Choosing, their wedding, the reception, the hotel room, and then...

Zanri.

Gods-damn him. Brynleigh had guessed he was a feline shifter. Something about the way he carried himself was a tell.

Zanri had shown up, and then... he shot her. He must have had a special gun in the bag his cat carried.

She remembered the bang and then the flash of pain.

Her hands flew to her abdomen, and she felt for a wound. Her stomach was tender to the touch, but there weren't any open injuries. She was wearing a shirt, though. The material was itchy and unfamiliar. She didn't have time to worry about that right now because she remembered what happened after

Zanri shot her, and then...

She fell to the ground. Shouts. A scuffle. Another gunshot. Ryker crying out.

"No," Brynleigh moaned. "No, no, no."

Her handler must've killed Ryker after he shot her.

Was that what he meant when he said rules are rules?

It was the only thing that made sense.

He shot Ryker, and then he... did something to Brynleigh.

Where was she? Part of her wished she could keep her eyes closed a little while longer and remain oblivious, but she couldn't. She needed to know. To understand.

Ice coated Brynleigh's veins as she opened her eyes despite the pain. A whimper rose in her throat. The shirt wasn't a shirt at all, but a black jumpsuit. That wasn't the worst of it, though.

Gray and black stones rose above her on three sides. Iron bars blocked the only entrance on the fourth wall. There were no windows. There was no light except a single violet Light Elf orb suspended from the ceiling. Condensation dripped down the stones, falling onto the ground in the rhythm she'd heard earlier. Something resembling a toilet and a sink sat in one corner. No bed. No blanket. Nothing else.

A fucking dungeon.

Brynleigh scrambled into a sitting position, moving to the corner of the cell so she could see if anyone walked by.

Her heart was a mallet shaking her entire body, but she didn't cry out to Isvana or Ithiar. There was no point in begging the goddess of the moon or the god of blood for help. She'd gotten herself into this mess, and there was no one to blame but herself.

Brynleigh didn't even realize they still had dungeons in the Republic of Balance. Their society was supposed to be evolved. They had technology now, for the gods' sake.

But this?

This place looked like it belonged in the stories of the fallen Rose Empire. Black manacles hung from the walls, the cell across from her looked like it housed a skeleton, and the breeze carried faint moans to her ears.

Yes, this was definitely a dungeon, and she was definitely a prisoner.

Because Ryker was...

He was...

He was...

Dead.

Brynleigh's breaths started coming in short gasps. Her head pounded. She drew her knees to her chest and hugged them close. Tears burned her eyes.

Captain Ryker Waterborn was dead.

Because of her.

This was all her fault.

Dead.

The word echoed in her mind, getting louder and louder and louder.

She wheezed, sipping air as a fist compressed her lungs.

Something strange happened in her chest. An ache grew in her heart. She tried to ignore it, to gather the emotion and shove it away, but she couldn't.

The box was broken.

She was broken.

Her lungs squeezed, squeezed, squeezed until they were on the brink of exploding. Her heart boomed. Tremors ran through her, and she rocked back and forth.

Then her gaze dropped, catching on the ring on her fourth finger.

A shuddering, broken gasp escaped her.

Her soul *cracked*. Fissures spider-webbed from that point, spreading through her.

Agony engulfed her.

Dead.

She shattered into a million pieces. It was like she'd been shot all over again. The pain of a thousand wooden stakes being shoved into her exploded inside Brynleigh's heart.

She screamed, but the cry soon contorted, becoming a twisted, mangled keening wail.

Anguish flooded her, stemming from her broken heart. It filled every crevice, every crack, every fragmented part of her soul. It wasn't a quiet trickle of grief or a blanket of despair like she'd felt when her family died.

No. This was different. Deeper. Darker. More complete.

This devastating, world-shattering pain would destroy her. There would be nothing left of Brynleigh after this.

Not that it mattered.

He was dead, and she was alone. Oh, gods.

Betrayal coursed a bitter path through her. Zanri did this to her. Jelisette abandoned her. Ryker died on her.

She was alone, and it was all her fault. She had no one to blame but herself.

Tears streamed down Brynleigh's face as she stared at the wedding ring. The jewelry mocked her as if it knew that she'd been married for less than a day before becoming a widow.

Alone.

She wept and screamed and cried until her throat was raw and her fangs ached. And then, when she had no more voice, she rocked back and forth.

A deluge of pain ran through Brynleigh, the grief a never-ending torment of betrayal and anguish and despair.

And she broke.

Minutes passed. Hours. Days. Time had no meaning.

No one came to see her.

At some point, she must've drifted off to sleep. Curse her young vampiric body for still needing rest.

She woke with a start, still living the same nightmare. Still betrayed. Still forsaken by her Maker.

There were more tears.

How could there be so many tears?

Ryker was dead because of her. He was a good man, a great one even, and she'd gotten him killed.

She never should've agreed to this stupid plan.

And to think she once thought this was nothing but a game.

She was a fucking fool.

Brynleigh should have told Jelisette the truth about River's involvement in the storm as soon as she learned about it. Maybe that could've saved Ryker's life. Maybe she could've stopped Zanri.

Maybe, maybe, maybe.

There were so many maybes, so many things she could have done, but none of them would save her from this fate.

Her mind ran in circles as she replayed the past few months repeatedly in her mind. She recalled the joy she'd felt when she first entered the Choosing. It was a terrible contrast to the pain coursing through her now.

She'd accomplished her goal. Captain Ryker Waterborn was dead. The Brynleigh from a few months ago would've been celebrating this news. But now?

She was wrecked.

For the first time in her entire life, Brynleigh had found someone who truly understood her.

And he was...

Gone.

She ran through every single scenario in her mind. Every interaction, every word, every moment they were together, searching for something she could've altered.

Time slipped on and on.

Her fangs ached, and her stomach hollowed.

Eventually, she realized she was hungry. How long had it been since she'd last had blood? She wasn't certain.

And then she felt it.

The air in the dungeon shifted. A cold breeze blew past her. Goosebumps pebbled on her arms.

Footsteps rang out, getting louder by the second.

And stupidly—so fucking stupidly that if she weren't broken, she'd have laughed at herself for being such an idiot—a spark of hope came to life in Brynleigh's stomach.

"Ryker?" she called out, her voice raspy from disuse. "Is that you?"

A bitter, malicious laugh that sounded like nightmares brought to life came from beyond her cell. It sent shivers down her spine.

"No." The voice was as melodic as it was deep and deadly. "He's gone."

It felt like she fell from the top of a high-rise as her stomach plummeted. She heard herself cry out and felt her heart shatter once more as a tall, black-haired fae approached her cell.

Two onyx manacles and a silver muzzle hung from his black-gloved fingertips. He wore fighting leathers, and though he had no visible weapon, she got the sense he could kill her in a heartbeat.

Swallowing at the sight of the fae, she pressed her back against the wall. Silver and vampires did not mix. Brynleigh wasn't entirely sure what the muzzle would do to her, but she didn't want to find out.

Violence glinted in the soldier's eyes as they swept over her. "You're in a lot of trouble."

"Please, I didn't do this." She shook her head, and more tears gathered in her eyes. This whole situation was her fault, but she didn't kill Ryker.

He laughed wickedly. "Oh, this will be fun."

Moving the muzzle to his left hand, he pulled a bag out of his pocket. Reaching in, he withdrew a shimmering black powder and blew it in her direction.

As soon as it hit Brynleigh's skin, fire erupted inside her.

He stepped into the cell, a malicious grin carved into his face.

And Brynleigh screamed.

CHAPTER 36
The Cost of Silence

Brynleigh would never leave this dungeon alive. Her immortal life would end here. She was certain of it.

The guard's powder was a mix of silver and prohiberis. She recognized it the moment it hit her skin. Like the black stones on the wall, it stole her magic. And the silver? It fucking burned. It ate her flesh. It was fire, and she was dying from its flames.

She tried to shake it off, but there was too much.

The fae stepped towards her, and she kicked at him weakly. Her leg hit his shin, and he cursed, "Vampire bitch. You won't escape what's coming for you. You're going to pay for what you did."

Brynleigh attempted to scramble away from him, but her body refused to respond to her commands.

A cruel, humorless laugh burst from the guard as he watched her struggle before seizing her roughly. He slammed the cuffs on her wrists before grabbing her head with both hands.

"Hold still," he snarled. "Or this will hurt even worse."

"Fuck. You." Even while she burned alive, Brynleigh wouldn't listen to him.

She raised her leg despite the pain running through her and

aimed for the precious bits between his legs. She missed, her knee connecting with his thigh.

"That was a fucking mistake." He knocked her head into the stone wall behind her.

Once again, darkness claimed her.

"Wake up, leech." That same cruel voice taunted her, pulling her from her painful nightmares.

Brynleigh moaned, shaking her head as she tried to remain asleep. At least then, the evil guard couldn't bother her.

A woman laughed. "Try this."

A grunt of approval came from somewhere to the right, and someone thrust a wet rag against Brynleigh's nose. An astringent, slightly sweet scent infiltrated her nostrils, swiftly followed by a bitterness that had her choking. Her eyes flew open, and she coughed as though she were hacking up her insides.

The moment her lungs felt somewhat normal, she looked around.

Oh, gods.

This was bad.

Worse, if possible, than the cell she'd first been in.

They'd put her in an iron chair in the middle of an otherwise empty stone room. The air was frigid. Suspicious rust-colored stains painted the cracked stones. A putrid stench that made her want to gag came through the air vents. One wall featured a black mirror, which she assumed was a double-sided window.

"Good morning." The soldier from before crouched in front of her. "Did you sleep well?"

Brynleigh snarled and lurched forward. Or at least, she tried to.

In reality, the moment she opened her jaw wide, her skin connected with the silver muzzle. Flames exploded within her.

Fire burned around her mouth. She screamed. And her hands? They clawed at the iron chair, manacles binding her to the seat.

"I'll take that as a no." The guard stood, watching her carefully as he stepped back. "That's alright. It'll only make this more fun."

It was not the kind of fun Brynleigh enjoyed; she was certain of that.

Then she noticed they weren't alone. Two people stood behind the first guard, and their gazes were also trained on her.

The man on the left was clearly an elf. His curling black ram-like horns rose above his head, making him nearly as tall as Ryker had been. He wore fighting leathers on the bottom and a black t-shirt, highlighting the red swirling tattoos running up his arms.

A Death Elf, then.

How very... predictable.

Beside the elf stood the source of the feminine voice Brynleigh had heard earlier. The woman had long strawberry-blonde hair and glowing blue eyes. She stared at Brynleigh with malice, and it was clear she would not be of any help.

This was fucking bad.

The first guard canted his head. "Do you know why you're here?"

Honestly? No. Jelisette would never bring Brynleigh to a place like this. She would've killed her—painfully and slowly—before leaving her to rot. This wasn't her. Brynleigh was confident about that. Her Maker wasn't behind this imprisonment, but she had betrayed her and left her to die.

Brynleigh didn't say that, though. She stared at the inquisitor, unblinking. She might not have known there were still dungeons in the Republic of Balance, but she'd been trained in dealing with interrogations. After all, there had always been a chance her plan for revenge might end up with her in jail.

She'd assumed—wrongly, obviously—that they would put her in a more civilized prison with tables and water and lawyers.

She'd also assumed that Jelisette would promptly get her out of prison.

Evidently, she had been wrong on many fronts.

Betrayal was tart at the back of Brynleigh's mouth.

Her body surged with a primal need to destroy, yet she couldn't.

She was trapped. Vulnerable. Exposed.

And...

Alone.

The sting of loneliness had never been as strong as it was at that moment.

Even though nothing was civilized about this prison, Brynleigh knew what she had to do. She would have to unpack her betrayal later.

Right now, she needed to concentrate on surviving. She closed her mouth and glared at the menacing trio. She could do this.

Seconds stretched into minutes as they waited for her to say something.

She wouldn't be talking. She might have been betrayed and left alone, but she was strong. She'd survived her family's death, and she would survive this. Somehow. Or not. Without Ryker, it didn't seem to matter. Nothing seemed to matter.

Eventually, the woman snickered. "I don't think she wants to talk to you, Victor."

The guard who'd slapped the manacles on her—Victor—tilted his head. "No, it seems she doesn't." He tsked. "Shame. I thought we might be able to do this the easy way."

This was easy? Brynleigh didn't want to know what the hard way was.

"Did you?" the Death Elf drawled. "Because Emilia and I both know how much you love it when the prisoners aren't talkative."

Emilia snorted. "You mean he loves to torture them, Preston."

Brynleigh's heart stilled. Torture.

Oh gods.

Damn Jelisette and Zanri for abandoning her. Their betrayal had hurt before, but now it was like a knife to her heart. She could barely breathe, barely think. Fear caused her blood to run cold. Her nails curled into the armrest.

Brynleigh had done everything Jelisette ever asked—save for killing Ryker—and this was how her Maker repaid her. She abandoned her and left her alone to be fucking tortured. Brynleigh's eyes burned, and tears tried to force their way out of her.

This wasn't fair. None of it. Had she been such a lousy progeny that this was how she was repaid?

Ignorant of Brynleigh's mental turmoil, Preston laughed. "Yes, well, it's semantics, really. One person's torture is another's—"

"Enough!" Victor snapped.

The other two instantly fell silent.

The guard leaned close to Brynleigh, and her nose wrinkled at the horrible scent wafting from his mouth. Had this man never heard of personal hygiene? "Are they right, little one? Am I going to have to force the words out of you?"

"I'll never tell you anything," Brynleigh seethed.

Victor didn't seem worried about her declaration. If anything, he looked amused. He reached out and trailed his finger down Brynleigh's cheek.

It took everything she had not to shudder.

"She'll talk," the fae said confidently. "She's a vampire, and the prohiberis cuts off all her healing. All it will take is time."

"How much time?" Emilia questioned. "You know she's waiting for answers."

She? The Chancellor, probably. It didn't matter, though. Not really. Nothing would ever matter anymore.

"Not long." Victor flicked his wrist, pulling a silver blade from a hidden sheath on his thigh. "I'd give it a day. Two at the most."

Then, faster than Brynleigh could follow, he spun the weapon in the air, grabbed the hilt, and slammed the dagger into her leg.

Black stars filled her vision as she cried out.

Four fucking days. Give or take. Keeping track of time was getting harder and harder as the hours passed. But at least four days had passed. Maybe five.

She was alone in the cell... for now.

They let her out of the chair when they left, and she would relieve herself before curling up on the stone floor and trying to sleep. It was a nearly impossible task in this place that reeked of death. Every sound, both real and imagined, woke her up as she waited for them to return.

They *always* came back.

Victor, Preston, and Emilia were a trio of torturers. They hit her, broke her bones, stabbed her, and made her wish she'd never been Made.

They never gave up, never stopped. Each time they returned, they brought more questions for Brynleigh. So many fucking questions.

Who sent you? Who do you work for? Why did you do it? Was this always your plan?

Those, at least, she understood.

But then others left her feeling more confused than ever.

Tell us about the rebellion. Who is your leader? What do you know about the Black Night? How many of you are there? Why are you targeting Representatives?

Brynleigh didn't understand those questions. Wasn't she here about Ryker's death? What did that have to do with the rebels? They'd almost killed her with their bomb at the Masked Ball. Of course, she wasn't one of them.

If she were talking to her torturers, she'd tell them they were way off track.

But she wasn't doing that.

It took everything Brynleigh had, but she kept her mouth shut. They'd come in and out, ask their questions again and again, but she was silent.

Broken—but silent.

Sometimes, she felt like someone else was watching her, but the only three people she ever saw were the torturers.

Her heart was bitter and icy and cold.

Her tears had dried up days ago. She was too tired, too sore, too hurt to cry.

Brynleigh stared at the closed door, wondering who would come through next. Would it be Victor with his knives? Preston with his deadly red magic? Or would it be the true devil of the trio, Emilia?

It hadn't taken Brynleigh long to realize the other woman was a powerful witch. Emilia's magic was blue, tinted with strands of black, and it felt *wrong* as it danced over Brynleigh's skin. It wasn't until the magic sank into her that the real torture began, though. One moment, Brynleigh was on fire. The next, she was ice.

It was more than physical discomfort. More than pain.

Emilia played with Brynleigh's mind, sending her image after image of death and destruction until it was the only thing she could see. The only thing she felt. There wasn't a single part of her that didn't feel broken.

Every day, they came and played and tortured her.

Every day, she bled and screamed.

Every day, she refused to speak.

And every day, without fail, she grew weaker and weaker. Brynleigh needed blood. She wasn't sure how much longer she would last without it.

She wasn't even sure she wanted to.

The trio had all but confirmed Ryker's death. Jelisette had abandoned her. Zanri, too. Brynleigh assumed there wasn't anyone else who even cared about her. Not really. Hallie was her friend, but what could the Fortune Elf do?

Upon reflection, Brynleigh realized she'd been the perfect pawn in Jelisette's game. She had no family, no friends, and no connection to anyone.

She'd been *played*.

Every time her heart throbbed, it sent pulses of anger, betrayal, and grief through her.

She grieved for Ryker, for their love, and for the life they could have led. She mourned what they had and wished there was something else she could have done. That grief would remain with her for the rest of what would likely be a very short life.

But the rest of it? The hurt at Zanri's betrayal? The shock that Jelisette wasn't coming to save her?

It was gone. It had vanished around the same moment Victor used her thighs as pincushions, stabbing several silver-tipped daggers into them and leaving them there while Brynleigh screamed.

Now she was fucking furious.

If she ever got out of here, she would destroy her Maker. Brynleigh considered herself to be a somewhat intelligent woman, but Jelisette had completely fooled her.

Brynleigh spent every moment she wasn't being tortured rethinking the past six years. She studied each interaction through a new lens. Jelisette had used Brynleigh and then discarded her like a piece of garbage.

Fuck her.

Brynleigh stared at the door, fists clenched, and waited for it to open.

She wouldn't talk. Not today. Not tomorrow.

Not ever.

CHAPTER 37
Questions and Answers

"I'll admit, I never expected you to last this long." Victor tapped the flat end of his blade on Brynleigh's bloody thigh, where another silver dagger was embedded in her flesh.

She breathed through her teeth, her nostrils flaring as a stab of pain ran through her. She was back in the chair, enduring another session of torture.

Don't cry out, she told herself.

Today was worse than yesterday. Every day was worse than the one before. She thought three weeks had passed, but she couldn't be sure.

Brynleigh was *so* hungry. Her stomach was a hollow void. She barely recalled what it felt like to feed. Her skin was shrinking in on itself. Her fangs were burning. It was getting harder and harder to remember why she wasn't talking.

Victor rocked back on his heels, his evil gaze studying her shrewdly. "Yes, I definitely underestimated you." He pursed his lips. "Or maybe we haven't given you the right incentive to speak."

Brynleigh stared at the fae. The artery in his neck pulsed so beautifully. She wondered what he would look like with his head removed from his shoulders.

Her stomach twisted.

Leaning forward as far as her restraints allowed, her lips pulled back to reveal her fangs.

Victor met her gaze and smirked. "Are you hungry?"

What kind of question was that? Of course, she was.

Victor didn't wait for an answer. He stood and wiped his hands on his black jeans, and walked to the door. He was gone for mere seconds before he returned with a bag of blood dangling from his fingers.

Brynleigh couldn't help it. She reacted instantly, snarling and fighting against the prohiberis manacles.

Hunger was a living, breathing monster within her.

She pulled against the cuffs locking her to this damned chair. She snarled through the muzzle, hating the silver they'd forced onto her.

A slow, pernicious smile crept along Victor's face. "Ah. I see. That's wonderful. Why don't we play a game?" He swung the blood, keeping it just out of her reach. "Every time you answer a question, I'll give you a sip."

Brynleigh's chest heaved as she stared at that crimson liquid. It called to her in a way that nothing else did. She needed it.

Every cell in her body strained towards his offering.

She just hurt so much, and she was so hungry.

It felt like years passed in the time it took for her to dip her head.

"Good." Victor pointed to the muzzle. "I'm going to take this off, and you won't bite me. Understood?"

Not fucking understood.

Brynleigh would kill Victor the moment she got the chance. But she was also a realist. She needed blood to survive, and right now, this was her best chance to get it.

Her gaze dropped to the silver knife sticking out of her leg.

He chuckled. "I won't be removing that, my dear. I need to keep some assurances you'll behave."

Brynleigh closed her eyes for the briefest moment. How had this become her life? Hating herself for it, she nodded again. She had no choice. Not really.

Victor rose to his feet and walked around her. His fingers worked quickly as he removed the muzzle. The moment the silver was off her face, Brynleigh felt like she could breathe for the first time in weeks.

A tear came to her eye, and she couldn't stop it from rolling down her cheek.

"There." Victor returned to where she could see him and leaned against the wall. The bag of blood hung from his fingers, taunting her. "The first question is easy, so you can get a taste of what you'll get if you behave."

He paused, and Brynleigh raised a brow as if to tell him to get on with it. She was hungry, but she wouldn't beg him for the blood. She wasn't that far gone yet.

"Where were you born?" Victor asked.

"Chavin." The word was raspy coming from Brynleigh's mouth, and she winced at the effort it took to force it out.

"Good." The fae stepped towards her slowly, uncapping the bag.

She stared at it, salivating as the precious drops she needed to live came nearer and nearer.

"Open," he said, as if she were an animal.

Gods help her, but she did. She opened her mouth like a bird, waiting for sustenance.

A solitary drop of blood landed on her tongue. It was the ambrosia of the gods, the first ray of sunlight after a long winter, a crisp drink of water after a dry, hot summer day. It was everything Brynleigh needed.

She swallowed and went for more, but he'd already pulled back out of her reach. "Now, now, you know the rules. One question, one drop."

A whimper slipped out of her.

"Where were you Made?"

"Chavin."

Another drop. Not enough.

"How old are you?"

"In human years? Twenty-three."

A drop.

"When were you Made?"

"Six years ago."

Another drop.

On and on they went, the questions getting incrementally harder. Each bead of blood was at once everything Brynleigh needed and not nearly enough. It took the hardest edge off the blade of starvation that had lodged itself in her stomach, but she was realizing that the blood in that bag wouldn't be enough. Not after what she'd endured.

She was just so gods-damned hungry.

The questions shifted gears.

"Why did you enter the Choosing?"

Brynleigh blinked. She could lie. She *should* lie. Every ounce of her training and every rule she'd ever learned told her that concealing the truth was the best way out of this. But was it really? She was in prison and had been tortured for the better part of a month. She was cold and dirty and hungry.

Lying hadn't gotten her anywhere. If she'd stopped doing it earlier, maybe Ryker would still be alive. Maybe she wouldn't have gotten him killed. Maybe they'd still be together.

Brynleigh had thought a lot about her husband over the past three weeks.

It was Ryker's face she pictured while Victor slammed endless silver blades into her. Ryker's voice that soothed her as the Death Elf wrapped red cords of magic around her neck, squeezing tightly. Ryker's fingers that grazed her flesh while Emilia sent deadly magic into her skin and twisted her mind.

She missed her husband more than she ever thought was possible.

"My goal was to kill Captain Ryker Waterborn," Brynleigh whispered, hating the words as they left her lips.

Shock flickered through Victor's eyes. "Come again?"

She repeated, "I entered the Choosing to kill Ryker."

He stepped forward and gave her several drops of blood.

"Why?" he asked.

Tears welled in Brynleigh's eyes, and despite her best effort to blink them away, she couldn't. "I thought..."

"What did you think?"

Those hot tears streamed down her cheeks. "I thought he was responsible for the death of my family. The flood that took out Chavin six years ago. His magic is powerful, and I just... I lost everyone."

She kept going. Now that she'd started stopping seemed impossible. She poured out her entire story to Victor. He didn't even give her blood for it. She started at the very beginning and explained it all. Her Making, the Choosing, even her confusion when she met Ryker. The way she didn't understand how someone so evil could be so good. River. All of it. She didn't hide anything. Why fucking bother?

When Brynleigh was done, she sagged in the chair. Her eyes closed, and tears fell down her face.

"I could have loved him," she admitted, mostly to herself. "I think maybe I did. And now, he's gone."

For the longest time, silence stretched in the room. She felt Victor's gaze on her, but he didn't say anything. Neither did she.

Her words echoed in the quiet. Her admission lodged itself in her broken heart. She hadn't thought it was possible to hurt even more than she already had, but she was wrong.

She was still hurting, still in pain, still broken.

And Ryker was still fucking dead.

What did it matter if Brynleigh regretted everything she'd done?

He was gone.

"Do whatever you want with me," Brynleigh muttered. "I have no one and nothing."

Victor didn't say anything.

Minutes stretched by. The weight of everything she'd confessed fell around her.

She wept and wept and wept.

Someone banged on the wall. Footsteps shuffled. The door closed.

She didn't bother moving or opening her eyes. Victor would be back, or maybe it would be Preston or Emilia. It didn't matter. They would bring more pain, more torture, and more questions about the rebels that Brynleigh didn't know how to answer.

This was her life now until they decided to put her out of her miserable existence.

When the door creaked open again, Brynleigh sighed and waited for the next burst of pain.

It never came.

There were two other people in the room. She could hear their breaths in this too-quiet place of agony, and she felt their gazes on her.

She didn't know who they were.

Once, without the prohiberis blocking her magic, she could've scented them. Right now, her nose worked like a mortal's. Those drops of blood hadn't been nearly enough to heal her, let alone restore her former strength.

Footsteps circled Brynleigh. A hand grazed the back of her shoulders. She stiffened. The touch was oddly familiar, but she couldn't place it.

Then, the pair left. She knew they were gone because the air in the room lightened. She exhaled, keeping her eyes shut. Why bother opening them?

When Victor came to release her from the chair, she'd look at her injuries long enough to catalog them before taking care of her personal needs and curling up in the corner to sleep.

The door opened again. That was strange. Usually, they didn't return so soon. Maybe they'd forgotten something?

"Open your eyes, Brynleigh."

That voice. She knew that voice. She'd been speaking with it for weeks. It haunted her dreams and, more recently, her nightmares.

Was she hallucinating? Was this the end? Maybe the blood had been drugged. Maybe they'd decided to kill her after all.

"Look at me," they commanded. There was a hint of apology in their voice, as if they felt bad for her. But that couldn't be true. Brynleigh was alone, and no one cared about her.

For a moment, she didn't reply. She couldn't. She sat frozen, shock running through her like ice. And yet, she had to know.

What if...

She didn't finish the thought. She couldn't let herself hope. That was dangerous. Deadly. This was another trick. It had to be.

Brynleigh knew that, and yet, she slowly peeled open her eyes. Because... What if?

The two words echoed through her head. *What if, what if, what if.*

She had to know.

Time crawled to a stop as her vision adjusted.

Disbelief coursed through her like a raging storm. Breathing was impossible.

A cry tore out of her chapped lips. Her heart slammed against her ribs. Her broken fingernails dug into the iron chair.

She rasped, "Ryker?"

The end... for now

Thank you for coming along with Ryker and Brynleigh for the first half of their journey.

Reviews mean the world to indie authors like me. If you enjoyed this story, it would mean the world to me if you could leave one.

Want to talk about this ending? Come hang out with me and my readers on Facebook! Join Elayna R. Gallea's Reader Group

A Heart of Desire and Deceit

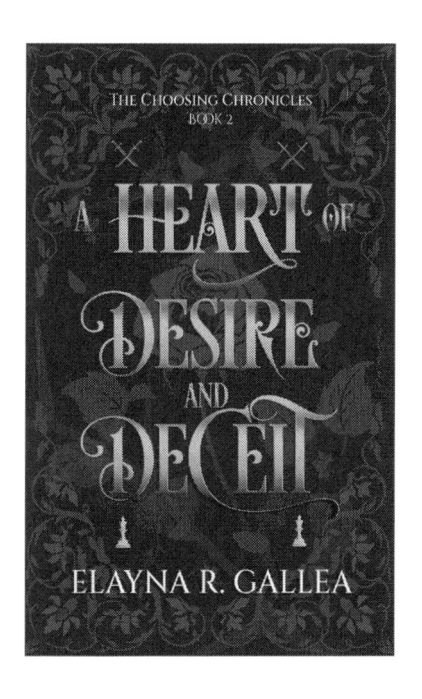

The second half of Brynleigh and Ryker's story is coming on July 22, 2024 in A Heart of Desire and Deceit.

Keep reading for a sneak peek of the first chapter.

Staring at his broken wife through what he hoped were dispassionate eyes, Ryker attempted to quell the racing of his aching, broken heart. For three weeks, the fae captain had existed in a state of disbelief, unwilling and unable to accept the truth of what had occurred on his wedding night.

His beautiful, smart, intriguing vampire had lied to him.

Worse than that, she'd played him for a gods-damned fucking fool.

Ryker knew that was true. He understood it in the same way that someone understood that the sky was blue, that flowers bloomed in the spring, or that the sun rose in the east every morning.

That understanding did nothing to dispel the absolute agony coursing through him like a raging river in the midst of a thunderstorm. It did not heal his brokenness.

Every breath was like inhaling shards of shattered glass. Every pulse of his pulverized heart was like throwing salt in an open wound. Every single second was worse than the last.

Broken.

They were so fucking broken.

Once, they'd been whole. Better than that, they'd been *one*. But Brynleigh had taken what they'd carefully formed during the Choosing and shattered it.

Ryker didn't know how to fix this. He didn't even know if it could be done. When he surveyed the shattered pieces of his heart, which had been a daily endeavor since their wedding night, all he felt was soul-deep pain. He had no idea how to put his heart back together. Was it even possible to pick up the remnants of his life after the one person he'd mistakenly trusted had obliterated it?

He had no idea.

Brynleigh's black eyes were wide, and she was staring at him as though he were a ghost. Her face, pale on a good day, was as white as a fresh snowfall. Her hands trembled against the bindings locking her to the chair, and her chapped lips opened and closed repeatedly.

She rasped, her voice rough and scratchy like she'd been screaming for hours, "You... you're dead."

By the Obsidian Sands, Ryker wished that were the case. Death would have been easier than this.

Agony was a spear lancing through him, stealing his breath, as he really, truly looked upon the woman he'd married for the first time since entering this gods-forsaken place.

A galaxy of black and blue bruises mottled every exposed inch of Brynleigh's skin. Dried blood crusted her face and arms. One of her eyes was nearly swollen shut. Her hair was matted and greasy, and the once-blonde ends were rusty. Her black, ill-fitting jumpsuit was covered in dirt and other substances.

She looked... bad.

Ryker had been around enough prisoners to know this was normal, but to see the woman he loved like this—

No.

The prisoner before him wasn't the woman he'd fallen in love with. This wasn't the woman he'd Chosen. *That* woman, the one he'd spoken with for hours on end and broken rules for, was a different person. One who, apparently, had never existed.

The entire Choosing had been a gods-damned lie.

Ryker repeated the words to himself again and again, just as he had over the past three weeks. They still didn't ring true. It didn't matter how often he told himself Brynleigh had played him; he still couldn't believe this nightmare was real.

How had everything turned out so horribly?

"No, I'm not dead." His voice was a low rasp, yet it seemed to echo in the windowless cell as he answered her previous question.

Ryker had to get a grip. He was a soldier, for the gods' sake.

Forcing a mask of composure on his face, he hardened his eyes and steadied his heart. Even though his hands twitched at his sides with the need to rip the silver shackles off Brynleigh, gather her in his arms, and take her out of here, he was a statue.

He had to be because this...this was wrong. His chest tightened, and his heart raced. Breathing was barely possible.

If Ryker had known Victor Orpheus had been put in charge of the fucking interrogation, he would have stopped it earlier. The sadistic fae couldn't be trusted with anyone, let alone Ryker's... his... Brynleigh.

But Ryker hadn't known. He hadn't wanted to know.

Grief had been an ocean, and he'd been drowning in it for three weeks.

He'd barely breathed, barely slept, barely thought. All he'd done was work, work, work.

He'd allowed his soldierly duties to bury him. Better that than to feel his emotions.

He hadn't even seen his wife until now. He hadn't asked about her, which in fucking hindsight, was a grave mistake.

Fuck, he hadn't even known she was being held in The Pit.

Like a gods-damned idiot, Ryker had assumed Brynleigh would be incarcerated in either Silver or Black Prison. If that had been the case, he would've come and dealt with her eventually.

But The Pit?

Gods-damned awful, terrible, nightmarish things happened here. This place was reserved for the worst of the worst criminals in the Republic of Balance.

And his wife was here.

A prisoner who, if the bruises and prohiberis manacles were any indication, was being tortured daily.

His heart twisted into a painful knot as he studied his wife.

His lying, deceitful wife.

Conflicted was too simple of a word to describe how he felt about the hell he currently resided in.

Ryker hadn't known a heart could hurt like this. He hadn't known that love could so quickly evolve into a monster hell-bent on destroying him from within.

Brynleigh inhaled sharply, the sound drawing Ryker from his

thoughts. She blinked, a trail of crimson running down her leg from where a silver knife was lodged in her thigh.

She asked, "H-h-how?"

How indeed.

Stepping back, he forced that steel mask he'd donned earlier to remain in place. He had replayed those moments with horrifying clarity a hundred times since that fateful night.

Still, the words tasted like ash as he forced them out of his dry mouth. "I wasn't asleep."

Time and again, he'd analyzed that night, but it still felt like the worst kind of nightmare.

The dipping of the mattress drew Ryker out of his slumber. The fae captain cracked open an eye and watched as his beautiful vampire strode towards the window with predatory, silent grace. Gods above, she was stunning. His cock hardened as he studied her. He'd had her twice before they fell asleep a few hours ago, but he still wanted her. He suspected he'd always want her.

She was his.

Brynleigh drew the curtain shut and turned towards the bed. But instead of coming back, she froze. Her back straightened, and she sharply inhaled.

The air in the room shifted, a too-quiet calm before a storm.

Ryker opened both eyes and followed Brynleigh's gaze. A frown tugged at his lips when he saw a cat in the room. Strange. He blinked, wondering if he was dreaming, but the feline was still there when he looked again.

His magic swirled in his veins. A warning. A harbinger. A premonition of what was to come.

But it was too little, too late.

Before he could act or even cry out, a flash of white light erupted from the cat-that-wasn't-a-cat.

In a heartbeat, Ryker's world turned upside down once again.

This was the moment he couldn't stop thinking about, the one that had haunted his nightmares, the one that had him questioning every single thing she'd ever told him.

A redheaded man stood a few feet away from Brynleigh, and she... wasn't screaming. Why wasn't she fucking screaming?

Ryker's heart thundered like a wildcat banging against the bars of its cage. He recognized the newcomer from the Masked Ball as the man who'd danced with Brynleigh.

Danger, danger, danger.

A roaring filled his ears.

Shocked, he listened as Brynleigh didn't yell at the shifter or command him to leave. Instead, they conversed. As if she knew him.

As if she had... expected him.

Icy horror coursed through his veins, freezing him in place and forcing him to watch as his new wife of less than twenty-four hours betrayed him. The one person he thought he could trust, the one person to whom he'd given his heart, took it and ripped it to shreds.

He couldn't move, couldn't think, couldn't do anything at all except listen.

"Love makes us do stupid things," the shifter said. "I should know."

What did that mean?

Brynleigh reached out a hand towards the shifter as if in protest. "What? Don't—"

"I'm sorry, B." The man's voice hardened, the promise of violence clear in his voice.

Danger, danger, danger.

His magic's warning was louder than ever. The fae captain gave up pretending to be asleep and threw off the blanket.

He was too late.

Brynleigh shouted, "No—"

A flash of silver filled the space, and then something popped. Brynleigh screamed, the high-pitched sound forever ingraining itself in Ryker's memory. She fell to the ground with a loud thud, her limp body covered in blood. The life-giving substance streamed endlessly from her chest. He'd always remember that, too.

How could he forget the worst moments of his life?

The next few minutes were a blur.

He formed ice daggers, one for each hand. He leaped out of bed, and instincts took over his movements. The shifter came at him, his murderous intent clear. Ryker didn't even remember fighting the other man.

All he knew, all he cared about, was that he won.

The shifter was still alive when Ryker was done with him, but he would probably wish for death soon enough.

After Ryker knocked the shifter out and tied him up, he called for backup. He managed to get the request out without his voice shaking, which was a gods-damned miracle.

And then he went to Brynleigh's side.

Crimson rivers flowed from her chest, staining everything in sight. There was so much fucking blood.

Ryker didn't stop to think about what he was doing as he fell to his knees. He didn't think about her betrayal because if he did, he might break.

His military training had him reaching inside her chest and pulling out the prohiberis bullet. He didn't think the magic-blocking metal could kill a vampire, but he didn't want to find out.

Even now, after everything, she was still... his.

Ryker chucked the bloody bullet across the room. It clinked, colliding with the wall. He didn't bother to see where it had landed.

He gathered Brynleigh in his arms, her blood coating them both as the wound in her stomach slowly stitched itself together.

They had one, maybe two minutes before the others arrived.

Pressure built behind Ryker's eyes, and finally, he allowed the full weight of what happened to hit him. The shifter came to kill him, and Brynleigh knew.

She *knew*.

He stared at his vampire through a watery curtain, brushing back her hair with a trembling finger. "How could you do this to us?"

He thought he knew her. He thought he loved her. He thought she was his.

Wrong. He'd been fucking wrong.

There was no response. She just lay in his arms, looking far too broken for someone who had caused him so much pain.

With every beat of Ryker's heart, an ache expanded in his chest. It started small but yawned until it was the size of a canyon.

A tear fell on Brynleigh's cheek, and Ryker whispered, "How could you break us?"

Preorder here

Acknowledgments

A Game of Love and Betrayal came to me one day in the summer while I was driving with my husband. As soon as the idea popped into my head, I knew I had to write the story. What I didn't expect was the way the world would quickly evolve and grow into what has now become the Republic of Balance.

Part of me felt bad for smashing the Four Kingdoms into pieces to make this dystopian future, but I had so much fun writing this book that it didn't last long.

I am so grateful to everyone who has come alongside me while I wrote this book. It flowed. It poured out of me. It became a part of me. I'm fairly certain there were several moments where I forgot to eat or sleep, but my husband helpfully reminded me those were important. Thank you for caring for me when I'm in the depths of my writing cave.

There are so many people I'm thankful for. My readers, of course. I wouldn't be able to do this without you.

My writer's group, for listening to my many ideas. Thank you for always being there.

My alpha and beta readers, for seeing this story in its raw form and helping me shape it into what it is today. I appreciate every single comments.

My proofreader, for catching those sneaky little last minute errors that pop up. Thank you.

And to you, my reader. Thank you so much. I wouldn't be doing this if it wasn't for you.

Also by Elayna R. Gallea

The Binding Chronicles (*A high fantasy arranged marriage vampire romance series in the Four Kingdoms*)

Tethered

Tormented

Treasured

Troubled

The Ithenmyr Chronicles (*An interconnected series that takes place in the Four Kingdoms at the same time as Tethered*)

Of Earth and Flame

Of Wings and Briars

Of Ash and Ivy

Of Thistles and Talons

Of Shale and Smoke

Legends of Love (New Adult Standalones)

A Court of Fire and Frost (a Romeo and Juliet Retelling)

A Court of Seas and Storms (a Little Mermaid Retelling)

A Court of Wind and Wings (a Hades and Persephone Retelling)

About the Author

Elayna R. Gallea lives in beautiful New Brunswick, Canada with her husband and two children. They live in the land of snow and forests in the Saint John River Valley.

When Elayna isn't living in her head, she can be found toiling around her house watching Food Network, listening to broadway, and planning her next meal.

Elayna enjoys copious amounts of chocolate, cheese, and wine.

Not in that order.

You can find her making a fool of herself on Tiktok and Instagram on a daily basis.

Made in the USA
Columbia, SC
12 June 2025